TOM CLANCY was the author of eighteen New York Times bestsellers. His first, *The Hunt for Red October*, sold briskly as a result of rave reviews, then catapulted into the bestseller list after President Reagan pronounced it 'the perfect yarn'. Clancy was the undisputed master at blending exceptional realism and authenticity, intricate plotting, and razor-sharp suspense. He passed away in 2013.

DON BENTLEY spent a decade as an Army Apache helicopter pilot, and while deployed in Afghanistan was awarded the Bronze Star and the Air Medal with "V" device for valor. Following his time in the military, Bentley worked as an FBI special agent focusing on foreign intelligence and counterintelligence and was a Special Weapons and Tactics (SWAT) team member.

ALSO BY TOM CLANCY

The Hunt for Red October
Red Storm Rising
Patriot Games
The Cardinal of the Kremlin
Clear and Present Danger
The Sum of All Fears
Without Remorse
Debt of Honor
Executive Orders
Rainbow Six
The Bear and the Dragon
Red Rabbit
The Teeth of the Tiger
Dead or Alive (with Grant Blackwood)
Against All Enemies (with Peter Telep)
Locked On (with Mark Greaney)
Threat Vector (with Mark Greaney)
Command Authority (with Mark Greaney)
Tom Clancy Support and Defend (by Mark Greaney)
Tom Clancy Full Force and Effect (by Mark Greaney)
Tom Clancy Under Fire (by Grant Blackwood)
Tom Clancy Commander in Chief (by Mark Greaney)
Tom Clancy Duty and Honor (by Grant Blackwood)
Tom Clancy True Faith and Allegiance (by Mark Greaney)
Tom Clancy Point of Contact (by Mike Maden)
Tom Clancy Power and Empire (by Marc Cameron)
Tom Clancy Line of Sight (by Mike Maden)
Tom Clancy Oath of Office (by Marc Cameron)
Tom Clancy Enemy Contact (by Mike Maden)
Tom Clancy Code of Honor (by Marc Cameron)
Tom Clancy Firing Point (by Mike Maden)
Tom Clancy Shadow of the Dragon (by Marc Cameron)
Tom Clancy Target Acquired (by Don Bentley)
Tom Clancy Chain of Command (by Marc Cameron)
Tom Clancy Zero Hour (by Don Bentley)
Tom Clancy Red Winter (by Marc Cameron)
Tom Clancy Flash Point (by Don Bentley)
Tom Clancy Command and Control (Marc Cameron)

TOM CLANCY
WEAPONS GRADE

SPHERE

SPHERE

First published in the United States in 2023 by G. P. Putnam's Sons,
an imprint of Penguin Random House LLC

This paperback edition published in Great Britain in 2024 by Sphere

1 3 5 7 9 10 8 6 4 2

A CIP catalogue record for this book
is available from the British Library.

ISBN 978-1-4087-2775-1

Printed and bound in Great Britain by Clays Ltd, Elcograf S.p.A.

Papers used by Sphere are from well-managed forests
and other responsible sources.

Sphere
An imprint of
Little, Brown Book Group
Carmelite House
50 Victoria Embankment
London EC4Y 0DZ
An Hachette UK Company
www.hachette.co.uk

www.littlebrown.co.uk

PRINCIPAL CHARACTERS

UNITED STATES GOVERNMENT

JACK RYAN: President of the United States
MARY PAT FOLEY: Director of national intelligence
ARNOLD "ARNIE" VAN DAMM: White House chief of staff

THE CAMPUS

JOHN CLARK: Director of operations
DOMINGO "DING" CHAVEZ: Assistant director of operations
GAVIN BIERY: Director of information technology
JACK RYAN, JR.: Operations officer / senior analyst
LISANNE ROBERTSON: Former director of transportation
MASTER SERGEANT CARY MARKS
SERGEANT FIRST CLASS JAD MUSTAFA

ISRAELI DEFENSE FORCES SPECIAL OPERATIONS TEAM

ELAD MORAG: Team leader
NIMROD DISKIN: Second-in-command
DAVID MILLER: Drone operator
YOSSI COHN: Sniper
BENNY KOKIA: Communications expert

UNITED STATES MILITARY

GENERAL CLYDE WOLTMAN: Chairman of the Joint Chiefs
of Staff

COLONEL BOB "LORENZO" BEHLER: SR-71 pilot

CHARLIE: SR-71 sensor operator

SHANNON KENT: Air Force Special Projects Office

IN TEXAS

LEON KRUGER: Mercenary leader

HENDRICKS: Mercenary

OFFICER BRADSHAW: Detective with Briar Wood PD

BRIAN: Patrolman with Briar Wood PD

AMANDA: An eyewitness

BELLA: Her daughter

ISAAC BLACK: Former Third Special Forces Group Green Beret

KYLE HOGAN: Former Army Black Hawk helicopter pilot

PROLOGUE

LEON KRUGER'S HAND BURNED WITH AN UNHOLY FIRE.

The pain shot up his muscular forearm in pulses, each one stronger than the one before. The sensation felt like a cramp that originated in the palm of his left hand and radiated along his forearm. Leon grimaced as he rotated his wrist. He desperately wanted to jab the scarred knuckles of his right hand into the fleshy section of his left, but he couldn't.

Because his left hand didn't exist.

Leon eyed the flesh-colored prosthesis that peeked from his long-sleeved shirt.

Though the fingers were made of plastic and rubber instead of flesh and bone, the appendage looked real, and he could do a respectable job controlling the fake digits thanks to the biometric sensors arrayed across his forearm muscles. Twenty years of combat paired with exponential advances in body armor technology and trauma medicine had produced some unforeseen offspring. Horrific injuries that would have ended their recipients' lives even a decade earlier were now survivable, which meant the prothesis business was booming. His computer-augmented prothesis was quite literally the best money could buy, but it wasn't real.

A fact that his central nervous system never stopped reminding him of.

The phantom pain seemed to correlate with Leon's emotions, particularly stress. The greater his worries, the more frequent the phantom pain episodes and the greater the discomfort.

At the moment, Leon had stress in spades.

A car turned in to the gravel driveway, raising a cloud of dust as the vehicle transitioned from pavement to rock.

Leon was a native of South Africa, and he loved his homeland's breathtaking coastlines and near-perfect weather. That said, even he found it hard not to like California. Most non–California natives thought of the Pacific's cold waters or miles of sparkling beaches as being unparalleled, but he considered South Africa to be the equal to the Golden State in these areas. However, the beauty currently surrounding him was like nothing he'd ever seen.

The sky was a special shade of blue. A cobalt pastel mixed with just a hint of cerulean at the point where sky touched earth. The shade steadily deepened to a dark azure the higher Leon's eye tracked above the horizon.

The terrain itself was a study in contrasts.

Toffee-colored rolling mountains were interspersed with pines, oaks, and cedars. Knee-high wild grass gave way to clumps of shrubbery. The vista gave the impression of something wild but not intimidating. A strip of nature that could be explored and enjoyed by rugged outdoorsmen and weekend hikers alike. Were it not for the Tesla slowly rolling toward Leon's rental car, he might just lose himself in the undulating terrain for an hour or two in an effort to release the stress-induced ache lodged between his pectoral muscles. But he couldn't afford to lose focus.

The sleek sedan concealed a particularly reprehensible human being.

Leon was something of an expert when it came to reprehensible human beings.

He was waiting among the stubby trees that lined the granite path winding up the hillside. Though not officially part of Ritter Ranch Park, the pull-off granted access to the four thousand–plus acres of beauty through what had once been a homestead. A sign planted next to the turnoff proclaimed the spot as the future home of a Baptist church, but if the rusted, corrugated steel siding and sagging roof on the standalone garage were any indication, it had been years since this stretch of land had been inhabited.

It would have been easier and quicker to meet the Tesla's driver in the gravel lot, but Leon had no intention of doing so. Though he'd lost his hand, he'd managed to keep his head, which was more than some of his fellow captives could say. This was because—contrary to the public persona often cultivated by those in his chosen profession—he was a cautious man and this caution extended to the plethora of cameras that littered the Tesla's body.

Leon was also old, and in his profession, age either came with wisdom or not at all.

The vehicle eased to a stop. The driver exited, closed his door, and then opened the gull-wing passenger door.

Over the course of his five-plus decades of life, Leon had cultivated expertise in a very narrow skill set and he would freely admit that this knowledge did not extend to luxury cars. Even so, he couldn't help wondering about the extravagance of gull-wing doors. He thought that this was an exercise in vanity more than a utility.

A sign that the driver wanted to be noticed.

While Leon couldn't say whether this observation was true of all Tesla owners, the analysis certainly fit the bill for the man rummaging around the backseat. Upon their first meeting, Leon's initial impression was the man could have been a human Ken doll. He was six feet tall with an athletic frame, sun-bleached blond hair, tan skin, and blue eyes that popped from his handsome face. His hair, while neat, had a shaggy feel. As if he were deliberately challenging the stereotypical stodgy norms assigned to men in his chosen vocation.

Today, the man was dressed California casual in a short-sleeve untucked white shirt, brown chinos, and loafers. Not exactly hiking attire, but Leon didn't care if the short walk was uncomfortable for his visitor. Though Leon's world was populated by degenerates, the Tesla's driver was in a class all his own.

The gull-wing door eased closed on silent hinges. The man pulled on the windbreaker he'd removed from the backseat, but he didn't leave the Tesla. It was as if he sensed that he was on the edge of a precipice. Or perhaps he just didn't want to get his sockless ankles dusty. The man was called Daniel, but unlike the biblical prophet for whom he was named, he did not possess the intestinal fortitude to brave the lion's den.

This was not to say that Daniel was free of convictions.

He wasn't.

He just lacked courage of any sort.

Leon gave Daniel a wave. The man acknowledged the gesture with a short bob of his head before starting toward Leon.

Daniel's blond hair fell in curls across his forehead, perfect ringlets worthy of a hair product advertisement. Daniel had it all—money, looks, and charisma. Men wanted to be him and women wanted to be with him. In no scenario should he have been meeting Leon in an abandoned pull-off in a remote park.

But Daniel was here all the same.

The Tesla's driver was the living example of the truism to never judge a person by their outward appearance. Daniel might look like the definition of American success, but his soul was a corrupted, soiled husk.

Leon knew this firsthand.

"Why all this cloak-and-dagger bullshit?" Daniel said, stopping a few feet away. "Traffic heading back into Santa Clarita is going to be a bitch."

Leon took perverse pleasure at the thin layer of dust coating Daniel's moccasins. The supple leather was probably hand-tooled lambskin. Now, bits of debris and dirt clung to the moccasins' shiny surface, fouling the sheen and crusting across Daniel's tan ankles.

Leon ignored the question just as he ignored Daniel's aggressive posturing.

The early thirties software engineer was a good two decades younger than Leon. His frame reflected the toned muscles that came from a tailored diet coupled with an expensive personal trainer. Any excess calories not expunged during gym sessions were undoubtedly burned away during his thrice-weekly jiujitsu practice. In a bar fight against another cubicle dweller, Daniel would be a formidable opponent.

This would not be a bar fight, and Leon was not a cubicle dweller.

Hopefully this was not a truth Daniel would have to be taught the hard way.

"Change of plans," Leon said with a smile.

Leon had spent the majority of his life in Southern Africa. In addition to English, he spoke French, Swahili, and Afrikaans. His exposure to such diverse languages had given Leon a natural ear for pronunciation and dialect. Knowing that he'd be working in the United States, Leon had spent several weeks watching American television and films, repeating each line of dialogue until he could mimic the speaker.

As a result, his South African accent had softened, the vowels and consonants losing their hard edges. He wasn't going to pass for a midwestern newscaster anytime soon, but neither would he be remembered for his speech.

At least that's what Leon hoped.

"What do you mean?" Daniel said, a frown splitting his handsome features.

"I mean that the request for information has changed."

"This meeting is over," Daniel said. "I told you before—I'm willing to provide you with boardroom insight, but not anything that can be traced back to me. This is nonnegotiable."

Leon kept his face carefully blank even though he desperately wanted to belly laugh. He'd been grooming Daniel for weeks. Their first contact had been in the guise of a corporate recruiter inquiring about the engineer's employment strategy via a direct message on LinkedIn.

As a software engineer, Daniel was in high demand. In Silicon Valley, people with his skill set bounced back and forth between the tech giants every couple of years, usually earning hefty raises in the process, though Daniel worked for a defense contractor instead of a cash-heavy social media behemoth. People with his qualifications were relentlessly pursued—even though the engineer's LinkedIn profile didn't suggest that Daniel was looking for work, profiles like his received a steady stream of messages from recruiters.

The one Leon had sent appeared no different.

But it was.

"Everything is negotiable, my friend," Leon said, this time

allowing his smile to peek through. "But I always feel that it's easier to close a deal once both sides understand the stakes."

Leon removed an iPhone from his pocket, scrolled through the photo reel until he found the one he wanted, and then selected the image.

"Remember her?" Leon said, angling the screen so that Daniel could see it.

The software engineer eyed the device as if unsure whether to come closer.

Leon remained still.

This was a key moment in Daniel's recruitment. An inflection point for the would-be asset. Two paths branched away from this encounter.

One led back to Daniel's Tesla and his old life.

For a pitch to be successful, the asset had to believe that he was in charge of his destiny. This was why Leon waited patiently, holding the phone at eye level like a lure dangled in front of a hungry trout.

For a long moment Daniel resisted the iPhone's siren call.

Then, he bit.

Bridging the distance between them with a single stride, Daniel took the phone and peered at the image.

The change in the engineer was instantaneous.

A moment before, Daniel had been the master of his destiny. As the lead engineer for his company's most lucrative project, he was someone of importance and he acted the part. He drove a luxury car, lived in a ritzy townhouse, and ate at the right restaurants. Independent headhunters openly pursued him while his current company's corporate rivals extended feelers in the form of congratulatory emails and random encounters at trade shows that weren't so random.

With his good looks and apparent wealth, Daniel had no

shortage of options when it came to female companionship. But in this regard, Daniel was as picky as he was with his mode of transportation or footwear. While he indulged in the occasional office romance and frequented the local watering holes from time to time, Daniel needed a very specific kind of woman.

A woman like the one staring back from Leon's iPhone.

"Who is this?" Daniel said.

Leon was impressed.

The engineer's tone conveyed just the right amount of skepticism. If he ever decided to give up writing code, Daniel might have a future in espionage. Assuming of course he learned to master his physical reaction in the same manner in which he controlled his voice. Leon had been intently watching the engineer, genuinely curious to see Daniel's reaction.

Leon hadn't been disappointed.

It was almost as if he could see the exact instant awareness hit Daniel's brain. In a fraction of a second, the healthy color drained from the engineer's face, leaving his skin a chalky hue. His posture stooped, and the charisma and confidence that seemed to ooze from Daniel's pores leached away like air from a punctured balloon.

Daniel looked deflated.

Which was exactly how Leon wanted him.

"Come now," Leon said with a chiding tone, "let's not play games. I told you from the beginning that I represented a serious client with serious resources. You were being offered a director position and sizeable stock options that would immediately vest. We found this as part of our due diligence."

"Found what?" Daniel said, handing back the phone. "A picture of a pretty girl?"

"Fine," Leon said with a sigh. "Just remember you chose this bit of unpleasantness, not me. The picture isn't just a pretty girl. Maria Gonzalez is a fourteen-year-old citizen of the state of Zacatecas, Mexico. She and her mother left with a convoy of twenty-five others for the arduous trip to America. Her mother did not survive the journey. Unfortunately for Maria, the coyotes facilitating her cross-border transfer were not the most noble of men. After arriving in El Paso, Maria was handed off to a par- ticularly nasty man who runs several brothels staffed almost ex- clusively by underage girls. These brothels cater to a certain clientele. A clientele consisting almost exclusively of men like you."

Leon's words hit Daniel like physical blows. The engineer's shoulders tensed, and his fists tightened. He stepped closer, en- croaching into Leon's personal space. Leon had anticipated a fight-or-flight reaction, but not one this pronounced. Rather than wilt, the engineer looked ready to go to fisticuffs.

This prospect didn't particularly concern Leon.

After surviving machete-wielding Boko Haram Islamists, Leon feared no man who walked the earth. Even so, Leon was grateful for California's restrictive handgun laws. Frightened men did stupid things and Daniel was frightened.

This was why Leon had chosen the California wilderness rather than the Four Seasons bar, the site of their previous meeting, to confront Daniel.

"This is ridiculous," Daniel shouted, his voice echoing across the craggy hills. "She told me she was eighteen. You can ask her!"

"Actually, I can't," Leon said as he thumbed to another image.

"Why not?" Daniel said.

"Because she's dead."

Leon again offered the phone to Daniel.

The engineer's fingers shook as he took it.

If seeing the first image of Maria had deflated Daniel, this image crushed him. The phone showed an obviously dead girl with vacant eyes staring heavenward with a dime-sized hole just above the bridge of her nose.

"You can swipe left for a profile shot if you'd like," Leon said helpfully. "I think there's also a picture of the exit wound, but I wouldn't recommend it on a full stomach. Hollow points really make a mess of things."

"I had nothing to do with this," Daniel said, dropping the phone in the dirt. "Nothing."

"Of course you didn't," Leon said as he retrieved the device. "But I doubt the police would share your opinion. My understanding is that you don't much care for condoms, which means your DNA was all over poor Maria's body."

"What is this?" Daniel said, backing away. "Who are you?"

"You already know the answer to that," Leon said. "I am a partner in an executive search firm. I told you that our firm was different. We protect our client's investments. In this case, that investment is you, which is why Maria's body was completely sanitized and then disposed of. In the unlikely event that some forensic piece of a fourteen-year-old girl from Zacatecas is ever discovered, there will be nothing that connects her to you. Not a thing."

Leon watched as hope warred with disbelief on Daniel's face. Like a drowning man who'd just been tossed a lifeline, the engineer wanted to latch on to what Leon was offering.

But he wasn't stupid.

"What do you want?" Daniel said.

"Want?" Leon said with a laugh. "You misunderstand things. I don't want anything from you. I'm here to give you something."

"Give me what?"

"A signing bonus," Leon said. "My firm's client chose us for a number of reasons. One, we have a reputation for procuring the industry's top talent. Two, we are discreet. My client neither knows nor cares what happened to a random Mexican girl in Middle of Nowhere, Texas. They are only concerned with your acceptance of their employment terms. If you agree to them, you will be paid a signing bonus of one hundred thousand dollars."

Daniel stared at Leon in silence. No doubt his agile mind was running through a million permutations as he viewed what was unfolding from a thousand different angles. For a long moment his features were wrinkled with confusion.

Then he understood.

Or at least he thought that he did.

"What will your discretion cost?" Daniel said.

"Nothing," Leon said. "I don't get paid unless you take the job."

"Then why did you say the request for information has changed?" Daniel said.

"My client wants you to start work immediately."

"Why?" Daniel said, the look of suspicion returning.

Leon made a show of considering Daniel's request before replying.

"I told you," Leon said, parsing out the words one by one, "my client must remain anonymous until you leave your current employer. Even so, I'm sure you're smart enough to guess who I represent. Let's just say that the media's legal analysts believe that a certain appeal is going well and that a ruling that will reverse the government's initial shortsighted decision will be issued imminently."

Leon didn't specify which appeal.

He didn't have to.

For Daniel and his coworkers, there was only one appeal. Daniel's current employer had just been awarded a contract in excess of two billion dollars on the strength of their prototype's performance. A sole-source contract. Understandably, their chief competitor and rival for the contract was less than pleased.

While working in the defense space could be extremely lucrative, it was not a business for the squeamish. Competition was fierce and there was only one customer—the United States government. Consequently, when a contract of substance was awarded to a single defense contractor, the losing company almost always appealed the decision. Though the government tried to discourage these lengthy and costly legal battles by assigning the losing party monetary penalties, a million-dollar adverse judgment was pennies compared to a multibillion-dollar contract.

And in this case, the losing corporation's appeal seemed to have merit. For reasons that only made sense to the in-house counsel charged with interpreting the government's bizarre and often contradictory acquisition regulations, the lucrative sole-source contract might have been awarded on improper grounds.

This was a topic that Daniel would be closely following.

"So your client is gearing up in anticipation of a split award?" Daniel said.

"I'm not in a position to violate my nondisclosure clause," Leon said with a smile, "but I can't prevent you from drawing your own conclusions. Now, if you're ready to formally come on board, I'm prepared to transfer your signing bonus to the bank account of your choice. Immediately."

Daniel made another show of thinking over the offer, but

Leon wasn't fooled. Daniel had taken the bait and now the hook was firmly lodged in the engineer's jaw.

"Okay," Daniel said. "Where do I sign?"

"No signature required," Leon said. "This is a sensitive situation. My client does not want to be accused of poaching rival engineers. We need to keep your hiring completely aboveboard in case the government audits my client's hiring records. This is why your payment will come from my firm rather than your new employer. Instead of signing a letter of intent, my client is requesting a show of goodwill."

"No," Daniel said, shaking his head. "I told you. I won't commit industrial espionage."

"Nor would my client expect you to," Leon said. "What they want could be obtained through open-source research, but that would take both time and considerable effort. They want you to save them the trouble by providing it yourself."

"What?"

"A list of the program's vendors," Leon said. "My client needs to be ready to execute the moment the appeal is decided in their favor. Obviously, they have a robust supply chain, but as you may know, the program's technical milestones are . . . aggressive. My client would very much like to have a repository of potential secondary choices should their primary vendors face difficulties scaling their production quickly enough to meet the government's timeline."

Daniel scratched his five o'clock shadow as he weighed Leon's request. Obtaining another company's list of second-tier suppliers certainly fell into a gray area. While it was nowhere near as sensitive as design specs or testing data, vendors were closely held information. Oftentimes a manufacturer would insist that their subcontractors sign nondisclosures to prevent poaching by competitors. That said, as Leon had intimated, it was possible to ferret out a company's vendor list. The prime contractor had to disclose their subcontractors to the government, and as a result, it was publicly available information if someone wanted to go through the headache of filing the appropriate paperwork.

Most people did not.

"I could provide you with my functional area's vendors," Daniel said, "but I don't have access to the program-wide database."

"I understand," Leon said, reaching into his pocket, "but there's a workaround."

"Explain," Daniel said, his eyes narrowing.

"The automated maintenance reporting feature," Leon said, handing Daniel a metallic business card holder. "Have this in your pocket when you do the next firmware update. When the prototype accesses the internet, this will record the data dump."

"And the list of vendors," Daniel said.

"Exactly," Leon said.

Daniel turned the innocuous-looking box over in his hand.

"I just carry this with me when I do today's update? That's it?"

"That's it," Leon said.

"And then I get paid?"

"No," Leon said. "Your signing bonus is based on your verbal commitment to resign from your current position and join my client as the director of engineering. Say the words and the money drops into your account."

"If you pay me now, how do you know I'll follow through?" Daniel said.

Leon shrugged.

"You're about to become a member of my client's C-suite. If the executive team didn't think they could trust you, the interview process would have ended long before now. Remember, I don't get paid unless you get paid, and I intend to get paid."

Daniel looked from the device to Leon and back again.

"Okay," Daniel said, "I'll do it."

Of this, Leon had no doubt.

1

BRIAR WOOD, TEXAS

THE MUSTANG'S HEADLIGHTS CUT THROUGH THE NIGHT AS JACK RYAN, JR., DROPPED the six-speed manual transmission into fourth, accelerating through the winding turn. Between the roaring 450-horsepower V8, the wind in his face, and the mild Texas weather, he didn't even try to temper his broad smile. In fact, the only thing making this night drive less than perfect was the empty passenger seat beside him.

As if on cue, his phone rang.

Jack eyed the caller ID on the console, and though he wouldn't have thought it possible a moment ago, his grin somehow grew even wider. Where the caller's contact information had once been a first and last name, the personal details now bore just a single word in all capital letters.

FIANCÉE

Jack liked the sound of that.

"Hey, baby," he said, answering the call as he eased off the gas, allowing the throaty engine noise to drop to a low rumble. Renting a muscle car convertible was a fine way to tool through the Lone Star State, but the ambient noise was hell on phone conversations.

"Hey yourself. I'm lonely. Know anyone who'd want to keep me company?"

Lisanne Robertson's husky voice sent shivers down Jack's spine. His right foot wanted to nudge the accelerator at the thought of the raven-haired beauty sitting alone in their Rainey Street hotel room. But as much as he wanted to free the horses lurking beneath the Mustang's hood, he resisted the urge. Flooring the pedal might get him back to Austin a couple of minutes sooner, but that would be at the expense of listening to his future bride tell him how much she missed him.

Not a trade Jack was willing to make.

"Lisanne Robertson," he said, catching the slight slur in his fiancée's words, "are you tipsy?"

"Get your cute self back here and find out."

This time it wasn't just the engine's RPMs Lisanne's words set racing.

Looking at the Mustang's dashboard clock, Jack did some quick math. He was currently heading west along Highway 79, somewhere in the no-man's land between the tiny towns of Rockdale and Thorndale. While the scenic ranches and farmers' fields had been quite beautiful when he'd made the drive to College Station earlier today, there wasn't much to see this time of the night.

That said, each of the little towns along this stretch of two-lane highway functioned as a de facto speed trap. While Jack could legally do seventy miles an hour on the meandering back road, the speed limit dropped to thirty-five within each city's incorporation limits. Texas cops were both professional and polite, but they were also quite happy to capitalize on the municipal payday offered by lawbreaking out-of-towners. Still, the longer he listened to the raspy words coming from the other end of the line, the more a speeding ticket seemed like a fair bargain if the money meant seeing his future wife that much sooner.

"You told me you weren't drinking tonight," Jack said.

"That was the plan, but Dawn & Hawkes were playing at Karlie's favorite bar, so we went to see them. Karlie may have told the bartender that I'd just gotten engaged, so he tried to buy me shots. I passed."

"But?" Jack said.

"But some college kids tried to pick us up," Lisanne said. "Somehow they didn't see my shiny new ring."

As a former college kid, Jack thought Lisanne might have been giving her would-be suitors far too much credit, but he was enjoying the sound of her voice way too much to interrupt.

"What happened next?" Jack said.

"I told those frat boys that I was waiting for my *fiancé*."

"How'd that work?" he asked.

"Not well," she said. "They started buying drinks for Karlie instead."

He smiled as he touched the brakes.

Karlie was Karlie Dill—Lisanne's college roommate and still one of her closest friends. After she'd shared the happy news with her parents, Lisanne had called Karlie. Never one to miss an opportunity, Karlie had suggested that Lisanne bring her fiancé to Austin so that she could meet the lucky boy.

While Jack loved traveling, he hadn't been so keen on accompanying Lisanne to a girls' weekend until his future bride had uttered the magic words—*Texas A&M football*. The Fightin' Aggies were at Kyle Field, and better yet, tickets were still available.

In a quick fit of negotiations that Jack thought boded well for their future nuptials, he and Lisanne had hammered out an agreement. They would fly from D.C. to Austin Sunday morning and rent a room at the famous Van Zandt near Rainey Street. Jack would drive over to College Station for the football game while Lisanne spent Sunday afternoon and evening catching up with Karlie. Jack would return after the night game ended, and they would meet Karlie for lunch on Monday and then grab the evening flight back to D.C.

Simple.

Or maybe not.

"Still haven't heard the part about you getting tipsy," Jack said.

"I'm getting there," Lisanne said. "After Karlie sent the UT kids packing, we were about to call it a night. But the bartender said he was working on a new drink, and he really wanted some feedback. He begged me to try it, Jack."

Jack just bet he had.

Lisanne Robertson had inherited her olive complexion, thick black hair, and deep chocolate eyes from her Lebanese mother. Her American father had bestowed upon her a desire to serve that took the form of a couple of years as an active-duty Marine followed by a stint in law enforcement before coming to the attention of an organization named The Campus. Lisanne's lean, athletic frame reflected her vocation.

So did the fact that she was missing one arm below the elbow.

The bullet that had taken her arm had nearly ended her life. For Lisanne, like Jack, physical fitness was a job requirement, not a hobby.

When he'd left for the football game, Lisanne had been wearing a fitted Longhorns T-shirt and tight jeans that showcased miles of legs. That outfit, coupled with her smile, had been enough to cause Jack to reconsider his sojourn to College Station. Knowing his fiancée, Lisanne had significantly upgraded her wardrobe before hitting the concert with Karlie. Pretty girls certainly weren't scarce in the legion of bars that called Sixth Street home, but Jack thought that Austin wasn't altogether ready for the phenomenon that was Lisanne Robertson.

He sure wasn't.

"What did he make you?" Jack said.

"He called it the McConaughey. It was like a margarita, but spicy. It was *so good*."

The emphasis Lisanne put on her last two words made Jack chuckle as he wisely refrained from asking just how many of the concoctions she'd sampled before rendering her verdict.

A drink named after Austin's favorite son had to be good.

"Is that why you called?" Jack said. "To rub it in?"

"No," Lisanne said. "I called because I miss you *and* I'm tipsy. Are you here yet?"

Jack very much wished he was *here yet* for more reasons than one. If he was being honest, he would have to admit that their weekend of fun was born of more than just a trip to see Karlie. He and Lisanne had come to a relational fork in the road. A fork that led down two very different paths. The weekend in Austin was meant to give them time together to think, and while he was no closer to solving their impasse, he did know one thing—life was much better in Lisanne Robertson's arms.

Unfortunately, the laws of physics cared neither for slightly intoxicated fiancées nor the rumbling of Detroit's finest engine. As much as he wished otherwise, Jack still had a good fifty minutes before he'd be handing the Mustang's keys over to the Van Zandt's valet. If experience was any guide, Lisanne would be fast asleep by then.

He opened his mouth to tell the woman he loved as much, when everything changed.

The crash happened so quickly that Jack almost missed it.

Though he was less than fifty yards from the colliding vehicles, the violence was still hard to follow. The impact quickly morphed into a tangle of metal and a cloud of debris. Like dancers joined at the hip, the two sedans spun from the winding Texas road into the surrounding brush. One moment, the stretch of blacktop had been the scene of crushing metal, skidding tires, and flashing headlights. The next, the two-lane highway was clear, all signs of violence erased from the double yellow lines as if an artist had wiped the entire scene from his slate. Unexpected violence and the chaos accompanying it had a way of confusing the senses and jarring the observer's sense of time.

Especially if the person witnessing it was unaccustomed to such things.

Jack Ryan, Jr., was not such a person.

Even so, it still took a moment or two for his OODA loop to run its course. For his brain to move from one stage to the next. And while Jack was not in a fighter jet's cockpit like the cycle's originator, he was in the driver's seat of a Ford Mustang GT. The car's snarling engine propelled him toward the accident at eighty-eight feet per second. Meaning in the time it took the average person to inhale, he had to process what had just happened and decide on a course of action. Under these harsh time constraints, Jack could have been forgiven for continuing past the wreck as his brain turned sensory inputs into thoughts.

Jack did not continue.

Though he was no more race car driver than fighter pilot, he was a member of a cadre of men and women who were arguably even more elect. This was not the first time Jack's mind had been required to analyze the unexpected and render a series of life-or-death decisions.

Nor would this probably be the last.

But Jack did not dwell on the oddities of his chosen profession any more than he considered what the crash's implications might mean for his already compressed schedule.

Instead, he acted.

Jack downshifted, transforming the engine's growl into a full-fledged roar even as he activated his hazard lights and angled the Mustang toward the shoulder.

"Hey, baby," Jack said, "I've got to go. I just saw a wreck."

"Watch yourself," Lisanne said.

Her previously flirty tone was a thing of the past.

There was a reason for the change.

Like Lisanne, Jack was an operative for an off-the-books intelligence organization known as The Campus. While he and Lisanne were in Austin purely for recreation, The Campus's long and distinguished list of adversaries weren't much for vacations.

"Always do," Jack said.

"Give me a call once you're back on the road," Lisanne said, her voice clear and her diction precise. "I love you."

"Love you too," Jack said.

As he hung up with his future bride, Jack had two thoughts. One, Lisanne wasn't anywhere near as intoxicated as she'd pretended to be. Two, a random car crash on a moonlit highway was not cause for concern for a normal person.

John Patrick Ryan, Jr., was not a normal person.

2

BACKCOUNTRY TEXAS ROADS WERE A TREAT, ESPECIALLY IN A CONVERTIBLE WITH power to spare and a traffic-free road. Fields of hay and grain were interspersed with wooded lots full of mesquite, live oaks, and cedar. Rolling hills dotted with cattle sat on either side of winding gravel paths that led to ranch houses. Some of the structures were fit for the set of *Yellowstone*, but most were simple affairs of river stone and wood and had probably been in the same family for generations.

Out here, motorists adhered to an unwritten courtesy that was a far cry from the Darwinian rules of the road followed by commuters in Austin, Houston, or Dallas. Though the highways were single lane for long stretches, people pulled off to the shoulder so that faster traffic could pass them by. But even the most polite driver couldn't dodge a car they couldn't see. And while the country's mild mannerisms and slower pace were delightful, there was nothing mild or slow about a three-thousand-pound mass of steel and plastic striking another at seventy miles per hour.

In a collision of that magnitude, even airbags wouldn't be of much help.

Jack's headlights played across the gravel shoulder as he brought the Mustang to a stop.

A light rain had fallen earlier in the evening and the roads were still slick with a rehydrated slurry of grime, oil, and the dirt and grit that were the typical by-products of vehicular traffic. As a Maryland native, Jack had grown up learning to drive on snowy roads. Accordingly, he'd snickered when a Texas native had warned him about driving in the rain, but Jack's arrogance hadn't lasted long. The black ice that terrorized his fellow northerners had nothing on Texas roads after a rainstorm.

In this case, the slick road had netted at least two victims. Though Jack had been certain the collision was between a pair of vehicles, he couldn't see anything beyond a vehicle-shaped hole in the underbrush lining the side of the road. Based on the way the terrain sloped downward, Jack guessed that a ravine or perhaps a creek lay at the bottom of the embankment.

This was no mere fender bender.

The portion of his brain that understood battlefield calculus suggested that what lay beyond the crushed limbs and broken bushes would rate far more serious than just bruises and bumps. Jack thumbed a button on the steering wheel and instructed the robotic voice that answered to call 911. Though the Mustang was a rental, he had still taken the time to sync his iPhone.

Driving the Texas back roads was a lot of fun.

Navigating them was a different matter.

"Nine-one-one, what is the nature of your emergency?"

"I need to report a multiple vehicle accident on Highway 79," Jack said. "I'm about ten miles west of Milano. The accident is on the north side of the road. Both vehicles have disappeared into the brush, and I'm afraid they've tumbled down an embankment."

"I'm dispatching EMS now. If it's safe for you to do so, can you take a look at the crash and describe it for me? I need to know if either vehicle is on fire."

"Just a minute," Jack said.

With the Mustang's top down, he'd elected to squirrel his phone away in the compartment between the front seats. Motoring down a back road with the wind in your face and Parker McCollum on the radio was great until an unexpectedly sharp turn sent your phone tumbling out into space.

Not that this had ever happened to Jack, of course.

But while the sports car's open roof indirectly hindered Jack's ability to reach his phone, it had the opposite effect on his hearing.

Or more precisely, the hearing of an all-too-familiar sound.

Gunfire.

3

JACK DID NOT HOLD AN ORDINARY JOB.

To be fair, not much about his life was ordinary. His father was President of the United States, and his mother had survived an assassination attempt by the Irish Republican Army. But compared to his career, these abnormalities were but blips on the radar. Jack's choice of vocations was difficult to describe. He worked for an organization that didn't officially exist doing things that didn't officially happen.

As a result, he was intimately familiar with both gunfire and the weapons that produced it.

He exited the Mustang and drew the SIG Sauer 365 SAS micro-compact holstered beneath his untucked shirt. While the organization that employed Jack was associated with the US intelligence community, it did not bestow upon its employees the authority to carry guns while traveling on commercial airlines.

That was fine.

Having found himself on the receiving end of ambushes a few too many times, Jack had arrived at a declaration of sorts. Namely, that he would never travel unarmed again. Accordingly, he'd checked his pistol and ammunition with his luggage and reunited with them both in Austin. Some people might have called this practice conspiracy minded.

Those people had never spent a day in Jack Ryan's shoes.

At six foot two and two hundred and twenty pounds, Jack was not physically insignificant, and the hours he'd spent sweating and bleeding in The Campus's fight house had well equipped him to use the advantages good genes and fierce sessions in the weight room had gifted him.

Even so, only a fool relied on physical prowess to win the day.

A firearm in the hands of a trained shooter always trumped fists or feet.

Jack led with the SIG as he followed the unmistakable tracks from the collision. He heard two distinct weapon reports: the short *pop, pop, pop* belonging to a pistol and the deeper barks associated with an assault rifle.

Probably an AK-47.

Whatever was transpiring in the underbrush was not a result of simple road rage. Texans might be well armed, but everyday motorists did not routinely pack long rifles for their daily commutes.

Jack flowed forward, resisting the urge to quicken his pace, and instead concentrated on maintaining a stable shooting platform. While there was much to be said for listening to subconscious cues from his lizard brain, sometimes they needed to be ignored. He felt an almost overwhelming need to run toward the sound of gunfire, but doing so would put him at a distinct disadvantage.

The kind of disadvantage that could lead to death.

Instead, Jack forced himself to steady his breathing and concentrate on the sounds of the battle. In his haste, he hadn't bothered to hang up his phone. With a little bit of luck, the 911 operator might hear the gunfire from the Mustang's mike and react accordingly. But as he'd learned long ago, luck, as with hope, was not a method nor a combat multiplier.

With a little help from his SIG, Jack intended to make his own luck.

The pistol's staccato rhythm ceased as Jack reached the underbrush. The significance of this event could be interpreted in a number of ways, but in moments like this, he'd found it useful to apply guardrails to his thinking. What were the worst- and best-case scenarios?

Best case—the pistoleer had eliminated the threat.

Worst case—the pistoleer was out of ammunition.

Or dead.

A chorus of male voices echoed through the woods. They were speaking English, but with an accent. Not British, but probably a distant cousin. Jack filed away this interesting tidbit for deeper consideration later in favor of devoting his mental energy to something much more pressing—staying alive.

As he'd suspected, the road did drop off, but not very far. The two vehicles occupied a meadow of sorts about five feet below him. Judging by the violence of the collision he'd witnessed, Jack expected to find the cars still locked together.

They were not.

Instead, the lead vehicle, a four-door sedan, was about ten yards in front of the second vehicle, a midsize SUV with a prominent brush guard. Jack registered the positioning of the vehicles and noticed that the sedan was facing the SUV.

Then he understood why.

The sedan was oriented in that manner because the SUV had conducted a PIT maneuver, which had sent the lead car into an uncontrolled spin.

The crash had been intentional.

Much like what was happening now.

Three gunmen were positioned outside the SUV, facing the sedan. The trio were wearing black balaclavas and were armed with assault rifles. But not the kind of beat-up specimens typically seen in the hands of gangbangers or cartel wannabes. No, these looked like the newer AK-47 variants, and they sported holographic sights, Magpul magazines, and tricked-out handguards. The SUV's driver and the front-seat passenger were using the vehicle's doors as cover even as they fired alternating bursts into the sedan's windshield. The third gunman was maneuvering under the covering fire, flanking the sedan to the left.

He moved with the rolling walk that mirrored Jack's own.

A gunfighter's walk.

Jack took a fraction of a second to assess the situation. He was about to enter the scenario with deadly force. There would be no take-backs or redos. He needed to be right, but his quick survey only reinforced his earlier assessment. Three men wearing black masks and armed with assault rifles had intentionally wrecked a second car. Aside from the brush guard, their vehicle had none of the telltale signs he would have expected from a low-profile law enforcement vehicle. No subdued red and blue lighting hidden in the grille or behind tinted windows, no antenna tree farm sprouting from the roof, and no spotlight incorporated into the driver's-side mirror.

Just an ordinary Tahoe.

While Jack didn't know whether the sedan's occupants were still alive, the gunmen weren't taking any chances. With another stride or two, the moving shooter would be able to fire through the driver's- and passenger-side windows, enveloping the car's interior in a deadly crossfire.

The men themselves were dressed in outdoor clothes. They didn't wear overt gear like plate carriers or tactical harnesses. Neither did their outer garments offer the uniformity of a SWAT team effecting an arrest. On that note, nothing Jack had heard or seen gave any indication that the men had given the sedan's occupants a chance to surrender before opening fire.

The commands the men were shouting matched what Jack expected to hear from a team in contact. No words were directed toward the pistoleer taking cover in the sedan. No orders to throw out his weapon or offers for him to surrender. Instead, the trio were firing into the vehicle with the discipline of professional soldiers. The gunmen didn't intend to arrest the sedan's occupants.

They intended to kill them.

The maneuvering gunman paused, settling into a shooter's stance.

Game time.

Jack centered the SIG's front sight post on the man's back, aligned the rear sights, and smoothly pressed the trigger to the rear. The countless hours spent expending tens of thousands of rounds on the range allowed him to complete this process in a fraction of a second.

The shot broke.

Jack took the slack out of the trigger as the pistol's sights came back onto target. His second shot came milliseconds after the first.

The gunman dropped to the ground.

Then things went sideways.

4

YOU CAN TELL A LOT ABOUT A SHOOTER'S TRAINING BY THE MANNER IN WHICH they react to an ambush. The gunmen Jack was facing were good.

Very good.

Unfortunately for Jack, he'd been forced to engage his targets from a position of limited cover. And by limited, he meant none.

Zero.

A gunfight is the ultimate example of playing for keeps. Jack had hoped that since he was approaching the gunmen from behind, that he'd be able to drop two, if not all three of the men, before they realized what was happening. This was not an unreasonable expectation if the men were simply killers rather than soldiers.

Based on their collective reactions, this was not the case.

With a fluidity that reminded Jack uncannily of the martial skills he'd seen exhibited by his Campus brethren, the gunmen firing on the sedan transitioned targets. By the time he tracked the SIG's sights from the shooter he'd dropped to the remaining pair, Jack was already looking down the barrel of an AK-47. More than likely two barrels, but in a bit of luck, the SUV's frame kept the driver from immediately engaging Jack.

The same could not be said of the SUV's passenger.

Jack was in the process of pressing the SIG's trigger when three sensory inputs demanded his attention seemingly simultaneously: a flash from the AK's barrel, the bark of a rifle shot, and the pinching of fabric across his torso as a high-velocity round passed within a hairsbreadth of his ribs.

The analytical portion of Jack's brain couldn't help but be impressed. In the space of just seconds, the gunman had heard Jack's shots, taken up a shooting position in a completely different azimuth, and put rounds on target.

Fairly accurate rounds.

These were not men to be trifled with.

Fortunately, the larger portion of Jack's mind was on autopilot, and in this case, autopilot equated to muscle memory. In the ultimate form of chicken, Jack continued pressing the trigger even as he minutely adjusted his sight alignment, compensating for the drift of his first shot, which had shattered the vehicle's door rather than the gunman's chest.

Jack was outmanned and outgunned. Attempting to seek cover now would only give his skilled opponent the opportunity to riddle his fleeing body with bullets. He had to kill or be killed.

It was the ultimate battle of skill.

And perhaps luck.

Though the odds were stacked against Jack in the firepower department, he had one important attribute in his corner.

Initiative.

Jack had begun the engagement, meaning that he'd had greater time to adjust to his new target. This meant that while both men's first shots had missed, Jack's second round impacted squarely on target. As did his third and fourth. The shooter folded in half and slid to the ground. The lopsided engagement had just shifted in Jack's favor.

He continued to believe this fairy tale for about two seconds.

That's how long it took for a new rifle to join the fight.

Dropping to one knee, Jack panned right looking for the rifle fire's source. He found it. The first gunman Jack had shot was very much alive.

Body armor.

Which meant that all the riflemen were probably wearing body armor.

Swearing, Jack rolled for the bushes to his right as dirt clods erupted to either side of him. Surprise and violence of action were the hallmarks of close-quarters battle, and he routinely employed both tenets to great success.

But not today.

Jack snuggled up next to a mesquite tree as he tried to become one with the earth. The bush's scraggly, narrow branches wouldn't offer much protection from flying bullets, but with a little luck the gnarled limbs might help to obscure Jack's outline. And that would have to do because luck and nine-millimeter rounds were about all Jack had to call on.

Twigs, leaves, and the ever-present Texas pollen rained down as Jack wormed farther to the right, intending to use the sloping ground to mask his vulnerable body. If he played his cards right, Jack thought he could follow the descending trail to some thicker vegetation he'd glimpsed earlier. From there, he could work his way back toward the sedan where perhaps the pistol's owner might be in a position to help. At the very least, the vehicle's metal frame would offer a better defense against the hail of 7.62mm rounds than flimsy scrub brush.

As if to reinforce this point, a flurry of rounds slapped into the tree to Jack's right, splintering the wood and blanketing him with choking dust. For all its benefits, this part of the Lone Star State was a haven for allergies, and Jack fought to keep from sneezing.

So much for following the terrain to the right.

Jack eyed the hill to his left, considering his other option.

Taking and holding the high ground was a tenet of ground combat, but to do so he would have to cross a stretch of open terrain.

That was a nonstarter.

Every action the gunmen had taken thus far had only reinforced Jack's estimate of their competence. With three skilled shooters focused on him, he knew he had zero chance of making it back to his car unscathed.

Which left his final choice.

Staying put.

Jack stretched out in the leaf litter, taking up a prone position. He pressed against the scraggly tree in an attempt to narrow the avenues of approach the gunmen might use when they came. Three professionals would not run the risk that he was still out there somewhere, waiting. The gunmen would attempt to flush him from the brush and finish the job they'd started.

The job Jack had interrupted.

Branches crackled.

The men were coming.

5

JACK TOOK A DEEP BREATH AS HE DROVE HIS RIGHT ELBOW INTO THE DIRT, STEADY-ing his aim. The SIG's tritium-coated night sights glowed a lime green as he prepared for the final act. The prone supported position was one of the most accurate platforms for pistol fire, and Jack would need all the accuracy help he could get. To have any hope of surviving the coming assault, he would need to make head shots. In a perfect world, staying hidden would force the gunmen to come to Jack, thereby negating the range advantage of their rifles while simultaneously allowing him to fire first.

In a perfect world.

Nothing about the last several minutes could be construed as perfect. Even so, Jack was glad this was about to be over. In kinetic operations, the buildup was often worse than the firefight. Jack was playing the bad hand he'd been dealt in the most advantageous way possible.

Now it was time to get on with things.

Another twig snapped.

Walking through the woods quietly was much harder than it looked, especially at night in unfamiliar terrain without the aid of night vision goggles. Added to this was the fact that the body's senses grew sharper during moments of duress. Under normal circumstances—with the sun shining, birds chirping, and joy in his heart—Jack probably wouldn't have even noticed the *crack* of wood splintering. But in his current state, with a thundering heart and death on his mind, every sound was magnified.

Or was it?

Jack resisted the urge to orient his pistol toward the sound, knowing that the human eye was keenly attuned to motion. He was also conscious of the fact that had he been in the shooters' shoes, he might have employed a little misdirection to get them looking one way while he hit them from another.

Very conscious.

Another *crackle* sounded from the same direction. Keeping his hands and the SIG motionless, Jack turned his head ever so slightly. Stalking an enemy at night was a science all its own.

A science happily taught to Jack by his boss, John T. Clark.

Clark had earned his stripes hunting NVA soldiers in the jungles of Vietnam and the lessons he'd imparted to his progeny were numerous. But one of the most important applied here. In darkness, using peripheral vision was the best way to detect targets. Jack was hoping that by tilting his head, he could bring the portion of his eye much better suited to darkness into play.

His plan worked.

But not the way he'd envisioned.

One moment Jack was holding his breath, listening for the slightest of footfalls as he tried to pierce the darkness with his straining eyes. The next, the sound of an engine roaring to life cut through the air. A looming black shape followed.

An SUV.

An SUV that was headed straight for him.

Dropping the SIG, Jack pushed off the ground with both hands as he scrambled to find purchase. He didn't have time to stand so he didn't try. Instead, with something that would have looked at home in a tumbling demonstration, Jack launched into the air from a pushup position, rolling down the incline as branches raked his face and cheeks.

The SUV roared by, shredding foliage like a charging rhinoceros, and a single spinning tire passed close enough to spatter Jack's face with mud. The engine revved, and Jack prepared himself for another pass, but it didn't materialize. Instead, the SUV's throaty roar faded as the vehicle motored down the road.

Cautiously, Jack got to his feet, found the SIG, and holstered the pistol.

While he didn't understand what would have caused the shooters to retreat instead of pressing the attack, Jack wasn't going to look a gift horse in the mouth. Maybe he'd be able to get out of here without any further drama.

And then he heard sirens.

6

LIKE MOST LAW-ABIDING CITIZENS, JACK DID NOT FEAR POLICE SIRENS.

Normally.

Tonight, Jack thought that the appearance of law enforcement might make an already confusing situation even less comprehensible. And when confusing situations involved men with guns and dead bodies, police officers tended to respond with their guns drawn and index fingers near the trigger.

Not ideal.

The best way to avoid this type of misunderstanding was to have someone else verify your side of the story.

Like the sedan's occupant, for instance.

Getting to his feet, Jack raced down the incline toward the damaged car.

"Friendly," Jack yelled as he approached. "Friendly coming in."

Surviving the gunfight had been a result of equal parts luck and skill. But luck was a fickle mistress, and Murphy's law applied doubly so to combat. If there was a patron saint of firefights, Jack thought that the man was a bit of a cynic. Jack wouldn't put it past the old guy to help him through the craziness of the last several minutes, only to allow him to catch a bullet from the unseen person he'd been risking his life to help.

"Hello in the car," Jack said, drawing even with the passenger door. "I'm here to help."

Nothing.

The silence could be because the car's occupant was incapacitated or dead. The fact that the pistoleer had stopped returning fire at the trio of gunmen seemed to lend credence to this theory. On the other hand, the driver could be waiting to shoot until they had the greatest possibility of hitting their intended target.

Which was exactly what Jack would have done.

Decisions, decisions.

The sirens grew louder, and blue and red flickers danced across the trees. The police were coming, which meant the window in which Jack could shape his pending encounter with them was closing.

Time to go all in.

"I'm opening the passenger door," Jack said.

His benign words aside, Jack approached the car from the rear, trying to put the passenger's window column between himself and a potential flurry of pistol rounds. The sedan's window was tinted, rendering the inside of the car a cavern of shadows. Jack thought he could see the outline of a body slumped in the driver's seat, but he couldn't be sure.

Taking a deep breath, Jack grabbed the door handle and pulled.

The door swung open, accompanied by the tinkle of falling glass.

Jack took a quick peek into the sedan's interior, taking a mental snapshot before ducking back out of the line of fire. He had used this simple but effective technique during countless gunfights, and judging by what he saw, the tactic might have just saved his life again.

A man lay sprawled across the front seat.

A man with a pistol gripped firmly in his right hand.

"Put the gun down," Jack said. "I can help you, but you've got to put the gun down."

Jack didn't know whether it was his tone or the sirens and headlights of the arriving patrol cars that prompted the man. It didn't really matter. The important thing was the dull *thud* of a metallic object hitting the car's floorboards that rang through the night. Jack edged around the door until he could see the pistol resting on the rubber floormat. Then he crawled all the way in.

The driver was in a bad way.

His chest and shoulder were a mass of blood, and his lips were flecked with crimson. Jack didn't know how many times the man had been hit, but his wounds appeared to be extensive. In a situation like this, there was just one prerogative—stop the bleed.

"You're gonna be fine," Jack said, searching the man's chest for the entrance wound. "The ambulance is right behind me."

Jack didn't know if this was true, but that didn't matter. Gunshots were unpredictable things. Wounds that were immediately incapacitating in some victims didn't have the same effect on others. More times than not, survival came down to the victim's mindset. If they believed they stood a chance, they did. If not, shock and blood loss helped the victim's negative thoughts become self-fulfilling prophecies.

"Help," the man whispered. "Help me."

A red mist accompanied his words as the man's fingers tried to find purchase on Jack's jeans. Jack brushed the driver's hands away as he tried to assess his wound. Blood in the airway suggested damage to one or both lungs. If this was the case, there was a good chance the driver had what was known as a sucking chest wound—a condition in which air enters the pleural cavity as the patient inhales. Ambulance or not, unless Jack found the entry wound and closed it, the growing pressure imbalance would collapse one or both lungs and kill the patient.

"I've got you," Jack said, unzipping the driver's sweatshirt. "I've got you."

The car's interior went from a dimly lit scene of shadows and indistinct forms to the clarity of an operating room as a floodlight burned through the windshield. The beam originated from behind Jack, revealing the driver in stark detail.

The man was not what Jack had expected.

Though adventures with guns and masked shooters tended to be a young man's game, the driver was the exception to the norm: middle-aged with a sharply receding hairline, wispy beard, and thick glasses. His fleshy cheeks and jowly neck seemed at home with the faded A&M sweatshirt and worn jeans. This guy didn't scream paramilitary operative so much as accountant.

Or dad.

Looking back at the sweatshirt, Jack found the source of his intuition. PROUD AGGIE FATHER was stenciled across the maroon fabric in black script. Had it not been for the pistol on the floorboard, Jack would have thought he'd mistakenly jumped into the wrong car.

Well, that and the hissing coming from the man's torso.

"Hold tight," Jack said, fishing his money clip from his pocket.

While just about anything could be used as a field-expedient bandage, only something capable of maintaining an airtight seal would stop the influx of air into the wound.

Almost anything plastic would work.

Jack pulled a Costco membership card from his money clip. Laying the plastic strip flat against the entry wound, he held the card in place with one hand as he removed his outer shirt and fashioned it into a makeshift pressure bandage with the other. The fabric wasn't designed with halting a hemorrhaging wound in mind, but he was able to knot the ad hoc dressing tight enough across the man's chest to keep the plastic in place. Ideally the plastic needed to be taped down to the man's skin on three sides, but Jack figured a compression bandage and a Costco card were better than nothing.

He was right.

The change in the driver was immediate.

The man had been gasping for breath before, but now his respiration seemed steady. The driver would need a chest tube to vent the excess pressure still compressing his lungs, but Jack's quick work had just ensured the problem wouldn't get any worse.

Now to see to the rest of his wounds.

"You, in the car, get out with your hands up. Slowly."

While Jack had been expecting to hear a similar command from the moment the floodlight had pierced the sedan's darkness, the way in which it was delivered was still a surprise. Rather than from a police officer standing just feet away, the words were projected from a loudspeaker. Meaning that whoever was speaking them was still sitting in his patrol car rather than coming to help.

"I'm unarmed," Jack shouted, raising his bloodstained fingers into the light, "but I'm treating a badly injured man. He's been hit at least twice in the torso. He needs a medic."

"Get out of the car with your hands up. Now."

Jack bit back the reply he wanted to make, putting himself in the police officer's place instead. In a town this small, there was probably just one officer on shift. With no partner to watch his back, it made sense that the person on the other end of the spotlight would call Jack out of the vehicle rather than take chances at what was obviously still an active crime scene.

"Okay," Jack said. "Okay. I'm coming out."

The driver was drifting in and out of consciousness, but his blue eyes seemed particularly lucid as Jack cinched the bandage one notch tighter.

"Help me," the driver said, his fingers again fluttering against Jack's jeans. "Please."

"Don't worry," Jack said, gently but firmly pushing the grasping digits away, "I'll be right back. Promise."

"Last warning," the loudspeaker echoed ominously.

"Keep your pants on," Jack said, "I'm tightening the bandage."

The driver's lips seemed to be working to form another word, but Jack shook his head. "Save your strength," Jack said, placing his hand on the man's chest. "Right back."

Then, to the cop, Jack said, "Coming out. I'm coming out."

Jack eased backward out of the passenger seat, his bloody hands shoulder high.

He backed two steps away from the car, debating whether to wait for commands or to just turn toward the light in the interest of getting this show on the road. While his close interaction with the driver had engendered in Jack a protective feeling for the man, Jack had no intention of joining him on a hospital gurney.

"Take three steps to your right. Now."

Jack complied, moving slowly and with exaggerated motions. He took extra-large strides, hoping that clearing a pathway to the sedan and the injured driver might provide the police officer with an impetus to move things along.

It did not.

Instead, the spotlight swung with Jack, ensuring he remained centered in the beam.

Which was stupid.

Jack clearly had nothing in his hands and his T-shirt was tight across his muscular chest. The real danger in this situation, had there been any, would be in the unknown factor—the car. The car that was now shrouded in darkness. While Jack's assessment of the officer's courage was still up for debate, it was clear this man was never going to win the spelling bee.

"Turn toward me."

"Can we speed this up?" Jack said, squinting as he faced the spotlight. "The guy in that car needs help."

"No, he doesn't."

The words came from behind Jack.

Apparently, the cop did have a partner.

"What do you mean?" Jack said, turning toward the sound of the voice.

A second police officer straightened from where he'd been peering in the car.

"I mean, he's dead."

7

"RUN ME THROUGH IT ONE MORE TIME."

"No," Jack said, eyeing the man seated across from him. "I'm done."

"You're done when I say you're done."

"That's actually not how this works," Jack said. "Unless I'm under arrest, my presence here is voluntary. And if I am under arrest, I want my lawyer. Now."

The officer stared back without speaking, as if his silence would somehow compel Jack to talk.

It did not.

Like many paramilitary operatives, Jack had attended a variant of the military's survival evasion resistance and escape, or SERE, training. While the course had not been one he'd ever voluntarily repeat, the days and nights he'd spent subjected to mock torture sessions and not-so-mock interrogations had been enlightening. Jack had learned as much about himself as he had how to resist questioning under duress. His opponents had been some of the most skilled interrogators the intelligence community had to offer.

This small-town yokel wasn't in the same league.

"Here's the thing," the officer said, speaking with deliberate slowness, "not much happens around here, and the people who call Briar Wood home like it that way. What passes for a busy night on my watch is usually a couple of high schoolers getting a little too rowdy at an impromptu bonfire. The last time someone was shot here was ten years ago when Old Man Sellers blew his finger off while cleaning his .22. Since Tim was drunk at the time, we decided to call that even. And then you came along."

The officer punctuated his statement by taking a bite of the pastry resting by the stained coffee mug to his left. Jack's was sitting on the table untouched, as was the cup of java the officer had so thoughtfully poured. After washing down his food with a swallow of coffee, the cop resumed his conversation as if he'd never left yet another conversational empty space that Jack had declined to fill.

"Part of me thinks that I should make a call to my friends at the FBI and let them handle things. I get along fine with the folks from the College Station Resident Agency. I'm sure they could be here in a couple of hours, Mr. . . . . Richardson."

The police officer handled Jack's driver's license as he spoke.

Jack's fraudulent driver's license.

Though he was not doing anything that even approximated work for his employer, Jack was traveling on one of several legends supplied by The Campus. A recent run-in with a Chinese wet work team had definitively proven that Jack could no longer use commercial transportation under his true name and expect to keep his movements hidden from adversarial governments. As a result, he'd taken to booking travel using one of several false names under the assumption that just because he didn't consider his trip to be work-related didn't mean that a foreign government with an axe to grind would feel the same way.

The driver's license the police officer held in his crumb-laden fingers would certainly withstand official scrutiny, but a search of Jack's assumed name in national crime databases would raise eyebrows at his day job. Not to mention that Jack preferred not to put his interrogation resistance training to use against an actual FBI agent.

This was not so much because Jack had something to hide as the fact that the interaction would cause more complications. At a minimum, his legend would be burned, and contrary to spy thrillers, backstopped false identities did not exactly grow on trees.

And then there was the pending paper trail that would come from the interview.

The FBI agent would take notes, as FBI agents did, and these would go into a computer system, forming an entry that would be shared across the federal law enforcement community. This was not to say that the interaction couldn't later be purged—it could. In fact, Gavin Biery, The Campus's IT director, had a protocol for doing just that. But all these things would take the collective eyes of The Campus's limited staff off the operational ball. Given the choice, Jack would like to spare his comrades any additional work.

But the small-town police officer didn't know any of this.

Or at least he shouldn't know any of this.

Which made Jack wonder if perhaps there was more to Officer Bradshaw than met the eye.

"Call whoever you want," Jack said, getting to his feet, "but unless you're arresting me, I'm leaving."

The officer's thick lip curled into a snarl, but he didn't say anything.

Jack took the man's silence as acquiescence.

With a final nod, Jack edged past the police officer and strolled out of the room.

The room in question didn't seem to have been built with interrogations in mind. At least it didn't look that way to Jack. Instead, the space was more of what he would have termed a huddle room. A place where someone could go for a private phone call or to have a quiet conversation. To be fair, Jack couldn't imagine that Briar Wood was the type of place where interrogations needed to happen in a controlled room wired for sound. Judging by the tiny police station and the single jail cell, the questioning of suspects probably happened in the field after Briar Wood's tiny force responded to whatever misdemeanor call had warranted their attention.

Judging by the strange looks from the station's other two occupants, Jack's assessment didn't seem to be too far off the mark. A woman was manning the phones as well as the front desk. She was dressed in a uniform that matched the style worn by Officer Bradshaw, but she lacked the requisite badge or utility belt. Probably a combination dispatcher and secretary.

The second person looked to be barely out of high school. The man had to be at least eighteen to be a police officer, but his baby face and bright brown eyes would have been at home on a high school student. What could charitably be called a mustache graced his upper lip, but the scraggly whiskers gave the officer the look of a boy trying to be taken for a man rather than the air of maturity he was no doubt cultivating. The hard stare he gave Jack only lent itself to the image of a schoolboy playing dress-up.

"Morning," Jack said with a smile.

The woman gave Jack a cautious nod while the boy/man did his best to look tough.

Jack chuckled as he pushed through the door into the night air.

For better or worse, he was done with this town and its people. As he had countless other times in his life, Jack had played the role of Good Samaritan and then paid the price for his kindness. Though the ambush outside of town was hardly a normal day at the office even for Jack, he'd done all he could for the driver and given what passed for law enforcement in Briar Wood a description of the shooters and their vehicle.

Whether Officer Bradshaw did anything with that information was not Jack's problem.

Okay, so that wasn't precisely true.

A man had been brutally murdered by a team of professionals. While his role in this scenario was over, Jack would not be content to leave the dead man's fate in Bradshaw's hands. Jack tried to live his life as if he was just another guy, not the eldest son of the most powerful man on earth. That said, sometimes he used his famous last name to tip the scale in favor of those who didn't have his connections. Once he got back to D.C., Jack intended to follow up with an FBI friend. Bradshaw might not be up to the task of solving this murder, but innocent blood had been spilled. This was Texas, by God, not a third world country.

In America, the rule of law applied to everyone, or it applied to no one.

Jack believed this concept with the whole of his being, but he was no masked crusader. Yes, he was often called to serve as the stick when those who enacted American foreign policy failed to sway bad actors with the carrot, but the continental United States was not his beat. Besides, the woman who loved him was waiting in a hotel less than sixty miles away.

Jack's time in Briar Wood was through.

Reaching in his pocket for his car keys, Jack found something else.

A paper.

Jack pulled off a paper clip before unfolding the stationery and angling it so it caught the glow given off by the mercury light hanging above the door. The spidery writing was difficult to read, and the dark splotches made the words even less legible.

Still, Jack saw enough.

A name, a time, and a place.

AMANDA, 4 AM, THE TIPSY CHICKEN

Jack thought about his final minutes in the sedan, battling to save the driver's life. The note gave new meaning to the man's furtive efforts. He'd thought the man's flailing arms and desperate attempt to speak had been driven by fear, but maybe Jack had been wrong. Maybe the victim had been trying to tell him something.

With a sigh, Jack remembered the driver's panicked look.

His blood-flecked lips.

His parting words.

Help me, please.

Could it have been that the man's plea corresponded to the slip of paper he'd shoved into Jack's pants pocket? Jack had no way of knowing. What he did know was that the driver had just reached out from beyond the grave to deliver a message.

Now the ball was in Jack's court.

The easy, not to mention legal, course of action dictated that Jack should march back into the office and hand the bloody note to Officer Bradshaw.

After all, America was not his beat.

Then again, Jack wasn't much for taking the easy way out.

Jack pulled out his phone and entered *The Tipsy Chicken* into Google Maps. It was a greasy spoon diner open twenty-four hours and located just two miles away.

Jack yawned as he looked at the time on his phone.

Three thirty-five a.m.

Bradshaw had let Jack cool his heels in the interrogation room for several hours before coming in to take his statement, but Jack hadn't realized it was this late. Or early. Either way, he was long past due for Austin.

Help me, please.

With a sigh, Jack got into the Mustang and started the engine.

Hopefully the Tipsy Chicken made a mean plate of biscuits and gravy.

8

SAGHAND URANIUM MINE, IRAN

NOT FOR THE FIRST TIME, DAVID MILLER FOUND HIMSELF RECONSIDERING HIS LIFE choices.

For a barely twenty-one-year-old, this was something of a novelty.

David was much too young for a midlife crisis and his grounded midwestern upbringing had helped to ensure he hadn't made life-altering decisions in the areas of love or finances. In fact, up until his nineteenth birthday, he would have categorized his existence as ordinary.

Painfully ordinary.

His mother and father were still happily married, his brother and two sisters were out of the house and pursuing lives of their own, and the small suburb outside of Cincinnati where he grew up had not disowned him. As the baby of the family, David had been offered a certain amount of latitude that his siblings had not been. Rather than following in their footsteps by attending college at the Ohio State University, he'd elected to take a gap year. The gap year had led to something else.

Which had led David here.

Here was a far cry from the relaxing adventure he'd envisioned.

To be fair, *here* was a far cry from anywhere.

"What do you think?"

The whispered question came from David's team leader, Elad Morag.

David hesitated before replying.

The pause wasn't born out of fear, though his team leader could be plenty intimidating. Israelis tended to be shorter than Americans, but Elad was short even by his country's standards. But within a moment or two of meeting the commando, David had felt himself shrink. Elad carried himself with a gravitas that made him seem eight feet tall. Though he was quick to smile, when it came to his teammates, Elad radiated intensity. He was part mother hen and part wolverine, but David's respect for Elad was not what caused him to hesitate.

David paused because Hebrew wasn't his first language.

Or second.

Or third.

But it was the language of his adopted people and David had been working nonstop for the last eighteen months to master it. Fortunately, the topic that Elad was asking David to weigh in on involved a tongue he'd spoken since childhood.

Persian.

"Those are the trucks we're looking for," David said, choosing his words carefully. "The license plates match."

Hebrew was a tricky language and David's exposure to it thus far had mainly centered on the masculine tense. Though Israel's laws required that both men and women serve a mandatory term in the IDF, or Israel Defense Forces, combat arms branches were not integrated by sex like the American military.

In the almost two years David had spent in the IDF's special operations pipeline, he'd been almost exclusively in the company of men, and his Hebrew had developed accordingly. While this idiosyncrasy usually produced nothing more serious than a few chuckles from his male counterparts, it had served as a great hindrance in David's primary extracurricular pursuit—hitting on Israeli women.

Fortunately, David had been taught Persian by his Iranian mother and expected to speak it to his maternal grandparents who lived nearby and visited often. The flowing script on the tanker truck's license plates came as natural to David as breathing.

Would that conversing with Elad were as easy.

"Are you sure? We only get one chance."

This time the speaker was Nimrod Diskin, the element's second-in-command. Nimrod and Elad were mother and father to the five-man-strong long-range reconnaissance unit, and they behaved like an old married couple. Though the men had grown up together on a small *kibbutz*, or farming collective, and were the best of friends, the pair bickered incessantly.

Or maybe that was just because they were Israeli.

After two years, David still wasn't certain.

"I'm sure," David said, putting the spine in his voice that he knew was needed to convince Nimrod. "The trucks are from the Isfahan Province."

Though Nimrod was a telephone pole to Elad's fire hydrant, the commando carried with him an intensity that exceeded even that of his huskier friend. Or maybe it was just a seriousness of purpose. Nimrod's older brother had been felled by a Hezbollah bullet during the disastrous 2006 Lebanon War, while his father had finally lost his struggle with the mental ravages inflicted on him when he was a tank crew member during the 1973 Yom Kippur War.

Nimrod understood the cost of keeping his homeland safe in a way that even most of his Israeli countrymen did not.

David was beginning to understand it, too.

"*Isfahan* means *Natanz*," Elad whispered. "David is right."

Natanz.

Home of a once secret, but now declared, Iranian uranium enrichment facility.

"Come on, let's do this."

The speaker was Yossi Cohn.

The sniper was the fourth member of the five-man team and the most temperamental. Though to be fair, the security of his nation and the livelihood of his people could very well rest on Yossi's ability to hit a moving target at a distance of almost a kilometer under less than ideal environmental conditions.

Saghand was a tiny village located in a mountainous region of Iran more than two thousand kilometers from Tel Aviv. David was a long way from his adopted home, as the eight days his team had spent getting to this abandoned plateau on the side of a mountain could attest. Over the course of his journey, David had lost count of the number of conveyances he'd employed to cross this vast distance, but the Mossad asset who had facilitated the final leg had dropped them off at the base of the mountains two nights ago. Now, he and his fellow commandos were in a hide site overlooking the Saghand uranium mine.

David was wearing a camouflage uniform that had been developed precisely to match the soil on which he and his team were lying, but the Israelis weren't the only ones who knew how to hide in plain sight. If the Mossad's intelligence was correct, the Iranians had repurposed the mine's abandoned tunnel complex for something else. David and his team were tasked with validating that intelligence assessment.

Assuming that Yossi was ever permitted to take his shot.

"Benny, what do you think?" Elad said.

Unlike the US military, the chain of command in Israeli military units was a somewhat amorphous concept. In a country of only nine million people, everyone was family, and everyone served at least two years in the IDF. A collective familiarity had replaced the ironclad discipline associated with American military units.

This was doubly so in the special operations community.

Elad was the team leader and ultimately the one in charge, but he would be loath to give orders without first hearing the consensus of his teammates.

"We've been in place twelve hours already," Benny said. "If we don't take the shot now, we will have to reposition or risk discovery. I say do it."

Benny Kokia was the final member of the squad.

Benny was facing the opposite direction of the other four commandos in order to provide security for their tiny element. Benny was a communications guru, and it would fall to him to call in the results of their operation to headquarters. Accordingly, he was keenly aware of the ever-changing location of the satellite constellation that permitted his sparse communications back to Israel as well as the efforts of the Iranians to intercept or locate his data bursts.

Benny was a pessimist by nature and served as a useful counterbalance to Yossi's exuberance.

"Okay," Elad said. "We're a go. David, get the bird in position."

In addition to being the resident Farsi expert, David was the team's drone operator. This was less because he had a natural affinity for aviation and more because he was the most junior, and therefore least experienced, commando. David did not mind his assignment. He liked flying the drone, but more important,

David agreed with Elad's assessment. He had a long way to go before he was ready to operate on the level of his much more seasoned teammates.

Reaching to the bundle lying beside him, David checked the drone's optics package and power indicator a final time, then he lofted the UAV into the sky. Unlike the more common quadcopters, this drone resembled a traditional glider with its skinny fuselage and long wings. It had been designed with clandestine operations in mind, and the drone's ultraquiet electric motor and lift-efficient body allowed it to stay aloft undetected in denied environments.

Or so David hoped.

Transitioning to the small tablet that controlled the device, David confirmed that the drone was tracking to the waypoint he'd input earlier before activating the aircraft's camera payload.

A moment later, a side view of the idling tanker truck swam into view.

"Target identified," David said. "Position confirmed. It's over the sensor."

The sensor David was referencing had been emplaced along the side of the road by a different Mossad asset. Like David's uniform, the sensor was housed in an outer casing designed to look like a rock that perfectly matched the texture and color of the surrounding terrain. Except that the "rock" had been coated with a special chemical compound that fluoresced in a discrete spectrum visible only to the camera beneath the drone's nose. Without the white flash running alongside the sensor's housing, David wasn't sure he would have been able to pick out the "rock" from the surrounding roadside rubble.

"Take the shot," Elad said.

Yossi let his rifle speak for him.

The soda can–sized suppressor attached to the muzzle of

Yossi's IWI-manufactured DAN bolt-action rifle did much to minimize the weapon's report.

Still, nothing could erase the acoustic signature completely.

A *pop* announced the shot, followed by the metal-on-metal *clank* as Yossi worked the DAN's action to chamber another round.

"Miss," Nimrod hissed. "Low."

A second *pop* sounded, followed again by the sound of the bolt sliding home.

"Hit," Nimrod said. "Hit."

"Confirmed," David said.

The drone's thermal camera allowed him to see both the minute flash as the .338 Lapua Magnum round impacted the truck's cylindrical cargo hold as well as the distortion as a vapor cloud leaked from the newly made hole. The gaseous mixture resembled the heat-induced mirages seen over blacktop in the summertime. The distorted air flowed across the ground, coating the still fluorescing rock.

This was the moment of truth.

"Positive confirmation from the sensor," Nimrod said.

"*Kus emek,*" Elad said. "Call it in, Yossi. Just once, I wish our Mossad brothers and sisters would get it wrong."

David didn't understand his team leader's sentiment then.

He soon would.

9

MARY PAT FOLEY MOVED THROUGH THE WEST WING, CONSCIOUS OF HER STRIDE. AS she wound past the closet-sized offices, she nodded to coworkers and smiled at the occasional intern even as her flats clicked across the floor like a metronome. Even though she was in her mid-sixties, Mary Pat could outwalk many a twentysomething West Wing staffer. Early in her career, she'd learned the importance of physical fitness and her focus on her health was now paying dividends.

But her insistence on maintaining an even cadence wasn't because Mary Pat was worried about leaving her assistant behind or because she was trying to keep pace with a longer-legged coworker. As the director of national intelligence, or DNI, she was a high-level member of the President's cabinet and one of his closest friends. If she ran through the White House, people would notice and tongues would wag. This wouldn't do, even if the news she was about to dump in the lap of one of her oldest friends merited a little running.

But Mary Pat was a former spy and spies were experts at masking their emotions.

"Morning, Mary Pat. Everything okay?"

Or maybe not.

"Good morning, Pete," Mary Pat said. "Just another Monday."

She forced a smile as she spoke, but the man standing post outside the Oval Office didn't seem fooled. His face might be wearing an answering smile, but his eyes were tight and his hands restless. While his fingers had been hovering near his waist, they had now drifted up toward his chest. This wasn't because the man regarded Mary Pat as a threat as much as he was instinctively reacting to the news she carried in the orange-and-white-striped folder clutched against her chest.

Apparently even old spies couldn't get one past the Secret Service.

"Five a.m. is an awfully early start for just another Monday," Pete said.

Mary Pat ceded this round with a slight nod as she stowed her mobile in one of the wooden cubbies mounted to the wall. Though she most often came out the loser, Mary Pat enjoyed the little sparring sessions with the men and women entrusted with keeping the most powerful man in the world safe. Like iron sharpening iron, she believed that trying to get one over on the Secret Service kept her case officer skills fresh, while trying to get a read on Mary Pat helped Pete.

Not to mention that this exchange served as a warm-up for the main event.

"Got some interesting stuff in today's PDB," Mary Pat said.

"I hate interesting," Pete said.

So did Mary Pat.

Mary Pat entered the Oval Office to find President John Patrick Ryan and his chief of staff, Arnie van Damm.

"Happy Monday, MP," Ryan said. "Coffee?"

"No, thank you, sir," Mary Pat said as the door to the Oval Office eased closed behind her. "I've already had my fix."

Though his smile remained as broad as ever, Ryan's blue eyes narrowed. As was his custom, he'd risen from his seat behind the Resolute desk when Mary Pat entered. This was partly because when it came to his behavior toward the opposite sex, Jack still had old-fashioned sensibilities.

But only partly.

Like Mary Pat, the President had begun his civilian government service in the Central Intelligence Agency. While she'd made her bones as an agent runner, Ryan had gravitated toward the analytical side of the business.

Neither of their careers had progressed along traditional paths. Though the details were still closely held from the general public, Ryan and Mary Pat had actually served together on more than one paramilitary operation, and as was often the case with warriors who faced combat side by side, their friendship had deepened into something closer to a familial bond than a work relationship.

As a result, Mary Pat knew that Jack was genuinely happy to see her this morning.

She also knew that what she was about to relay from today's PDB would cause her friend anguish. On the whole, Mary Pat considered their joint history a positive thing, but on days like today she sometimes wished her relationship with the President of the United States was a bit more formal. What she had to say wasn't something she'd relish dumping on any superior.

When that superior was Jack Ryan, it hurt even more.

"Got an early start then?" Ryan said.

"Yes, sir," Mary Pat said. "Some reporting came in last night that has thrown us a bit of a curveball."

"I see," Ryan said. "Is there anyone else we should bring in?"

The fact that Mary Pat was delivering the briefing herself at this early hour wasn't lost on Ryan, but he was too professional to remark on it. His trust in his DNI manifested in a multitude of ways, but this was the one that she treasured the most. Rather than trying to preempt her briefing with a series of questions, Ryan throttled his inner analyst. He trusted his friend and allowed her to present without interruption or helpful suggestions.

But that didn't mean Mary Pat was without her blind spots.

As someone whose time in government spanned multiple decades, she'd served under several administrations and interacted with countless elected officials and political appointees. Though she certainly exercised her opinions as a citizen at the ballot box, at work she tried her best to be apolitical. Mary Pat's job as the nation's top intelligence official was to present the unvarnished truth and recommend courses of action independent of their potential political consequences. In a perfect world, politics and intelligence would be treated as two separate topics.

This wasn't a perfect world.

Mary Pat had long ago come to terms with the truth that her boss was a politician. As such, Ryan needed a balanced approach to the information she presented. Someone to remind him that there were other stakeholders in the room, even if they couldn't be seen or heard.

About three hundred and thirty million of them.

If Mary Pat was the good angel sitting on Ryan's right shoulder, then the role of bad angel often fell to his long-suffering chief of staff, Arnie van Damm. Though she and Arnie shared an amenable relationship, they often came at a problem from different angles. Mary Pat knew that her boss was well served by this diversity of thought even if scraps with Arnie weren't always fun. Unlike the Secret Service agent standing post outside the Oval Office, Arnie didn't always surrender after he'd been beaten.

Then again, neither did she.

"I don't think so, sir," Mary Pat said, "but if Arnie disagrees, we can convene a larger group. The material I'm about to present is sensitive, and I would prefer that as few ears as possible heard the first draft."

"You okay with that?" Ryan said, eyeing Arnie.

Like the President, Arnie had risen at Mary Pat's entrance, but she had a feeling this was more because the longtime political pugilist sensed a coming fight and wanted to be on his feet for the brawl. Though Ryan would always place the safety of the American people before all else, his role was more than just that of commander in chief.

Jack had run for his second term because he had a vision for America, and in a constitutional republic, enacting that vision took buy-in from Congress. Accordingly, the influence that Arnie and Mary Pat both exerted over their boss waxed and waned with the legislative tides. When Ryan was attempting to woo members from the legislative branch of government, he tended to give Arnie's musings more weight. When his agenda was lost in the congressional morass, the President gravitated more toward Mary Pat.

It had taken her a while to get used to the idea that her boss's priorities were always attempting to reach equilibrium, but now Mary Pat embraced the push and pull. The truth of the matter was that Jack Ryan worked for the American people, and she was okay with that.

Even if this reality sometimes made her life more difficult.

"Yeah," Arnie said, drawing out the word. "Mary Pat doesn't make statements like that lightly."

As usual, Arnie looked as if he'd wadded his suit up into a ball and jumped on it before donning the coat and jacket. At first Mary Pat had found the chief of staff's perpetually rumpled look off-putting. Now she thought differently. Like Columbo and his trench coat, Arnie's disheveled appearance had caused more than one political adversary to misjudge the longtime operative.

That was a mistake people only made once.

Arnie's wrinkled and sometimes mismatched wardrobe concealed a once-in-a-generation political mind, and though it had taken her a while to come around to this opinion, Mary Pat now viewed the political insight the chief of staff provided as the twin to her intelligence briefings. Besides, if this presentation went the way she anticipated, Arnie would soon be hard at work.

"Great," Mary Pat said, opening the folder. "It'd be easier if you came over to the desk, Arnie. Sam's busy turning the raw product into a PowerPoint presentation, but I didn't want to wait for him to finish."

The remnants of Ryan's grin slid from his face as Mary Pat's sobering words registered. Though he would have preferred otherwise, Ryan was rarely afforded the opportunity to peruse raw intelligence product. This wasn't because he lacked the ability to dissect the raw data. In fact, the opposite was true. Though he'd been a politician for years now, at his core Ryan was and would always be an intelligence analyst. He was most comfortable with his sleeves rolled up and head down, paging through documents while scribbling notes in a yellow legal pad.

But that was no longer his job.

Accordingly, Mary Pat had slowly acclimated her boss to the high-level PowerPoint summaries that most politicians expected. She allowed him to dive into the weeds when the situation merited, but tried to shepherd his limited time so that the majority of his formidable intellect was devoted to making decisions rather than analyzing and drawing conclusions. On the rare instances when she violated this arrangement, Ryan knew something in the world was deeply amiss.

"The Israelis shared this with us at 0200 Washington time,"

she said, circulating a pair of glossy photographs between the two men.

"You were at your desk then?" Ryan said, hunching over the first photograph.

"No, sir," Mary Pat said. "I was lying next to Ed, fast asleep. Fortunately, the director of the Mossad and I have an understanding. If intelligence reaches a certain threshold, he calls me at home."

"What's Ed think of that arrangement?" Ryan said with a grin.

Mary Pat smiled.

Ed Foley, her husband, was also a former CIA case officer. But unlike his wife, Ed had retired years ago. Ryan's question was part of an ongoing joke between the two. A way to defuse the tension inherent in one of the world's most difficult jobs. This morning she welcomed the President's efforts even more than usual. By the time she finished laying out what Shahar Abuhazira had told her, they would all need a bit of levity.

Or a stiff drink.

"What are we looking at?" Arnie said, the attempt at humor completely lost on him.

Arnie was a bulldog and most days Mary Pat found his singular focus endearing.

Not today.

"Pictures of a convoy of tanker trucks transporting compressed gas," she said. "Please excuse the quality. The photos were taken by an IDF Shaldag special operations team. My understanding is that the unit doesn't have an exact equivalent in our armed forces, but they are similar to the British SAS. Shaldag specializes in long-range reconnaissance."

"How long?" Ryan said.

"About twelve hundred miles," Mary Pat said.

"Iran," Ryan said.

She nodded. "Saghand, to be exact. The Israelis have long suspected that the Iranians were secretly constructing a clandestine enrichment facility. Now they have hard evidence."

"This again?" Arnie said with a huff. "The Israelis have been pushing that theory for the last twelve months. Long on speculation but short on proof."

"How's this grab you for proof?" Mary Pat said, laying down another set of glossies.

This time the photos showed a thermal image of a transport truck leaking an aerosol.

"What does that tell us?" Arnie said.

He pointed a stubby index finger at the picture, but refused to touch it, as if hoping that whatever the image signified would stay in the two-dimensional world of film rather than contaminate and destroy the delicate Iranian proposal he'd recently brokered between warring factions of his political party.

"This is a transport truck *entering* Saghand uranium mine," Mary Pat said. "A truck carrying uranium hexafluoride gas."

"Damn it," Ryan said. "The Israelis were right."

"Could one of the two of you explain whatever this is to me so that I can also express the appropriate amount of outrage?" Arnie said.

Mary Pat wanted to laugh but couldn't. Even though she'd known what the images represented the moment she'd seen them, the information hadn't seemed real until just now.

No, that wasn't right.

While she hadn't doubted the intelligence's veracity, it wasn't significant until this moment—the instant when the leader of the most powerful nation on earth saw the pictures and would be compelled to act.

"These are trucks carrying uranium hexafluoride, or UF_6," Mary Pat said. "It's the feed gas that is refined in centrifuge cascades to produce enriched uranium. There is absolutely no reason for a feed gas to be transported to a uranium mine."

"Unless the mine is hiding a clandestine enrichment facility," Ryan said. "I've got to hand it to the Iranians, they are sneaky bastards."

"Still not following," Arnie said.

"The entire world knows about this mine," Mary Pat said, "so the Iranians have no reason to hide the trucks coming back and forth to the facility or the security surrounding it. Uranium is dug from the earth there, and then transported to plants in Fordow and Natanz to be prepared for use in Iran's supposedly peaceful nuclear power program. But if trucks are arriving *from* Natanz full of feed gas, then something else is happening at the mine. The Israelis believe that the Iranians have constructed a clandestine enrichment site in one of the mine's abandoned tunnels. The Iranians are shipping the feed gas in, enriching it, and then sending the weapons-grade material back out as if it were uranium dug from the mine."

"We're sure there's no other reason feed gas would be needed at a uranium mine?" Ryan said.

"Positive," Mary Pat said.

"Wait a minute now," Arnie said, squinting at the image. "Those are just trucks. That leaking vapor could be anything."

"It could be," she said, "but it's not."

"How do you know?" Arnie said.

She laid the final sheet of paper on the Resolute desk.

"This is the chemical composition of what leaked from the tanker truck," Mary Pat said. "When uranium hexafluoride gas encounters the atmosphere, it breaks down into two compounds: hydrofluoric acid and a dustlike aerosol. The Israelis had a sensor emplaced on the ground beneath the truck. The sensor collected and analyzed the aerosol that escaped. It's a match."

"Beneath the truck?" Ryan said. "The Israelis are some gutsy sons of bitches."

"Mossad is very thorough," Mary Pat said.

For a long moment, neither man spoke, though Mary Pat thought their collective silence was for different reasons. Ryan's eyes jumped from the images to the Mossad-provided summary, dissecting the data as his analytical mind double-checked his DNI's conclusions.

Arnie looked at the intelligence products, too, but his expression more resembled that of a person who'd just witnessed a deadly car crash and was trying to come to terms with the horrifying images. An intelligence professional Arnie was not, but he hadn't survived in the political arena this long by not being able to recognize a disaster. If Mary Pat had to guess, she'd say that the chief of staff was running down his mental Rolodex, already counting votes and trying to mitigate this disaster in the making.

"What's your confidence in the Israeli reporting, MP?" Ryan said.

The question was that of an analyst, not a politician. When the cards were down, Ryan defaulted to the critical thinking skills he'd learned at the Agency.

"High, sir," Mary Pat said. "Director Abuhazira offered to send me the physical samples the Shaldag team collected once they're back on Israeli soil."

"The Israelis are still out there?" Arnie said.

"That's what *long-range* means, Arnie," Ryan said.

"Lord knows I don't always see eye to eye with my Israeli counterparts," Arnie said, "but those boys have some big brass balls. What do you want to do, sir?"

After a final look at Arnie, Ryan straightened and turned his attention to his DNI.

"MP?" Ryan said.

Mary Pat paused, searching her conclusion for fallacies one last time.

She found none.

"It's the real deal, sir," Mary Pat said. "The Iranians are going for breakout."

"I agree," Ryan said with a sigh. "Round up the principals, Arnie. We've got a decision to make."

10

COLONEL BOB "LORENZO" BEHLER WAS A DINOSAUR.

But not in the way his wife thought.

To his bride of forty years, Bob was a dinosaur in the way that all men eventually devolved into prehistoric creatures. Bob's hair had receded, and his waist had expanded. His eyesight wasn't what it once had been, and he frequently found himself consulting his children when it came time to navigate the unending software upgrades to his mobile devices. The bands of his childhood now released only greatest hits compilations if they released anything at all, and the inevitable reunion tours more resembled a bingo night at a nursing home than a rock and roll concert.

There were no two ways about it: Bob was getting old.

But that isn't why Bob agreed with his wife's assessment. Sooner or later, everyone grew old.

That didn't mean he had to become extinct in the process.

"Snake, this is Main, confirm ready for transition, over."

Snake was the aircraft's call sign, and Bob knew his backseater would answer, but like any good pilot, he still ran a quick cross-check over his instruments. And while Bob might be three quarters of the way to fossilization, one thing was still true—he was a good pilot.

A very good pilot.

"Main, this is Snake, optics are cued, and tape is rolling. Confirm visual of Corvair. We're ready to rock and roll, over."

Bob winced at what passed for radio protocol from his backseater. Then again, he really shouldn't expect too much. Aside from the three-plus decades that separated him from his sensor operator, there were a number of other important differences between the two men. Charlie was not a pilot or even a current or former member of the military. Instead, the twentysomething wunderkind was a mechanical engineer with a penchant for vintage rock T-shirts, tattoos, and more piercings than Bob could count.

At their first meeting, Bob had been thoroughly unimpressed.

To be fair, the feeling had probably been mutual.

At the time, Charlie had been much in demand as a propulsion expert. He'd learned the fundamentals at Aerojet Rocketdyne before moving on to a brief stint at SpaceX, where he'd quickly climbed the ladder to become the senior engineering manager. After making a name for himself there, Charlie had been lured away by a company intent on doing the impossible—inventing a passenger airliner capable of traveling in excess of five times the speed of sound. To finance this insane endeavor, the company had looked to an entity that coupled larger pockets and a higher risk tolerance than even Silicon Valley's bravest investors with no desire to receive a monetary return on their investment.

The federal government.

This was where Bob came in.

Bob had retired from active duty ten years ago, and his days as a fighter pilot were over a decade before that. Most former officers his age spent their days on the lake or a golf course. Bob would be there, too, but for one thing: He'd once flown the SR-71 Blackbird. To support the company's attempt to accomplish the impossible, the world's fastest air-breathing plane had been called out of retirement along with her last serving pilot.

"Snake, this is Main. Yippee-ki-yay. Prepare for transition countdown, over."

Bob grimaced, but he didn't voice his displeasure. Though pilots and mission specialists often bantered about who was the more important human component to their aircraft, in this case Bob knew the truth—he was nothing more than a glorified bus driver.

But what a bus it was.

Though officially known as the SR-71 Blackbird, the men who piloted her called the aircraft by a different moniker—*Habu*. The name referred to a deadly viper the Blackbird was said to resemble, and the speed demons who pushed her to the edge of space thought it an apt descriptor of their mistress. Bob's call sign of *Lorenzo* was similarly based on his need for speed, and the Habu satisfied that yearning in spades.

But that didn't mean she was easy to fly.

The slanted viewports that framed his cockpit were admittedly hard to look through. The quartz windows were two inches thick and rated to six hundred degrees Fahrenheit. Right now, the forward-looking panes had taken on a reddish glow thanks to the air screaming by at a velocity that was slightly faster than a bullet fired from a rifle. Bob knew from countless hours spent aloft that the heat radiated through the glass with enough intensity to warm up the meatloaf-in-a-tube that he sucked through a feeding straw for lunch. At more than eighty-five thousand feet in altitude, the view up here was heart-stopping, but as visually tempting as the vista was, Bob didn't spend much time woolgathering.

His aircraft wouldn't allow it.

The SR-71 Blackbird was unique among Air Force combat aircraft in that not a single copy had ever been lost to enemy fire. But flying her was dangerous all the same. Of the thirty-two Blackbirds designed and manufactured at Lockheed Martin's legendary Skunk Works facility, twelve had been lost to accidents.

The Habu was not a forgiving mistress.

But in Bob's experience, few women worth having were.

"Snake, this is Main, transition in five, four, three, two, one, execute, execute, execute."

Bob turned his head to the right at the word *execute*. The fifty-pound space suit he was wearing made the gesture difficult, but he was betting that the reward would be worth the effort.

He was correct.

Just off his right wing, at a distance of one hundred feet, a dark pinpoint against the black sky flared to life. The engineers who'd designed the craft had christened her *Corvair* in what they thought was a funny take on Ralph Nader's book about the 1960s Chevrolet Corvair. The automobile had a sordid history of accidents, and Mr. Nader had appropriately titled his book *Unsafe at Any Speed*.

Bob certainly hoped this version of the Corvair didn't live up to its name.

Twin jets of blue-tinged flame shot from the Corvair as its modified Pratt & Whitney J58 engines did what was once thought to be impossible.

Transitioned from turbojet to ramjet.

For a moment, the Corvair continued to fly in formation with Bob's Blackbird. Then the unmanned aerial aircraft did something that no other jet-propelled aircraft had ever accomplished.

It pulled away from an SR-71.

Though Bob was screaming through the atmosphere at more than three times the speed of sound, the Corvair nosed forward, slowly at first, and then, like a horse getting its feet beneath it, ever more rapidly. Within a handful of seconds, Bob could see only the superheated exhaust as the world's first combined-cycle engines turned compressed ram air into thrust.

Then, the Corvair was gone.

"Snake, this is Main, transition complete. Corvair is hypersonic. We are at Mach four and climbing to Mach five, over."

Bob smiled at the three seemingly innocuous words even though the gesture was invisible behind his faceplate. Almost sixty years after the Blackbird had made its first flight, the Habu's airspeed record had finally been broken. And if that was the end of today's demonstration, this fact alone would have been cause for celebration.

But demonstration day was just getting started.

"Main, this is Snake," Charlie said. "Roger that. We are beginning our turn now. Call inbound, over."

Bob obediently eased the stick over into a right turn, remaining well below the Blackbird's bank limitations of forty-five degrees at night. At this speed, the aerodynamic forces acting on the Blackbird's needle-like fuselage were extraordinary. The reconnaissance bird was not meant for flashy maneuvering, and in a bit of less than illustrious history, a Blackbird pilot had once pulled more than the allowable three Gs and bent the Habu's frame in the process. But even with Bob's slow and steady application of the SR-71's control surfaces, making the turn at Mach 3.2 meant Bob looped through two hundred and thirty miles.

The Habu didn't exactly corner on a dime.

But that was okay.

After verifying his position with the aircraft's Astroinertial

Navigation System, otherwise known as the R2-D2 by the Habu's pilots, Bob rolled the jet's wings level. In another testament to the previous century's engineering chops, the Astroinertial System had been developed to allow the reconnaissance aircraft to accurately navigate in the world that existed prior to global positioning systems.

The Blackbird flew too high to utilize standard radio navigation and its speed and mission didn't allow for the margin of error inherent in dead reckoning. At an altitude of more than fifteen miles, Blackbird pilots weren't worried about midair collisions, but if the SR-71 happened to wander across a Cold War foe's border, the airspace could still become crowded quite quickly.

Crowded with telephone pole–sized surface-to-air missiles.

"We're on course and in position," Bob said.

"Roger that," Charlie said. "Slaving the video to your display now. It should be a good show."

While the aircraft was for the most part the same model that had last flown for NASA in 1999, certain modifications had been made to allow the Blackbird to function in its new role of test bed rather than spy plane. The most extensive changes had been to the backseat. Gone was the old analog display screen and most of the controls that went with it. In its place was a state-of-the-art monitor capable of utilizing GPS fixes to train the similarly updated sensor payloads to exactly where they needed to point.

While retrofitting the entire backseat instrumentation would have been prohibitively expensive on a project with an already astronomical budget, a rack had been constructed for Charlie's tablet as well as a dock for his laptop. The engineer had whined and complained a fair amount about not being able to type in the manner to which he was accustomed, but a single video showing what would happen if the cockpit ruptured while he was not wearing his pressure suit's gloves had put his bellyaching to rest.

Turns out a person will endure an inconvenience or two if it keeps their blood from boiling.

Never one to let a little thing like the ergonomics of a space suit keep him from doing his job, Charlie had quickly found workarounds for his less than stellar dexterity with a combination voice-to-text software program and a large joystick he operated like a mouse. With the same commitment to detail, Charlie had found a way to bolt a small tablet in the center of the pilot's cockpit.

Initially Bob had resisted the idea.

A multipurpose display with an integrated moving map and approach plate would have been great, but Bob could make do with flying the Habu the same way he had thirty years ago. But as much as he wanted to pretend otherwise, Bob had become quite enamored with the tablet that displayed the imagery Charlie was collecting. Though before today the Corvair had never exceeded Mach 3, he loved to watch that little thing zoom across the sky, even if each successfully completed flight was just one more step in Bob's transition to relic. While Bob firmly believed that the unmanned combat aerial vehicle, or UCAV, would eventually speed through Mach 5 and beyond, it would be doing so without human company.

The days of manned piloting were coming to an end.

Bob was a dinosaur.

"Snake, this is Main, Corvair is turning inbound. Attack run to commence in sixty seconds, over."

"Main, Snake," Bob said. "Vector established. Ready for attack run, over."

As per the preflight briefing, Bob had brought the jet around in a wide arc so that he was now flying a course that took him from north to south across the western sky. To his left, the East Coast and Manhattan beckoned, a trip he could make in sixty-one minutes. To his right lay the region known as the Nevada Test and Training Range to the military and Area 51 to the wider world.

Located about eighty miles northwest of Las Vegas, the remote strip of desert had been home to some of American aviation's brightest successes and stunning failures. Here, the U-2, SR-71, and other unnamed X-planes had been secretly tested. The F-117 Nighthawk, the aircraft that had ushered in the stealth age, had made its maiden flight over this barren landscape. And while the secretive base had never hosted aliens to the best of Bob's knowledge, what would occur tonight at a hastily erected compound on a sandy expanse in a remote corner of the range might prove just as revolutionary.

Assuming everything worked.

This was not a foregone conclusion.

"Ready back there, Charlie?" Bob said.

His backseater responded with a grunt. The millennial engineer had yet to embrace the fighter pilot culture he'd reluctantly joined. That was not Bob's problem. While the aircraft of tomorrow would undoubtedly be controlled by ones and zeroes, today the entity with the stick in one hand and the throttle in the other was still flesh and blood.

"Words, please, Charlie," Bob said.

"Cameras are slaved to target," Charlie said. "Telemetry from the vehicle is all nominal. We are *go* for the attack run."

Bob's Habu played two roles during the test sequences. As the only other aircraft capable of exceeding Mach 3, Bob flew in formation with the Corvair in order to live stream the most hazardous portion of the flight envelope—the transition from supersonic to hypersonic.

But that was only part of Bob's mission.

Charlie also served as a safety officer of sorts.

Though the data radioed from the vehicle traveled at the speed of light, Charlie's proximity and ability to keep pace with the Corvair gave him a situational awareness that the ground-based team in Palmdale, California, just didn't have. It was the engineer's job to certify that the vehicle was performing within acceptable limits and clear the final phase of the demonstration. The tremendous aerodynamic forces at play, insane heat generated by the high-speed flight, and the sheer complexity of the Corvair meant that every part of this test was dangerous.

But the final portion was dangerous to more than just the UCAV.

Bob let his eyes drift across the instrument panel.

After almost ten thousand total flight hours—several thousand of them spent in the Blackbird—Bob's cross-check was driven more by intuition than a rote adherence to the checklist. The bird was flying fine right now, but as the thirty-seven-percent accident rate could attest, *just fine* for the SR-71 sat awfully close to catastrophic failure.

And even the noncatastrophic events were no walk in the park.

The Blackbird's engines were prone to flameouts or, in pilot speak, un-starts. Except that when flying at a speed that allowed you to cover one mile per second, these engine failures produced a yaw rate sharp enough to smash your head against the glass.

Bob didn't so much fly the Habu as coexist with her.

Like a circus trainer who worked with tigers, Bob constantly had to remind himself that though his aircraft seemed tame right now, a wild beast lurked in her soul.

One that wouldn't hesitate to kill him if the opportunity presented itself.

Bob lingered on the attitude indicator before finishing his sweep across the engine instrumentation. The number one engine was running a little warm, but the deviation was still within acceptable norms.

Whatever that meant.

Even when it had been first flown more than half a century earlier, the SR-71 had lived in the narrow space between pushing the envelope and the destruction of both man and machine. Now the aircraft had the finicky nature and creaky joints of a senior citizen. Except that if the jet developed the equivalent of a bum knee at this speed and altitude, there would be little left but plasma.

Still, that was the job and Bob was happy to do it.

"Main, this is Snake," Bob said. "All systems nominal. You are go for throttle up."

"Snake, this is Main, acknowledge all. Stand by for—"

A wave of distortion made the rest of the radio transmission unintelligible, but Bob didn't bother asking the speaker to repeat herself. He didn't need to. Like a meteor streaking in from the heavens, a thermal flash at the edge of the horizon demanded Bob's attention. Even in the thin air sixteen miles above the earth's surface, traveling at almost four thousand miles per hour generated friction.

A lot of friction.

Bob had been briefed to expect a thermal plume, but the comet streaking toward him was insane. At first, Bob was convinced that he was watching the vehicle's disintegration.

Then the shouts of joy across the intercom convinced him otherwise.

Switching his attention to the tablet, Bob saw the source of Charlie's cheers. Though the thermal plume generated by the hypersonic vehicle was probably too dense for the visual cameras to pierce, Charlie had switched spectrums to thermal. The results were spectacular. While a white-hot plume still enveloped the UCAV, the sensor's algorithms were able to render the aircraft in startling detail. Looking like a seed visible through a translucent husk, the Corvair's fuselage was revealed in high definition. For a long moment, Bob forgot about everything but that tiny, perfect form streaking through the air at a never before achieved velocity.

The SR-71's fifty-year speed record had just been broken.

"Snake—"

Bob fiddled with the radio's gain and level, but there was no filtering the distortion. The friction between the Corvair's airframe and the surrounding atmosphere was throwing off energy across a variety of wavelengths, including RF.

No matter.

The smart boys and girls in mission control had foreseen some level of radio interference and planned accordingly. The next phase of the test would be driven by the operational timeline. In the case of radio failure, Bob was to maintain current course and speed and continue to observe. And while the light show the UCAV was generating was pretty amazing, it was nothing compared to what should be happening right about—

"Weapon release," Charlie said.

Now.

A sliver of white broke away from the seed, angling sharply downward.

It happened so quickly that Bob wasn't sure he would have been able to catch it with his naked eye had Charlie not announced the event. The tablet video evenly divided into two side-by-side frames. The imagery to the right continued to track the UCAV, while the picture to the left focused on the rapidly descending sliver.

"Good trajectory," Charlie said. "The weapon is maneuvering."

To call the sliver a weapon was misleading.

While the ten-foot length of tungsten was a weapon in the classical sense of the word, this was true in the same way that a hydrogen bomb was also an explosive. The tungsten rod was a kinetic kill vehicle. A length of metal meant to destroy hardened targets without the use of explosives. Instead of relying on energetics, the dart used its incredible speed and mass to achieve an explosive power roughly equivalent to five tons of conventional TNT explosives upon impact.

But its destructive power was only part of what made the rod amazing.

Rather than a "dumb" projectile like a sabot round fired from a tank or even the primitive slugs that were shot from prototype rail guns, the sliver had both a control surface and a GPS-enabled guidance system. Though calling the ingenious method of controlling the sliver's flight path control surfaces wasn't accurate. Unlike the SR-71 or even the UCAV, which made use of ailerons and flaps, the sliver changed course via a series of strap-on maneuvering thrusters located at the rear of the projectile. In the same manner in which a space rocket relied on jets of gas to control its attitude, pitch, yaw, and roll, the tungsten projectile was kept on course by tail thrusters.

"Entering terminal phase," Charlie said.

Disposable tail thrusters.

Though the projectile had begun to slow the moment it dropped away from the UCAV, the tungsten rod was still streaking through the atmosphere at better than Mach 4. At that speed, the air friction, which only increased the lower the projectile dropped in altitude, could melt steel. The tail thrusters couldn't survive the heat of reentry for long.

Fortunately, they didn't need to.

Even at its more leisurely speed, the projectile covered distance quickly. Not to mention that at its hypersonic speed, the sliver was basically immune to such pedestrian concerns as the Coriolis effect, ballistic coefficient, and gravity's pull. Like a high-velocity rifle round fired at a fifty-yard target, the speed was too great and the distance too small for the projectile to drift off course once its pointy head was aimed at its intended point of impact.

At least that was the theory.

"Impact in five seconds," Charlie said.

"Roger that," Bob replied. "Banking."

Bob added right stick until he had a fifteen-degree angle of bank and then adjusted the throttle to hold the turn. When the engineers had struggled to find a sensor gimbal capable of surviving the Blackbird's operating environment, Bob had suggested a simple fix—a shallow but steady turn. This maneuver, while admittedly hard to hold in the almost nonexistent atmosphere, would ensure the suite of cameras would have the largest possible viewing angle at the moment of impact. The target was a desolate mountainside ten miles from the base. The combination of the extreme speed coupled with wide target area had given rise to the fear that the Blackbird might miss the kill shot.

"Impact in three, two, one, strike," Charlie said.

For a long moment Bob saw exactly . . . nothing.

Then, a brilliant flash split the night sky.

"Holy shit," Bob said.

He had to resist the urge to roll the wings level and jam the throttle forward. In his previous life, flashes on the ground signified SAM missiles clawing their way skyward with the intent of burying their stubby nose cones into his Blackbird's soft underbelly. But this was not a combat mission, and the flash had been much too bright for a missile launch.

Bob looked back inside the cockpit just in time to see the sensor feed displayed on the tablet slowly regain resolution. The heat and energy released when the kinetic slug had impacted the mountain had washed out the image into a sea of white static. As the afterimages died away and the electronic buffers compensated, Bob could begin to make out details again.

"Damn it," Charlie said. "I must have slaved to the wrong coordinates. Let me pan out and—"

"No," Bob said. "Hold it right there."

For once, the difference in age between the two unlikely crew members worked in Bob's favor. Unlike his twentysomething backseater, Bob had been alive during the Vietnam War. In fact, he'd flown more than one mission to conduct a battle damage assessment after a BLU-82 daisy cutter strike.

He knew exactly what he was seeing.

"Pan out one field of view," Bob said.

"Why?"

"Do it."

With a very audible sigh, Charlie complied. As Bob had explained in no uncertain manner during their first pre-mission crew brief, Charlie might be the mission specialist, but Bob was in charge of the airplane. The image on the tablet blanked and then resolved into something recognizable as Charlie changed the field of view from zoom to medium.

At least it was recognizable to Bob.

"See?" Charlie said. "We're slaved to that depression instead of the target."

"That depression *is* the target," Bob said. "Or at least what's left of it."

For once, Bob's backseater was speechless.

Bob thought he could get used to the change.

11

BRIAR WOOD, TEXAS

JACK JUNIOR SAT IN THE PARKING LOT OF THE TIPSY CHICKEN, CONSIDERING HIS options.

Just before 4:00 a.m. Texas time equated to almost 5:00 at Campus headquarters in Alexandria, Virginia. The northern Virginia area didn't exactly espouse the dawn-to-dark work ethic of the Midwest, but there were still some earlier risers even among the government set. Even so, few normal people would answer their phone at zero five hundred.

Nothing about Gavin Biery was normal.

The perpetually chubby keyboard warrior had proven himself to be a force multiplier more times than Jack could count. In fact, it would not be an exaggeration to say that Jack owed his very life to The Campus's director of information technology.

But that did not mean Gavin was ready to save the world quite this early.

To be fair, this was not because the digital ninja was averse to daylight. Gavin worked late into the night because those were the hours his fellow hackers kept. Though Jack knew that Gavin wouldn't hold it against him if he called with an operational requirement, Jack wasn't sure that what he had qualified as an operational requirement in any sense of the word. Sure, Jack had witnessed a murder, and not just any murder. After seeing them in action, Jack would put the trio of shooters who'd almost punched his clock against any of the paramilitary operatives he'd fought against over the years. The hitters were technically proficient, well outfitted, and disciplined.

But that didn't mean the men had anything to do with Jack.

As much as his professional life seemed to indicate otherwise, sometimes Jack really did just happen to be in the wrong place at the wrong time. And while Jack had felt morally obligated to help the driver in the same way he would have felt obligated to save a floundering man from drowning, that didn't mean he should engage Campus resources for what was likely a simple coincidence.

Then again, Jack was in the middle of Podunk, Texas, about to meet a mystery woman named Amanda for coffee. As Jack's mentor Domingo "Ding" Chavez had pounded into Jack's head on more than one occasion, a fight often went to the better prepared rather than the more skilled pugilist. Besides, the Campus OPTEMPO had been a bit slow as of late. With nothing active and no operations in the hopper, Gavin might be getting an early start monitoring the activity of some nefarious computer hackers somewhere on the other side of the Atlantic.

At least that was what Jack told himself as he dialed his friend's number.

The phone rang.

And rang.

And rang.

Jack was just about to hang up when a very sleepy Gavin answered the phone.

"Jack?"

"Hey, buddy," Jack said, "sorry to wake you. Late night fighting bad guys?"

"What?" Gavin said. "Oh, no. Nothing Campus related. I was taking a personal day."

A personal day?

The last time Jack could remember Gavin taking a random vacation day was . . . never.

"Everything okay?" Jack said.

"Honestly, no," Gavin said. "I've been waiting for this moment for so long that now I'm not sure I can go through with it."

In spite of himself, Jack was intrigued.

Over the course of his many unscheduled calls with Gavin, Jack had interrupted his friend in the middle of a plethora of activities. From practicing for a Call of Duty tournament to brushing up on his ukulele technique, Gavin's antics were a constant source of amusement.

But this was the first time Jack had found his friend reticent about his activity.

"What are you thinking about trying?" Jack said.

"There's no thinking about it," Gavin said. "I took the next two days off, put my phone on do not disturb, and left an out-of-office note on my email. The fridge is stocked with beer and the freezer is full of chicken wings. I'm ready, Jack. Completely ready, but I just can't commit."

Jack waited for a beat, giving his friend time to fill in the silence. But the old interrogation technique didn't work any better on Gavin than it had on Jack. If he wanted to know what was going on, Jack knew he would have to bite the bullet.

And boy did he want to know.

"Can't commit to what, Gav?" Jack said.

His mind raced with possibilities as he waited for Gavin to reply.

"The new Dragonlance book."

As always, his conversation with Gavin felt jarring. As if the world in which Jack existed was a distant cousin to the one the IT specialist inhabited.

Which might just be true.

"Say that again," Jack said.

"Dragonlance. Surely you've read the books, Jack? Weis and Hickman just released their latest volume, but what if they've lost the magic? What if by reading this one I ruin everything that I loved about the series?"

"That's a tough one, buddy," Jack said as a dirty pickup truck pulled into the parking lot. "Maybe I can help."

"How?" Gavin said. "Are you talking about reading some of the Amazon reviews? Because if so, don't. Some of those people are *savages*."

The pickup nosed into a spot before shuddering to a stop. Since the driver had elected to pull, rather than back, into a parking spot, Jack was willing to bet the occupant was a woman. In his experience, cops and pickup-driving men were the only people who went to the trouble of reversing into a spot in an otherwise empty lot.

"No," Jack said. "But how about this—I've got a little research project I need help with. Maybe knocking that out could help ease some of your trepidation?"

"If you needed help, why didn't you just say so?" Gavin said. "If I've told you once, I've told you a thousand times, when you field guys are working, I'm working. What do you need?"

The driver's door of the pickup opened, and a woman hopped out of the cab wearing what probably passed for business casual here—cowgirl boots, jeans, and an A&M T-shirt. The streetlights on either end of the parking lot had seen better days, but the weak light was enough to give Jack a general impression of her appearance—brunette, thin, probably mid-thirties.

She took in the parking lot with a long glance, eyes settling on Jack's Mustang for a beat. Then she headed for the restaurant's front door.

"I appreciate you saying that," Jack said, "but this isn't exactly Campus business. Not yet, anyway."

"Is this about the wedding shower?" Gavin said. "I already told Ding that I was not breaking into Lisanne's email calendar just so he would know when to schedule it."

"The what?" Jack said.

"Wedding shower. It's for Lisanne. Though I guess you could come, too."

"What are you talking about?" Jack said.

"Hmmm . . ." Gavin said. "Maybe you weren't supposed to know. Better act surprised just to be sure."

"I need you to focus, buddy," Jack said as the woman entered the restaurant. "Things have gone a little sideways, and I need you to do some digging."

"The kind of sideways where Lisanne calls off the wedding? Because if that happens, I won't be in trouble with Ding for ruining the surprise. Or are we talking the usual kind of sideways— dead bodies?"

Jack took a deep breath as he bit back his immediate response.

The truth of the matter was that his calls to Gavin often occur after a fatality or one kind or another. As to the bit about Lisanne, maybe Jack's fellow Campus operators hadn't been completely joking when they'd reacted to news of the engagement by asking what the raven-haired beauty saw in him.

To be fair, Jack still asked himself the same question.

"The second option," Jack said, even though he wanted to dig a bit more into the first. "I'm late for a meet, so I don't have time to explain, but I need information. Fast."

"No problem," Gavin said. "What do you have?"

"Not much," Jack said. "The dead man was driving a car with this license plate." Jack gave Gavin the series of numbers and digits he'd memorized as well as the car's make and model and then listened while his friend confirmed the data.

"That's it?" Gavin said. "A dead guy driving an old Subaru?"

"Not exactly," Jack said. "There was also a team of three shooters. Well trained and equipped. They were wearing masks, so I couldn't see their ethnicity, but they spoke with a familiar accent. Not British, but close."

"South African?" Gavin said.

"Maybe," Jack said. "Why do you ask?"

"An educated guess. What you're describing isn't street muscle, and British-sounding accents rule out cartel. You have a good eye for talent, Jack. If you think the shooters were good, they're probably high-end mercenaries. And the country with the reputation for the world's best mercenaries is—"

"South Africa," Jack said. He was a bit irritated that he hadn't made the connection himself, but the cocktail of adrenaline and nervous energy that accompanied combat had a way of clouding a person's thinking. "I think you're onto something, Gav. The accent certainly could have been South African. Hit the usual searches and see what your queries turn up. Oh, also add this license plate to your mix."

Jack read off the beat-up pickup truck's license plate and then gave Gavin a description of the driver.

"Got it," Gavin said. "Who's the girl?"

"Don't know. But I'm about to find out."

12

"I HAVE A QUESTION," SERGEANT FIRST CLASS JAD MUSTAFA SAID.

Master Sergeant Cary Marks sighed as he considered how to respond.

Though Cary and the Libyan American shared a brotherhood forged in the crucible of combat, like any siblings, they occasionally squabbled. This admittedly rare occurrence usually began with one of Jad's infamous questions. The kind of questions Cary didn't want to answer, often because he was wondering the same thing himself.

"What?" Cary said.

His response came out harsher than he'd intended. This was not so much because he was irritated with his teammate, though Cary had no doubt this would be the case the moment Jad responded. No, Cary half shouted for another reason.

He could barely hear.

This disability was not the result of the damage to the eardrums that men in Cary's profession often suffered. Though he'd logged more time on the range than the average soldier spent standing in formation, Cary had thus far escaped the ravages of tinnitus, the medical name for a constant ringing in the ears.

Even the training sessions on the demo range or with the team's 120mm EMTAS mortar system hadn't wrecked Cary's hearing.

But tonight's venue might just succeed where the loudest the military had to offer had failed.

"Does it seem loud in here?" Jad said.

A grin split his teammate's face and Cary had to chuckle.

Together, the two men had deployed to untold countries in combat zones both acknowledged and otherwise. As snipers, their accommodations in operational theaters were not what anyone would consider five-star. During a particularly turbulent tour of duty in Iraq, Cary had endured almost twenty hours nestled in a makeshift sniper hide site hollowed out of a garbage heap with Jad at his side to interdict a particularly troublesome Shia militant. Sometimes he still awoke at night shuddering with memories of what he'd encountered among the decaying refuse.

Cary would have traded his present locale for that one in a heartbeat.

"Maybe the next song will be quieter," Cary shouted back.

"Or maybe the rapture will happen," Jad said.

Cary looked at his friend in surprise. "I didn't know Muslims believed in the rapture."

"If it gets me out of this place, I'll throw in with anyone."

Cary understood how his friend felt.

Though the two men hailed from widely different backgrounds, their differences reinforced their friendship in the same way that the finest steel was made from diverse ores. Physically, the two Green Berets couldn't have been more dissimilar. Cary Marks was a blue-eyed, blond-haired farm boy from New England whose vowels gave away his Yankee roots under duress.

Jad Mustafa's dark complexion and SoCal surfer accent lent itself to kidding from his teammates, who often accused him of being a SEAL in disguise. Jad's affinity for hair gel and fashionable clothes didn't help in this regard. Despite the men's differences in skin color and ethnicity, after more than half a dozen shared combat deployments, Cary and Jad were brothers in a way that transcended birth parents or family lineage.

Cary agreed with his spotter's assessment wholeheartedly. If he was forced to spend much longer in this Vegas nightclub, Cary might have to resort to violence. As the Iraqi Shia militant had discovered, violence wrought by the two Green Berets was not a trivial matter.

"When this is gone, so are we," Cary said, pointing to the Jameson and ginger ale he'd been nursing for the last hour. The glass was a little less than half full, but bubbles still floated to the surface, seemingly jostled loose by the music's thumping bass line. The beverage was one of Cary's favorites, but he'd still consumed the cocktail with an eye toward staying alert. Though the mixture tasted as good as ever, he and Jad weren't here for fun.

The commandos were on the job.

Reaching past his longneck, Jad grabbed Cary's glass, and drained the mixture in one long swallow.

"Problem solved," Jad said, slamming the empty on the table.

Cary chuckled.

Green Berets were unique among the greater special operations community in a number of ways, not the least of which being their mission. Unlike Army Rangers who specialized in direct action or Navy SEALs who were great at . . . well . . . being Navy SEALs, Green Berets were charged with fighting by, with, and through the Indigenous soldiers they trained. Where most special operators kicked in doors, shot the bad guys in the face, and then helicoptered away to fight another day, Green Berets lived with foreign fighters in locales that were often thousands of miles from the flagpole. Accordingly, the psychological profile Special Forces candidates were screened against was equally unique. Prospective Green Berets had to be creative thinkers with a wide independent streak.

Sometimes a little too wide.

"Okay, okay," Cary said, conceding the fight. "Our guy isn't going to show. Let's call it."

Though he wouldn't admit his feelings to Jad upon pain of death, Cary was glad to be quitting the nightclub. This had never been his scene, and as a happily married father of three in his mid-thirties, an evening spent listening to head-splitting music in a smoke-filled room surrounded by posers and wannabes while sipping overpriced drinks was not his idea of fun. In fact, Cary's only solace had been that the government, rather than he or Jad, was picking up the tab. But even the satisfaction of sticking Uncle Sam for the cost of their VIP table and booze wasn't enough to justify another moment spent in this circus.

Cary's fun meter was pegged.

"Best news I've heard all night," Jad said. "I'll flag down the waitress and . . . wait a minute now, boss."

The word *boss* made Cary's skin tingle.

Though Special Forces culture was purposely less formal than the rest of the military, this did not mean that the men who wore the Long Tab were undisciplined. In fact, the opposite was true. Every member of an Operational Detachment Alpha, or A-team, was at least an E-5 sergeant and most were even more senior. Unlike the Ranger Regiment where the vast majority of shooters were twenty years old and under, experience was a prerequisite for wearing the green beret. Typical military customs were relaxed because the highly disciplined commandos knew when saluting was appropriate and when it was not.

Case in point, the two men were on a first-name basis even though, as the team sergeant of Operational Detachment Alpha, or ODA, 555, Cary was Jad's boss. But in Triple Nickel, as ODA

555 was called, the informality the two men enjoyed did not supersede the military's chain of command. Jad had his own way of letting Cary know when he was thinking about the business.

The word *boss*.

That noun changed everything.

Though the amount of alcohol Cary had consumed had been minimal, the oppressively loud music, pulsing lights, and parade of scantily clad women had still abraded his alertness. On more than one occasion, the monotony of lying near motionless in a hide site while watching a bad guy's compound had lulled Cary into a dormant state.

Tonight, the sensory overload had produced the same effect.

Not anymore.

13

"WHERE?" CARY SAID, HIS VOICE CALM EVEN AS HIS HEART BEGAN TO ACCELERATE.

The Green Berets had taken a table in the club's VIP section located on a balcony perched above the plebeians jostling for space at the bar below. The roped-off section gave the illusion of privacy when in fact the booth's prominent position was clearly meant to incite envy from those not well-off enough to pay the exorbitant seating fee. As the pair had moved to occupy their perch, Jad had proven to be just a bit fleeter of foot. This meant that he had secured the coveted seat that put his back to the wall. Cary would now have to rely on his spotter to talk him onto target, which, come to think of it, was not all that different than their normal state of affairs.

"Just came in from the VIP entrance," Jad said. "Dressed in Eurotrash casual. Skinny pants, and a black silk shirt unbuttoned to his navel. Can't see his shoes, but I'm willing to bet he's not wearing socks."

"Don't hate the man because he's beautiful," Cary said. "Maybe you two could swap fashion tips."

"Sheee-it," Jad said. "I've got more style in my baby toe than that boy has in his walk-in closet. I don't hate him because he's beautiful. I hate him because he's a dirtbag mercenary. And he's coming this way."

Though Cary instinctively wanted to tense at Jad's announcement, he forced himself to relax. Slouching deeper into the leather booth, he turned with his now-empty glass as if in search of a waitress. According to their legend, he and Jad were just two more soldiers for hire blowing off steam after the Soldier of Fortune conference.

Cary needed to act accordingly.

"Are you Jad?"

"Who wants to know, buttercup?"

Jad's response to the accented question might have been a little out of place in polite company. Nothing about the company filling the nightclub was polite. That went double so for Hans Schmidt. Calling the man Eurotrash was an insult to Europeans everywhere. A former member of the German Kommando Spezialkräfte, or KSK, Hans had turned in his maroon beret in order to put his skills to use in more profitable endeavors. Plenty of Cary's friends had done the same thing after enduring the burn of countless deployments for low pay. Becoming a soldier for hire did not automatically make you a dirtbag.

But in Hans's case, the moniker was well deserved.

"The railroad man," Hans responded.

The mercenary's seemingly nonsensical response was the correct password to Jad's rather unorthodox use of the challenge word *buttercup*. Still, the exchange of bona fides did nothing to ease Jad's demeanor. If anything, the surfer's expression grew harder and the earlier merriment that had danced in his eyes vanished. This was Jad's business face. That was probably just as well. Cary had a feeling that the nightclub had only been a warm-up for what he was about to endure next.

Turning in his seat, Cary got his first look at Hans in person.

Like many private military contractors, the German's appearance suggested that he'd exchanged the cardiovascular requirements of his former life for more time in the gym. His shirt's sheeny fabric strained at the mercenary's shoulders and biceps. Hans's sleeves were rolled, exposing forearms with tendons that rippled beneath his skin like steel cables. As someone whose vocation demanded an elite level of fitness, Cary was no stranger to gym rats, but Hans's body reflected the type of sculpting that suggested chemical help.

"You're late," Cary said before turning back to Jad.

Knowing that the mercenary was standing behind him had Cary's tactical sixth sense sparking like a live wire, but still he forced himself to face Jad. By turning his back on the German, Cary had unequivocally communicated two things. One, the power dynamic inherent in this relationship rested with Cary. Two, physically imposing though Hans might be, Cary did not consider the man a threat. For someone who sold his sword for a living, there could be no greater insult.

That was the point.

Cary's gesture would anger Hans, and angry men made mistakes.

Since his glass was now empty, Cary reached for Jad's longneck. He could feel the seething energy from the gorilla lurking behind him, but Cary took a leisurely pull as if he'd already dismissed Hans from his universe. Even though he was languidly swallowing a mouthful of Pacifico as if he hadn't a care in the world, Cary's gaze was locked on his spotter's face.

Jad's features were flat, and his expression carved from stone. Though Jad's slouch was the epitome of indifference, Cary knew that his fellow Green Beret could bridge the distance between them in a blur that would make Bruce Lee look slow.

Cary just hoped Jad wouldn't have cause to demonstrate his skills.

After draining the bottle, Cary set the empty on the table. Ignoring the tension radiating like heat from the potbelly stove behind him, Cary eyed his spotter.

"Want another?" Cary said.

"Sure," Jad said.

Cary was in the middle of raising his hand to signal the waitress when Hans dropped into the adjacent chair, ending the Mexican standoff.

"Oh," Cary said with surprise, "I didn't know you were still here."

"I heard you two wanted a job," Hans said, leaning forward.

"You heard wrong," Cary said. "My partner and I are entertaining offers. Serious offers. Whether you are serious remains to be seen."

Cary was walking a fine line, and judging by the slight widening of Jad's eyes, he was treading awfully close to the edge. But that couldn't be helped. Cary didn't know Hans, but he knew the type. There was always a certain amount of posturing that took place when operators from rival services met. Like two wild dogs crossing paths in a back alley, shadow warriors had to sniff each other out. To understand the capabilities and limitations of a potential operational partner. This went doubly so for those looking to cashier their national service into personal gain. Before work could begin, a pecking order had to be established. Cary needed Hans to acknowledge who was chasing whom in this dance.

Or at least who appeared to be chasing whom.

Jad and Cary had spent the last two days in Vegas for one reason and one reason only—to secure a meeting with the

European mercenary fuming in the adjacent chair. Though the two Green Berets were technically still on the rolls of Triple Nickel, they were currently on a leave of absence. How long that leave extended was still up in the air. After a chance meeting with Jack Ryan, Jr., in Syria, the commandos had been drawn ever closer into The Campus's operational web.

Case in point, they were currently in Las Vegas at the behest of The Campus, not the United States Army. The forty-eight hours in Sin City was not even close to Cary's idea of fun, and while he was ready to be done with this place, he couldn't act that way. Appearing too eager to leave would shift the advantage to Hans. If only half of what Cary had read in the soldier of fortune's targeting folder was true, Cary was going to need every advantage he could wrangle. Even so, judging by the merc's look, Cary was worried he might have pushed things too far.

And then Hans spoke.

"I had to make sure your résumés checked out," Hans said.

"That's your problem, not ours," Cary said. "Look, we're here as a courtesy to Billy. He vouched for you, so my partner and I made time in our busy schedule. If you have an opportunity to discuss, speak. If not, piss off."

Cary again made to raise his hand for their server.

Hans grabbed his wrist.

"Listen to what I have to say," Hans said. "If you're not interested, I'll buy the next round. If you are, you won't be drinking any more tonight."

A surge of excitement shot through Cary, but the tone he used with Jad was positively bored.

"What do you think?" Cary said.

"I think he'd better let go of your arm before he loses his fingers," Jad said.

The statement was delivered in a casual manner, but the air

resonated with Jad's words. Though he was not Jad's intended target, Cary still had to suppress the urge to flinch. Hans had no such protection. The mercenary dropped Cary's arm as if he'd been scalded.

Nobody projected violence better than Jad.

"Fantastic," Jad said after stifling a yawn. "I'm all ears."

Hans's face flushed but he was wise enough not to reply with snark of his own. Billy must have provided one heck of a recommendation for the two commandos, which was ironic because neither Cary nor Jad had ever met the man. This was by design. While the Green Berets certainly had the operational chops to back up any bragging on their behalf, Billy did not know that.

This was because Billy was working as an asset for The Campus.

The American special operations community usually lived up to the reputation afforded them by the media, but this was not to say that they were infallible. Any population, no matter how selective, was bound to have a few bad apples. That these instances of malfeasance occurred among special operators at a much lower rate than the general public spoke to the military's vetting and selection processes.

Even so, no one was immune from temptation.

In Billy's case, this temptation took the form of a Chinese American girlfriend. A Chinese American girlfriend who turned out to be an undeclared Chinese intelligence officer working for the Ministry of State Security.

To Billy's credit, rather than take the easy way out by committing the required act of espionage when his girlfriend had made her pitch, he'd honored the oath he'd sworn to protect the Constitution against all enemies foreign and domestic and confessed his transgression to his chain of command. Even though he'd not completed his betrayal, Billy had strayed too far from the path of the righteous to be redeemed.

He'd expected a court-martial followed by a prison term.

He'd been wrong.

Billy was a good soldier who'd done a bad thing and his chain of command were determined to give him a second chance. Billy's team sergeant had friends in the intelligence community and had made a few calls. Turns out there was an opportunity for Billy to mitigate the stain on his soul. At an unnamed intelligence community member's request, Billy had answered an ad placed by a company looking for men with a particular set of skills. After learning more about the opportunity, Billy demurred, but he offered to arrange a meeting for the recruiter with two of his friends who had similar qualifications.

Their names were Cary Marks and Jad Mustafa.

"I'm looking for a pair of instructors to teach high-angle shooting," Hans said. "Preferably graduates of the Special Operations Target Interdiction Course."

"We're graduates of SOTIC," Jad said.

"Along with hundreds of other people," Cary said. "Maybe you could talk to one of them. We're looking for something a bit more . . . exclusive."

"What do you mean?" Hans said.

"He means we have a very unique set of skills," Jad said. "Based on our conversations with other interested parties, these skills command a high value on today's market. We intend to monetize them."

"And you will," Hans said. "Once I have the opportunity to assess your skills personally."

"Nope," Jad said.

"What?" Hans said.

The European's accent thickened when he grew angry. Given that the *w* on *what* had become a pronounced *v*, Hans was getting good and angry.

Perfect.

"What my partner is trying to say," Cary said, "is that our résumé speaks for itself. Did Billy tell you which unit we came from?"

"*Ja*," Hans said.

"Good," Cary said. "Then you won't take this the wrong way when I say that you can fuck all the way off when it comes to vetting our skills. Men better than you decided we both had the necessary skills a long time ago."

"No offense," Jad said.

Judging by the fact that the flush that had begun on Hans's neck had now reached his ears, the mercenary wasn't heeding Jad's advice. The European opened his mouth.

"Let's not go saying things we'd each regret," Cary said, before Hans could speak. "You came to us, remember? We already have several offers on the table."

"Fine offers," Jad said.

"So tell us what you really want and how much you're willing to pay or we walk," Cary said. "Last chance."

Hans looked from Cary to Jad, his blue eyes sparking.

Once again, Cary was worried that he might have pushed things too far. Though he'd never seriously entertained making a living as a soldier of fortune, Cary knew the type. Braggarts were easy to find, but the true professionals let their qualifications speak for them. If Hans was going to bite, Cary had to play the part.

At least that's what Cary told himself.

His thundering heart begged to differ.

"Okay," Hans said, his voice hitching lower, "okay. I have a client who is looking for discreet individuals with your skill set."

"What's the job?" Jad said.

"A rendition," Hans said.

Now they were getting somewhere.

When a government snatched people it was called a rendition. But when the kind of guys who hired Hans wanted it done, it was a kidnapping, plain and simple. Still, kidnapping someone wasn't exactly rocket science. Shove a gun into an unarmed person's face and throw them in the back of a panel van.

There had to be more to Hans's job.

"Why do you need someone with our skills for that?" Jad said, reading Cary's mind.

"Because the target is well protected, and the environment is nonpermissive," Hans said.

"What's the fee?" Jad said.

"Twenty-five thousand," Hans said. "Each."

"Where's the job?" Cary said.

"No," Hans said, shaking his head. "You agree first. Then you get the details."

Cary looked at Jad both for confirmation and to give himself a chance to think.

This endeavor was picking up steam fast. He and Jad's tasking had been to attend the conference, meet with whoever it was that was trying to hire American SOF members, and report back to The Campus with what they'd found. Nowhere in that mission set had been a writ of permission to engage in an illegal operation. That said, if Cary ended the farce now, what would he have to report? A shady-sounding military contractor was looking for ex-shooters to take part in a shady-sounding job.

That wasn't exactly news.

Across the table, Jad was making a show of considering Hans's offer by rubbing his chin. In reality, the gesture meant something quite different. As part of their mission set, the men of Triple Nickel had to be prepared to operate in denied environments. This was a fancy way of saying that in a future conflict, the twelve-strong A-team would more than likely be working in a theater in which they were under constant surveillance.

A theater like China, for instance.

Accordingly, the men had been instructed in the use of non-verbal communication with a standard set of gestures that the Green Berets had immediately modified for their own use. While he couldn't remember what rubbing your jaw meant when applied to the approved military system, Cary knew exactly what it signified when Jad made the gesture.

Call the ball, Maverick.

Most days Cary liked his job, but even on the suckiest missions, he always loved the men he worked with.

"Okay," Cary said, "we're in. What are the details?"

"A man has something my client wants," Hans said. "You two are going to get it for him."

"That doesn't sound very challenging," Jad said.

"We'll see," Hans said. "He's in the next bar over. You have ten minutes to prep."

Then there were days when Cary wished that he sold car insurance.

14

"COFFEE, HONEY?"

The combination waitress/cook asked the question as Jack entered the restaurant. Though her tone conveyed an appreciable amount of southern hospitality, Jack thought it might also contain more than a hint of desperation. Besides the woman seated in a corner booth at the far end of the dining area—the woman from the parking lot—Jack was the only customer.

"Please," Jack said with a smile. "With cream and sugar."

"Coming up," the waitress said. "Sit anywhere you like."

Now came the tricky part.

The woman in the booth had noticed Jack's entrance, but she wasn't paying him much attention. Which meant she knew who she was here to see and that person was not Jack. Things were about to get awkward. Jack crossed the room smiling his biggest smile, hoping his actions would set her at ease.

They didn't.

The woman stiffened as Jack approached, and her eyes slid from him to the door. Though Jack admired her spunk, there was no way she was getting past him. The restaurant's décor suggested that it had once been a Waffle House. The seating area consisted of small booths with plastic bench seats centered around tables with cracked laminate finishes. A long counter divided the seating area from the small kitchen and a tiny hallway led to the bathrooms. There was just one way in and out, and the exit was on the other side of Jack's linebacker-sized frame.

"Hi," Jack said, standing just short of the woman's table. "You Amanda?"

"Who are you?" the woman said.

"That's going to take some explaining," Jack said. "But my name's Jack. Mind if I sit?"

Now that he was closer, Jack could see that she looked older than he'd originally thought. It wasn't that her face was wrinkled from smoking or that her hair was beginning to gray. No, if Jack had to put a word to her appearance, it would be *worn*. This was the kind of mileage that came from learning way too young that life was not all rainbows and unicorns. Her ring finger was empty, and her eyes had the tired look of someone who went to bed late and got up early. The appearance of a single mom doing her best to put food on the table and keep the lights on.

Which made her role in this situation all the more strange.

"Everything okay, Amanda?"

The question came from the waitress. Her tone wasn't nearly as warm this time, but it made Jack smile all the same. He liked the idea of two hardworking Texas women looking out for each other. While the waitress sounded concerned, her question wasn't flavored with fear, making Jack think that the woman's side of the counter probably held something a bit more potent than coffee.

"So far, so good, Shirley," Amanda said, never breaking eye contact with Jack.

"Good," Shirley said, setting Jack's coffee and cream on the table. "If that changes, let me know."

The waitress's reply had a fortifying effect on Amanda. The single mom's expression was still serious, but her posture eased. Slightly. She shuffled something on the bench seat just out of sight.

A purse.

A purse that, like Shirley's counter, probably contained something other than lipstick.

God bless Texas.

Since neither woman had pointed a pistol at him, Jack took the détente as an invitation to sit. He'd spent more time in hostile environments than he cared to remember, but voluntarily putting himself in a crossfire between two aware and equipped Texans didn't make it easy to relax. If the mood in the diner didn't thaw quickly, Jack would have no need of the coffee to stay awake.

"Nice to meet you, Amanda," Jack said, using the steady, non-threatening tone he might have taken with a stray dog. Jack was a big man, and no amount of sweet talk was going to change that. But by keeping his actions nonthreatening, he was hoping to put her at ease.

"You've got five minutes," Amanda said. "If I don't like what I'm hearing, I'm walking. Don't try to stop me."

"How about sixty seconds?" Jack said. "If I can't reassure you in less than a minute, then I'll leave you and Shirley to your coffee."

Some of the wariness drained from Amanda's eyes. The woman's right hand was still nestled inside her purse, but she hadn't drawn the hidden pistol.

Progress.

"Okay," Amanda said as she glanced at her watch. "One minute. Go."

Jack had hoped that the woman might view his self-imposed

limit figuratively. That did not appear to be the case. But that was okay. He was up to the challenge.

Hopefully.

"Here's the deal," Jack said. "Someone asked that I meet with you."

"Who?" Amanda said, eyes narrowing.

"I don't know his name," Jack said. "He gave me this."

Jack reached into his pocket, withdrew the paper, and unfolded it. Turning the scrap so Amanda could read the man's precise writing, Jack slid the paper across the table. Amanda took it with her left hand. Her right remained out of sight. She smoothed out the wrinkles and studied the words, puzzling over them much longer than the simple phrase required.

"Where is he?" Amanda asked, looking from the paper to Jack.

"Dead," Jack said. "Three gunmen ambushed him on the road."

Amanda seemed to shrink as she processed Jack's words. While not an expert at body language, Jack judged people for a living and he found the woman's response interesting. While she was surprised at the news, her reaction skewed more toward disappointment than sadness. Jack had assumed that Amanda knew the driver. That they were partners in whatever had caused three South African assassins to end the man's life.

Now, Jack wasn't so sure.

About anything.

"Who are you?" Amanda said.

"That's a longer story," Jack said. "For now, let's just say I'm a concerned citizen."

"How do I know that anything you've said is true?" Amanda said.

"Call the police," Jack said. "Play the nosy neighbor role and ask them what happened. Or drive out there yourself. If I had to guess, the evidence response team is still processing the scene. Even if they're not, you'll still be able to find the skid marks from the crash, broken glass, maybe even some shell casings. Two vehicles were involved in a crash and five men had a gunfight. If you know what to look for, you'll see the signs."

Amanda stared at Jack in silence for a beat. The woman was obviously making a judgment call of some sort or another, but without knowing what she was weighing, Jack didn't bother trying to influence her decision. Instead, he added cream and sugar to his coffee and took a sip.

Surprisingly good.

"This is fantastic, Shirley," Jack said over his shoulder.

"One of our town's many secrets," Shirley said. "It's a local blend."

Jack raised his cup in salute.

"You don't know about the reward?" Amanda said.

"I don't know about anything," Jack said. "I was just in the wrong place at the wrong time."

"Then why are you here?"

Jack sighed. "Here's the thing, Amanda, I really don't know. I'm not from here, and I have no idea what's going on. I saw a man in trouble, and I couldn't pretend I didn't notice. My parents raised me better than that."

"So what," Amanda said, "you're some kind of superhero?"

"No," Jack said, shaking his head. "Just a man trying to do the right thing. I know that sounds old-fashioned, but it's true. Now, I've more than taken up that minute I asked for and I'm sure you have places to be. Tell me what you know or don't. It's all the same to me."

"You're not in it for the reward?" Amanda said.

"Lady, I don't even know what *it* is," Jack said. "Hey, Shirley, can I get a to-go cup?"

"Sure thing, honey."

Jack reached in his pocket for his money clip, peeled off a twenty, and left the bill on the table next to the scrap of paper.

Then he stood.

"Have a nice day," Jack said.

"Wait," Amanda said, reaching across the table to grab Jack's arm.

Her fingers were small but strong. Like a falcon's talons. Jack paused. He made no attempt to pull away, but neither did he move to sit down.

What happened next would be up to Amanda.

"I called Jeff's tip line and arranged a meeting," Amanda said.

"Who's Jeff?"

"Jeff Wellington," Amanda said. "I'm assuming that's who you saw get killed."

"Why did you set up a meeting with Jeff?" Jack said.

"The reward. I've got a teenager at home, and a mortgage I can barely pay. Things have been hard since her dad split. Lately, they've been even harder. Not all of us can afford to be noble."

Amanda's face flushed as she spoke, but she didn't break eye contact. Jack eased back into his seat. He was no biblical scholar, but twelve years of Catholic school had made it crystal clear where his responsibilities to widows and orphans lay. The least he could do was hear Amanda out.

"Look," Jack said, "I didn't know about the reward until this second, and I don't need it. I'm just trying to honor a promise to a dying man. That's it."

"You going or staying?" Shirley said, setting Jack's to-go cup of coffee on the table.

"That's up to her," Jack said, gesturing at Amanda.

Amanda stared at Jack for another long minute. Then she looked to Shirley.

"He's staying."

15

"HOW MUCH DO YOU KNOW ABOUT THE TROY WELLINGTON CASE?" AMANDA SAID.

"Nothing," Jack said. "I'm from D.C. My fiancée is on a girls' trip to Austin, and I came along to watch A&M play the Lobos. "

"What do you do for a living?" Amanda said.

"I'm an accountant."

"You don't look like an accountant."

"I've heard that before," Jack said. "Tell me about the case."

Amanda nodded.

"Troy Wellington was a twenty-one-year-old A&M student who disappeared while passing through Briar Wood on his way home for summer break. Jeff is his father. Was his father. I called Jeff's tip line because I had information about Troy's disappearance."

Jack nodded, considering the shoot-out in a new light. No wonder the driver had been so adamant about providing Jack with the details about this meeting. Information about his missing son would outweigh just about anything in a parent's life.

Including their own.

"What exactly?" Jack said.

"Let me give you a bit of background," Amanda said.

Now that she'd decided to talk, the woman acted as if she had all the time in the world. Or maybe as a parent herself, she understood the need to get this right. Either way, Amanda took a long swallow of coffee as she collected her thoughts.

"Troy was reported missing after he failed to make it home. Jeff found Troy's car just outside Briar Wood's city limits after retracing his son's likely route. The vehicle had crashed into a tree and was abandoned. A trace amount of blood was found at the scene along with a backpack, clothes, and Troy's cell phone. Nothing more. That was four months ago."

"If you had information about Troy's disappearance this whole time, why are you just talking now?" Jack said.

"Because I didn't realize I had information until recently."

"What do you mean?"

"I live here," Amanda said, "but I work outside of town. I run the register at a gas station about ten miles east of here. On Fridays I pull the night shift. Anyway, this case was huge. This is Briar Wood, Texas. We might have a couple of bar fights and some petty theft, but for the most part, this is about as close to Mayberry as you can get. The disappearance of a college kid made national news. For a while it was all anyone could talk about."

"And then?"

Amanda shrugged. "And then, other details started coming out. DPS did a poor job processing the scene."

"DPS?" Jack said.

"Department of Public Safety," she said. "The stateys. They're Texas's version of the highway patrol."

Jack nodded.

"Rumors started that the kid might have detoured off his route because he was up to no good. They found weed in his backpack, and the local PD leaked the idea that he might have been trying to score drugs. Once the media ran with that angle, people started caring a whole lot less."

"Why?" Jack said.

Amanda shrugged, her shoulders narrow and bony beneath her thin shirt.

"Texas is a border state," Amanda said. "A lot of drugs flow through here. But that's only half the story. A couple years back, the high school had a once-in-a-lifetime quarterback. Real *Friday Night Lights* stuff. We thought he was going to put our town on the map."

"Didn't work out?" Jack said.

"We'll never know. He ODed. Fentanyl. It was like someone ripped the heart from our collective chest. Folks around here *hate* drugs."

Jack nodded. "So once people thought that Troy was just another out-of-town college boy looking to score smack, he dropped off the radar."

"More than that," Amanda said. "With the media and outside law enforcement crawling all over Briar Wood, it dredged up a lot of bad memories. And the papers and TV made us out to be a bunch of backward rednecks. Locals were tired of it, so they stopped helping. Truth be told, more than a few residents worked to make things more difficult. Pretty soon Jeff was the only one still pushing the investigation. Folks assumed he'd eventually give up."

"But he didn't," Jack said.

"No, he didn't."

Amanda fiddled with her coffee mug. "I don't know why anyone who's a parent thought he would. If my daughter was missing, I'd be screaming at the police until they hauled me away. Anyway, the attention did die down for a bit until Jeff announced a reward for information. A big one."

"How much?" Jack said.

"Fifty thousand dollars."

Jack nodded as his mind raced. While not a fortune, that sum was not insignificant. Around here, that amount of money probably represented close to a year's wages. Maybe more. Rewards that large had a way of making people remember things they might have otherwise forgotten.

"The reward wasn't the reason I came forward," Amanda said, as if reading Jack's thoughts. "Or at least not the only reason. When Jeff announced the money, the Briar Wood Police Department doubled down on the drug theory. The lead investigator is a guy named Bradshaw. Anyway, he claimed to have new evidence showing that Troy was clearly high right before he disappeared."

Bradshaw.

Jack wasn't surprised that the same cop who'd raked him over the coals was somehow part of this.

"What evidence?" Jack said.

"Cell phone video. Apparently, Troy was trying to take a selfie while driving and he hit record instead. Anyone who looks at the footage can tell that he's blitzed out of his mind. Except he wasn't."

"What do you mean?" Jack said.

Even though they were the diner's only customers, Amanda still leaned forward before she spoke. As if she and Jack were in hostile territory.

Maybe they were.

"Troy filled up his gas tank just before driving into Briar Wood. He stopped at my station."

This time it was Jack who stared in silence.

Jack had conducted enough debriefs to understand that there was an art to drawing out a person's story. Sometimes the process necessitated leading questions from the interviewers. Other times, it was better to let the witness process through the information in their own way.

This was one of those times.

"Of course I told the police about this during the initial investigation," Amanda said, answering Jack's unasked question. "But back then, they were simply trying to retrace Troy's steps."

"To establish his timeline," Jack said.

Amanda nodded.

"The credit card reader on the number three pump was on the fritz at the time," Amanda said, "so he had to come into the store. He paid for the gas and bought a Red Bull."

"And you could tell he wasn't high just from that interaction?" Jack said.

"He was wearing an A&M hat," Amanda said. "I always wanted to go there, so I asked him about school. We talked. He said that he was heading home early to surprise his mom. For her birthday."

Amanda's eyes watered.

Jack reached across the table to squeeze her hand, and she smiled.

"Anyway," Amanda said, "he paid and drove off. That was that."

"Does your store have security cameras?"

"Yeah. I assume the owner handed them over during the initial investigation."

"You don't know?" Jack said.

Amanda shook her head. "The station's not franchised. It's owned by some corporation. When I heard about the case, I contacted the police. My boyfriend, Brian, is on the force. He doesn't think much of Bradshaw, so he gave me the number of a detective. The investigator called me back and took my statement. I told him about the video surveillance during the interview. I don't know if he ever followed up."

Jack wondered the same thing.

Obtaining the surveillance video wasn't as easy as just asking the owner for a copy. To cover their backside, most people would insist upon a subpoena, and this process would be even more difficult if the local police had to navigate a corporation's legal department. Back when Amanda had given her statement, the case must have seemed pretty cut and dried. At least her participation in it would have been. The kid had stopped for gas, verifying the location information law enforcement had undoubtedly ascertained from his phone or service provider. Obtaining the gas station's video had probably been deemed more hassle than it was worth.

Until now.

"You're positive Troy wasn't high?"

Amanda's eyes narrowed. "I know a thing or two about addicts. I was married to one for the five longest years of my life. I can't say whether Troy got high the moment he pulled out of my parking lot, but he was clean when we were talking. And this was ten minutes *after* the selfie video was supposedly recorded."

Jack deliberately breezed by the word *supposedly*.

Americans have always loved a good conspiracy theory and were fascinated by police procedural work as the slew of *CSI* and *Law & Order*–type shows could attest. Engaging in a discussion about whether the video could have been faked was pointless. Jack was all too familiar with the capabilities of so-called deep fake videos.

Could the imagery released by police have been falsified?

Sure.

But this was way beyond his expertise. Instead, Jack wanted to keep the conversation centered on what Amanda could swear to in court—her interaction with Troy.

"How are you certain about the time?"

Amanda sat back and wiped her misting eyes. "Because I

called my daughter, Bella, the moment Troy walked out the door. She didn't answer so I left a message. She called me back, but I was dealing with a customer so her call went straight to voicemail. Her message was sweet for once, so I decided to keep it."

Taking out her phone, she scrolled through the voice message section and pointed to an entry. The contact was titled YOUR FAVORITE CHILD and the time and date were clearly visible.

"You have kids?" Amanda asked.

Jack shook his head.

"Then you probably won't understand."

That's where she was wrong.

Jack might not have any children, at least not yet, but that might not be true for too much longer. His thoughts flashed back to the discussion between him and Lisanne that had turned into an argument.

The fork in the road.

Lisanne had a sister who made bad choices. Bad choices in men, bad choices in careers, and bad choices with drugs. She also had a fourteen-year-old daughter, Emily. Child protective services wanted to remove Emily from her mom and Lisanne wanted to fight for custody of her niece.

Jack wasn't sure about that plan.

Becoming a husband was a big step. Becoming an instant dad to a teenager was a gargantuan one. But it wasn't just that Jack was becoming a dad. Lisanne would be becoming a new mom to a broken daughter who might not even want any part of the arrangement.

Jack wanted time to think it over.

That had not been the right answer.

Lisanne had seen his hesitancy as a lack of commitment, or more specifically, a lack of commitment to her.

That had not gone over well, either.

Pushing aside his relationship problems, Jack brought his focus back to Amanda.

"So once you realized you had something, what did you do?" Jack said.

"Called the reward hotline. I left my name and number and said I had information about Troy, but I would only provide it to Jeff."

"Why the secrecy?" Jack asked.

Amanda's gaze grew flinty. "Look, I might work at a gas station in middle-of-nowhere Texas, but that doesn't mean I'm an idiot. Whatever happened to that boy, it wasn't because he got high, wrecked his car, and wandered off. We live in the kind of surveillance state that Orwell imagined. Each of us voluntarily carries a tracking device wherever we go. Not only that, even the smallest of these towns has traffic cameras and almost every mom-and-pop store has a surveillance camera. But with all of that, Troy somehow still managed to disappear off the face of the earth. And then, the moment when his case gets a shot of new energy in the form of a fifty-thousand-dollar reward, a previously unreleased video gets leaked to the press. Somebody powerful does not want that boy found."

Jack agreed.

While he didn't know enough about the circumstances surrounding Troy's disappearance to comment on them, Jack did know what he saw—three professionals carrying out a sophisticated hit on a single man. A man who was on his way to meet with a woman who claimed to have evidence that would shed new light on his son's disappearance.

This could not be a coincidence.

"Besides the reward hotline, did you tell anyone else what you just relayed to me?" Jack said. "Anyone at all?"

"Why?" Amanda said.

"Because somebody wanted to keep Jeff from meeting with you," Jack said. "They succeeded. But there's still a loose end."

Amanda's eyes widened. "Me?"

"I don't know," Jack said. "But I'd rather be safe than sorry. Who else did you tell about your tip?"

"My boyfriend."

"The Briar Wood cop?"

She nodded.

Well, shit.

"Is your daughter home?" Jack said.

She nodded again. "She's in high school, plays varsity soccer, and has a part-time job. Our schedules don't always overlap so she's used to hanging out alone."

"Call her. Now."

Amanda's fingers trembled as she punched the contact and put the phone on speaker. It rang multiple times before going to voicemail.

"Do you ring through her do not disturb?" Jack said.

"Yes."

"Let's go," Jack said.

"Where?"

"Your house. I'll drive. You keep dialing."

Amanda didn't argue.

16

AMANDA LIVED ON A LONELY PLOT OF LAND ON THE OUTSKIRTS OF TOWN. A RUSTED barbed wire fence delineated the property lines with a sprawling farm on one side and a dense copse of mesquite, cedar, and an assortment of Texas shrubs on the other. Based on what he'd seen during his journey along the Lone Star's back roads, Jack thought the wooded area probably bookended a cattle ranch. Texas herds were free range and larger ranches often left patches of woods that served as a refuge for the roaming longhorns during the summer's oppressive heat.

In any case, Amanda's dwelling was a single-story domicile at the end of a gravel driveway. Tufts of grass sprouted from the bare spots where the rock fragments had been washed away, and the house's exterior had been bleached by the sun and scoured by the wind. But the yard was trimmed and the wraparound front porch freshly swept. Amanda might not have the money for much, but she took care of what she had.

"Pick up," Amanda hissed, stabbing her iPhone for what seemed like the hundredth time. "Come on."

Jack kept his mouth shut, concentrating on navigating the pot-holed driveway instead. The first couple of times Amanda had asked if he thought her daughter, Bella, was okay, Jack had tried his best to reassure her. By the sixth time, he no longer bothered. The truth was he had no idea what they were going to find inside the plain home and Amanda was smart enough to know that. But when it came to a mother's concern for her child, intelligence didn't factor into the equation.

"See anything out of place?" Jack said, triggering the Mustang's brights. Twin pools of halogen light swept across the porch before centering on the carport.

"Like what?" Amanda said, turning from the phone to Jack.

"A vehicle that doesn't belong," Jack said. "Or an open door or window that you'd left closed."

Amanda hunched forward in her seat, her phone forgotten. She bit her lip as she squinted at the house.

"Not that I can tell," Amanda said.

Her words sounded plaintive.

Unsure.

Jack covered the last fifty yards in a blur of groaning shocks and crunching gravel. Rather than following the driveway to the carport on the left, he continued straight, transitioning from stone to what passed for grass. The Mustang was not what anyone would term an off-road vehicle, but the big engine offered power in spades. Jack downshifted, sending the RPMs redlining as he compensated for the fishtailing the torque induced. The maneuver was not going to be kind to Amanda's front lawn, but if she had thoughts about her landscaping, the single mom didn't voice them.

"You have your keys ready?" Jack said, clutching and braking.

"Yes."

"Good," Jack said as the muscle car's front wheels rolled up to the porch. "Unlock the door and stay behind me."

She gave a terse nod, her lips set in a thin, hard line. The keys were already in her fingers, ready to go. Jack had expected more resistance to the idea of her staying back as he entered the house, but maybe he shouldn't have.

After explaining that he worked for the Department of the Interior, Amanda had examined his fake creds with an admirable amount of attention but she'd declined to ask the obvious question—What was a Department of the Interior employee doing in Texas? Instead, she'd seemed to accept that he was the professional, or at least the only one of them who'd been trained professionally how to employ a pistol. And while Jack was thankful that she hadn't put up a fight, his motivation for going through the door first went beyond mere tactical considerations. Her house sat at the top of a sloping section of land at the end of a long driveway. With no way to approach the house discreetly, Jack had made the decision to trade stealth for speed. If someone was waiting in ambush, they would know Jack was coming.

But this wasn't the only reason he wanted to go first.

The men with whom Amanda was now at least peripherally involved were professional killers. If the mercenaries had already paid a visit to Amanda's house, Jack didn't for a minute think the shooters would balk at killing a teenage girl.

This was the real reason Jack wanted to clear the house first.

He might be too late to prevent Bella's death, but if things had played out for the worst, Jack wanted to find the crime scene first and control the way the soon-to-be-grieving mother learned that her only child was dead.

Jack actioned the emergency brake, but left the engine running and high beams triggered. The brights stabbed through the bay window at the front of the house, illuminating the room where Jack intended to make entry. He would have loved to have a flashbang or two about now, but the headlights were better than nothing. Opening his door, Jack drew his SIG and then flowed around the front of the car with Amanda following. He mounted the porch in two quick strides, covering the bay window to his right even as he heard Amanda fit her key to the lock behind him.

"Here's how this is gonna go," Jack said. "You're gonna unlock the door. When I say so, I want you to open it and then step out of the way. Got it?"

"Got it," she said.

Her voice quavered, but the fingers holding her keys remained steady. When it came to displaying courage in the face of danger, a grizzly bear had nothing on the mother of a teenager.

"Good," Jack said. "Unlock the door and turn the handle. I'm gonna count down from three. Open the door on one. Okay?"

"Sure," Amanda said, her voice already sounding steadier.

While the single mother wasn't going to be auditioning for the role of breacher anytime soon, she was calm under pressure and could follow directions.

Jack could work with that.

"Here we go," Jack said. "Three, two, one."

With admirable efficiency, Amanda keyed the lock and opened the door.

Then she stepped into the entryway.

17

"BELLA?" AMANDA CALLED, STANDING IN THE FOYER. "HONEY?"

Jack wasn't mad at Amanda. He was mad at himself. He should have anticipated her reaction. As a mother, there was no way she wasn't going into the house first.

Jack found her courage admirable.

If misguided.

The majority of casualties that occurred during close-quarters battle, or CQB, happened during entry. This was why all doors, and the front door in particular, were known as fatal funnels. Nothing focuses a shooter like an open door, so assaulters were trained to transit through the fatal funnel with speed and violence.

Pretty much the opposite of what was happening now.

Jack blasted through the front door like a runaway freight train, knocking Amanda aside with a well-placed shoulder. The unexpected impact sent the petite woman sprawling, which might just have been the best tactical move she could make. Jack mentally winced as his peripheral vision caught her tumbling across a recliner, but the single mother's well-being would have to wait. Jack's entire being was hyper-focused on the SIG's stubby front sight post.

Panning across the room, Jack sought out human forms.

He didn't find any.

The small living room gave way to an equally small but neatly kept kitchen.

Or at least mostly neat.

The front sight post flickered past a half-empty gallon of milk along with an open peanut butter jar sitting next to a bag of rice cakes. The detritus of crumbs, utensils, a milk-stained glass, and a coffee cup suggested that someone had enjoyed breakfast without bothering to clean up after themselves.

Or maybe their breakfast had been interrupted.

Jack assumed the door on the far side of the kitchen opened into the backyard, but that area could be cleared later. First, he needed to finish the house. Pivoting left, Jack followed the narrow hallway that led from the kitchen.

A door on the right led to a bathroom. Jack peeked across the threshold to find it empty with a steam-clouded mirror. Bunched towels littered the floor.

"Bella?" Amanda said, desperation filling her voice. "Bella!"

Her tone was heartbreaking.

The sound of a mother anxious for her child.

"Which room is hers?" Jack said, yelling over his shoulder as the SIG's front sight post floated between the two closed doors at the end of the hallway.

"Right," Amanda said, her reply breathless. "The one on the right."

Jack had given up the option of a stealthy entry the moment he'd roared into the front yard with the Mustang's high beams blasting through the bay window. But just because he wasn't trying to hide his approach didn't mean he wasn't going to proceed with caution. The long, claustrophobic hallway was the definition of a fatal funnel. A gunman waiting in ambush in either room wouldn't have to be any sort of marksman to hit Jack. A shotgun fired through the center of the door would bring this little tactical situation to a rather abrupt end.

Jack eased up to the door, placing his left hand on the doorknob, and switched the SIG to his right. Serving as both the breacher and lead assaulter was not ideal. Of course neither was having Amanda wander across his gunline. But the single mom's unreliability wasn't the only reason Jack was heading through the door first. His muscular frame was large enough to dominate the entryway, preventing Amanda from entering the room until he moved. And until Jack knew what was waiting on the other side, there was no way he was allowing Amanda past him.

The small bedroom could hold a shooter.

Or something much, much worse.

Jack squeezed the SIG's grip until his knuckles whitened before easing back on the pressure in an effort to bring his nerves under control.

Then he turned the doorknob and entered.

The view on the other side of the door was difficult to process. It felt as if he'd stepped into some sort of three-dimensional kaleidoscope. The room's overhead lights were off, but strings of white Christmas lights hung from the ceiling and climbed up the walls. A bookshelf was light on books and heavy on soccer trophies, but it was the walls of Bella's room that really gave Jack pause. Rather than album covers or movie posters, the drywall was decorated with snapshots.

Hundreds of them.

The pictures were artfully arranged in geometrical patterns, which the lights highlighted. Rather than the *Beautiful Mind*–type chaos, the snapshots were like shards from a shattered mirror, each one reflecting an aspect of the girl whose room they dominated.

Jack knew this because Bella lay on the bed situated on the far side of the room.

For reasons Jack couldn't quite fathom, the mattress rested on the floor where two of the walls met at a right angle. Here again the teen's interior decorating chops banished the expected effect. Instead of looking like a college flophouse, the made-up bed gave off an elegant vibe. Like something pieced together from an influencer's Instagram post.

Bella was curled against the wall, peering at her phone. Her head was tilted forward and her eyes were masked by the kind of thick, blond ringlets that would have made Rapunzel jealous. The teen didn't so much as twitch at Jack's unexpected appearance, and despite his training, he paused in the doorway, trying to make sense of her reaction.

Then he understood.

Earbuds.

The teen must have been listening to music or watching a video. If Lisanne's niece was any guide, Jack had no doubt that the volume pumping out of the device was loud enough to keep Bella oblivious of anything up to an earthquake.

"Bella," Jack said, lowering the SIG. "Hey."

When his words didn't garner a response, Jack stepped into the room and tried again.

"Bella!" Jack said.

This time, he accompanied the words with a wave from his left hand, as he held the SIG alongside his leg with his right. The one–two combination did the trick. Bella looked up from her phone, her eyes widening.

"It's okay," Jack said. "Your mom's right behind me."

He turned to point over his shoulder, hoping that his tone and movements proved soothing.

They didn't.

A moment ago, Bella's hands had held only her phone.

Now they held something else.

Bear spray.

"Wait," Jack screamed, holding up his hand, palm out.

It was the universal signal for *stop*.

But not in this house.

Bella eyed him over the top of the can, like a cannoneer sighting down the barrel at a pirate ship.

Then she pressed the trigger.

18

"PACKAGE IS INBOUND."

Cary acknowledged the transmission with two clicks of the radio's transmit button.

For a Eurotrash-looking has-been, Hans was surprisingly well outfitted. Or maybe not so surprising, considering the level of talent he was trying to recruit and the wages he was willing to pay to recruit them. Case in point, the communications gear Cary and Jad were using was strikingly similar to the low-profile kit they employed during Campus missions. Though he couldn't speak to the combination cell phone/radio's encryption, Hans's words echoed in Cary's ear with perfect clarity.

Which was unfortunate.

Cary would have loved to have a gear-inspired loss of communications right about now.

"Package confirmed."

The radio call came from Jad, who was situated at the far end of the promenade. Though it was early morning, several pedestrians wandered the stretch of concrete proving that while Las Vegas might tone down its act, it really never slept. Right about now, Cary would have traded his right arm for a little less atmosphere.

Or a couple of additional operatives.

After almost fifteen years with Triple Nickel, Cary was good at his job.

Very good.

And his skill set went beyond just putting steel on target with his Barrett Advanced Sniper Rifle. Though doctrinally his mission set had never changed, what Cary and his teammates had been tasked to accomplish during deployments ebbed and flowed as the War on Terror waxed and waned. The surges in Iraq and Afghanistan had lent a direct action focus to Triple Nickel's mission set, while the subsequent reset and shift toward near-peer adversaries like China saw the Green Berets perfecting entirely new skill sets. Like many team sergeants, Cary had shifted his team's training to focus more on low-profile surveillance and asset meets in complex urban environments.

Like Beijing.

Or Las Vegas.

"Give me a talk on," Cary said, straining his eyes to pierce the semidarkness.

The promenade where the kinetic action was to take place was one of the many pedestrian areas linking Vegas namesakes. In the same manner in which a casino could never be exited without first following a meandering path through gambling machines galore and visual distractions of every conceivable type, the footpaths that wormed to and fro along the strip were constructed to present a person ample opportunities to part from their cash in the form of eateries, bars, casinos, and the like. As a result, navigating the many Vegas side streets was more akin to following a wandering cow path than a crow's straight-line flight.

This promenade was no exception.

Though the walkway traveled in a generally east-west direction, it was neither straight nor straightforward to traverse. Cary was seated at an outdoor metal table on the south side of the cobblestone thoroughfare with his back against a brick wall in typical Green Beret fashion. The fact that the brick wall formed the exterior of a coffee shop that had long since closed for the day was an added bonus. For a man who made his living by the sword, the feeling that came with knowing that your back was protected could not be beat.

Unfortunately, the other cardinal directions were more problematic.

To the west, and Cary's left, lay the north-south-running Las Vegas Boulevard. The normally busy two-lane street was absent most vehicular traffic at this time of the night, but a healthy contingent of tourists still swarmed past the Caesars Palace monstrosity located on the road's western banks. To the east, the promenade wound by a number of storefronts and attractions before dumping into the High Roller observation wheel, Vegas's answer to the London Eye Ferris wheel.

Everything might be bigger in Texas, but Vegas wasn't far behind.

The package was supposed to be exiting a bar on the north side of the promenade about one hundred yards to Cary's right. While this distance should have been visible to Cary, the rat warren of a path twisted due north before turning again to the east, effectively creating a blind spot in between two buildings.

A blind spot Cary intended to use.

"Roger," Jad said. "Target is a singleton proceeding west. He's dressed in a white, untucked button-down shirt, blue jeans, and black shoes. He's Caucasian with close-cropped brown hair and no facial hair. Mid to late thirties, six feet tall, and big. Probably close to three bills."

"Roger that, 2," Cary said. "Break, 7, this is 1. Confirm this is the target? I thought we were looking for someone who was about one hundred and fifty pounds, over."

"One, this is 7," Hans said, his German accent more pronounced over the radio. "That is the target. I must have been mistaken."

And the hits just kept on coming.

Cary's plan to interdict the target was admittedly simple, but he'd learned long ago that the best plans were. Leaders too often try to account for every variable and the result is a concept of the operation that is complex, cumbersome, and goes out the window within moments of first contact with the enemy. That said, there's a difference between providing a framework that gives a trained operator the latitude to do what they do best, and a ready, fire, aim concept that sends men off on a wing and a prayer. In this case, Cary had devised a pretty good course of action considering the limited time before the hit and his constrained resources. But there was still quite a difference between interdicting someone with the lean build of an endurance athlete versus the dump truck on wheels Jad had just described.

Time for an audible.

"Two, this is 1," Cary said. "Break station and follow the target toward me. Stand by to flex to Octavia, over."

"Two copies all," Jad said. "Standing by for Octavia, over."

"One, this is 7," Hans said. "You never briefed an Octavia contingency."

"Sorry," Cary said. "Must have been an oversight."

The sputtering that came over the radio in response was gratifying, but Cary couldn't take too much joy in the German's anger. He had other things to consider.

Like what in the hell was Octavia.

19

"ONE, THIS IS 2," JAD SAID. "TARGET IS FIFTY METERS AND CLOSING. SHOULD BE coming into visual range any minute."

"Roger," Cary said, getting to his feet. "Stand by to execute."

Jad replied with two clicks of the transmit button.

While Cary had no doubt that the German mercenary was fuming, Hans had the sense not to ask what was happening. Which was good, because at this point, Cary wasn't sure how he would have answered. Their objective was to appropriate the target's driver's license. For two burly commandos versus a relatively slight man, this was a difficult, but infinitely doable task. But the human dump truck changed Cary's math.

But perhaps all was not lost.

Just because he weighed nearly three hundred pounds did not mean their target was a force to be reckoned with. After all, America was fast becoming the most obese nation on earth, and Las Vegas was a city that specialized in indulgences of all forms. It was not unthinkable that the man who was about to appear at the far end of the promenade might be a grotesquely overweight tourist visiting Sin City for the famous all-you-can-eat buffets.

And then Cary saw their target.

Describing him as muscular didn't do justice to the word. The target could have been in Vegas to participate in a bodybuilding competition. Come to think of it, maybe he was. Instead of the outright bulk of a football lineman, the man walking toward Cary carried his mass like a dancer.

Though the majority of the target's frame was hidden by his shirt and jeans, what Cary could see didn't bode well. The target's neck could have doubled as a tree trunk, and his shoulders were wide enough to serve as helicopter landing zones. But it was the man's torso that really signaled trouble. The target had the perfect V shape—a broad chest, heavy shoulders, and wide back that tapered to a narrow waist. Though the exact military units Cary had discussed with Hans were lies, he hadn't exaggerated his operational experience. Cary had tangled with men this size before, and as targets went, they represented the worst of both worlds—strong and agile.

In other words, trouble.

Swiping to the text app on his phone, Cary found the thread he was looking for and thumbed in a short message. Then he hit send and hoped for the best.

"Two, this is 1," Cary said, masking his lips with his hand. "Execute, execute, execute."

Cary got to his feet without waiting for Jad's reply.

One way or another, it was going down.

The human dump truck keyed off Cary's movement, turning toward the Green Beret.

Cary didn't like what he was seeing.

This wasn't the casual glance one pedestrian might give another. Cary felt himself being appraised in a familiar manner. The man's gaze swept over Cary from head to toe, lingering for a moment on Cary's hands, before returning to the Green Beret's face. The target was more than just a juiced-up meathead. An appraisal like that came from practice. Cary was facing another operator.

Fantastic.

Cary gave the man a cautious nod before transferring his attention to the bar across the narrow promenade. The bar the target was just coming abreast of. As if on cue, the glass doors opened, and the bar's ambient noise spilled out.

The target oriented on the new stimulus, as did Cary.

For good reason.

While beautiful women in Las Vegas weren't exactly uncommon, a man was still hardwired to react to external stimuli. And there was plenty about the pair of blondes who strutted onto the promenade worth reacting to. That they were working girls, strippers, showgirls, or all three wasn't in doubt. But knowing how they earned their money didn't make the women any less captivating. With skirts as short as their heels were high and tops that left little to the imagination, the women showcased plenty of tan skin paired with accessories that had to be the handiwork of Sin City's best plastic surgeons. But as with their chosen profession, knowing that the woman's assets were fabricated rather than God-given did nothing to lessen their appeal.

The target's eyes were drawn to the pair like a moth to the flame. In a testament to his training and profession, the human dump truck's gaze didn't linger long.

But it was long enough.

In two quick strides, Cary halved the distance.

With the speed of a striking viper, the target's head snapped back to Cary as his face hardened. The target's right hand drifted toward his waistband as his left hovered about chest high. This stance gave the target the flexibility to create space by shoving Cary out of the way or clear his shirt for a quick draw.

He was good.

"Want to party?" the closest blonde said, laying a hand on the man's shoulder.

"No," the target said, shrugging off fingers tipped with pink manicured nails.

"Come on," said her partner. "We're running a special—two for the price of one."

"I said no," the target said.

The steel in his voice left no room for argument.

"Fine," blonde number one said. "No reason to be a dick."

The conversation had lasted just seconds, but the target realized his mistake. He spun back toward Cary.

Too late.

The Green Beret was already abeam the man. Except Cary wasn't paying attention to the target or his two new friends. Instead, the commando was focused on the man emerging from the shadows.

Jad.

"Hey," Cary said, catching his voice loud enough to carry over the ruckus. "Are you Amir Albazi?"

Jad slowed his walk with an exaggerated sigh. "Yeah, but lower your damn voice. I'm trying to keep things on the DL."

"I told you he was here," the first blonde said, elbowing her friend.

"Your last fight was amazing," Cary said. "You absolutely crushed that guy. Can I get a picture?"

"Yeah, okay," Jad said. "But make it quick. I've got places to be."

"Thank you," Cary said. "I really appreciate it. Taking his phone from his pocket, he prepared to assume the selfie pose when he looked at the posse behind him. "Hey, man, could you take this?"

Cary thrust his cell toward the target, who instinctively accepted the device.

"Thanks, bro," Cary said, wrapping his arm around Jad's neck. "Really appreciate it."

"Can we get in, too?" the first blonde said.

"The more the merrier," Cary said.

The ladies sidled up next to the Green Berets and the target dutifully snapped a few pictures before handing the phone back to Cary.

"Hey, you want to get in?" Cary said, motioning toward the group. "I can text you the pic."

"No," the target said, his expression more sneer than smile. Spinning on his heel, the man strode down the walkway and out of sight.

"What's his problem?" the first blonde said.

"Don't know," Jad said, "but I bet you could fix it."

The ladies thought that was funny.

Hans apparently did not.

"Debrief at the Peppermill," Hans said, his voice crackling from Cary's earpiece. "Thirty minutes."

"He doesn't sound happy," Jad said.

"Join the club," Cary said.

20

BRIAR WOOD, TEXAS

JACK WAS NO STRANGER TO CHEMICAL IRRITANTS. OVER THE COURSE OF HIS CAM-pus employment, Jack had been on the receiving end of mace, tear gas, and pepper spray.

None of them held a candle to bear spray.

One moment he'd been trying to reassure Bella of his noble intentions. The next he was doing his best not to claw his eyes out as what felt like an army of fire ants attempted to eat their way out of his sinus cavities. Saying that his eyes, nose, and throat burned had about as much in common with what was transpiring in his mucous membranes as lighting a match equated to an erupting volcano.

Both events involved heat, but the scale between the two just wasn't comparable.

"Your mom's right behind me," Jack shouted.

Or at least tried to.

Between a tongue that was suddenly the size of a watermelon and a throat that had constricted to the diameter of a soda straw, the noises that left Jack's swollen lips were less than intelligible.

Fortunately, Amanda was still able to speak.

Barely.

"Bella," Amanda yelled between coughs. "It's me. *It's me.*"

Backing out of Bella's room more by feel than sight, Jack holstered his SIG and then stumbled down the hall.

"Mama?" Bella said.

"Yes," Amanda said, hacking. "For the love of God, honey, yes."

"Oh," Bella said. "Sorry. But you always said to shoot first and ask questions later."

Of course she did, Jack thought. He expected no less of a Texas girl. But instead of saying that, he tried to voice something more positive. "Dish soap."

"What did he say?" Amanda said between coughs.

"I don't know," Bella said. "Sounded like *fish rope.*"

Jack's mother, the indomitable Cathy Ryan, had a saying for situations like this one. Actually, as a world-class ophthalmologist often sought after for the most complex surgical procedures, Cathy was more than familiar with the frustrations that accompanied failure. That said, Jack wasn't sure that his mother had ever been rendered blind and dumb by bear spray. Even so, one of her mantras seemed particularly poignant at the moment— *when you can't laugh, cry.*

Except with Jack's tear ducts in their current state of enragement, he wasn't entirely sure he could do either.

Instead, Jack enunciated his words and willed his leaden tongue to cooperate.

"Dish. Soap."

"Wish hope?" Bella said.

Jack blindly pounded his fist against the wall as he shook his head.

"Wait," Amanda said. "I think I got it that time—*dish soap?*"

Jack nodded.

Violently.

"Why didn't he just say so?" Bella said.

"Because he just mainlined half a can of bear spray thanks to you," Amanda said. "God, that stuff's awful. Make yourself useful and start opening windows while I take our friend to the kitchen."

Jack's eyes were now completely swollen shut and the napalm attacking the mucous linings in his nose and throat seemed to be in no hurry to burn out. Even so, Amanda's words felt like a cool balm. Though he'd never been doused with bear spray, he'd been hit with pepper spray enough times to know the remedy—Dawn soap. Bear spray was chemically formulated to cling to a person's skin like a pit bull. Attempting to wash away the mixture with just water was useless without giving the oily compound something to bond with.

Like dish soap.

"Sink's this way," Amanda said.

Jack felt her fingers circle his biceps. Amanda tugged him forward and Jack allowed himself to be led down the hall as he tried not to harbor murderous thoughts toward Bella.

In this endeavor at least Jack was successful.

Mostly.

"SO, YOU'RE HERE TO PROTECT MY MOM FROM BAD GUYS?"

The question was asked with the sort of innate skepticism that only a teenager can properly muster. A tone that conveyed the stupidity of the question's recipient and the superiority of the questioner. But as much as Jack wanted to respond with a bit of righteous rage, the teenager had a point. Though a liberal application of Dawn soap had tamped the volcanic eruption across his mucous membrane to a low simmering, Jack would not be up for the Liam Neeson role in the *Taken* franchise anytime soon.

"Bella," Amanda said from across the kitchen. "Be nice."

Jack's vision might be somewhat degraded, but he would have

to be blind to miss the eye roll that Amanda's admonishment prompted in her daughter. That was fine. He was seated at the kitchen table, sharing coffee with a surly teenager and her mom. In the greater scope of things, this was a much better outcome than Jack had envisioned as he'd been driving hell-bent along Texas back roads.

"I saw that," Amanda said, washing the soap from her face.

Though she hadn't experienced the pleasure of a direct hit of bear spray like Jack, some of the splatter had still landed on Amanda's shirt. At Jack's urging, Amanda had performed her ritual cleaning under the kitchen faucet. Though her eyes were still closed as she toweled herself dry, Bella's mom's sight seemed to function just fine.

"I'm just saying that I had the situation well in hand," Bella said. She glared at Jack as if daring him to say otherwise.

Rather than engage with the surly teenager, he winked.

Bella scowled.

Perhaps the legendary Ryan charm wasn't quite as invincible as Jack's father had led him to believe. Or maybe teenage girls were just immune.

"Don't you need to get dressed for school?" Amanda said, eyeing her daughter.

"I am dressed," Bella said, her early haughtiness burning away under her mother's scrutiny.

Amanda's eyes settled on her daughter's midriff-baring tank top before traveling to her low-slung jeans that crested a good deal south of her belly button. The single mother's face took on the appearance of a gathering storm cloud, growing darker with every inch her gaze traversed her daughter's bare skin. After a thorough inspection, Amanda directed her attention back to Bella's face.

"I don't think so," Amanda said.

"Mom—"

"Change," Amanda said. "Now."

The exchange had a familiar feel to it, and judging by her reaction, one that Bella hadn't expected to win.

"I don't have time," Bella said, crossing her arms beneath her breasts. "Jeremiah will be here in two minutes."

"Jeremiah?" Amanda said.

Amanda's question seemed innocent enough, but her tone suggested otherwise. A chill settled in the air and Jack could feel the cold settle onto his burning eyes. Where a moment before Bella had looked to be in the throes of victory, her face had now turned ashen.

Jack recognized the expression.

It was the look of defeat.

"Yeah," Bella said, trying for nonchalant, but her tense shoulders and flushed cheeks suggested otherwise. "You headed out early this morning, so I asked Jeremiah for a ride."

"Jeremiah doesn't go to your school," Amanda said. "In fact, he doesn't go to school at all."

"What do you expect me to do?" Bella said. "Walk?"

"There's a big yellow bus that drives right by our house," Amanda said.

"Mo-om," Bella said, somehow squeezing two syllables from the word. "I'm a *senior*. I can't ride the bus."

"Change," Amanda said. "Now. I will take you to school."

"But, but," Bella said, her hazel eyes darting back and forth, "you'll be late for your shift."

"Now."

A moment ago Jack wouldn't have believed it possible, but the chill in the room grew even more pronounced. Bella hugged herself, as if she could feel the cold. She opened her mouth. Jack expected another salvo, but the spunky blonde didn't launch it.

Instead, her eyes clouded with tears.

"You just don't get it," Bella said before storming down the hall.

Amanda tracked her daughter's progress in silence. Only after the sound of a door slamming cracked down the hall like a rifle shot did she speak.

"Actually, I do," Amanda said. "That's the problem."

She stared after her daughter for another long moment and then turned to Jack.

"Sorry about that," Amanda said.

"Don't apologize," Jack said. "My fiancée has a niece."

"Then you know," Amanda said.

Jack shook his head. "I think only a parent can really know. I see a bit, and I hear the frustration in my fiancée's voice, but I don't feel it here." Jack tapped his chest. "Not like you do with Bella."

Amanda nodded, folding a hand towel before hanging it neatly from the oven. "My parental struggles aside, what's next?"

That was a very good question.

Up until this moment, Jack had been operating primarily in react to contact mode. And while he felt quite comfortable executing this battle drill, simply reacting would not allow him to resolve whatever was happening here. Even worse, staying reactionary meant that Jack would always be one step behind whoever was pulling the strings.

In his experience, this was a great way to wind up dead.

But that did not mean Jack knew what to do next. In a lesson that had been even harder to learn, Jack had slowly come to realize that while having a bias toward action was good, he still needed a vector. Too often Jack's desire to do something, anything, to regain the initiative had resulted in unforced errors. That he'd emerged from this philosophy relatively unscathed was more a testament to luck than skill.

Not that long ago, his luck had nearly run out.

After an operation in the Philippines had gone wrong, Jack's cousin and fellow Campus operative, Dom Caruso, had suffered a grievous injury that had almost resulted in his death.

An injury for which Jack considered himself responsible.

That his boss, John T. Clark of Rainbow Six fame, didn't agree was irrelevant.

At least to Jack.

If nothing else, that moment in a dank warehouse smelling of fish offal and death had seared a lesson into Jack's psyche. As a team leader and full-fledged operator in the Campus's ranks, Jack's actions had repercussions that extended well beyond just his own personal well-being. To say that Jack had become indecisive as a reaction to what happened was too strong of a description.

But without a doubt, he had grown more conscious.

"I'm not sure what's happening here," Jack said, rousing from his introspection, "but I do know this—a man was murdered. Until I'm sure that he wasn't killed because of what you know, I want to take some precautions."

"What's that mean?" Amanda said.

"It means that the people I work with are pretty good at getting to the bottom of things," Jack said, "but we'll need some time to sort things out. Time to shake the trees and see what falls out. I want you and your daughter to go somewhere safe while we work."

"So the Department of the Interior handles murder cases now?" Amanda said.

Jack smiled.

Amanda might be working the swing shift at a gas station, but she wasn't dumb.

Not by a long shot.

"Not exactly," he said. "But what went down on Highway 79 wasn't road rage or a carjacking gone wrong. Those shooters were professionals."

"Takes one to know one," Amanda said.

Jack smiled again, but this time the grin felt a bit forced.

"Bottom line," Jack said, "nobody's gonna make you do anything. I can walk out that door right now if you prefer, but I'd like you and Bella to come with me. I'll put you up in a fancy hotel in the city of your choice—Houston, Austin, I don't care. Stay there for a day or two and order all the room service you can eat. I think the men who killed Jeff are foreign mercenaries, but regardless of who they work for, they're not common criminals, which means they won't be sticking around. Once I'm sure they're gone, it'll be safe for you and Bella to come home."

"If you don't think they'd stick around, then why do we have to leave?" Amanda said.

"Because thinking so isn't the same as knowing so and I'm not going to bet your life or your daughter's on a hunch."

Jack felt the force of Amanda's gaze as she stared at him.

Once again it felt as if she were weighing his words. Or, more likely, weighing his character. If Bella was sixteen, then Amanda must not have been much older when she'd given birth. The single mom had probably been forced to get good at judging people's character very fast.

"I'll need to call my boss," Amanda said with a sigh. "I can afford to miss a day or so, but not more than that."

For a moment Jack didn't understand.

Then he got it.

"Don't worry about losing the hours," Jack said. "I'll make sure you're paid."

Amanda's expression hardened. "I don't need charity."

"Good," Jack said, "because that's not what I'm offering.

147

Consider it sort of like the witness protection program. You're missing work at the government's request, so it's incumbent on my agency to make things right. This isn't a handout."

Amanda stared at Jack again, but this time he must have been ready for the scrutiny because the silence seemed less awkward. Or maybe Amanda truly was taking less time to make up her mind.

"Okay," Amanda said. "Let me get some things and tell Bella."

"Want help?" Jack said.

Amanda shook her head. "If you thought *I* was a tough sell, just wait. Hurricane Bella's about to make landfall."

"Really?" Jack said with a laugh. "I figured she'd jump at the chance to blow off school."

"Not my daughter," Amanda said as she got to her feet. "She sees school as her ticket out of here. Bella's enrolled in all AP classes, and she's taking two sciences this semester. She about has a breakdown if she misses even a day of classes. I don't suppose your agency can do anything about that?"

"Even the federal government has limits," Jack said.

"That's what I was afraid of," Amanda said, sliding past Jack and heading down the hall. "Bella? Honey?"

Jack looked from the chipped mug in front of him to the carafe of coffee sitting temptingly within reach. At this point he couldn't remember how much java he'd consumed, which was a good indication that it was time to call it quits. While he didn't usually get jittery, the caffeine seemed to stay in his system for longer. If he had another cup now, Jack was worried he wouldn't be able to sleep until sometime next week.

"Bella?"

Jack heard the teenager's door creak open.

And then a scream.

21

JACK'S LEGS CARRIED HIM TOWARD AMANDA AS HIS HEAD TRIED TO PREPARE HIS heart for what he might find. The gas station attendant had lived a hardscrabble life as a young, single mom eking out a living as she cared for her child. Though she'd been concerned when Jack had intimated that men might want to kill her, Amanda had taken the news in stride. Jack couldn't imagine that there were too many things that would make a woman with Amanda's grit scream.

The things that might were almost too terrible to contemplate. But contemplate them Jack did.

Jack sprinted past the bathroom, and then he was at Bella's door. Amanda was still standing in the threshold, and Jack placed his hand on her back to shepherd her out of the way. Her body seemed to be vibrating beneath his fingers, like a glass on the brink of reaching its resonant frequency and shattering.

Steeling himself for what he was about to see, he surveyed the room.

Though he was ready for it this time, the kaleidoscope effect was still jarring. But Jack kept his eyes moving past the photos, hand-drawn pictures, and dangling lights in favor of the room's occupant. His eyes settled on one—a fat orange cat resting in the center of Bella's bed. The feline regarded Jack through slitted eyes, a pointed meow telling Jack that trouble would be had should he make the ill-conceived choice to disturb her.

But of the cat's owner, Jack could find no sign.

"Where'd she go?" Jack said.

He kept his eyes moving across the room, searching for the clue he'd missed as he waited for Amanda's reply. Though he hadn't noticed the cat the last time he'd charged into the teenager's room, Jack couldn't imagine the feline was the source of Amanda's angst. Besides, the cat didn't seem at all surprised to see people in the room, which led Jack to believe that he, not the tabby, was the visitor here.

"Out the window," Amanda said, her voice sounding defeated.

Jack registered the cool breeze across his skin the moment his eyes found the bedroom window. The blinds were still lowered, but an inch or two separated the pane from the sill.

Jack moved to the window, and the cat's meow took on a warning tone.

"Relax," Jack said. "I'm not going to touch you."

The cat didn't answer, but Jack gave the bed a wide berth all the same. The window sat low on the wall at a height easily surmountable by a teenage girl. Jack parted the blinds in time to see the glow of red taillights disappearing down the drive.

"Who do you think has her?" Jack said.

Amanda settled against the wall with a sigh. "Jeremiah."

The change in the single mom nearly broke his heart. Before he'd seen an indomitable woman who'd been knocked around by life but had refused to stay down.

No longer.

Amanda sagged against the drywall.

"Do you want to go after her?" Jack said.

Amanda shook her head.

"Though she'd never believe it, I know my daughter. They'll go out for breakfast, but she'll make him take her to school. She has a calculus quiz every Monday. There's no way she'd miss that."

Jack glanced at his watch. "What time does school start?"

"Seven," Amanda said. "Which means they have plenty of time to be up to no good between now and then."

The single mom gave another deep sigh, wrapping her arms across her chest as if she were hugging herself. "That boy is three years older than her and good for not much beyond drinking beer and getting into trouble. Bella took the ACTs this summer and scored high enough to win a Pell grant. The offers from colleges are piling up on the kitchen counter. If she can just hold on until the end of the school year, she can have a whole different life. One outside this nowhere town and the nowhere men who call it home."

Jack said nothing.

It did not take a genius to understand that Amanda was seeing more than just Bella's potentially wasted life as she spoke. He had to imagine that her daughter's path was mirroring Amanda's and now the mother was desperately trying to prevent her little girl from making a life-altering choice that would keep her anchored to Briar Wood. The pain on Amanda's face was hard to look at. The raw emotion made her seem older.

Tired.

"What do you want to do?" Jack said.

"I'll call Brian," Amanda said. "He'll keep an eye out for them. I'd love for him to pull that boy over and check the expiration date on his truck's registration, but Brian hassling Jeremiah over nothing would probably do more harm than good. Bella ran away, but I know she'll still end up at school. If she thinks her relationship with Jeremiah is at risk, she might just choose that boy over everything else and run away for good."

Jack nodded, again feeling woefully unprepared to be a parent.

The fortitude needed to raise a teenager made the profession of espionage look like a fairly straightforward vocation. Baiting a potential double agent with an enticing dangle had nothing on navigating the relational pitfalls intrinsic to parenting a teenage girl.

"These men who you think might be after us," Amanda said, making eye contact with Jack, "would they be a danger to Bella while she's at school?"

Jack considered the question in silence before slowly shaking his head.

"I don't think so," Jack said. "My guess is that they're here to clean up a mess, not make a new one. They'd come after you here or maybe at the gas station."

Amanda looked at Jack with a confused expression on her face.

Then her eyes widened.

"A robbery gone bad?" Amanda said.

Jack nodded.

"Maybe I should call Brian," Amanda said. "What do you think?"

"I'm in no position to offer parental advice," Jack said. "But I do know something about bad men and the way they think. If it were up to me, I'd take you both to a safe house for the day until I could figure out what's what. Keeping out of sight might be all that it takes for the men hunting you to move on. Chances are they were intending to take care of both you and Jeff and then disappear. No matter how much the locals want to brush it under the rug, Jeff's death is going to draw attention. Attention the shooters don't want."

Amanda nodded, eyeing the rug.

Jack could almost see the wheels turning in the woman's mind. The risk-reward equation of irrevocably damaging her already fragile relationship with her daughter versus the possibility that Jack was right and dangerous men were hunting them. After a moment longer spent in silence, Amanda dug into her jeans and removed her phone.

"Come on," Amanda said as she began to dial, "we'll drive by where they like to eat breakfast. If I don't see Jeremiah's truck, I'll give Brian a call. I hope you're right."

So did Jack.

22

THE BUZZING OF HIS PHONE STARTLED LEON FROM HIS THOUGHTS.

One moment he'd been contemplating what higher being would tolerate a world that produced both savages armed with machetes and men who hid their madness behind luxury cars, Italian loafers, and two-hundred-dollar haircuts. The next, he was reliving the instant in time that had altered his life forever. As his iPhone thrummed like an angry rattlesnake, Leon looked for a place to pull off the road. His prothesis worked quite well for many daily activities, but he didn't trust himself to drive with it one-handed.

Especially in California.

Even at three a.m.

Leon could have answered via the rental's Bluetooth system if he'd paired his mobile with the car. He hadn't. Again, contrary to the popular stereotype of men who thrived in Leon's chosen profession, he was a cautious man. He didn't take unnecessary chances, and while his injury hadn't made him timid, it had reinforced the consequences of mistakes.

Leon was not an accountant.

When he made the wrong call, men died.

Or were horribly maimed.

As Daniel would soon demonstrate, there were consequences every time a smart device paired with a network. Like a knight lowering his castle's drawbridge, joining a network meant opening a portal into the device. Most of the time, this portal amounted to a temporary breach that was bricked over as soon as the linkage to the network was terminated.

Most times.

But like enemy sappers of old, sometimes digital warriors were able to turn that breach into an entry point through which they could funnel their attacking troops. And even when this wasn't the case, electronic devices left digital footprints, which lingered long after the pairing ended. As with anything electronic, these signs were almost always there for a trained tracker to find. Leon hadn't paired his phone because he didn't want to open the device to exploitation or provide the inevitable hunters anything that could be used to track him in the physical world.

But like all good tradecraft, this practice came at a price.

The cell shuddered a final time before giving up the battle, but Leon was not fooled. In keeping with his leave-no-trace mentality, the contacts section of the burner phone was empty, but Leon recognized the 512 area code. There was only one person who would be calling him from Texas, and he wasn't phoning to chitchat.

As if hearing his thoughts, the phone jittered again, rattling the cupholder and filling the car with the noise of a swarm of buzzing wasps. Leon found himself accelerating, his subconscious responding to the sound like one of Pavlov's dogs. Trusting the wheel to his prothesis for an instant, Leon grabbed the phone and tossed it onto the seat, where it continued to tremor, though far more impotently.

Fortunately, Leon didn't have to war against the urge to answer much longer. After winding a long curve, he saw an exit leading to a rest area. He followed the turnoff into the parking lot and eased the rental to a stop. Switching off the ignition to better hear, Leon snagged the still-dancing phone and answered.

"Hello."

"Captain, it's me. We've had trouble."

An SUV pulled into a slot on the opposite side of the parking lot. The license plate denoted the occupant as a disabled veteran. A moment later the doors opened revealing a man, a woman, and two small children. Before shutting the SUV's door, the man extracted a pair of crutches.

Then he hobbled toward the bathrooms, his little family in tow.

Not for the first time, Leon wondered at the direction his life would have taken if his country had some sort of stipend for old campaigners such as himself. But as with combat, wistful thinking in life led to nowhere. South Africa was a country on the brink of becoming a failed state. Taking care of their population of aging and often disabled veterans was nowhere on the national priority list. This was why Leon was in California meeting with repugnant men like Daniel and undoubtedly why his subordinate was on the phone.

But that was okay.

South Africa had a troubled history and struggled for decades to add anything of value to the world stage. But there was one commodity that the nation of almost sixty million produced in great numbers.

Warriors.

And warriors did not sit idly by as former comrades slowly faded.

They fought.

"Talk to me, Hendricks," Leon said.

"Our attempted cleanup has resulted in an even bigger mess."

"How big?" Leon said.

"Beyond our ability to sanitize. Another Good Samaritan intervened. He was decidedly more effective than the boy."

Leon closed his eyes and rubbed the bridge of his nose.

What was it about Texas and the men and women who called that state home? This entire mess had begun when a college kid had regrettably interfered in something that should have been none of his concern. Though to be fair, the mishap probably could have still been contained if Graham hadn't overreacted. But part of providing men like Graham meaningful work meant dealing with their disabilities—both visible and less pronounced. If Leon was correctly reading between the lines, Hendricks's attempt to sanitize the situation had backfired.

"What's your assessment?" Leon said.

The family of four reached the door and the man stumbled as he tried to open it. His wife caught him, supporting his weight on her shoulder. The former soldier wobbled and then got his canes back on solid ground. With a determined set of his shoulders, the man continued inside.

Hendricks had led the quick reactionary force that day in Namibia. While he hadn't arrived in time to save Leon's hand, he'd prevented the machete-wielding psychopaths from removing additional body parts. The assaulting mercenaries had found their captain missing a hand, but still fighting for his life.

At least that was the story.

The truth was that Leon had been about to beg when the *crack* of the assaulter's automatic weapons had convinced him to take another path. While the image of a sweat-soaked African holding a newly severed hand in one hand and a bloody machete in the other still haunted Leon's dreams, this sequence was not his greatest night terror. No, that honor belonged to the eternal shame he would have borne had the quick reactionary force found him groveling in the dirt for his captor's amusement. Sometimes the difference between victory and defeat was a gossamer margin, the breadth no thicker than a spider's web.

Leon trusted Hendricks implicitly.

If his lieutenant thought the operation blown, so be it. Much was riding on successfully executing this contract, but Leon would abandon the lucrative deal in an instant if it meant compromising his men. He was on a mission to provide work and dignity for his country's forgotten warriors.

But Leon would not trade their lives for dollars.

"The team has been compromised," Hendricks said, "but we were able to tie off some loose ends here. Of even greater importance, I believe the operation is still intact. I recommend we pull up stakes here and stage for phase two. Assuming we're still on schedule."

Leon thought of the software engineer's handsome face and corrupted soul. A fourteen-year-old girl was dead because of Daniel, and the man was concerned only with his stock options and signing bonus. Daniel had done what was asked of him and received his thirty pieces of silver. Like Judas, Daniel probably wouldn't have long to enjoy his newfound wealth, but that wasn't Leon's concern.

"Agreed," Leon said. "I'm on my way to the airport now. Position your men for phase two. I'll be there soon."

"Of course, Captain," Hendricks said. "It will be smooth sailing from here. See you on the high ground."

"On the high ground," Leon said before ending the call.

He hoped Hendricks's optimism was well placed.

But if experience was any guide, it probably wasn't.

23

JACK PULLED INTO YET ANOTHER PARKING LOT.

Besides the obligatory Pizza Huts and Dairy Queens that seemed to be staples in every small Texas town, Briar Wood sported a surprising number of eateries along the four-lane road that served as its main street. The quest to find Jeremiah and thereby Bella had taken Jack past three Mexican restaurants, a greasy spoon like the one where he and Amanda had first met, an establishment advertising fresh fish and hot burgers, and a single McDonald's strategically located in front of the town's lone stoplight. For a town of perhaps eight thousand on a good day, its citizens liked to eat.

Jeremiah's truck wasn't at any of them.

Amanda didn't seem surprised.

"These places only serve tourists this early," Amanda said as they motored through the flashing yellow stoplight. "For locals, there's only one place for breakfast."

That place had a storefront that was uninspiring, to put it kindly.

Located between a two-pump gas station and a darkened beauty salon, the structure was more storage shed than restaurant.

It was constructed of sheet metal that seemed held together by entropy rather than rivets. The walls sagged and the door was rusted. The windows were cloudy and didn't emit much in the way of light. But the parking lot was jammed full of pickup trucks and dusty cars.

After opening his door, Jack understood why.

The smell of rich, clingy woodsmoke mingled with slow-roasted meat filled the air.

"What is this place?" Jack said.

"About as close to heaven as you're gonna find in Briar Wood," Amanda replied with a small smile. "Officially, it's a butcher shop."

"And unofficially?" Jack said.

"Unofficially, Ray's Meats smokes the best BBQ between here and Memphis."

"Smells like it," Jack said, savoring another deep breath. "But isn't it a little early for brisket?"

"Never too early for brisket," Amanda said. "Especially if it's chopped and put into a breakfast taco with eggs, cheese, beans, and potatoes. Like any Texas girl, Bella loves breakfast tacos. And that's Jeremiah's truck."

Jack followed Amanda's outstretched finger to see a dirty pickup occupying the corner of the lot. The frame was jacked up high enough that he wasn't sure how Bella managed to scramble into the passenger seat without the aid of a stepladder.

The tires were massive.

Not so much mere conveyances meant to support the weight of the truck as rubber-armored terrain shredders. The tread was jagged and enormous. A mouth full of black teeth waiting to devour anything foolish enough to linger in the truck's path. A rack of KC floodlights graced the top of the cab while a plastic snorkel wound from the engine before snaking up the left side of the windshield. A pair of iron testicles dangled from the truck's trailer hitch.

The steel monstrosity wasn't so much a vehicle as a statement.

"In case you're wondering," Amanda said as she watched Jack's reaction, "it's a perfect representation of Jeremiah."

Jack nodded.

He was interested in the truck, but not for the same reasons that Amanda probably thought. While he understood why she would be less than thrilled with her daughter riding off in such a chariot, Jack approached the gas-devouring spectacle from a different vantage point.

Finances.

While he wasn't a truck guy, Jack had friends who fit the bill. In fact, he'd once spent a weekend off-roading with a bunch of Jeep aficionados. The amount of money some of them put into their four-by-fours was truly mind-numbing, and Jeremiah's ride had all of the extras and more. The cost of the truck and its add-ons easily stretched into six-figure territory.

Where did Jeremiah get that kind of cash?

"How do you want to play this?" Jack said.

"Jeremiah's an asshat, but he's never openly bucked me," Amanda said. "The dining area stretches around behind the counter to the rear of the store. There's a separate entrance in the back. I'll go in that way. Give me a sixty-second head start, and then come in the front door. With any luck, Bella and I will be on our way out to meet you."

"And if you're not?" Jack said.

"You've got that shiny set of creds," Amanda said. "Use them."

24

WHILE THE IDEA OF USING HIS CREDS TO INTIMIDATE JEREMIAH INTO STAYING OUT of what was clearly a mother-daughter moment wasn't without appeal, Jack didn't think that approach was going to carry much water. From its coal-black brush guard to the metal spikes protruding from the hubcaps, Mad Max–style, to the stick graphic of a cartoon character peeing on the Ford emblem stenciled across the rear window, Jeremiah's ride screamed conflict. If Jack's creds had proclaimed him a member of the FBI or another similarly known federal law enforcement agency, the intimidation plan might work.

Not so much for the Department of the Interior.

The creds were meant to be official without being memorable, but that distinction wasn't an advantage in this situation. Not to mention that life in a small town often was one of comfortable monotony. Jack was willing to bet that the same five or six people had breakfast at Ray's most days and that the most interesting thing that happened during said breakfasts might be a run on the BBQ sauce. If Jack started waving around his creds, people would remember the interaction and talk. That was a nonstarter.

He would have to come up with a Plan B.

Fortunately, Jack specialized in Plan Bs.

Sliding his cell from his pocket, Jack snapped two pictures of the truck, including one in which the license plate was clearly visible. He thumbed both images into a text to Gavin:

> Run this and give me everything you get on the owner and vehicle.

As much as he enjoyed his conversations with the eccentric keyboard warrior, Jack knew that sometimes it was better to just engage Gavin via his preferred medium—digital.

Besides, Jack didn't have time for a phone call.

His sixty seconds were up.

"CAN I HELP YOU, SIR?"

The question came from the pretty redhead on the other end of the register. Jack guessed her to be in her late teens. Probably a recent high school graduate working to save money for college.

At least he hoped that was her story.

After spending the last several hours with Amanda, he was no longer quite so optimistic. Small towns made for great country songs and fantastic television backdrops, but sometimes they also had a darker side. As Amanda could attest, their gravitational pull could be hard to escape. Big dreams died slow deaths in the glow of Briar Wood's single stoplight.

"How about a couple of brisket breakfast tacos," Jack said. "Egg, cheese, potatoes, and beans."

"You bet," the redhead said. "Corn or flour?"

Jack checked himself just before he said *flour*. One did not go to Baltimore in search of crabcakes only to buy them from a chain restaurant. He could get flour tortillas anywhere. This was

Texas, by God, and he would make his culinary choices appropriately.

"Corn," Jack said.

"Excellent choice," the redhead said with a smile. "They'll be up in ten minutes."

He paid with his debit card, and then moved out of line, making way for the pair of men who'd trooped in from the parking lot while he'd been ordering.

For a restaurant in a small town, Ray's did a surprisingly brisk business. If the smell lingering inside the dilapidated building was any indication of the taste, Jack could understand why. Though he'd grown up all over, Jack was an East Coast boy at heart. He understood the concept of BBQ, and was no stranger to smoked sausage and ribs, but this establishment took things to a new level. The perfect combination of woodsmoke mixed with slowly cooking meat permeated everything. The oily odor should have been overpowering.

It wasn't.

Like a toddler's first sample of ice cream, Jack's stomach rumbled almost uncontrollably at the thought of what the eclectic combination would taste like as it exploded across his palate. The anticipation was almost enough to make him forget why he was here in the first place.

Almost.

The entrance to the establishment was bare-bones. A counter with the redhead who worked the cash register and charmed customers with equal ease and a swinging door behind her that Jack assumed led to the kitchen.

To the left, a smaller counter held loaves of store-bought white bread, barbecue sauce in squeeze bottles with hand-lettered labels, plastic containers loaded with onions and pickles, as well as an aging fountain drink station that offered Coke, Diet

Coke, and Dr Pepper. A bubbling coffeepot guarded the drink station's right flank while to the left sat two gigantic silver thermoses, one labeled SWEET and the other UNSWEET.

Tea.

The southern version of water.

Jack angled toward the drink counter, nodding to several bystanders also patiently waiting for breakfast tacos. As Amanda had stated, two or three laminated picnic tables offered limited seating in this section of the building, but the real action was through a second set of swinging double doors.

The eating area followed the same minimalist décor as the rest of the building. Seven or eight rows of picnic tables dominated the space with each table featuring a trio of BBQ sauce squeeze bottles and a prominently displayed roll of paper towels. The floor was rough concrete and the walls were wood framed with transparent plastic tarps serving as windows. The tarps looked like they could be rolled up in good weather, while a wood-burning stove nestled in the corner stood ready to combat the cold in what passed for winter in this part of Texas.

Though the swinging doors were currently closed, large glass windows provided a vantage point into the eating area. The benches were mostly empty, with singletons here and there devouring their food. The exception being the picnic table at the end of the room nearest the second entrance Amanda had described. Though her back was to him, Jack had no trouble picking out Bella's blond braids. Amanda stood to one side of her daughter, and judging by the woman's posture, the conversation wasn't going well.

But Jack wasn't so much concerned about the ladies. He'd been in Amanda's company long enough to feel confident that the single mom could handle herself. No, he was focused on the smirking man-child seated across from Bella.

Jeremiah.

As Jack should have guessed, Jeremiah was a big 'un. Defensive lineman big. Jack was no shrinking violet, but Jeremiah took things to another level. Though Bella's boyfriend had yet to stand, Jeremiah's T-shirt stretched tight against massive shoulders and bulging biceps and his thick fingers dwarfed the fountain drink he held in one hand.

Jack sighed.

Just once, he'd love to run into a troublemaker who fought in the welterweight division.

In the eating area, things were growing more heated. Amanda was trying to ignore Jeremiah as she engaged in a conversation with her daughter, but the big boy wasn't having it. His mouth was moving and even though Jeremiah's voice didn't carry through the windows, Jack could see the effect of the man's words. Amanda's face flushed as her shoulders tightened. She reached for Bella's arm. Her daughter flinched and Jeremiah lumbered to his feet.

Jack had been wrong earlier.

The boyfriend wasn't big.

He was massive.

While Bella undoubtedly needed a boost to climb into Jeremiah's truck, her boyfriend would have no trouble. He stood at least six foot five. While Jeremiah didn't overtly threaten Amanda, his size was menacing. The smirk on his stubble-covered face was more sneer than smile. He said something else to Amanda and she responded by digging into her pocket. Her fingers appeared a moment later clutching her phone and she showed the device to Jeremiah. Amanda's message was clear— my daughter is coming with me. If you attempt to interfere, I will call the cops.

A reasonable strategy.

But wrong.

Faster than Jack would have thought possible given his size, Jeremiah lashed out. His paw connected with Amanda's delicate hand and the phone went flying. Amanda shrank, but Jeremiah was too smart to carry things further. Heads had begun to turn. After directing a final sneer at Amanda, Jeremiah crumbled the remains of his taco wrapper and tossed it into the garbage can. Then he walked to the door in two giant, distance-eating strides. Shouldering it open, he turned back and locked eyes with Bella.

The moment of truth.

Would the teenager stay with her mother or follow her trainwreck of a boyfriend into the unknown? While Jack didn't know what was going on in Bella's head, he had reached a decision of his own. There was no way Amanda's daughter was getting in the truck with that maniac. How that played out would be up to Jeremiah, but Jack intended to conduct the next bit of business in the parking lot, away from prying eyes.

Now he just needed a reason to leave the restaurant.

"Excuse me, who owns the Mustang convertible?"

Jack turned toward the speaker to see a man holding open the front door.

"Me," Jack said.

"Can you come outside?" the man said. "I dinged your bumper backing out of my spot."

"Gladly," Jack said.

25

JACK'S MIND WAS ON MANY THINGS AS HE FOLLOWED THE SLIGHTLY BUILT MAN OUT of the restaurant and into the parking lot. Damage to his rental car didn't make the list. Judging by the haphazard arrangement of vehicles and nonexistent lines denoting individual spaces, Jack thought that dings and scratches were probably a daily occurrence as customers cycled through the tiny eatery. If his conveyance had been a dusty pickup instead of a sparkling new Mustang, the offending party probably would have just shrugged off the nick as the price of doing business.

Either way, Jack wasn't concerned.

Even if the man had screamed into the parking lot at ramming speed and had rendered the Mustang an unrecognizable pile of metal, it was no skin off Jack's back. Thanks to a run-in with a Chinese band of mercenaries, Jack was more attuned to his digital trail than ever. The car, like his plane ticket, had been booked under a false name and paid for with a credit card that drew funds from one of The Campus's many shell corporations. Other than the inconvenience of filling out an accident form when he returned the Mustang, Jack was certain that everything would be fine.

The developing situation between Amanda, Bella, and Jeremiah was a different matter.

While Jeremiah wasn't the sort of problem Jack had envisioned protecting Amanda against, he was still a problem. As an espionage professional who made snap judgments about people's character for a living, Jack knew a bad actor when he saw one. Jeremiah's treatment of his girlfriend's mom had only reinforced this sentiment. Jack had already decided that Bella was not leaving the parking lot in Jeremiah's company.

Raised voices echoing from the rear of the restaurant added a sense of urgency to Jack's dilemma. While he appreciated the fact that the slender man had unwittingly provided Jack with the excuse he needed to walk outside before his tacos were ready, he was also very much aware that his presence was needed elsewhere.

Now.

It was time to bring this encounter to a close.

"Hey," Jack said, reaching out to grab the man's shoulder, "no worries on the ding. I'm sure everything's fine."

As he touched the man's back, Jack realized two things. One, the man wasn't as slender as he appeared. Shoulder muscles bunched beneath Jack's fingers, concealed by a bulky shirt. Two, the man's overemphasized diction was attempting to erase an accent.

A South African accent.

The slender man spun in a tight circle, locking Jack's arm at the elbow. Jack instinctively stepped back and to the side in an effort to relieve pressure on the joint as he loaded his weight in preparation for launching a left hook into the man's liver.

He didn't get the chance.

Additional hands grabbed Jack from behind.

Jack fired an elbow blindly, trying to create space. He felt bone connect with flesh and heard the *whoosh* of an expelled breath. A prick flared at the side of his neck followed by a blast of cold as something flowed beneath his skin.

Then Jack felt nothing at all.

26

LISANNE ROBERTSON AWOKE WITH A START.

The sky outside her undrawn shades was still dark, but the sound of morning commuter traffic was already buzzing against the windowpanes. She'd only meant to close her eyes for an instant, but her nap had apparently lasted several hours. Turning, she looked at the other half of the king-size bed.

It was empty.

Picking up her phone, Lisanne checked for missed calls from Jack.

None.

On one level, this should not have surprised her. In the short but meaningful time Lisanne had known Jack Ryan, Jr., she had often found herself waiting for his call. This was not because Jack was a forgetful or inattentive boyfriend. In fact, the opposite was true. Jack went out of his way to make her feel special, and she deeply appreciated that when they were together, she was the center of his world.

Therein lay the problem.

As paramilitary operatives working for a very busy intelligence service, she and Jack were not often together. This was doubly so after a catastrophic injury permanently removed her from the active-duty roster. Not yet ready to hang up her spurs and find a normal job, Lisanne had been slowly matriculating toward an operational support role. She had an agile mind, was a great multitasker, and her admittedly brief career as a shooter still gave her a particularly keen insight into what the men and women on the pointy end of the spear were experiencing.

Taken in sum, these qualities made Lisanne an excellent battle captain.

Unfortunately, this role meant that she now spent most of her time waiting for a phone to ring, a text to ping, or a radio call to crackle across her earbuds. While manning The Campus's operational cell still beat the career in real estate her mother envisioned, Lisanne could now sympathize with Tom Petty—the waiting really was the hardest part.

But this was not an operation.

Her phone showed the time as just before five a.m. Lisanne stabbed Jack's number in a flurry of motions.

The call clicked to voicemail.

Pressing the end button, she employed a bit of magic that had never been available to her mother when she'd had to determine whether Lisanne's Marine father was truly working late or just down at the O-Club for a beer with his friends.

The Find My app.

Lisanne touched the appropriate icon and was rewarded with an image of Jack's picture and the words NO LOCATION FOUND. She redialed Jack's number and listened again as the call went straight to voicemail. Then she tried the Find My app again with the same result.

NO LOCATION FOUND.

Her heartbeat accelerated.

Lisanne had long ago come to terms with the notion that life with her fiancé was never going to be anyone's definition of normal. Setting aside that his father was one of the most famous men in the world and his mother was a renowned surgeon, Jack had a career that could be charitably described as eclectic. Lisanne had never been one prone to worry, but with Jack, the silly fears that many wives entertained about their husbands' safety weren't so silly.

Unlike the spouses of firefighters or cops, Lisanne wasn't really able to breathe a sigh of relief when Jack was *off*. This was partly because Campus operatives were never truly off, but more so because with a career as long and noteworthy as Jack's, trouble had a way of finding him even when he wasn't actively courting it.

Case in point, Jack stopping to help a potentially stranded motorist on a lonely stretch of Texas highway should not be a great cause for alarm. Lisanne's fiancé was well trained, armed, and had been humbled enough never to assume that the first two qualities would allow him to best an unexpected adversary. That he wasn't answering his phone didn't mean he was in trouble. Helping with the car wreck could have gone longer than anticipated, and Jack might have just decided to crash at a local hotel rather than continue the drive back to Austin.

But the twisting feeling in her gut didn't think so.

She might be new to the role of fiancée, but Lisanne had been working in operational roles for most of her career. As a cop, would she have been worried if her partner wasn't answering the phone under similar circumstances?

Her subconscious answered without hesitation.

Yes.

Lisanne confirmed again that the location of Jack's phone was still unknown. Then, she scrolled through her contacts looking for a name she hadn't thought about in years. In her life, people were segregated into two groups—civilians and *others*. Civilians were the folks who lived normal lives. Those for whom a bad day at work might mean a disagreement with a coworker or the loss of a customer. While not trivial, this definition of *bad day* still ended with everyone returning to their loved ones alive.

Not so with the *others*.

This word signified the collection of like-minded individuals Lisanne had befriended during her service in the military, law enforcement, and now as a Campus paramilitary officer. Though her time as a patrol officer had been brief, she had excelled at being a cop. Accordingly, when the FBI had offered a seminar for local law enforcement on the hallowed grounds of Quantico, Virginia, Lisanne's supervisor had recommended that she attend. To be fair, as she was a Virginia state trooper, the seminar hadn't been much of a commute, and while the topics were bound to be interesting, not many of her fellow officers were jumping up and down at the chance to spend five days in a classroom.

But Lisanne had gladly accepted.

This had been driven as much by the high-quality content she knew that she'd receive as by another less tangible benefit—the chance to network with fellow law enforcement professionals from across the nation. One of those professionals had been Paul Embry, a Texas state trooper. In the way of state troopers, Lisanne and Paul had quickly bonded, going so far as to exchange contact info at the class's conclusion. He had promised her a home-cooked meal and a chance to meet his wife and children if she ever found herself in Texas, and Lisanne had reciprocated.

That conversation had been five years ago.

But the great thing about *other* relationships was that they never ended. Selecting Paul's number, Lisanne hit *call* and once again listened to the phone ring.

This time her call was answered.

27

"HELLO?"

The Texas accent flavoring the word set Lisanne at ease. People in her *other* category might expect early morning calls, but they still didn't relish them. Even so, there was something calming about the sound of Paul's voice.

"Paul? Hey, it's Lisanne. Lisanne Robertson. We met a couple of years ago at Quantico."

"Trooper Robertson, how the hell are you?"

"I'm doing well," she said. "Thanks for picking up."

"Of course," Paul said. "I'm assuming you aren't calling this early just to shoot the shit."

"Can't get anything past you Texas boys," she said. "It's no longer *Trooper*, but I do have a job-related issue. Got a minute?"

"As long as you haven't gone over to the dark side and become a fed, I've got all the minutes in the world. Whatcha need?"

Lisanne was reminded of one of the many reasons she'd loved being a cop. Police officers were a different breed—part social worker, part enforcer of societal norms, and when the occasion merited, part warrior. Only another cop truly understood this world, and she was grateful to be talking to one of her brothers in blue.

"I've got something a little strange going on," Lisanne said, composing what she was about to relay as she spoke. "My fiancé and I are down in Austin for the weekend. He drove out to College Station to see the game."

"Beautiful country," Paul said. "Terrible football team."

Lisanne found herself smiling despite the anxious feeling in the pit of her stomach. Paul was a good cop. "I'm not going to wade into that, but I can tell you he enjoyed his time at Kyle Field. Anyway, a couple of hours ago he called to tell me that he was stopping to assist with a car crash along Highway 79. I haven't heard from him since."

"Where exactly along 79?" Paul said.

While his voice still had the comforting Texas twang, the earlier levity was gone. Though Paul's sudden seriousness did nothing to calm her rising sense of disquiet, the trooper's response did offer Lisanne some vindication.

She was right to be worried.

"He didn't tell me exactly," Lisanne said. "He just said that he was on his way back to Austin. I've tried calling him, but it goes straight to voicemail."

"That's not unusual," Paul said, though his serious tone suggested otherwise. "That stretch of road is known to have cell dead spots. Most of the tiny towns between Taylor and College Station aren't exactly bustling metropolises. Spotty cell coverage is sometimes the price you pay for country living. Tell me about your fiancé."

"What do you mean?" Lisanne said.

"Come on, Lisanne," Paul said, "once a cop, always a cop. You know what I'm asking."

Lisanne sighed, trying to decide how far she wanted to go

with her answer. The work she and Jack did was classified, and while The Campus was now a quasi-member of the intelligence community, its operatives were not acknowledged intelligence officers. Then again, she had called Paul, not the other way around. If she wanted the trooper's help, she needed to give him something to work with.

"We're coworkers," Lisanne said. "Not law enforcement, but similar. He's armed and can handle himself."

"Okay," Paul said, drawing out the word. "Describe him."

"His name is Jack," Lisanne said. "Mid-thirties. Athletic build."

"Race?" Paul said.

"Caucasian. Black hair and blue eyes. Are you putting out an APB?"

"No," Paul said, "but I wanted to verify something."

Lisanne frowned as she tried to make sense of his reply.

Then she understood.

"You know something about the crash," Lisanne said. "The one Jack said he was stopping to help with."

"I do," he said. "Your fiancé wasn't hurt in it."

"But someone else was," Lisanne said. "What's going on, Paul?"

"Not over the phone," Paul said. "Can you meet me somewhere?"

"Sure," Lisanne said.

"There's a bar named Revelry about forty miles west of College Station. It's at the edge of a town called Briar Wood. Meet me in an hour, okay?"

"A bar at this time of the morning?" Lisanne said.

"Revelry's open twenty-four hours," Paul said. "Lots of Briar Wood folks work rotating shifts at the semiconductor factory a couple of towns over."

Lisanne typed *Briar Wood* into Google Maps. The town was about forty-five minutes away.

"Okay," she said. "I'll meet you there."

"Good. Keep checking Jack's phone. If it comes back online, let me know, okay?"

"You bet."

"Great," Paul said. "If you get to the bar before me, you can wait in the parking lot if you don't want to deal with drunk cowboys. Just do not go to the police station, okay?"

"Why?" Lisanne said.

"I'll tell you everything in person," Paul said. "You armed?"

"Yes."

"Stay that way. See you in an hour."

Lisanne had a thousand questions, but she wasn't going to get the chance to ask them. At least not yet.

Paul had already hung up the phone.

28

JACK WOKE UP IN STAGES, LIKE HE WAS SWIMMING TOWARD THE SURFACE AFTER being dropped in a murky pond.

He noticed his mouth first.

Or to be more specific, the absence of anything approaching moisture in his mouth. Jack had been overserved a time or two, but he'd never had a case of hangover-induced dry mouth like this.

Next came the pounding headache.

As with the cotton mouth, he was no stranger to alcohol-fueled headaches, but this one was a doozy even by college standards. With a start, Jack realized he had an even bigger problem— migraine and dry mouth aside, he had no idea where he was or how he'd gotten here. To make matters worse, his skull was throbbing in time to something. A long, high-pitched tone that seemed intent on driving ice picks through his eyeballs.

An alarm of some kind.

Or a whistle.

A train's whistle.

This did much to answer why his eyes were on fire. The brilliant light lancing through his stubbornly closed eyelids wasn't some kind of migraine-induced hallucination. It was as real as the tracks vibrating beneath him and the tornado sound of thousands of pounds of steel hurtling toward him.

Jack opened his eyes, and the white light seared his retinas, making him gasp in pain. Then he tried to get to his feet.

And failed.

The sluggishness infecting his thoughts wasn't just limited to his brain. The amount of alcohol he'd consumed must have been mind-numbing. Never before could he remember being so drunk that he couldn't stand. Abandoning the complex muscle movements he'd been attempting, Jack settled instead for something more primal.

Rolling.

If a person on fire could summon the mental wherewithal to stop, drop, and roll, surely he could do the same. But it wasn't that simple. Jack shifted his bulk, but the motion was aborted when his shoulders struck something cold and unyielding.

The metal rails.

He was lying lengthwise between the railroad tracks.

Jack bit the inside of his lip hard enough to draw blood. The pain was electric, shocking his nervous system. The resulting jolt of adrenaline helped him reach his muscles through the chemical fog. Grunting, he rolled sideways again, twisting at the shoulders. The metal rail bit into his torso and face. For a moment he tottered on the vibrating rail.

Then he was on his back, staring at the sky.

Jack tried for another roll, desperate to put more space between him and the rumbling monstrosity, but like he'd driven into a fogbank, his nervous system refused to respond.

And then the train was beside him.

While he wouldn't exactly have termed his life thus far as *dull*, Jack had never been as terrified as he was in that instant. For a long moment, he was convinced that the engine had somehow jumped the tracks as wheels three feet in diameter rushed by inches from his face in a blur of hot steel. He'd once thought that sitting in a SEAL delivery vehicle as it slowly filled with seawater was the definition of fear.

No longer.

The train seemed alive—a breathing, screaming leviathan spoiling to crush Jack's flesh. The ground shook as the *clack, clack, clack* of passing cars drowned out the engine's shrieking whistle. The train wasn't so much next to him as inside his chest. His heart thundered in time to the singing metal as his lungs spasmed, desperately wanting to draw a breath that Jack was afraid to take. Were it not for his sluggish muscles, Jack might have accidentally rolled back into the train's path. Like a drowning swimmer who could no longer tell up from down, he had no existence beyond the artificial hurricane roaring by a hand's breadth away.

Then it was gone.

"Holy hell," Jack said, as much to prove that he was still alive as to vent the terror still gripping his body.

Jack touched his extremities with trembling fingers. With ears still ringing and heart still shuddering, he was dangerously close to going into shock. He began a series of four-count breaths, trying to lower his raging pulse as he continued to verify that his body parts were still where he expected them to be. Then he patted down his pants.

His crotch was still dry, so hadn't pissed himself.

Always a good sign.

On the other hand, his pockets were empty, which was a mark in the *not so good* column. Jack still didn't know where he was or how he'd gotten there and with no pocket litter, wallet, or phone to consult, he wasn't any closer to solving that mystery.

Jack closed his eyes, trying to think, but was rewarded with an afterimage of the train's searing lamp.

He shivered.

That was much too close.

Groaning, Jack pushed himself into a sitting position. The world tilted slightly, but it did him the favor of not spinning. He could work with that. After a moment or two spent verifying that his uneasy truce with his hangover was going to last, he rolled onto his hands and knees and slowly pushed himself to his feet.

Which was when his hangover mounted a sneak attack.

Bending at the waist, Jack retched, narrowly missing his shoes. After a couple of stomach-twisting convulsions, he wiped his mouth with the back of his hand and tried his luck a second time. While the world still felt a bit tilted, his stomach seemed to have surrendered. Or perhaps the first bout of nausea had only been the opening shot in what would prove to be a long and protracted war of attrition. Either way, it was time to get the inevitable over with. Jack might be unsure of his whereabouts, but he was reasonably certain of one thing—he couldn't stay here.

But that didn't mean he was cleared to leave.

At least not yet.

As much as his still gurgling stomach and pounding head tried to convince him otherwise, Jack knew he couldn't abandon the scene of the crime without examining what had almost become his final resting place. Though he couldn't imagine that anything that might have slipped from his pockets would have survived an encounter with the locomotive, he had to check. Maybe a scrap of paper or two had fallen out of his jeans and blown to the other side of the tracks. Or better yet, perhaps his missing cell had taken refuge in the rock-lined rail bed, beneath the tracks. Jack knew the likelihood wasn't great, but maybe he was due for a little luck.

Or a little *more* luck, to be precise.

Jack had no idea how many drunks passed out on a set of railroad tracks and lived to tell the tale, but he had to figure the number was in the single digits. Squaring his shoulders, he trudged toward the tracks as he cleared his throat and spat, trying to rid his tongue of the taste of bile. His efforts didn't exactly leave his mouth feeling minty fresh, but they did produce a belch.

A belch without the lingering hint of alcohol.

That was strange.

Jack pushed into his foggy recollection, for the first time trying to make sense of his predicament. Even during his college days, he had never been one to head out to a bar solo or get mind-numbingly intoxicated by himself.

Where were his friends?

The thought of friends brought with it an image of Lisanne. For a moment, Jack could feel something just on the other side of his mental haze. Something about Lisanne. Then the recollection was gone, chased away by the piercing echo of another whistle.

Trains must be pretty frequent here.

Doubling down on his efforts, Jack crossed the remaining distance and then settled to his knees, safely on the far side of the tracks. The full moon provided a fair amount of light, and while he would have liked to get a closer look at the gravelly patch of ground, the world was still exhibiting a distinct list. Jack decided he was better off conducting his search from a bit farther away from what had almost been his grave. It was better to be lucky than good, but only a fool pushed his luck twice.

Especially when it came to trains.

As if on cue, a locomotive rounded the bend to Jack's left. The engine's spotlight blasted the tracks revealing the futility of his task in monochromatic detail. While he could easily pick out the disturbed rocks that showed where he'd been lying, Jack wasn't able to see anything else. The scraps of paper had been a long shot. Even if they'd somehow survived getting chewed up by the train's churning wheels, the accompanying wind would have surely blown them away. But Jack had been hoping for the shiny reflection of his iPhone's Gorilla Glass screen.

No dice.

A second, more prolonged whistle prodded Jack to his feet. Apparently, the engineer had seen the idiot peering at the tracks. Or maybe this stretch of railroad was a known collection point for drunks.

Either way, it was time to go.

But where?

Turning his back on the man-made thunder, Jack trudged toward the street that paralleled the railroad tracks. His walk had become more shuffle and less stumble, but he was clearly still not firing on all cylinders. That said, he was increasingly beginning to question his initial assumption that his present circumstances were due to alcohol. Too many things didn't add up. With a start, Jack realized that his pants fit looser than he expected. He was missing something even more important than his phone.

His SIG.

The more Jack thought about it, the less the absences seemed accidental. Sure, a receipt or two could have fallen out of his pockets along with his money clip. His phone could have theoretically suffered the same fate. But his pistol and holster? Wasn't going to happen. His personal items had been removed.

But by whom and for what purpose?

A car appeared. The headlights illuminated the far side of the tracks for the first time, revealing a series of simple homes. The ranch-style houses were small and old with postage-stamp yards and the cookie-cutter construction reminiscent of 1950s subdivisions. Judging by the crumbling brick buildings on his side of the tracks and the worn-down homes on the opposite, this was no one's idea of a bustling metropolis.

Jack paused, eyeing the approaching vehicle. For a reason he couldn't put into words, the SUV's silhouette gave him a sense of unease. The vehicle continued past him, before turning left and coming to a stop. As it passed abeam him, the ambient light caught a decal stenciled on the SUV in brightly colored letters.

POLICE.

In an instant, he remembered everything.

Jack dropped to his stomach, hoping to reduce his silhouette as he wrestled with the memories that swept over him like floodwaters from a ruptured dam. Jack's confusing physical ailments now made a lot more sense. He wasn't waking up from a bender. He was recovering from being drugged.

Drugged and almost murdered.

As if to underscore Jack's conclusion, the spotlight attached to the SUV's driver's-side mirror flared to life. The beam lanced through the misty darkness, spilling over the railroad tracks as the driver walked the spotlight back and forth.

The cop was looking for something.

Or someone.

Cursing, Jack crawled toward the deeper shadows cast by the buildings to his right. Leaving his unconscious body sprawled across the railroad tracks had been a stroke of genius. With no identification and little beyond chewed meat once the train got through with his body, Jack's murderers wouldn't have needed to worry about forensic evidence. Cops were trained to look for the most simple explanation because, conspiracy movies aside, the Occam's razor way of looking at crimes was generally correct. Case in point—a man found passed out along the tracks was probably exactly that. Either way, it made a hell of a lot more sense than a random stranger who'd stumbled across something he shouldn't have seen and now had to be silenced.

But that was exactly what had happened.

After apparently not finding what he was looking for with the spotlight, the SUV's occupant opened the driver's door and stepped onto the pavement. The vehicle's interior light illuminated someone male in appearance and roughly the same age and build as Jack. Leaving the halo of light centered on the tracks, the cop moved toward the railroad, his hand on his holstered pistol.

Jack waited for the man to pass him, and then headed for the crumbling building at a fast walk. While his sense of balance was slowly returning, the ground was littered with chunks of rock, bottles, and general debris. The last thing Jack needed was to catch his foot on an unseen obstacle and face-plant.

After reaching the safety of a bit of landscaping that had seen better days, Jack squatted amidst the scraggly bushes. The thin foliage wasn't the world's best hiding spot, but the shrubbery would break up his distinctively human outline and allow him to observe the police officer. The cop skirted the edges of the beam of light, staying close enough to benefit from the illumination while taking care not to spotlight himself.

A dozen or so strides brought the officer to the railroad tracks. Once there, the cop withdrew a flashlight from his utility belt and triggered the beam. He swept the light back and forth across the rail bed as he searched for what should be there but clearly wasn't.

Jack realized his mistake.

The cop had either been the one who'd positioned Jack's unconscious body on the tracks, or he'd been told what to look for. This meant that, unlike a normal police officer responding to a call about suspicious activity, he wasn't going to just shrug his shoulders and drive away when he didn't find bits of Jack spread across the railroad.

Not good.

Jack surveyed his surroundings.

He was currently crouched in the shadow cast by a monstrous, pyramid-shaped storage silo. The tin building was one of several scattered across the open area, no doubt constructed to take advantage of the prolific railroad traffic. Though he hadn't managed a look around the northern side of the building, the occasional passage of headlights coupled with the sound of traffic led Jack to believe that a road was on the far side. If this place was indicative of the other one-stoplight towns Jack had passed through on the way to and from College Station, that road was probably the main street.

The structures on the cop's side of the railroad tracks were predominantly houses with small yards and tired-looking fences. A copse of trees to Jack's left paralleled the railroad tracks, and another series of grain silos stood like silent sentinels in an adjacent lot to his right. A quick glance at the horizon showed that dawn was probably an hour or so away. This was both a hindrance and a help. As someone who'd been on the run a time or two, Jack would have normally welcomed the darkness and the anonymity that came with it.

Not now.

This was not a Beirut slum or a Syrian back alley.

Unless Jack had been unconscious for a day instead of a couple of hours, he was still in Texas. While the Briar Wood police might be corrupt, the same could not be said of all the law enforcement professionals who existed beyond this city's limits. A main street behind him equaled stores, which equated to people and phones. Jack only need make one call and the cavalry would come riding to his rescue.

Even in the unlikely event that every single person in this one-horse town was also facilitating illegal activity, the next map dot was at the most ten miles down the road. While this was a bit farther than Jack typically went for a recreational stroll, he had every belief that three hours of hard walking would land him somewhere much less sympathetic to the notion of drugging strangers before tossing their bodies onto the town's railroad tracks.

But first he had to ditch the cop.

The problem with a small town was that it was by nature small. While this descriptor referred to the city's population, the town's municipal footprint generally corresponded with the number of its citizens. A rural city like Briar Wood might cover a large geographical territory thanks to the acres of farm and ranchland, but its downtown would naturally be smaller. As far as Jack could tell, he was located in the middle of downtown and his options to hide from a local police officer who knew every alley and abandoned building like the back of his hand were admittedly limited. Here, darkness would help as fields and ditches could be fashioned into makeshift hide sites, but the utility of many of these places would melt away in the morning light.

Jack's choices were simple—find a place to hide until dawn or begin his trek to the next town now. He wasn't much on hiding and this course of action was even less appealing in his current state. With no phone and, more important, no weapon, a hidey-hole could quickly become a trap. Not to mention that the South

Africans would probably not try something quite so tricky as the accidental death they'd engineered this time around.

For criminals, daylight equaled desperation.

The next attempt on Jack's life would be much more direct— a bullet to the head.

If he had any idea he was being observed, the police officer gave no sign. Instead, the man diligently searched the tracks, his flashlight's beam bouncing from one section of the rail to the other. Twice the officer crossed in front of his SUV's headlights or the spotlight's halo, revealing himself in flashes. Jack glimpsed a short, stocky man with close-cropped brown hair. He walked with the gait of someone who spent his time on the street rather than behind a desk. At one point, the man knelt in the middle of the tracks and shone his light down in each direction. The flashlight must have been one of the high-grade military models because the vast amount of track it illuminated was at odds with its small size.

After trekking a good fifty yards in either direction from the starting point formed by his spotlight, the cop paused to grab the mike affixed to his shoulder lapel. The distance was too great for Jack to decipher the officer's words but his body language and tone still conveyed quite a bit. Rather than the amped-up jittery movements Jack expected of someone who'd anticipated finding a mangled body only to discover the victim's absence, the cop's mannerism projected something else.

Frustration.

Unless he was a very cool customer indeed, Jack would have sworn that the police officer was irritated. Like he'd been dispatched to investigate something suspicious that had turned out to be nothing, much like most of the calls local law enforcement fielded in quiet little towns. Jack frowned as he considered what his subconscious was trying to tell him.

Did he have this wrong?

Perhaps the police officer was exactly what he seemed—an honest cop working an honest job. If this were true, then Jack's would-be murderers were the people who'd called in the suspicious report, not the single man sent to investigate it.

The more Jack considered this turn of events, the more it made sense. Who better to find his body than a cop who was above reproach? If he was right, Jack had no reason to trek ten miles to the nearest town for help or pass the rest of the night hiding in a rat-infested building. Instead, he could walk right over to the police officer and tell him his story. Or better yet, pass on the full story in favor of something less dramatic and the request to borrow a phone. With the President of the United States for a father and John T. Clark as his boss, Jack had no shortage of options available to him.

If he was right.

If Jack was wrong, the outcome wouldn't be anywhere near as rosy. While he could handle himself in a fight and was no stranger to the application of deadly force, he was not in the habit of waltzing into a deadly scenario unarmed and unafraid. At least not purposely, anyway. Maybe the smarter play here was the more conservative. Sure, his feet would probably be a little sore after hoofing it ten or so miles, but a couple of new blisters would be a small price to pay, all things considered.

His decision made, Jack lowered himself to a squat, resting his back against the building while he waited for the police officer to finish his search and drive off into the night. Even a town this small had to have its share of teenagers and a place where they could buy illegal beer. On a weekend in *Friday Night Lights* country, he was certain there was trouble for the cop to find somewhere else.

Except that judging from the shadows detaching themselves

from the grain silos to Jack's right, trouble might have found the cop. At first, he assumed the skulking figures were the teenagers he'd imagined earlier. But rather than skirt around the side of the tin building, heading toward town and safety, the trio rippled toward the oblivious officer.

Moonlight glinted off something metal in the lead shadow's hands.

It wasn't beer.

29

FOR A HEARTBEAT OR TWO, JACK ENTERTAINED THE NOTION THAT HE WAS MIS-taken. Or better yet, that the shadows were reinforcements responding to the police officer's earlier radio call. They had appeared only moments after the cop finished his transmission.

Not at all an unreasonable hypothesis.

Except reinforcements don't point weapons at the person they're supposed to be helping.

The lead shadow held a rifle to his shoulder.

The telltale curved magazine identified the weapon as an AK variant, but at the moment, Jack wasn't concerned with the rifle's nomenclature so much as where it was aimed. Namely at the unsuspecting police officer's head. Jack's grandfather had been a Baltimore city cop, and while he'd escaped the job relatively unscathed, the same couldn't be said for far too many other brothers and sisters in blue. Jack might not be entirely sure what he was seeing, and he was still a ways away from sorting out the good guys from the bad.

Even so, there was one thing he knew for certain.

No way was a cop getting shot in the back on his watch.

Without his SIG, Jack was at a serious disadvantage. But he

wasn't out of the fight. As John Clark had told him on multiple occasions, a man's deadliest weapon wasn't the one he carried in his hands. It was the organ between his ears. Still, in that moment Jack would have traded more than a few brain cells for his trusty suppressed MP5.

But beggars couldn't be choosers.

Putting his fingers to his lips, Jack blew for all he was worth.

Jack's father had many redeeming qualities. He was loyal, courageous, and a born analyst. Though he got a lot of credit for the crazy kinetic operations he'd participated in over his long and storied intelligence career, Jack Ryan Sr. was most famous for his intellect. As a young CIA analyst, he had instinctively known the significance behind a certain renegade Soviet submarine, and his intuition still served him well forty years later.

But Jack always thought that his father's best quality was a much less known talent. The man could finger whistle at a decibel level that shattered glass. While there were many things Jack had sought to learn from his dad, the Ryan whistle had been one of the most sought after. When he was seven, anyway. The whistle that he'd spent hours perfecting now ripped through the night with intensity that would have made his dad proud. It might not have been the equivalent of the earlier train whistle, but it was more than potent enough to garner the attention of the armed men.

Which was good.

What was not so good was the manner in which they reacted to Jack's presence. The shadow closest to Jack swung his weapon toward the unseen threat and mashed down the trigger. Fire erupted from the AK's barrel and bullets snapped through the air and punched holes in the tin inches from Jack's face. For the second time in the same night, he found himself flat on his stomach.

But that was fine.

Mostly.

Jack was operating off the assumption that a weapon pointed at him was a weapon not pointed at the cop. Since he was unarmed and the police officer had both a pistol and a radio, this had seemed like a good idea in the admittedly abbreviated planning session Jack had undertaken. Unfortunately, like most plans, what sounded good during the brief often didn't play out so well once things went loud.

Tonight was no exception.

Rolling away from the structure, Jack sought the darkness like a gopher diving for his hole. Contrary to TV, hitting a moving target is hard. Hitting a moving target at night under duress is very hard.

At least that was Jack's working theory.

Still, all the theory in the world didn't seem quite so reassuring when high-velocity rounds were buzzing through the air that was recently occupied by your internal organs. The gunmen were fifty yards away—too far to rush but well within the range that even a novice could successfully employ a rifle. If he was alone, Jack knew that all the running and dodging in the world wouldn't save him. If the shooters had discipline and even a paltry amount of training, they could end this Greek tragedy by maneuvering toward him as a squad with a support element providing cover fire while the assaulter advanced. In this scenario, Jack estimated he'd have a minute left on earth.

Maybe less.

But he wasn't alone.

The police officer who was the group's original target was still alive and kicking. Not only that, but by distracting the shooters, Jack had given the cop a golden opportunity to even the odds.

Assuming he took it.

Jack's shoulder smacked into the grain silo, and he edged around the corner trying to put as much of himself behind the metal as possible. While the thin tin wouldn't stop the heavy 7.62mm rifle rounds, it was hard to hit what you couldn't see. Unless of course you were three men equipped with automatic rifles. In that case the old spray-and-pray method of engaging targets worked pretty darn well.

Jack was just beginning to question the brilliance of his tactical plan when the *crack, crack, crack* of a pistol added a counterpart to the rifle reports. A scream echoed across the courtyard as the pistol reports continued in a marksman's controlled steady manner.

Hot damn.

Not only was the cop brave, he was a good shot, too.

Jack peered around the side of the building, trying to get a sense of where things lay. What he saw wasn't encouraging. He assumed that the dark-colored Escalade pressed against the building belonged to the gunmen, one of whom was now writhing on the pavement.

Unfortunately, his two brethren were doing just fine.

This was because the shooters were taking turns firing short disciplined bursts into the patrolman's squad car as they slowly moved away from each other, creating a crossfire.

This was not going to end well.

The clincher for Jack came about half a second later. The rifle belonging to the gunman closest to him fell silent as the AK's bolt locked to the rear. This was the moment of truth. The instant in which the firepower arrayed against the lone police officer was reduced by half. If he'd been hoarding his rounds in favor of expending them when the situation more clearly favored him, this was the moment the cop would use them.

But the firepower wasn't halved for long.

With a precision that only came from long hours on the range, the gunman ejected the spent magazine, reloaded a fresh one, and released the AK's bolt in one smooth motion. Jack spent his day job surrounded by elite gunfighters and he knew expert weapon-handling skills when he saw them.

Whatever was happening here was not the work of random gangbangers.

With seemingly languid movements that reinforced the maxim *slow is smooth and smooth is fast*, the gunman reshouldered his rifle just as the cop popped up from where he'd been taking refuge behind his SUV's open door. The officer led with his pistol, squeezing off a round almost instantaneously.

Almost instantaneously wasn't fast enough.

No sooner did the cop's head and arms appear around the side of the doorframe than a fusillade of rounds impacted, sparking off the vehicle's body and cratering the steel. Jack didn't see the telltale puff of fabric or the bloody mist indicative of a bullet strike to a person, but the officer still disappeared from view. If somebody didn't do something soon, the patrolman was a goner.

As usual, Jack was that someone.

With the police officer's SUV to his extreme left and the gunmen midway between their Escalade and his center point, Jack found himself as the base of a lopsided triangle. But while the gunmen's movement had taken them closer to the SUV and therefore farther from Jack, their repositioning had now cleared Jack's path to something else.

Their Escalade.

Jack broke from his hiding spot and sprinted for the Escalade. The adrenaline burning through his veins had done much to clear away the dregs of whatever he'd been injected with. He was actually running as opposed to stumbling, and the world had finally righted itself.

On the not-so-great side of the ledger, he still felt somewhat lethargic, as if he were moving through water rather than air. Gritting his teeth, Jack torqued his arms up and down, forcing his leaden legs to pick up the pace. After several agonizing seconds, Jack arrived at the Cadillac. Though he'd sprinted for less than half the length of a football field, his racing heart and heaving lungs seemed convinced he'd just turned in his fastest quarter-mile time.

No matter.

Jack was far more concerned about the sounds behind him. Or lack thereof. The rifle fire died away just as he grabbed hold of the Cadillac's door handle. But even more concerning, the pistol reports were missing.

He was running out of time.

Piling into the leather driver's seat, Jack ducked below the dashboard as he pressed the brake to the floor and jabbed the start button. He had a moment of terror as it dawned on him that the keys to the Escalade might be in one of the gunmen's pockets.

Then the V8 roared to life.

While the 420-horsepower rumbling beneath the hood was not the equivalent to Jack's MP5, it was a great place to start. Slamming the transmission into drive, he smashed the accelerator to the floor and activated the Cadillac's brights. The twin xenon beams pinned the two gunmen like cockroaches caught in the light. Jack swung the wheel to the right, angling the grille at the nearest man with the intention of ridding the world of two insects.

Here again the shooters proved that they were more than just hired help. The pair did not panic. Both actioned on Jack and dropped the hammer. Flames shot from their rifles, and the Escalade's windshield erupted. Fortunately, a vehicle that could do zero to sixty in 6.1 seconds could cover a lot of ground in a short amount of time. With a burst of acceleration that pushed Jack deeper into the bucket seat, the Cadillac narrowed the distance to the gunmen like a greyhound bounding after a rabbit.

But the shooters weren't so easily cowed.

The disciplined rifle fire continued, and while the safety glass didn't rupture completely, the windshield was now a mass of spiderwebs. Something scored Jack's cheek, prompting him to crouch lower. Whether the debris was silicon or a fragmented bullet didn't much matter to his sensitive eyeball.

Not to mention his sensitive body.

The seat bucked as rounds punched into the Escalade's cabin, sending bits of plastic and shards of leather everywhere. As much as he wanted to swerve, Jack stayed the course, keeping the hood centered on the gunmen in what was evolving into a high-stakes game of chicken.

For a long second Jack was convinced the pair were going to call his bluff.

Then the shooter to his right buckled.

The gunman slid to his left, beyond the reach of the Cadillac's hood, as he continued to fire. At first brush, the gunman's tactic was sound. By putting distance between himself and his partner, the man gave Jack two targets instead of one. Rather than rolling both men up on the Escalade's hood, Jack would have to choose.

But Jack had already chosen.

Angling the wheel left, Jack appeared to zero in on the opposite gunman. Like a matador facing a raging bull, the first shooter nimbly shuffled aside, intent on shifting his fire to the driver's window.

Jack had other ideas.

Rather than try to match the man's dodge, Jack did something unexpected.

He opened the driver's-side door.

With a dull *thud*, metal met flesh at just under fifty miles per hour.

Slamming on the brakes, Jack bailed out of the vehicle. He was on the gunman in a millisecond, securing the man's assault rifle as his partner continued to shoot into the still-moving but now empty Cadillac. Jack shouldered the rifle, waited for the Escalade to roll past, and then fired a burst into the second shooter's head.

The man toppled to the ground.

The surprised expression on his face might have been comical were the consequences not so dire. A groan brought Jack's attention back to the first shooter. Swinging the rifle back to his original target, Jack intended to warn the man against moving.

He didn't get the chance.

The remaining gunman was fumbling for the pistol holstered at his waist, forcing Jack to fire a second burst. While he would have liked to have had someone to question, Jack was somewhat relieved the shooter forced his hand. When dealing with a fellow professional, discretion really was the better part of valor. Especially when the said professional showed no inclination to give up the fight.

A metal-on-metal *crunch* sounded from behind Jack. Turning, he saw that the Escalade had used the police officer's SUV as a speed break. With a grunt, Jack took off for the wreck, anxious that the cop was still MIA. Jack eyed the third gunman as he ran past, but judging by the shooter's still form and blood puddled beneath him, the man was no longer a threat.

"Friendly coming in," Jack said, just short of the SUV.

After being on the receiving end of three trained gunmen wielding assault rifles, Jack had every reason to believe the police officer might be a bit amped up.

Assuming he was even still alive.

"Friendly," Jack said, yelling the word as he moved around the SUV.

He saw the patrolman's boots first.

Then the pool of dark crimson.

Cursing, Jack dropped the AK on the SUV's hood and bent to help. In the first bit of good luck, the officer was still alive, but for how much longer remained to be seen. The blood-soaked fabric on his right leg suggested he'd taken at least one round to that limb while his right hand was missing several fingers. His left held an Israeli one-handed tourniquet that he'd worked partway up his leg. Shock, blood loss, or both had prevented the man from properly employing the lifesaving device, and his pale skin and rapid breathing suggested that Jack had arrived in the nick of time.

At Jack's unexpected appearance, the police officer reached for the pistol lying on the concrete next to him.

"I'm here to help," Jack said, moving the pistol away from the officer's fingers. "I promise you can have that back, but let's stop your bleeding first."

While not a doctor, Jack had been through enough trauma medicine training to know that the hand wound, while gruesome, was not the most serious injury. Blood was still pumping from the officer's leg, leading Jack to think that the man's femoral artery might have been compromised.

"Stay with me," Jack said as he threaded the tourniquet around the officer's leg. "Did you call for help?"

The man's eyes began to glaze over, and Jack worked faster, riding the band as high up on the man's thigh as he could. With a grunt, Jack tightened the band, velcroed it, and then began to twist the windlass rod. The officer's body went rigid, but Jack kept twisting.

"Hang on," Jack said, "almost there."

After several more turns, Jack saw a noticeable decrease in the blood spilling from the bullet wound. He continued to ratchet the plastic rod, cinching the tourniquet tighter. The pain had to be excruciating, but Jack had no other way to stop an arterial bleed.

Finally, the blood flow ceased.

"How you doing?" Jack said.

The cop groaned, but he was still conscious. At this point, that was about all Jack could ask for. Jack reached for the mike clipped to the man's lapel, but stopped as the sound of police sirens echoed through the air.

Apparently help was already on the way.

Good.

Jack zipped open the man's med kit, found a pressure bandage, and did what he could for the officer's mangled hand. Satisfied that the bleeding from both wounds had been stanched, Jack shifted toward treating shock. Unfolding a space blanket from the med kit, Jack tucked the fabric around the officer. Then he stood, intending to see if he could find something in the cop's Tahoe that he could use to elevate the man's feet. Left untreated, shock was just as deadly as a gunshot wound.

Squealing tires and flashing headlights announced the cavalry's arrival. Blue and red hues danced along the shadows in time to the newcomers' strobing lightbars.

"Over here," Jack yelled, still focused on the wounded cop. "Officer down."

Doors slammed and voices echoed across the pavement as the responders rushed to help. Jack paused, considering how to play this. He could slowly stand with his hands raised, but quickly discarded the idea. He was covered in blood and looked a bit worse for the wear. With tensions burning hot as the officers responded to an officer down and a potentially still active shooter, Jack did not want to do anything that tested trigger discipline. Instead, he decided to stay where he was. Hopefully the sight of a citizen rendering aid to the downed policeman would dampen the operational temperature.

Hopefully.

"Don't move."

The command came from his right, and Jack resisted the urge to turn toward the voice. Instead, he froze with his hands resting on the officer's chest, fingers splayed.

"He needs help," Jack said, still unmoving. "I tourniqueted his leg and put a pressure bandage on his hand, but he's lost a lot of blood. I think he's going into shock."

"On the ground. Now!"

Suppressing a sigh, Jack did as he was told, lying facedown with his arms stretched out in front of him. He was rewarded for his compliance with a knee in his back.

"Easy," Jack said. "I'm the good guy, remember?"

"Give me your right hand. Slowly."

Jack followed the shouted instructions only to feel the familiar sensation of metal biting into his skin as handcuffs were ratcheted on his wrist. Without being told, he moved his left hand to the small of his back, hoping to get brownie points for being cooperative.

He did not.

Instead, Jack's wrist was twisted, putting his shoulder into a painful joint lock as the police officer secured the second handcuff.

Then he was jerked to his feet.

Jack had been arrested enough times to know that it was common practice to help a handcuffed subject up by supporting their shoulder or arm. Not this time. Instead, the police officer yanked on the handcuff chain, which had the effect of transferring the load directly to the nerve-rich area around Jack's wrists.

It hurt.

A lot.

Jack clenched his teeth against the jolt of pain as he stumbled, attempting to offload the pressure on his wrist bones. Though he'd tried to give the still-unseen officers the benefit of the doubt, this little bit of jackassery was a step too far. Clearly, the wounded officer had not bandaged his own wounds and treated himself for shock. While Jack understood the idea behind handcuffing everyone until the officers had control of the situation, this stunt was an exercise in pettiness.

"Hey," Jack said. "Ease up, will you? I'm one of the good guys."

The blow to his kidney was as sudden as it was unexpected. One moment Jack had been standing, the next he was back on his knees, hunched forward. Strikes to the face might look cool in YouTube highlight reels, but anyone who knew anything about boxing understood that body shots felled far more fighters than headshots.

"What the hell?" Jack said, his anger burning through the pain.

He turned to look over his shoulder.

That was a mistake.

He saw the silhouette of a fist in time to tuck his chin, but could do nothing to mitigate the power of the blow. And it was a doozy. As with the shot to his kidney, the person throwing the punch knew what he was about. Jack's teeth smashed together and his head snapped violently to the side. Dropping his chin allowed the corded muscles and tendons running down his thick neck to absorb some of the strike's power, but tiny pinpricks of light still danced in front of his eyes as he wobbled on his knees.

One more like that, and Jack would be done.

"You are not one of the good guys, asshole. Now watch what you've made us do."

The voice came from lips just inches from Jack's ear. Before he could make sense of the words, someone grabbed him by the hair, immobilizing his head.

A figure stepped into the light.

The man was not what Jack expected. Instead of wearing a police uniform, he was dressed in functional recreational clothes. Cargo pants, an outdoor shirt, and a ball cap over what appeared to be a shaved head. What Jack would have termed contractor casual. Slipping on a set of shooting gloves, the man squatted down over the injured officer and removed the space blanket. The ultra-thin material billowed in the wind, but the man was prepared. He snared the shiny blanket before it could fly away, pinning it beneath his foot.

Then he reached for the tourniquet.

"It's tightened as far as it can go," Jack said.

His efforts earned Jack a cuff to the back of the head.

Though not as powerful as the other strikes, the smack was enough to send Jack tilting forward. At first, he thought his captor was going to let him face-plant into the concrete, but an unseen hand grabbed him by the shirt collar and hoisted him back up, choking him in the process. The sense of alarm that had been slowly building erupted into full-fledged terror once his watering eyes focused. In the second or two when Jack had been trying not to kiss the cracked pavement, the crouching man's gloved fingers had been busy.

Uncinching the tourniquet.

30

JACK STARED AT THE SLACK STRAPS, TRYING TO COMPREHEND WHAT HE WAS seeing.

Then, he understood.

"Hey!" Jack screamed, throwing himself forward.

This time his nose was just centimeters from the asphalt when his fall was arrested. His captor yanked Jack backward, the effort accompanied by a grunt as he had to work harder to haul Jack's considerable mass upward. The effort was much less gentle than before, no doubt fueled by anger at Jack's antics.

Which was exactly what Jack wanted.

Instead of letting his captor bear his slack weight, Jack helped the effort by rocketing his head and torso backward. He was looking for a soft target for his skull. Perhaps a stomach or groin.

Jack didn't find one.

Instead, he heard the *crunch* of cartilage as the back of his head impacted his captor's nose. As Jack knew from experience, a person's natural reaction to having their nose broken was pretty much universal.

His unseen captor proved to be no different.

The instant Jack's head flattened the man's nose, the tension on Jack's collar vanished. This was certainly an improvement to Jack's situation, but he wasn't out of the woods.

Not by a long shot.

Still, as Ding had driven home over multiple sparring sessions in The Campus's fight house, when you have your opponent on his heels, don't give him a chance to get up. Spinning on his knees, Jack got to his feet, coming face-to-face with his captor for the first time.

Captors, actually. A pair of cops stared back at Jack.

But not just any cops.

Officer Bradshaw and the baby-faced officer Jack had seen at the Briar Wood police station.

Jack should have expected as much, but the notion of law enforcement officers standing by as one of their brothers bled out threw Jack for a loop. But he didn't hesitate. There would be time for sorting out whatever was happening here later. At the moment, Jack had just one goal—keeping himself and the wounded officer alive.

To do that, the corrupt cops needed to go down.

Hard.

Baby Face was closer and already bleeding from his broken nose. He would be first. If his hands had been free, Jack would have trapped Baby Face's neck in a Muay Thai clinch before delivering a knee strike to his devastated nose. But with his wrists chained behind him, Jack was wary of attempting a knee. It was easy to overshoot or miss completely, and unlike the fight house, here there would be no do-overs. Instead, Jack transferred his weight to his right leg as he roundhoused Baby Face's lead leg with his left shin like he was cracking a whip. In mixed martial arts fights, the bundle of nerves running along the outside of a person's thigh was normally the target for this kick.

But Jack was not engaged in a sporting event.

This was a life-or-death contest, and Jack adjusted his aim accordingly. Jack twisted his hips and drove his shin into the side of the cop's knee. He pictured himself snapping the other man's leg as if it were made of balsa wood rather than flesh and bone. While Jack didn't quite manage that, the results were still satisfactory. The joint collapsed with a sick-sounding *pop* and Baby Face howled as he spilled to the ground.

One down.

Jack turned, looking to engage Bradshaw.

He didn't get the chance.

Something slammed into his temple.

This time, he didn't have to fake a dive. Jack dropped to the ground like a pile of wet laundry, barely managing to hold on to consciousness. A high-pitched ringing reverberated through his skull as his pain receptors tried to make sense of what had just happened. As a high school linebacker, he'd once been blindsided by a particularly sneaky tackle who'd been pulling for a running back.

This felt like that.

Only worse.

While he wasn't certain what had been used to clobber him, Jack instantly knew the significance of the cold ring of steel pressing against the back of his head.

A rifle's barrel.

He was about to be executed.

In a strange twist of fate, Jack's collapse had left him eye to eye with the stricken cop. Though the officer had been fading in and out of consciousness earlier, something had brought him around. Perhaps the feeling of blood spilling out of his leg. Whatever the source, the officer seemed to understand he was dying. He clawed at the tourniquet with a shaky hand, his dexterity destroyed by the loss of blood. His desperate eyes found Jack's and his mouth tried to form a word, but no sound escaped his pale lips.

"I see you," Jack said past the spittle and blood leaking from his own lips. "You're not alone."

The officer nodded.

Then his head lolled to the side.

"You are dead men," Jack screamed. "Dead men walking."

Jack wondered if he'd hear the gunshot that would send him chasing after the officer's spirit. Or whether death would precede the physical sensations that would accompany the bullet that shredded his brain. He thought of Lisanne and the life they would have had together and how his mother would react to the terrible news. But mostly, Jack dwelt on the all-encompassing rage that lit his blood on fire. In that moment, his biggest regret wasn't the life he would never live. It was that he wouldn't have the chance to kill each and every one of these sons of bitches.

But when a sound did reach his ears, it wasn't the echo of a gunshot.

It was laughter.

"I do believe you'd try if we gave you the chance, *bru*."

The speaker had an accent.

South African.

"Uncuff me and let's see," Jack said.

"Not today, my friend. But soon. Soon."

Despite the speaker's words, the muzzle pressing against Jack's head didn't move.

"We're not doing him? Like the others?"

The new voice belonged to the triggerman.

"Nah. He's coming with us. Sort him."

The phrase might have been unfamiliar, but the connotation wasn't. As soon as the circle of steel left his skull, Jack made his move.

Or tried to. He turned on his side, intent on getting to his feet and giving the men a run for their money.

He didn't get the chance.

With the casual indifference of someone who dealt out violence for a living, the gunman standing over Jack reversed his grip on his AK and smashed the wooden butt downward. Jack tried to intercept the blow, but remembered too late that his hands were cuffed.

Instead, he saw a blur of brown and then a flash of red.

Then darkness swallowed him.

31

BRIAR WOOD, TEXAS

WHILE LISANNE DID IN FACT HAVE A WAY TO GET TO BRIAR WOOD, IT WAS NOT VIA her own car. She and Jack had only rented one and the Mustang, like her fiancé, was missing.

Lisanne debated calling Karlie, but didn't.

Her friend had been a bit more liberal with the free drinks than Lisanne. While she hadn't been stumbling-down drunk, Karlie had made the wise decision to take an Uber home, which meant that her vehicle was still at the bar. Assuming Karlie even heard the ringing phone, it would take her at least thirty minutes to make her way back to the bar, which was thirty minutes Lisanne didn't have. So she decided to call an Uber of her own. The forty-five-minute trip out to Briar Wood would allow her time to think through everything Paul had and hadn't said.

Maybe she'd even be able to work in a quick nap.

Lisanne had done neither.

Instead, she spent most of the drive calling Jack's phone, watching its unchanging status on the app, or attempting to dodge conversation gambits by her much too friendly Uber driver. To be fair, it was approaching six o'clock in the morning, and she was leaving the partying mecca that was Austin for a no-name bar located on the outskirts of a one-horse Texas town.

Judging by his fumbling, if persistent, inquiries, Lisanne gathered that the driver believed she was either an escort, a stripper, or perhaps both. He'd already dropped several none too subtle hints concerning his willingness to swap services, and Lisanne was beginning to wonder if she'd need to state her disinterest more forcefully. As she was debating whether to feign sleep with some obnoxiously loud snoring thrown in for good measure, the bar swam into view.

Though calling the dilapidated structure a *bar* might have been too charitable. Lisanne was no stranger to small towns and their antiquated watering holes, but this honky-tonk brought an entirely new level of seediness to the genre. The building actually looked the part of an Old West saloon with a wide front porch, double doors, and wooden façade. As the Uber driver's headlights spilled over the structure, she wasn't entirely sure that the place hadn't been constructed two centuries prior.

It was, in a word, *worn*.

The front porch and entrance both sagged in equal measure, drawn downward like an old man's droopy smile. The wood was an indeterminable shade of gray. Whatever hue of paint had once graced its surface had long ago been scoured away by the baking Texas sun and the dirt and grit kicked up from the road. REVELRY was spelled out across the entrance in a maroon-colored neon sign, but the *r* and *y* were both dark.

But dilapidated structure or not, the bar was hopping. Waves of percussion tempered by a wailing steel guitar slapped against the vehicle's windows, rattling the glass. The parking lot was brimming with a mixture of motorcycles, pickup trucks, and Jeeps with the occasional minivan and sedan sprinkled in for good measure. Unlike the yuppie Range Rovers that prowled D.C.'s mean streets, these off-road vehicles looked well used. Most quarter panels were crusted in road grit if not outright mud and many of the pickup trucks sported brush guards, while the collection of Jeep Wranglers, old Broncos, and Toyota Tacomas sprouted KC lights and window-mounted rifle racks like the northern Virginia suburbs grew Teslas.

This was a bar of and for the people.

The people of rural Texas.

"This it?"

Her Uber driver was speaking absent the innuendo he'd been plying for the last forty-five minutes. Lisanne thought she understood why. While his sky-blue Prius wouldn't garner a second glance in Austin, in the Revelry's parking lot, the hybrid vehicle was definitely an endangered species.

"Yes," Lisanne said, undoing her seat belt.

If her driver hadn't been so clearly a creep, Lisanne might have considered waiting for Paul in the Prius, but she was more than ready to part company with the man. While her concealed pistol made her more than a match for the driver's greater size, she didn't want to spend another second in his company.

"It's been fun," the driver said.

It had been nothing of the sort, but Lisanne didn't have a chance to voice her opinion. The Prius shot away almost before she was completely clear of the vehicle. If she hadn't been standing outside a bar at who knows when in the morning, Lisanne might have thought the man's hasty retreat funny. As it was, the passenger door wiggled back and forth in a pseudo wave as the hybrid turned west toward civilization. Presumably her knight in shining armor would stop to close the door at some point, but she had a feeling this would not occur until the lights of Briar Wood were a distant memory.

With a sigh, Lisanne dug out her phone, checking for a text from Paul. Seeing nothing, she thumbed him a quick note letting him know she'd arrived before sliding the device into her back pocket. Either the Prius had more under the hood than she'd imagined, or Paul had been delayed. In all likelihood, Paul had more than just her on his plate. With an active duty roster of less than two hundred men and women, the Texas Rangers were responsible for a state that had a landmass nearly twice that of Germany. Viewed this way, it was not at all unlikely that Paul might have run into something that would make him late to the party.

Lisanne took another long look at the bar.

While she had walked into a dangerous situation a time or two, she'd also learned long ago not to tempt fate. In her line of work, there was no need to go looking for trouble. Lisanne decided to enjoy the cool Texas early morning as she waited for Paul to arrive.

Or at least that's what she'd intended.

No sooner had she leaned against the old-timey horse hitch that had probably served as a lifeline to more than one inebriated patron than lightning rippled across the pre-dawn sky. Thunder followed almost instantaneously as did fat, Texas-sized raindrops.

As a Marine, Lisanne had been no stranger to what her Corps drill instructors had termed liquid sunshine. But she could also hear her practical mother's admonishment that even cows were smart enough to come in from the rain. With a sigh, Lisanne trudged up the warped wooden steps, grabbed hold of the sticky metal door handle, and prepared to enter her second bar of the night. Before boarding their plane at Reagan, she'd told Jack that she wanted an authentic Texas experience.

She had a feeling she was about to get her wish.

32

TO SAY THAT THE MUSIC STOPPED AT LISANNE'S APPEARANCE WASN'T ENTIRELY AC-
curate. King George continued to rattle the bar glasses at a volume only a couple of decibels lower than a jet fighter lighting its
afterburners. But this was only because Mr. Strait was serenading
the crowd via a corner jukebox rather than a cover band. Based
on the rest of the bar's reaction, Lisanne was pretty certain that
the music would have faltered mid-note if the small raised stage
had held real musicians.

To be fair, Lisanne's entrance was straight out of a spaghetti
western. After pulling the gritty steel door open on complaining
hinges, she had taken a step inside just as another peal of thunder
echoed across the sky. This time, the accompanying discharge of
electricity must have struck somewhere a little closer to the tiny
town's power grid. The bar's lights flashed in time with the thun-
derclap, causing George to stutter mid-syllable. And just to ensure that every single eye was facing her direction, a blast of
rain-drenched air slapped through the open door, blowing
Lisanne's hair into a cloud of midnight and scattering bar napkins
and cigarette packs. If she'd been looking to make an impression,
Lisanne couldn't have asked for better theatrics.

Unfortunately, that hadn't been her goal.

"Get you something, miss?"

The question came from the bartender. The shabby interior, dirty floor, and dim lighting were what Lisanne would have expected to find based on the establishment's exterior, but the man behind the length of faux wood was not. Rather than a tatted-up biker or a shady cowboy, the proprietor could have been an accountant. Late fifties with gray hair and a matching closely trimmed goatee, button-down shirt with the sleeves rolled up above the forearms, and khaki pants. Had their roles been reversed, Lisanne might have started their conversation with the old standby of *What are you doing in a place like this?* Instead, she viewed the unassuming man as an island of normalcy in the otherwise decidedly masculine crowd.

"Club soda, please," Lisanne said, stepping closer.

On closer inspection, the bar appeared to be real if well-seasoned wood. In contrast to the pitted floor, smoke-stained walls, and general air of dinginess, the length of oak had been well cared for. The wood was a rich camel brown and its polished surface reflected back the neon beer signs in puddles of crimson and blue. Like the man behind it, the bar belonged in a much nicer establishment, but its presence brought a sense of comfort all the same. As if not everything in the Revelry reflected Briar Wood's bleak future.

"Would you care for a lime?"

"Sure," Lisanne said, setting her clutch down on the bar.

Turns out that possessing just one arm wasn't a hindrance only to gunfighting. Tasks she hadn't thought about twice before now required double the effort. But if fumbling for her debit card was an embarrassment, Lisanne was glad no one had watched her struggle with putting on a bra one-handed for the first time.

"On the house," the bartender said, setting a glass on the bar.

"Why?" Lisanne said, the question coming out more pointed than she'd intended.

That she would take a while to deal with the physical limitations imposed by her injury was a given. What Lisanne hadn't anticipated was the emotional baggage that went with her disfigurement. Especially the one reaction she hated more than any other.

Pity.

"Because it's my bar and I can do what I want," the man said, a wide smile taking some of the bite out of his words. "Besides, you're a pretty girl with only one arm. If that doesn't get you a free drink, I don't know what does."

Lisanne studied the bartender's face as she stopped working the latch to her clutch. His expression remained as open and honest as it had been without the slightest hint of malice or sarcasm.

Besides, he was right.

She *was* a pretty girl with one arm.

Though it had taken her some time, Lisanne had finally come to realize that some part of other people's reaction to her injury partially depended on her. There was no hiding that one of her arms ended in a stump just below the elbow. The question lay in how she addressed the elephant in the room.

"Thanks," Lisanne said, abandoning her purse for the glass.

"Were you in the service?" the bartender said.

"Why?" Lisanne said, her eyes narrowing.

"Lots of patriotic folks around here," the bartender said. "Some of them are missing a limb. Besides, I have a financial interest in your answer. Veterans get free refills."

Lisanne smiled.

That the bartender was flirting with her was a given, but she was still impressed. Rather than the unartful come-ons she'd had to endure from the Uber driver or some of the less than subtle leers she could feel from the bar's other patrons, this guy was doing an artful job of flattering her without coming across as creepy—a more difficult task than most men realized.

"Marines," Lisanne said, "but I'll pass on the refill. Don't want to have to be carried out of here."

"You wouldn't be the first," the bartender said. Then his warm eyes hardened as he looked over her shoulder. "Back off, Willie. She's engaged and a Marine. In other words, she's out of your league."

Lisanne turned to see a skinny man with uneven teeth, a bad haircut, and a ratty T-shirt standing behind her. The man, Willie, smiled as he caught her eye, but his grin slowly dried up in response to her cop face. She'd learned a lot about how to handle herself during her time as one of Uncle Sam's Misguided Children, but the Virginia State Police Academy hadn't exactly been a finishing school.

"Take it easy, Jim," Willie said, his hands held up to shoulder level, "it's not like a girl looking like her walks in here every day."

"Or ever," Jim said. "Back to your table, Willie. Next round's on me."

Willie smiled as his eyes wandered across Lisanne. He clearly liked what he saw, but he must have liked the idea of a free alcoholic beverage even more. Or maybe there was more to the accountant turned bartender than met the eye. Either way, after tipping his hat, Willie meandered back to his two companions on less than steady legs.

"Don't take this the wrong way," Jim said once Willie was out of earshot, "but what are you doing here?"

"Waiting for a friend," Lisanne said as she pulled the club soda closer. "He should be here any minute."

"Now I have to tell you, miss, you're welcome to wait for your friend as long as you'd like, but I expect that offers of additional friendship from my patrons will only continue. These boys will behave themselves, but I don't reckon they're going to stop introducing themselves."

The obligatory mirror behind Jim confirmed his prognosis. While Willie and his two friends were still enjoying the trio of longnecks one of the waitresses had brought over, the occupants of the high-top adjacent to them were paying much more attention to Lisanne than their margaritas.

While Willie and his trucker-hat-wearing friends fit her stereotypical assumption of what a Briar Wood resident might be—hardworking boys who lived paycheck to paycheck and liked to blow off some steam on a Saturday night—the four men next to them were decidedly different. For one thing, their mannerisms were restrained compared to the back-slapping behavior of Willie and his friends. While the natives laughed, told loud stories, and poked fun at each other, the outsiders talked in low voices and took slow, deliberate drinks.

While their dress wasn't nearly as out of place as Jim's office attire, the mystery men's wardrobe did not equate to a night drinking with the boys or potentially spinning a girl around the sawdust-covered dance floor. Their cargo pants, hiking boots, and fisherman's shirts certainly reflected an outdoor motif, but of a different sort than the cowboy/farmer look of the locals. This, combined with the men's subdued manner, gave Lisanne the impression that the four were on the job.

Working.

But working at what?

The quiet foursome, more so than the trio of loud cowboys, had Lisanne's nerves on edge. It wasn't as much what they were doing as their presence. As a police officer, she had been trained to look for what didn't belong. Inconsistencies. Whether aberrations came in the form of gaps in a witness's testimony, or a high-end sports car cruising through a decidedly low-end part of town, the ability to spot what didn't belong was one of the qualities that made for a good cop.

Doing something about it was another.

Lisanne stood, fishing her phone from her back pocket as she watched her audience for reactions in the mirror. She was wearing her favorite pair of AG jeans. Actually, that wasn't true.

While she liked the feel of the jeans well enough, Jack was their biggest fan. Judging by the cowboys' actions, her fiancé wasn't exaggerating their appeal. Though the locals were probably not in the midst of the sort of conversation that results in life-changing revelations, talk tapered off while she dug into her back pocket. The three drunk rednecks certainly weren't who she'd had in mind when she packed the jeans yesterday afternoon, but it was nice to see that her over-thirty figure could still stop a male brain mid-thought.

Or at least most male brains.

The quartet of out-of-towners also had their eyes on her backside, but their gaze felt different. Colder. She kept watch as she slid the phone onto the thankfully freshly wiped bar and wiggled into her seat. The four shared a glance as she thumbed open her contacts. This was not the look guys tended to exchange before one mustered up the courage to approach a pretty girl. The man closest to her pulled out his phone. His shaved head and broad shoulders would have lent him a resemblance to Mr. Clean were it not for the red mustache above his upper lip. The man's thumbs went to work, the cell looking like a child's toy in his massive paws.

After a flurry of texting, Mr. Clean eyed his companion and nodded.

Interesting.

Lisanne brought up her phone, hoping to see a message from Paul.

She did not.

Their last exchange had been from her hotel room. He'd promised to arrive at Revelry in less than an hour. That had been seventy minutes ago. Keying in a message, Lisanne asked for an updated ETA.

She hit the send button as Jim materialized from the gloom.

"Anything from your friend?" Jim said.

Lisanne shook her head.

"I was afraid you were going to say that. Maybe you should wait for him somewhere else."

Lisanne looked back at Jim, waiting for an explanation.

It didn't come.

Usually, an uncomfortable silence provoked a response. Not this time. Either Jim knew the old interrogator's trick, or he had a more compelling reason not to voice his concerns.

Like fear.

Leaning forward, Lisanne closed the space between them to foment a sense of intimacy. "Why?"

Jim hesitated, eyeing the out-of-towners. But whether it was their close proximity, the innate male desire to help a pretty girl, or perhaps his moral compass, Jim seemed to overcome his reluctance. Leaning toward Lisanne under the guise of refilling her drink, the bartender uttered a few words.

But she never heard them.

Just as Jim opened his mouth, a squeal of tires was followed by a sickening metal-on-metal *crunch*.

"Shit," Jim said, his eyes widening. "Not another one."

"Another what?" Lisanne said, getting to her feet.

"Accident. The road goes through a pretty aggressive curve

out front. With the woods as a backdrop, the turn can be hard to see, especially at night. We get about a wreck a month."

The bartender headed toward the door and Lisanne followed, mentally preparing herself. While she was grateful for the excuse to leave the crash offered, she had worked enough accidents as a trooper to know that crashes at the back road's posted speed limit of seventy miles per hour often resulted in fatalities.

This was doubly so when alcohol was involved.

At this time of the night, alcohol was almost always involved.

Jim pushed through the door and stopped on the porch. Lisanne pressed past him, both to make way for the traffic she was certain was coming behind her and because she had no intention of turning her back on any of the bar's occupants. Instead, she continued down the steps, peering into the night. At first the darkness and a rising cloud of dust, smoke, and vehicle fluids conspired to limit her vision.

Then she saw a shape.

A familiar shape.

"Call 911," Lisanne said as she sprinted for the upturned vehicle.

While the damaged car wasn't one she'd seen before, she knew the type—a dark SUV with a prominent brush guard, a combination spotlight/mirror on the driver's side, and low-profile red and blue lights.

In other words, an unmarked cop car.

Jim called something, but his words were lost to the wind whipping by Lisanne's face. As she drew closer, her cop brain categorized the accident in a series of impressions. The SUV was on its roof and the driver's-side door was crumpled. This pointed to an impact with another vehicle, not an overshooting of the turn Jim had mentioned. She registered a pair of taillights disappearing in the dark, heading east out of town, but couldn't determine a make or model.

Glass sparkled in the moonlight behind the SUV, lending credence to Lisanne's collision hypothesis. But that could wait for later. At the moment she was singularly concerned with something much more important—the life of the driver.

In the same way in which an experienced homicide detective could conduct a quick survey of a crime scene and arrive at a sense of what had transpired, she registered the car's condition and had a pretty good idea of what she'd find in the cabin. Crash mitigation technology had grown by leaps and bounds since the advent of the lap belt, and while airbags and cabin crash space were lifesavers, these innovations could not negate physics. The immense force generated by a collision with a tree at seventy miles per hour was difficult to survive regardless of the SUV's safety features.

But as the crumpled door could attest, the upturned vehicle hadn't impacted a tree.

With a final burst of speed, Lisanne reached the SUV. She grabbed the door handle and missed, sliding across the slick pavement. People who made fun of Texas motorists for treating rain showers like snowstorms had never driven in the Lone Star State. Wet Texas roads were the southern cousin of a Midwesterner's greatest winter fear.

Black ice.

Lisanne slid across the pavement on her knees, barely managing to brace herself against the vehicle's frame before face-planting. Getting her feet beneath her, she stood, grabbed hold of the SUV's door, and pulled.

Stuck.

Gritting her teeth, Lisanne tried again to no avail.

"Let me help," Jim said.

Though he hadn't kept up with her reckless sprint, the bartender had still covered the distance at an admirable pace. More than that, Jim had two hands, which was double what she could bring to the task. Swallowing her irritation, she nodded and moved out of the way. Jim grabbed hold of the handle and wrenched backward, putting his weight behind the effort. At first, he had no more luck than Lisanne, but after a bit of rocking, the door squealed partially open.

"That's as far as I can get it," Jim said between huffed breaths.

The opening was nowhere near large enough to facilitate a full-grown man.

Fortunately, Lisanne was not a man.

Wiggling into the space, Lisanne came face-to-face with the driver. The man was hanging upside down, his extremities a limp bundle of flesh. The grotesque angle of his head told Lisanne all she needed to know, but she pressed two fingers against his carotid artery all the same.

Nothing.

The driver was dead, probably from a broken neck.

Pulling her phone from her pocket, Lisanne activated the flashlight feature and shone the light onto the man's face.

Paul's unseeing eyes stared back at her.

33

JACK AWOKE TO THE DULL *THUNK* OF FLESH COLLIDING WITH FLESH.

Unlike his previous journey into dreamland courtesy of whatever he'd been injected with, this time there was no amnesia as he regained his senses. Jack remembered everything.

Every single thing.

Rage burned through his veins as he saw the cop's pleading eyes while the last of the man's lifeblood fountained away in arterial spurts. Jack still didn't understand what was happening in this godforsaken town, but he knew one thing.

He was at war.

Another *thunk*, this time accompanied by a burst of pain.

In a flash of insight, Jack realized what he'd missed before. The *thunk* was the sound of a fist hitting someone's face.

His face.

"Enough. He's useless to us if you beat him unrecognizable."

"He killed Johannes."

"Aye, Graham. And he'll pay for that. But if you let your rage get the better of you, we'll be right back where we started."

Judging by the throbbing of his face, Jack thought his captors had been going at him for a while. The section of Jack's head where he'd been hit with the AK-47 was hot and swollen while his nose pulsed with every breath. Coughing, he hocked up a mouthful of blood. This earned him another punch, but this time the strike caught him in the side. A perfectly executed body blow that made him want to fold in half.

Except he couldn't.

His hands were cuffed behind his back.

"I told you to knock it off."

"I didn't hit him in the face now, did I?"

"Don't be a child. Johannes was a comrade, but he chose the way of the gun just like us. Don't dishonor his memory by thrashing the wanker who's going to help us all get free and clear of this godforsaken place."

The blood flowing into his eyes from the cut on his forehead, combined with the swelling on his face, made it hard for Jack to see, but the distinct accents of the two speakers helped. The first, South African if he were to guess, came from the front passenger's seat. The one arguing with him was Scottish and was seated next to Jack. A third man was driving.

None of them seemed to have his best interests at heart.

"What's the play then, Hendricks?" the Scot, Graham, asked. "Dump his body in a field and drive away?"

"That's what I love about you, Graham," said Hendricks, the South African. "Straight and to the point. No, we're going to use him. He'll be at the flesh house when the locals show. The evidence will lead the coppers right where we want them to go."

"Not if this one tells them otherwise," Graham said.

He punctuated his comment with a slap to the back of Jack's head. The blow was half-hearted, but still hard enough to send jagged lightning bolts of pain arcing through Jack's skull. He groaned and slumped forward, allowing the seatback in front of him to catch his head.

"I told you to leave him alone," Hendricks said. "I've been at this game longer than a day so give me a little credit, *bru*. I said the coppers would find him at the scene. I didn't say he'd be in any condition to speak to them."

"I get to do him," Graham said. "Johannes was me mate."

"Sure, sure," Hendricks said. "But first things first. Right?"

Jack felt tentacles of fear constrict his chest at the casual way the pair discussed his pending execution like it was just another day. Amateurs talk big, building themselves up for the act. Professionals let their actions speak for them. Not that he'd had any doubts after watching the gunmen acquit themselves in the lopsided gun battle against the Briar Wood cop, but these men were professionals.

Jack choked, cleared his throat, and spat a blood clot on Graham's pants. The gunman let loose a stream of expletives before hooking another right into Jack's midsection. The Scotsman had cinder blocks for hands. Jack doubled over in pain. The blow landed squarely in Jack's stomach, and he had to fight the urge to vomit, but hunching forward also conveniently brought his cuffed hands in close proximity to his back pocket.

Dipping his thumb and middle fingers into the tight fabric, Jack quested for the five-cent object that might be the difference between life and death.

His probing fingers found only denim.

He needed to dig deeper.

"I'm going to throw up," Jack said after another, not entirely faked, hacking cough.

"The hell you are," Hendricks said. "Stop the car. Now!"

Jack's face bounced off the seat in front of him as the driver slammed on the brakes. Previously unseen stars achieved supernova as the collision caused the broken cartilage in his nose to grind together.

He dry-heaved.

"Not in the car," Graham said as he scrambled out his side.

Jack clamped his lips together as bile filled his mouth, not sure he'd be able to survive the beating he'd receive if he really did desecrate the car's interior. His stomach spasmed, and he was on the verge of losing the struggle when his door opened, admitting a wash of cool air. Graham pulled him out of the car by his hair, and Jack vomited a bloody stream, some of which splashed against the mercenary's leg. The Scotsman fired a hook into Jack's kidney and he nearly pissed his pants as he sunk to his knees.

Jack drove his fingers into the depths of his pocket as he fell and nearly cried with relief when the tips touched metal.

The paper clip.

The paper clip he'd taken from Jeff's paper scrap and shoved into his back pocket what seemed like a lifetime ago. Hunching forward, Jack vomited a second time as he slowly withdrew the tiny bit of metal with trembling digits.

He had it.

"Are you done?"

Jack nodded.

He was done.

So were the gunmen.

34

PICKING A SET OF HANDCUFFS IS NOT EASY.

Picking a set of handcuffs while seated with your hands behind you in a jostling car accompanied by men with murder in their hearts was nearly impossible. But impossible beat the alternative. And Jack was under no delusions as to what his fate would hold if he didn't get his cuffs unlocked.

Death.

As Ding liked to say, death was a great motivator.

"How are we doing this?" Graham said.

The SUV had just pulled onto a gated driveway from the blacktop road they'd been following in a long, winding path. The wrought-iron sign that hung above the gate had proclaimed the property RRR Ranch, but if this stretch of land was still a ranch, it had fallen on hard times.

While the gate had seemed to open and close easily enough, the rest of the property could use some tender love and care. The SUV rolled from side to side like a trawler in heavy seas thanks to the never-ending potholes that the driver either couldn't or didn't try to avoid. On the rare occasions when the headlights washed over the surrounding land, Jack didn't see any sign of cattle. Instead, patches of mesquite and cedar trees dominated the rolling terrain intermixed with patches of overgrown scrub brush. Nothing had grazed this ranch in a long, long time.

"We'll keep it simple," Hendricks said. "Pop inside and sanitize the place. Then we add your American friend to the mix and leave town."

"You think that will tie up all the loose ends?"

Hendricks shrugged. "The coyotes who run this brothel are dangerous men engaged in a dangerous business. No one will shed any tears over a few dead sex traffickers or their equally dead john. We'll make sure the evidence points in the right direction and our friends at the Briar Wood Police Department will handle the rest."

Graham nodded and added something else, but Jack didn't pay attention to what the gunman said. He'd heard more than enough. Besides, Jack was devoting all his remaining brainpower to one not so insignificant task—fitting the paper clip into the handcuff's keyhole.

Easier said than done.

In a testament to the weekly prayers and candles his mass-attending mother lit on his behalf, Jack had maintained his hold on the paper clip while Graham helped him back into the SUV at the conclusion of his vomit fest. To be fair, *helped* was a much too charitable description of the Scotsman's efforts. While he adhered in spirit to Hendricks's instructions regarding not leaving additional bruises on Jack, Graham still found ways to express his displeasure.

Painful ways.

Graham kicked Jack once in the testicles, which, while not a lot of fun, was not the abuse that hit Jack the hardest. No, this honor was bestowed on the knife-handed strike Graham gave to the back of Jack's neck as the Scotsman pushed him back into the car. The attack was dangerous in its own right. A strong enough blow could do irreparable damage to the spinal cord, while a strike that hit the carotid artery and vagus nerve just right could render the receiver unconscious.

Jack was worried about something much more severe.

Maintaining control of his fingers.

Unlike the kick to his groin, Jack hadn't seen the knife hand coming. One moment he'd been stumbling into the car. The next, the pins and needles sensation that usually accompanied dinging his funny bone ran the length of both arms. The numbness persisted long enough for Jack to promise the Almighty that next Sunday he'd join his mother at mass were he to see fit to allow Jack to live that long.

The next, feeling returned to his fingers.

His empty fingers.

Then Jack felt a sharp jabbing sensation from the vicinity of his left ass cheek.

With a dexterity that surprised even him, Jack thrashed against the closed door and slid his fingers along the leather seat. Once again, he found and palmed the paper clip. Once again, Graham made him pay for his sins, this time by grabbing Jack's broken nose with his thumb and index finger and squeezing.

Jack howled, but only partly with pain.

He had the paper clip.

Now it was time to get to work.

"Want help?" Graham said.

"Nah," Hendricks said. "Me and Pieter will take care of it. Two men won't spook them. Three might. Besides, someone needs to keep an eye on our friend."

Jack tried not to let the words hammer at his confidence as he worked the paper clip against the locking mechanism. The instructor who'd given The Campus operatives a version of the escape-from-restraints block of instruction taught to candidates in the special operations pipeline had been truly sadistic. In addition to the normal vignettes on defeating duct tape, zip ties, and handcuffs, he'd added a practical applications phase.

As part of this scenario, students were wired with a TENS unit in addition to the restraints. As The Campus operatives worked to escape from their bonds, the instructor randomly administered electric shocks that increased in intensity the longer it took the student to escape. Jack had considered the practice to be a bit excessive at the time, but now he understood. If you could pick a set of handcuffs despite jolts of electricity turning your major muscle groups into slabs of marble at random intervals, you could do it while broken and bloody in the company of men who wanted to kill you.

In theory.

After what seemed like days of sweeping the lock with no effect, Jack finally found the torsion point. The only problem was that the metal-on-metal *click* of the lock disengaging would be unmistakable in such tight confines.

He needed another distraction.

For once, his captors obliged him.

"Be back in a jiffy," Hendricks said as he opened his door.

The driver, Pieter, silently followed suit.

Jack wasn't fast enough with the clip to catch the sound of the door unlatching. But he was ready when it closed. As the door slammed, he wrenched the clip and added a cough for good measure. The lock disengaged and the steel bracelet released its bone-cold hold on Jack's left wrist.

He was free.

Sort of.

While nothing put spine in a fighter like the prospect of death, Jack knew that anger alone was not enough to carry the day.

Graham had worked him over. Hard. And while he was confident in his abilities as a fighter, he wasn't stupid. A shot to his nose would be a shock to his system even if he was expecting the blow, not to mention the other beatings he'd received. Jack could not afford anything approaching a fair fight. To have any chance of surviving, he needed to end this engagement both rapidly and definitively. He needed to catch the Scotsman off guard, which meant Jack needed the man angry.

Fortunately, when it came to pissing people off, Jack was something of a savant.

Clearing his throat, Jack collected a sizable wad of mucus, blood, and snot in his mouth. Then he turned and spat the glob.

Directly into the mercenary's face.

"You little shit," Graham said.

Grabbing hold of Jack's bloody shirt, the Scotsman yanked Jack toward him with his left hand as he snapped a jab into Jack's face with the other.

Or at least he tried to.

As Jack fell toward the other man, he raised his left arm, cupping the left side of his head just above his skull. Graham's fist crashed against Jack's thick forearm, doing no damage.

The same couldn't be said of Jack's elbow.

Jack yanked the gunman toward him with his right hand as he drove the pointy end of the hardest bone in his body into Graham's unsuspecting face like a fencer impaling an opponent with a perfectly timed lunge. After finding himself on the receiving end of the Scotsman's wrath, Jack took quite a bit of pleasure in what happened next. Graham's anger, combined with his certainty that he had nothing to fear from Jack, had led the mercenary to rush toward The Campus operative with reckless abandon. Jack felt the impact generated from the collision run the length of his arm, into his shoulder, and across his back.

It was glorious.

Graham didn't agree.

Though Jack missed the Scotsman's nose, he buried his walnut-sized elbow into Graham's right eye socket and was rewarded with a dull *pop* as the orbital bone fractured. The mercenary screamed, instinctively pulling away. Once again, Jack added to Graham's momentum, this time by grabbing his forehead and smashing the Scotsman's head backward into the passenger's window.

Repeatedly.

By the second blow, Graham stopped struggling. The third cracked the glass. And the fourth, well, it was safe to say that the Scotsman wouldn't be administering any more kidney shots to handcuffed captors.

Ever again.

Though Jack's animal instinct desperately wanted to expend its pent-up rage on the captor's limp body, he had other concerns. Like the two armed men still inside the house. Jack relieved Graham of his pistol, press-checked the weapon to ensure a round was seated in the chamber, and then considered his options.

They were limited.

Two mercenaries had trooped inside the house with murder on their minds. In no way was Jack equipped to follow them inside and continue his quest for justice. As if to underscore this thought, a series of flashes strobed from the picture window at the front of the house, accompanied by pistol reports.

While Jack had still not pieced enough together to understand exactly what illegal activity had been taking place inside the small structure, he gathered that the flashes signified that the former proprietors were no longer in business. In fact, he suspected that his body was meant to join theirs in an effort to offer the Briar Wood police a tidy explanation for the startling amount of violence that had engulfed their town over the last several hours.

Which meant that the gunmen would be coming out to claim him any moment.

Jack didn't intend to wait around for that reunion.

Squirming past Graham's slumped form, Jack wiggled into the front seat and stabbed the start button.

The vehicle didn't turn over.

For a moment Jack seriously considered going back on his promise to attend Sunday mass.

Or perhaps doubling down on it.

Then he realized the problem.

He wasn't stepping on the brake.

Jack smashed the pedal to the floor and tried the button a second time.

The engine started.

Unfortunately, the headlights activated at the same time, sending twin beams of halogen light lancing through the large bay window. The same room in which the gunmen had just executed their expendable business partners. Throwing the transmission into reverse, Jack crushed the gas pedal. The tires spun before grabbing the earth, giving Jack a view of the front door swinging open.

Then he was in motion.

Jack triggered the brights and ducked beneath the dashboard as a fusillade of rounds cratered the windshield. Crouching lower, he blessed the backup camera as he steered by the grainy video while doing his best to ignore the high-velocity projectiles punching through the SUV's thin metal skin. After two or three seconds of driving backward at nearly forty miles per hour, the volume of fire slackened.

Still not willing to chance a look above the dashboard, Jack cranked the wheel to the right, swinging the hood one hundred and eighty degrees. That he managed to accomplish this feat on rough terrain, in the dark, while being shot at, was a testament to luck as much as his tactical driving training.

And perhaps his praying mother.

Jack peered through the spiderwebbed windshield until he found the gate, then floored the accelerator. Three seconds later, he smashed through the rickety metal and his tires were back on blacktop. He rolled down the windows as he turned right, heading back toward town. He told himself it was to vent the smells of blood and death from the cabin.

This wasn't the only reason.

As the engine roared and the house of death vanished behind him, Jack extended his left hand into the air and waved goodbye to his enemies.

With a single outstretched middle finger.

35

"WHAT ELSE CAN YOU TELL ME?"

The question was a valid one, but the expression of the man asking it suggested otherwise. As evidenced by the fact that he was at the accident scene talking to her rather than chasing the motorist who'd fled, Lisanne surmised that he was the most junior member of Briar Wood's law enforcement. Or maybe another officer was already in pursuit of the hit-and-run driver.

Either way, his mannerisms didn't jibe.

A totaled vehicle, a dead Texas Ranger, and a hit-and-run driver was not an everyday experience, especially in a backwoods town like this one. The Briar Wood officer should have been pissed about being left behind, amped up at the death of a fellow law enforcement professional, or excited that his normally mundane shift had just turned interesting. But if Lisanne had to sum up the Briar Wood officer's reaction, she could do so in just one word.

Bored.

Even with a crime scene being processed just feet away, her questioner might have been taking a statement for a fender bender. Maybe this guy was in the wrong line of work.

Or maybe something else was at play.

"Nothing," Lisanne said, keeping her face impassive. "I heard the crash and came out to see what happened. Just like everyone else."

The officer gave a slow nod as a long yawn escaped his lips. The man didn't have the grace to look embarrassed. An EMS recovery team was prying a cop's broken body out of his destroyed car less than twenty yards away, and this joker acted like he was ready for his midshift nap.

Unbelievable.

"Actually, you didn't react just like everyone else."

"What do you mean?" Lisanne said.

"Everyone else stood around gawking," the officer said. "You sprinted across the parking lot and tried to get into the car. With one arm. After someone pried open the door, you wriggled inside, assessed the driver's condition, and pronounced him dead. A reaction like that usually signifies a personal attachment to the victim."

The officer spoke in the same deadpan voice and his disinterested expression never changed, but there was something different about him all the same.

His eyes.

A flicker of intelligence sparked from their depths.

Or cunning.

Then again, maybe it had been there all along.

Maybe Lisanne had seen only what she'd expected to see.

Eyeing the police officer, she renewed her assessment of the man, taking in all the details with her cop eyes. Though only about six feet in height, the man's slim frame made him seem taller. He probably weighed in at less than one hundred and sixty pounds, but his uniform fit snugly across his trim build. A prominent Adam's apple protruded from his long neck and made him look perpetually sleepy.

The nametag on his pressed uniform shirt read BRADSHAW and it was precisely aligned with the fold in the pocket it hovered above. Officer Bradshaw was probably used to being underestimated. This was a great quality to have as a cop.

Especially when it came to interrogations.

"Yes," Lisanne said, screwing up her features in confusion. "I said all that in my statement."

Officer Bradshaw looked at Lisanne without speaking. She stared right back, letting the silence build as she allowed a hint of irritation to creep into her puzzled expression.

"I know," Bradshaw said after it became apparent Lisanne wasn't going to volunteer anything else. "I was wondering if you'd accidentally omitted anything pertinent."

"Like what?" Lisanne said, the irritation in her voice growing more evident.

Unlike the confusion, her irritation wasn't hard to fake. She was tired, anxious, and growing wetter by the moment. What had before been a drizzle was fast becoming a downpour. And unlike Officer Bradshaw, Lisanne had no waterproof ball cap to keep the fat droplets at bay. As if to emphasize this point, a particularly intrepid raindrop splattered against the back of her neck before charting a cold trail of wetness down her back.

This was getting old.

Fast.

"Like what you do for a living," Bradshaw said, his sleepy eyes never leaving her face.

"I work for Hendley Associates," Lisanne said, giving the standard Campus cover story. "It's a financial firm."

"Interesting job?" Bradshaw said.

"I like it," Lisanne said, moving her wet hair away from her face with her stump. "But I wouldn't call it interesting. Mainly shuffling paper."

Bradshaw's gaze noted the stump before moving back to her face. "See many dead bodies while you're shuffling papers?"

"Got my fill of those in Iraq," she said. "I was part of the second battle of Fallujah."

"Army?"

"Marines," she said. "Military police."

"Interesting," Bradshaw said.

"What?"

"That you didn't pursue a law enforcement career after you left the military," he said.

"Not really," she said, shrugging. "I saw enough during that deployment to last a lifetime. And I came home with this nifty souvenir."

Lisanne lifted her stump.

Bradshaw nodded.

His features might have been chiseled from stone for all the reaction he gave to her deliberate provocation. Just another small-town cop drudging through another boring shift.

But his eyes said differently.

"Anything else?" Lisanne said, giving an exaggerated shiver. "I'd like to get out of the rain."

A second and third droplet followed the path charted by the first, and Lisanne didn't have to exaggerate her next shiver. So far her thick hair was doing an admirable job of shedding the damp, but she knew it was only a matter of time before it collapsed around her head in a limp, midnight mess.

"Just one more thing," Bradshaw said. "What were you doing at the bar?"

Lisanne hesitated.

Though on the surface the officer's questions were completely natural, there was something about him that just felt . . . off. Lisanne was still relatively new to the paramilitary world, especially in comparison to legends like Clark and Ding, but as a Marine and then a Virginia trooper, she'd been living by her intuition for most of her adult life. Right now, that quiet voice was telling her that there was more to Officer Bradshaw than met the eye.

Lisanne intended to listen.

"Waiting for a friend," Lisanne said.

"He never showed?" Bradshaw said.

"*She* canceled on me," Lisanne said with a shrug. "You know how Texans are with wet roads."

Bradshaw gave a long, slow nod, again letting the silence build to see if Lisanne would say more. Once again, she returned his dead stare, determined to wait him out despite the rain's icy fingers.

"Okay," Bradshaw said. "I think that about does it. Do you need a ride?"

"No thanks," Lisanne said. "I've got it covered."

She did not in fact have it covered, but that was fine. She might not know exactly what was happening here, but she was sure of one thing. Lisanne would walk the four miles back to town in the rain before she went anywhere with Officer Bradshaw.

36

WASHINGTON, D.C.

THE ATMOSPHERE IN THE SITUATION ROOM WAS, IN A WORD, ELECTRIC. THOUGH the room's occupants had been gathered without much in the way of official notice, word of the meeting's purpose had still filtered out. If her years in the nation's capital had taught Mary Pat anything, it was that asking politicians to keep a secret was a fool's errand.

This truism was doubly valid when the secret involved Iran.

"Okay, people," Jack Ryan said, "let's get started. Mary Pat, you have the floor."

"Thank you, sir," Mary Pat said.

As per their usual arrangement, she was seated at the head of the table on Ryan's right and while she appreciated the trust and respect the President's gesture conveyed, she did not especially love that the conference table's other occupants were all facing her. When the attendees focused on the President, she saw them as the cabinet members and principals that they were. But when that collective attention was directed at her, Mary Pat felt like an elk that had been brought to bay by a pack of hounds.

No matter.

While it was normal for a spy to eschew the limelight, Mary

Pat had given up running agents a long time ago. Besides, she had a weapon available to her that was lacking in most of the faces staring back at her.

Ambition.

Or more specifically, a lack thereof.

Mary Pat was still in government service because her friend—the President—had asked her to stay. She had no plans to parlay her stint as DNI into a political career and no intention to join a think tank or form a consultancy and hang out her shingle. In a town full of people whose livelihoods depended on their ability to monetize their proximity to power, Mary Pat was an anomaly. She wanted nothing from the people arrayed in front of her, which meant that she could do something that was becoming all too rare among Washington's movers and shakers.

Tell the truth.

"Yesterday at 0930 Tehran time, we ascertained that the Iranians have constructed a clandestine uranium enrichment facility," Mary Pat said. "We assess with a high level of confidence that the Iranians are attempting to achieve nuclear breakout. If the facility continues to function uninterrupted, we anticipate that the regime will have enough fissile material to construct one to three nuclear devices within days."

During their quick huddle before the presentation, the President had told Mary Pat to be brief, succinct, and direct with her presentation. Ryan's reasoning was that the sooner they ripped the Iran Band-Aid off, the quicker they could get to the meeting's purpose—war-gaming options to deal with an apocalyptic theocracy about to cross the nuclear threshold. Mary Pat had structured her opening in accordance with her boss's wishes, but based on the cacophony of voices exploding from the table, ripping off the Band-Aid might have been the wrong analogy.

This felt more like chumming the water.

"I'm sorry, Mary Pat, but I don't understand how your timeline could be right. Even if Iran started enriching yesterday, they would need months to compile enough enriched uranium for a nuke."

The statement came from Scott Adler, the secretary of state.

As was often the case, he was seated on the left side of the conference table with his civilian counterparts while the uniformed military attendees occupied the opposite side. This divide wasn't mere happenstance. As of late, the military and civilian components of Ryan's administration increasingly came at issues from very different perspectives, and Iran was ground zero for their divide.

The Islamic Republic of Iran was a tough nut to crack. Once a vibrant country with a civilization that stretched back to 4000 BC, the nation had been under the bootheel of religious extremists since 1979, and the strain was showing. Though blessed with an abundance of natural resources, the nation's economy was abysmal. Unemployment was rampant, wages were stagnant, and the national outlook was bleak. With a government more concerned with exporting its vitriolic form of militant Shia Islam through its numerous overseas proxies and subduing its population with morality police and public executions, Iran was not a garden spot even without access to nuclear weapons.

With a nuke, Iran was an existential threat to the entire globe.

The ayatollahs who still guided the nation with the help of their gestapo-like enforcers known as the Islamic Revolutionary Guard Corps, or IRGC, were committed to an apocalyptic version of Shia Islam in which the Hidden or Twelfth Imam would only be revealed after the Iranians engaged in an Armageddon-style battle with the West and Israel.

This was why Israel, the Middle East's sole democracy, refused to see the near-constant barrage of threats that emanated from Tehran as just blustering from feeble old men. The Iranians were committed to bringing about the last battle and intended to use nuclear weapons to do so.

On this account, everyone in the Ryan administration agreed.

It was the way in which this threat should be countered that opinions varied.

Case in point, Scott was the nation's chief diplomat. His instinct was to solve the Iran problem through a coalition of the willing. A cadre of nations that would wield diplomacy in the form of economic carrots and sticks. He'd been building consensus for a kind of grand bargain aimed at convincing the mullahs that only through relinquishing their nuclear weapons program could they hope to improve economic conditions enough to stave off a popular uprising.

Seated on the opposite side of the table from Scott was General Clyde Woltman. The chairman of the Joint Chiefs of Staff was a grunt through and through. A Marine infantryman who'd begun his career as an eighteen-year-old boot in the crucible of Parris Island before rising through the ranks, attending college, and gaining his commission as an officer. While Woltman did not disparage diplomatic solutions, he considered such efforts beyond his purview. Woltman wielded the nation's sledgehammer—a fighting force designed to pummel an adversary into the dust. Unfortunately, Iran was the sort of problem that defied both military and diplomatic initiatives—as Mary Pat was about to remind them.

"In a traditional sense, you are correct, Scott," Mary Pat said. "The process of enriching uranium is a straightforward, well-understood task. Feed material in the form of gaseous uranium hexafluoride is fed into a series of linked centrifuges known as a cascade. The centrifuges spin at extremely high speeds, generating centrifugal forces that separate the heavier U-238 from the lighter U-235. This separation concentrates the U-235, enriching it to the ninety percent mark required for nuclear weapons. The time required to reach the quantity of material needed to construct a nuke was generally thought to be months."

"Except the Iranians cheated," Ryan said.

The President's remark was more statement than question, but Mary Pat continued her explanation for the group's benefit. Judging by the blank stares confronting her from both sides of the conference table, not everyone shared Ryan's understanding of the intricacies of the fabrication of nuclear weapons.

Or much else for that matter.

"That's correct, sir," Mary Pat said. "The two-to-three-month window Scott just quoted was based on the assumption that the Iranians would use feed material derived from uranium enriched at the three- to five-percent level. This is the level of enrichment required for uranium to be used as fuel for their nuclear reactors at Arak or Isfahan. The amount of time to further enrich U-235 from three to five percent to a weapons grade concentration of ninety percent is well baselined. But the Iranians figured out a way to circumvent the traditional process."

"I'm still not following you," Scott said.

Mary Pat resisted the urge to suggest that perhaps the secretary of state's confusion stemmed from the fact that he had yet to let her finish her explanation. While the Islamic theocracy sported a population of only eight to nine million, Iran occupied an outsized spot on America's priority list. The once proud nation known as Persia had proven extremely adept at waging war through proxies, and until the tragedy of September 11th, had been responsible for more American deaths than any terrorist organization. Though Iran was ranked eighteenth worldwide for population, it ranked within the top three threats from a US perspective.

All this to say that Scott's rudeness was understandable.

Iran had a way of getting under everyone's skin.

"The Iranians did not follow the conventional path," Mary Pat said. "Rather than attempt a breakout in one massive rush, the Iranians have spent the last several years incrementally enriching their feedstock to levels closer to sixty or seventy percent. Still below what is required for a weapon, but much higher than what traditional breakout models forecast."

"If we knew the Iranians were cheating, why didn't we stop them?"

This time the question came from Senator Colleen Brown.

Though Senator Brown was a recent addition to the legislature, she was already proving to be a force to be reckoned with. Smart, photogenic, well spoken, and unabashedly ambitious, Senator Brown had made waves among the nation's electorate. Her frequent television appearances produced no shortage of sound bites, as did her systematic takedowns of the talking heads brave enough to challenge her. Senator Brown's isolationist views on American foreign intervention put her at odds with many of her peers, and she wasn't afraid to take on senior members of her party on this topic.

Even if that senior member happened to be the President of the United States.

Senator Brown was here because she was part of Arnie's plan to bridge the gap between the party's warring factions and unite them around a common understanding and acceptance of the Ryan Doctrine. Even so, Mary Pat had argued against the woman's inclusion. To Mary Pat's thinking, the ambitious woman was too self-serving for such a delicate discussion.

Mary Pat had lost.

And now the senator was calling into question the Ryan administration's entire approach to containing Iran.

Mary Pat felt the President stir, but she placed her hand on his arm before he could respond. She knew her friend well enough to understand that his anger was righteous. Ryan valued loyalty above all else, and he was more than willing to go confront anyone who threatened his subordinates.

Ryan didn't back down from much.

At least not willingly.

As she'd often reminded him in private, the office of the presidency was bigger than them both. She was a political appointee who could be fired, but he answered only to the voters. Sometimes it was necessary to sacrifice a lesser chess piece to save the king.

"From a tactical perspective, striking Iran is not an easy lift," Mary Pat said.

"The Israelis do it all the time. Let them handle it."

Mary Pat regarded Senator Brown with a level stare, trying to put herself in the woman's position.

Had she ever been that cocksure?

That arrogant?

The simple answer was *no*. This was because unlike the senator, Mary Pat had spent her formative years running agents behind the Iron Curtain against the very best in the espionage business—the Russians. No matter how naively sure she felt in her abilities as a case officer after graduating from the Farm's grueling training regimen, a single tour in the field put that notion to rest.

In the real world, mistakes equaled dead agents.

And Mary Pat had made her share of mistakes.

"The Israelis can strike targets in Isfahan," Mary Pat said, "but they have yet to attack Iran's nuclear infrastructure."

"Why?" Brown said.

"Because they can't," Mary Pat said. "One, the distances are too great and Israel doesn't have organic aerial refueling assets. Two, they don't have a strategic bomber fleet capable of carrying the extensive ordnance that would be required to ensure the threat was removed. So even if we agreed to provide tankers for Israeli F-35s and F-15s, delivering enough ordnance to ensure the enrichment facility's destruction would require their entire air force making multiple sorties. Israel hitting Iran wouldn't be a surgical strike as much as a precursor to all-out war. The United States is the only Western nation capable of such a strike. But I'll defer to General Woltman on the analysis of military options. As to why Iran was allowed to slowly enrich uranium, that answer requires a nuanced understanding of the issue, but I'll try to frame my reply in more basic terms."

Mary Pat spoke with the clinical manner one might expect of an intelligence professional, but her eyes communicated something else—a willingness to show the little princess what life under Moscow rules had really been like. Judging by the quick squeeze of Ryan's fingers on Mary Pat's forearm, a bit of her feelings might have bled through.

"Iran has spent the last two decades dancing on the head of a pin," Mary Pat said. "For all their backward ways, the ayatollahs have become experts in pushing the envelope with regard to their nuclear program. Time and time again, they have walked the rest of the world to the point of no return, only to back down in exchange for sanctions relief or other concessions in return for the supposed mothballing of a part of their nuclear program."

This time it was Scott who looked uncomfortable.

The truth was that the Iranians were masters at playing diplomats for fools and the current secretary of state was only the latest in a long line of victims. But that didn't make the conclusion any easier to hear. Mary Pat paused for a second to give the nation's top diplomat an opportunity to speak.

The look he shot her was less than friendly, but Scott kept his peace.

Maybe Mary Pat's dressing down of Senator Brown had made Scott reassess his conclusion. Or maybe he was biding his time for an offensive later. Either option made no difference to Mary Pat. As Arnie was fond of saying, when it came to politics, if you weren't offending at least half the room, you probably weren't doing your job.

"The bottom line is this," Mary Pat said, "the consensus of those in this room, along with most of the rest of the Western world, is that a nuclear-armed Iran cannot be permitted. But there isn't much agreement on the red line that would precipitate action. Iran has taken advantage of this dissension by refining small quantities of uranium while the rest of the world dithered. One leading academic termed this strategy as the *creep out* strategy."

"I'm sorry, but I still don't understand why we knew this was happening and did nothing," Senator Brown said.

"*We* did do something," Ryan said, a flush building at the base of his neck. "My first administration instituted a campaign of maximum pressure against Iran using a variety of crippling sanctions. A subsequent administration took a different tack."

"The fact remains that the Iranians have reached the nuclear threshold," Senator Brown said. "This is unacceptable."

"You are correct," Mary Pat said, "but not for the reason you suppose. The crisis here isn't driven by the Iranians' gradual enrichment of their existing feedstock. It's that they built a clandestine enrichment facility that allowed them to secretly finish the job and the entire intelligence community missed it. As DNI, blame for that miss resides with me."

"I appreciate you falling on your sword," Senator Brown said, "but it's awfully convenient that news of this secret facility doesn't surface until now. Just as the American people are about to debate a major tenet of the President's foreign policy."

For an instant, Mary Pat wondered if the senator was really this stupid.

Jack Ryan might be a politician, but he didn't play political games, especially with national security. Surely she didn't truly believe that Ryan would use the most potentially catastrophic intelligence failure since 9/11 to distract the American people from an unpopular national discussion on entitlement reform.

Then Mary Pat saw the mirth lurking in Senator Brown's eyes and knew the truth.

The comment was a cheap shot. The type meant to generate the sort of viral social media videos that led to clicks and campaign dollars. Though there were no cameras or audiences to perform for in the Situation Room, Brown was no doubt testing the line she'd later use on the Sunday programs.

Not for the first time Mary Pat found herself wondering how they had gotten to this point as a nation and what it might take to engender some sort of shared purpose between America's politicians. But she didn't say any of this to the senator who would be president. As she'd told her boss countless times before, Mary Pat was not a politician nor did she aspire to be. Her job was to tell the truth and let the chips fall where they may.

So she did.

"We didn't find the facility," Mary Pat said. "Our allies did."

"Who?"

Mary Pat paused, considering how she intended to answer. Whatever Mary Pat might think of her, Brown was a duly elected senator. She had a constitutional duty to provide oversight of the executive branch and the agencies it controlled.

And yet.

And yet, the woman was a politician with an adversarial view of Israel. Would she deliberately compromise the operatives who had gathered this crucial intelligence? Mary Pat didn't think so. But as a former agent runner herself, Mary Pat knew that loose lips sank ships with no regard to whether the information was shared accidentally or intentionally.

"Madame Senator, I—" Mary Pat said.

"We're not going to answer questions on sources and methods," Ryan said. "You've been on this committee long enough to know how this works."

"I'm not asking you to reveal sources and methods," Brown said, "but I was invited here for a reason. In one breath you're telling me that this new development caught the intelligence community completely by surprise. In the next, you're asking me to trust that you now have your ducks all in a row. Which is it?"

Mary Pat found herself reappraising her opinion of the woman. People who underestimated the senator's intellect because of her propensity for fluffy social media posts or her photogenic smile did so at their own risk.

She would be a formidable candidate for the nation's highest office.

"Perhaps I can help thread the needle," Mary Pat said with a look to her boss. The glance was pure theatrics. Her relationship with Jack Ryan had long since progressed beyond the point where she needed his permission to share classified material. On matters of national security, the President trusted her judgment implicitly.

But Senator Brown didn't know that.

And by teeing up the interaction this way, Mary Pat had put Ryan in the position where he could appear to compromise. This gesture would both give Brown a victory and potentially build goodwill for the coming ask. Mary Pat might not be a politician, but she'd spent a lifetime perfecting the art of manipulating assets.

Politics wasn't much different.

Ryan frowned as if weighing the request before granting Mary Pat's wish with a slow nod.

Theater at its finest.

"What I'm about to reveal is classified at the code-word level," Mary Pat said. This time her tense expression had nothing to do with theater. If leaked to the wrong source, the information she was about to reveal could lead to the deaths of the Israeli reconnaissance team still on the ground in Iran. "The intelligence was derived from HUMINT sources. In addition to clandestine sensors, the operatives employed a unique collection device that obtained physical samples of uranyl fluoride, a dustlike aerosol that is a by-product of the chemical reaction that occurs when uranium hexafluoride gas escapes into the atmosphere. The findings have been verified by our laboratories. We can state with one hundred percent certainty that the Iranians are on the cusp of nuclear breakout."

"Is that clear enough for you, Senator?" Ryan said.

Brown nodded.

"Good," Ryan said. "Now we can get to the reason why we're actually here. I am not prepared to allow Iran to develop a nuclear bomb. Period. This facility and the enriched uranium contained within it represent a clear and present danger to the United States, Israel, and frankly, the rest of the world. We are going to remove this threat. I want to hear options, starting with the intelligence community. You're up, Jay."

Mary Pat eased back in her chair.

Ryan's choice to bypass her in favor of the CIA director was a purposeful one. While Mary Pat sat atop the intelligence community's organizational chart, her role was traditionally more administrative in nature. The amount of control the DNI exercised over the organizations under her office's umbrella ebbed and flowed in response to the DNI's personality and the manner in which the sitting president decided to employ the office. Because of her close relationship with Ryan, the DNI's influence had grown decidedly more pronounced during Mary Pat's tenure.

But there were directors that helmed each agency for a reason. In situations such as this one, Mary Pat better served her boss as his counselor rather than his subordinate. With this in mind, she'd given Director Canfield a heads-up that the boss wanted to hear directly from him during this session without Mary Pat serving as a buffer.

Hopefully he'd taken her advice to heart.

"Yes, sir," Jay said. "I'm sorry to say that my update is going to be fairly brief. From a clandestine or covert perspective, we have nothing that can be actioned in the timeline you've laid out, Mr. President. While we are working several initiatives to adversely affect the Iranian nuclear weapons program, our quickest flash to bang can be measured in months, not days. Short of using a Ground Branch team to conduct a raid on the facility, we have nothing to offer."

In spite of her best efforts, Mary Pat frowned at Jay's response.

While she had no reason to doubt the veracity of his assessment or the conclusion he'd reached, this was not how she would have gone about delivering the message. With the exception of Senator Brown, everyone in the room worked for the President. Their job was to provide the commander in chief with options, not explain what they couldn't do.

Then again, Mary Pat understood the man's frustration.

Over its storied, almost eighty-year history, the agency had pulled the proverbial rabbit from the hat more times than the American public would ever know. For an organization that traced its roots back to the daredevils who staffed the World War II–era OSS, the CIA hadn't acquitted itself badly during the War on Terror.

Even when the subject turned to Iran, the agency had either facilitated or directly undertaken scores of operations. These efforts had delayed the mad mullahs' quest for a bomb through assassinations, sabotage, and good old-fashioned trickery. When push came to shove, CIA officers had bought America's politicians time. Time to fashion a coherent strategy designed to keep the weapons of Armageddon out of the hands of those who would wield them.

Time that now seemed to have been squandered.

"I appreciate the honest assessment, Jay," Ryan said, "but I don't want to see the head hanging that went along with it. At its core, this is a leadership, not intelligence failure. Every President and senior elected official for the last twenty years knew that the Iranian nuclear program was a problem and every single one of them was content to kick that can down the road. It's not your fault that we ran out of road on your watch. Chin up."

"Yes, sir," Jay said. "Sorry, sir."

Ryan held the man's gaze for a beat longer before slowly nodding.

Then he turned to the chairman.

"All right, General," Ryan said, "run us through the tactical problem."

"Gladly, sir," Woltman said. "As Director Foley laid out in her opening remarks, destroying this site is going to take some doing."

The LCD screen mounted to the wall came to life, revealing a map of Iran.

"The Iranians chose the location well," Woltman said. "The

clandestine enrichment facility is located inside the Saghand uranium mine, probably in an abandoned tunnel. The shafts were literally bored into the side of a mountain. We estimate that facility probably is at least eight meters underground. Conventional fighter bombers cannot deliver the type of ordnance necessary to ensure the facility is destroyed. Neither can cruise missiles."

"Then what are we looking at?" Senator Brown said. "B-2 sorties?"

"Ordinarily, I'd say this would be the exact mission set for a B-2, but our prestrike intelligence workup has identified some challenges," Woltman said.

The slide changed to a pair of side-by-side images. The picture on the right showed a satellite view of the facility. Crimson, diamond-shaped graphics expanded from the facility in concentric rings. The image on the left showed the Russian SA-10 Grumble surface-to-air missiles.

Mary Pat had a feeling she knew where this was going.

"As expected, Iranians are protecting the enrichment facility with layered antiaircraft defenses. Since Saghand has long been known as a uranium mine, the presence of these systems was not out of the ordinary, which was another part of the genius in selecting this site as the facility's location. In essence, the Iranians were able to hide in plain sight."

"But those missiles rely on Big Bird radars," Ryan said. "Our B-2s have defeated them before."

Not for the first time Mary Pat found herself wondering how the President had found the time to keep abreast of Russian antiaircraft systems. She needed to run her traps to see if her boss had finagled his way into getting his hands on raw intelligence feeds again. She knew Ryan had an agile mind and a voracious appetite for military data, but surely there were more suitable subjects for his bedtime reading.

"That's correct after a fashion, sir," Woltman said. "But the worry here is the Big Bird radar, not the missiles themselves. DIA published a finding several weeks ago stating that the Russians had made tremendous strides with the targeting algorithms that interpret the radar's returns. The initial conclusions from Redstone's analysis suggest that the upgrades might give systems like this one the ability to detect and acquire our stealth platforms."

And the hits just kept on coming.

Mary Pat had skimmed the DIA analysis of the radar system's projected performance, but hadn't devoted much brainpower to the white paper. As the president's gatekeeper, Mary Pat spent almost as much time deciding what merited her boss's attention as sifting through finished intelligence products. She'd mentally flagged the topic for follow-up, but like many subjects in the world of intelligence, more often the topic of the day chose you, rather than the other way around.

"Let me get this straight," Ryan said, his voice taking on a harder edge. "Iran's about to cross the nuclear threshold, and short of a full-fledged war, we have no way to stop them. Is that what I'm hearing?"

Mary Pat took the question as rhetorical.

Someone else did not.

"Actually, Mr. President, there is another option."

The statement came from the cluster of chairs lining the Situation Room's rear wall. Mary Pat craned her head to get a look at the speaker. While she'd seen the woman in the scrum of aides and undersecretaries who often accompanied their principals to meetings, Mary Pat had never met her. She looked to be in her early thirties and was tall with fair skin, auburn hair, and a trim build. She was dressed in a conservative pantsuit, but the erect manner in which she sat and the confident yet respectful manner in which she addressed President Ryan screamed *military*.

"I'm sorry," Ryan said. "I don't believe we've met. Who are you?"

"My apologies, Mr. President," the woman said, standing. "My name is Shannon Kent, and I'm with the Air Force's Special Projects Office. Apologies to Director Canfield, but there's something we've been working on that was envisioned exactly for situations such as this. We call it Chaos."

"I can't say I'm familiar with that one," Ryan said.

"I'm not surprised, sir," Shannon said. "The program is still very much at the prototype phase, but given the urgency of the situation, it might be worth discussing, sir."

"You want to brief me on an unproven solution that no one in this room has heard of?" Ryan said.

"Yes, sir," Shannon said.

Mary Pat eyed the woman, intrigued.

Case officers made snap judgments about a person's character as a matter of course. Each meeting with an asset involved subjecting them to a sort of human polygraph examination. A series of observations designed to answer the most important question a spy couldn't ask: *Is the asset compromised?* For reasons she couldn't put into words, Mary Pat liked what she saw in Shannon. While the office of DNI wasn't exactly on a hiring spree, Mary Pat was always on the lookout for talent. Based on what her gut was telling her, Shannon Kent might just fit the bill.

If she survived this meeting.

"Okay, Miss Kent," Ryan said. "Lay it on me. I'm all ears."

Shannon smoothed her already wrinkle-free slacks.

Then she began to speak.

37

"I DON'T SEE ANYTHING, BOB."

Bob Behler swallowed his frustration along with the sarcastic comment lurking on the tip of his tongue. Though he was an old man by aviator standards, the gray-haired, hunched man standing next to him was positively ancient. Bob wasn't sure where exactly the program office had dug up Alec Van Tilburg, but his contributions to Lockheed's Skunk Works were legendary. Supposedly Alec had cut his teeth on the F-117 Nighthawk program before graduating to the F-22 Raptor and then a series of X-plane demonstrators that were still not officially acknowledged.

Though Bob couldn't figure out how to make that math work, he'd spent enough time with the engineer over the last several months to attest to a couple of things—Alec was wicked smart and the Coke-bottle-thick glasses he kept perched on the edge of his nose didn't miss much.

If Alec said there wasn't anything to see, Bob believed him.

But that didn't mean his aviator's sense was wrong.

Bob stretched out a gloved hand to feel the Blackbird's titanium skin.

Like all pilots, Bob was a bit superstitious. He believed he could discern the mysteries his aircraft sometimes whispered to him. While on the test sortie hours earlier, he could have staked his wings on the notion that there was feedback in the stick, meaning something about the control surfaces was out of whack. Bob was hoping that running his fingers across his bird's fuselage would bring another detail or two to the surface. Something that had perhaps lodged in his subconscious that the feel of his aircraft would jar loose.

At least that's what Bob would have told a nonpilot.

But the truth was he believed he could intuit things about his jet in the same manner in which a good horseman could sense things about his mount simply by laying a hand on its flank. Bob knew that Blackbird was trying to tell him something, but damned if he could figure out what.

And that was problematic.

Because while a bruised tailbone was usually the worst a rider suffered if he didn't understand his mount, a finicky SR-71 would do much more than just buck its pilot. Not for the first time Bob thought about the men who'd died piloting the world's fastest plane.

The Blackbird was a dream to fly, but she could also be a nightmare.

"Here's what I think," Alec said. "It's probably—"

A cheer echoing from the other side of the hangar interrupted the ancient technician. Bob turned toward the celebration and tried not to feel jealous. Unlike decades ago when he'd been flying sorties on the edge of freedom's frontier, his SR-71 was not the hangar's celebrity guest. That honor belonged to the sleek, black form that had just shattered the air-breathing speed record, which had stood for fifty years.

A pilotless, sleek black form.

Though it felt like cheating on his wife, Bob still let his gaze drift over the Corvair's clean, shadowy edges. The UCAV oozed sex appeal, no two ways about it. If given the chance, Bob would trade away years of his life for a chance to fly it. Maybe all of them remaining, if he were being honest. But no man or woman would ever sit in its cockpit as the thundering engines drove the vehicle to the ragged edge of speed.

Because the Corvair had no cockpit.

Unlike the rumored optionally manned B-21 Raider, the Corvair was designed to be pilotless. And while Bob understood the reasoning behind this decision from a head perspective, it was sometimes more than his heart could bear. Unless the Department of Defense radically changed course with its procurements, the days of manned flight were rapidly drawing to an end. He drew some comfort from the notion that the *manned* airspeed record would stand, but like his SR-71, Bob was a dinosaur, and his extinction event was looming.

"That's some plane, isn't it?"

Alec's comment broke through Bob's morose thoughts. He might someday go the way of the *Tyrannosaurus rex*, but thanks to this R&D effort, today wasn't that day. He was lucky to be standing in this hangar post flying the greatest airplane in history instead of sitting in his bass boat waiting for a nibble. He was a lucky man and he needed to start acting like it.

"It's okay," Bob said, inclining his head toward the Corvair and its crowd of engineers. "But they don't make 'em like this anymore."

"Amen to that," Alec said with a smile. "This beauty came together with slide rules and number two pencils."

"And a little bit of luck," Bob said.

"A whole lot of luck," Alec echoed.

"Excuse me, are you Colonel Bob Behler?"

Bob turned toward the voice to see a young woman holding a phone.

"I haven't been called anything near that nice in a long time," Bob said, "but I think you found your man. What can I do for you?"

"You have a phone call," the woman said, offering Bob the handset.

"From who?" Bob said.

"The White House."

38

WHILE THE PHONE CALL DID TECHNICALLY ORIGINATE FROM 1600 PENNSYLVANIA Avenue, the caller was not a resident of the West Wing.

But this did not make the conversation that followed any less unusual.

"Hello?" Bob said after accepting the cell and finding a quiet corner of the hangar.

With all the celebrating still going on around the UCAV, this was easier said than done. But as much as he wanted to be a curmudgeon about the whole thing, Bob couldn't begrudge the Corvair team their happiness. Granted, he had flown the SR-71 in a different era, but the celebrations he and his comrades had engaged in after a successful mission were legendary.

Or perhaps infamous.

The difference between those words was often in the eye of the beholder.

"Is this Colonel Behler?"

Bob paused before answering.

The voice sounded familiar, but he couldn't quite place it. Besides, there were operational security concerns to consider.

The Corvair developmental program had been moved to the black side of Department of Defense–sponsored research in response to the leaps forward in hypersonic technology Russia and China were both making and moved to Air Force Plant 42, the same secure facility located near Palmdale, California, which held the B-21 Raider. While he wasn't on the design team, Bob certainly had firsthand knowledge of the vehicle's performance and the nondisclosure he'd signed before reporting to work had been both long and unambiguous when it came to describing the penalties that would befall him should he violate its terms.

Then he realized the absurdity of his line of thinking. The unknown caller had dialed the number for a classified hangar and asked for Bob by his military title. The chances that this was some sort of espionage fishing expedition were slim to none.

"Yes, sir," Bob said, plugging his left ear as he pressed the phone against his right. "To whom am I speaking?"

"That's a hurtful question," the caller said. "I know you're getting old, but I'd still expect you to recognize the voice of your former backseater."

The answer coincided with a sudden dimming of the hangar's background chatter, allowing Bob to really hear the voice for the first time. And the unmistakable edges of a Boston accent the speaker had never been able to smooth out.

"Bean?" Bob said with a smile. "Is that you?"

"In the flesh. Good that you finally put that together. I was hoping the dementia hadn't completely sunk you."

Ed "Bean" Allie had been one of the last crops of Reconnaissance Systems Officers, or RSOs. Ed had reported to Beale Air Force Base as Bob had been on his way out. Though crew members with such disparate experience levels weren't usually paired together, Bob had taken the eager young officer under his wing. They'd flown several training missions together as well as a pair of operational flights over Central America.

"It's great to hear your voice, Bean," Bob said. "Seems like all the government money spent on speech classes finally paid off."

Bean's Boston accent mellowed in person, but over the radio it was especially thick when the RSO grew excited. After a flight with an ornery pilot who claimed that he'd missed a critical navigation cue from his backseater because he couldn't understand Bean, the issue came to a head.

Bob had always been suspicious of the circumstances, as the pilot in question had a reputation for fudging his waypoints, but there was no denying that the Blackbird's intercom system seemed to amplify Bean's dialect. The pilot pushed the issue to avoid a negative annotation in his officer fitness report, and a review panel recommended Bean sit down with a speech pathologist. The backseater gracefully agreed, and the pilot was later drummed out of the Blackbird crew roster when he missed another turn while paired with a different RSO.

But by then the damage had already been done.

Bean, short for Beantown in a nod to Ed's Boston hometown, had been given his call sign.

"I'd tell you what I think of your flying abilities," Bean said, "but I'm currently in mixed company. All bullshit aside, I have a question I need you to answer. A serious one."

The change in Bean's tone was impossible to miss, not that Bob needed a reminder that this was not just a case of two old comrades in arms catching up. The clarity of the call combined with the peculiar shifting of Bean's tone pointed to just one conclusion—their voices were being run through a digital cipher that encoded the signal.

Put more simply, this was a secure call.

Lifting the handset from his ear, Bob studied the device.

Though his expertise did not extend to cell phones, even he could tell the one he was currently holding was not an off-the-shelf model. The case was thicker than the slim models everyone carried, and the frame lacked a camera. More important, a piece of red tape stretched across the back of the device.

Bob scratched at the strip with his fingernail but couldn't so much as find a seam. Permanent red tape to let everyone know this was the phone designated for secure communications.

Bean was not calling just to shoot the shit.

"Lay it on me," Bob said.

"The UCAV—what's your assessment?"

Bob frowned as he thought. "Look, Bean, I'm on the program, but I'm not privy to the technical details. Hell, if I'm being honest, I'm more of just a highly paid chauffeur for the tech geek who rides in the back of my Habu. I'm not the one who should be answering this question."

"That's where you're wrong, old friend," Bean said. "You're precisely the one to answer this question. I don't want program speak or technical gobbledygook. I need a simple answer to a simple question. Is that bird ready for prime time?"

This time Bob's hesitation wasn't born of confusion. He understood exactly what Bean was asking. More than that, he understood exactly why he was asking it in this manner. In the almost fifty years since Bob had first donned a flight suit, technology had progressed at a staggering pace. What had once been the stuff of *Star Trek* episodes was now part of everyday life. But even with these exponential leaps forward, one truth remained constant—unless a conversation was conducted face-to-face inside the confines of a Faraday cage, it shouldn't be considered secure.

At least not completely.

Bob's old friend was now a four-star general, and four-star generals dealt with four-star problems. This wasn't a request for an off-the-record program update between former comrades in arms. This was the real deal.

"Here's what I think," Bob said, remembering the feel of the SR-71's still-warm skin beneath his gloves. "It's a fine piece of technology, but it's still a demonstrator. I flew a bird that killed a hell of a lot of pilots, so I don't make this declaration lightly, but if you're asking would I want to go into combat with it? My answer would be no. Or at least not just yet."

"Hey, Bob," a new voice echoed through the phone. "This is Jack. Can I chime in?"

Bob felt a flash of irritation at the intrusion. Old Bean could have at least let him know that they were on a party line. And who the hell was this Jack guy anyway?

The answer came a moment later like a bolt of lightning out of the blue.

Bob unconsciously squared his shoulders and sucked in his gut.

"Yes . . . sir," Bob said, trying to decide on the correct form of address. "Ask away."

"Good," President Ryan said. "You're an old guy like I am. You know what I like about old guys? They don't have time for bullshit. So I'm going to put this to you straight—if you had a problem and this bird was the only viable solution, would you use it?"

Bob turned as he thought, eyeing the UCAV. Like aviation enthusiasts everywhere, he'd kept abreast of the startling developments in hypersonic technology long before he was formally brought into the Corvair's fold. While some of the hype behind the proposed hypersonic missile mission profiles was pure showmanship as far as Bob was concerned, the need for a Mach

5–capable weapons delivery platform was easy to understand. A bomber could carry a much heavier weapons payload than a missile. It was reusable and its blazing speed allowed for purely kinetic kills as per the demonstration that Bob had just witnessed.

But that was only part of the draw.

The weapons system that the Corvair was trying to become would fill a new role in America's arsenal. For the first time in history, a Mach 5–capable bomber would be able to service time-sensitive targets anywhere on the globe with devastating effects. More than that, the combination of stealth and speed would deliver an unambiguous message to bad actors the world over.

You can't run and you can't hide.

If the President of the United States was asking Bob's opinion with regard to the viability of using a relatively untested prototype to deliver a lethal payload, this was not a cakewalk mission. In all likelihood, the bird would be flying into heavily contested airspace on a tight timeline to hit a time-sensitive target. Which meant that if Bob gave the thumbs-down, manned aircraft would have to be used instead. Fighters to take out the early warning radars and air defense systems, cruise missiles to destroy critical command and control nodes, and then finally a fleet of B-2 bombers to deliver the knockout punch.

Except that if the scuttlebutt was correct, B-2s weren't as invisible as they once had been, and at over a billion dollars a copy, the United States couldn't afford to lose them. Which meant the initial strike package used to set the conditions for the raid would be even larger. Which meant putting a lot of men and women into harm's way.

There would be casualties.

If it was the target set he was envisioning, Bob thought there might be lots of casualties. Viewed through this lens, the President's question wasn't much of a question at all.

"Sir," Bob said, "if you're asking what I think you're asking, I'd send the bird. But I'd also have one hell of a backup plan."

A long stretch of silence greeted Bob's reply.

Then the President spoke.

"Thank you for your honesty, Bob," Ryan said. "I know that put you in a tough spot."

"I might be a cranky old man," Bob said, "but I'm still a jet jockey at heart. Tight spots are where we live."

"I was hoping you might say something like that," Ryan said. "How'd you like to suit up for one more mission?"

Someday, Bob was going to follow his wife's advice and learn when to keep his mouth shut.

Today was not that day.

39

"HERE SHE COMES."

The excitement in Charlie's voice was palpable, and while Bob shared his backseater's joy, his emotions were also tempered by a bit of sadness. Bob was back in the saddle flying a combat mission of sorts, but he was no longer the main event. That honor belonged to the black wraith materializing out of the clouds above him.

"Tally Corvair at nine o'clock, our flight level," Bob said.

Though he was still trying to get his hippie crew member to adopt at least some Air Force protocols, Bob knew it was probably a losing battle. The kid was in full-on video game mode now, and he was just jazzed that his prototype was going on an actual mission. That the mission in question would result in the deaths of quite a few people if it was successful, and untold more if it wasn't, didn't seem to register with the engineer. To Charlie, this was just a proof-of-concept demonstration on steroids.

"Snake, this is Grip, are we clear for refuel, over?"

This radio call came from the KC-46A tanker that had been turning lazy circles in the sky for the last ninety minutes. While

269

the Corvair was performing well beyond what anyone had expected, it was still an experimental aircraft, and it came with experimental aircraft problems. No, that wasn't quite right. As jets had become steadily more complex, the number of issues that could ground a plane had grown right along with them.

The newest planes had some of the lowest fully mission–capable rates because of this quandary. This was the reason why it took a pit crew to keep a Formula One car running while the average passenger vehicle could go years without any maintenance more substantial than the occasional oil change. Complex problems required complex tools and the complex maintenance that went with them.

"Grip, this is Snake," Bob said after keying the radio transmit button on his throttle, "we're running a final diagnostic check now. Stand by, over."

"Roger, standing by."

The call from the tanker's boom operator was standard radio protocol, but Bob thought he could detect a bit of an undertone in the airman's voice. While tanker crew members understood that they played a supporting role to the warfighters, and that role often involved burning holes in the sky while waiting for their bomber or fighter customers to arrive on station, no one liked to aviate in poor weather.

The air was beginning to become choppy when Bob had arrived on station and begun his aerial refueling thirty minutes ago. Now, the rising and falling columns of air were buffeting both jets. Thunderstorm conditions weren't much fun to fly in and the turbulent air was downright frightening when it came to aerial refueling. While the Corvair had no passengers with sensitive stomachs, the same couldn't be said of the tanker's crew. Or Bob and Charlie for that matter. If he were in the boom operator's shoes, Bob would want to get this show on the road.

"We good to start the refueling, Charlie?" Bob said.

As was par for the course, Bob's backseater was head down, his attention focused on his computer. As was also the norm, he didn't seem to have much concept of the urgency surrounding their timeline. Bob had nothing but respect for the men and women who designed and maintained the flying machines that had given the United States unmatched aerial dominance for more than a century. Still, there was a time and place for engineering rigor and Bob was certain that an active combat mission fit that bill.

"What?" Charlie said. "Oh, yeah. Sorry. There was a slight anomaly in the maintenance telemetry, but I've got it sorted. Yes, the bird's ready to refuel. She's clear to enter the mission profile."

Like her elder sibling the Blackbird, America's newest hypersonic platform departed the runway with the bare minimum of fuel required to link up with her tanker. Over the course of this mission, the Corvair would have to tank several times. The next one would be over the Atlantic with no one but the tanker crew to watch. The op plan called for Bob to fly the Corvair's flight route, but since his top speed was almost forty percent slower, he wouldn't link up with the UCAV again until the Corvair was returning from Iran with its mission complete.

The Corvair's ingress aerial refuelings before that would be completely autonomous, which meant this was the only test. Conducting the first aerial refueling on a mission with zero margin for error had everyone on edge.

Well, everyone but Charlie.

"Roger that," Bob said before changing the radio selector to the SATCOM setting and thumbing the transmit button. "Main, this is Snake, Corvair is clear for refueling, over."

"Main copies all. Transitioning to autonomous."

Technically speaking, the Corvair was already operating autonomously. Using technology that had been perfected during twenty years of drone warfare conducted around the globe, pilots sitting in a bunker at Palmdale had flown the UCAV during the takeoff sequence. But as soon as the Corvair had passed through one thousand feet, the aviators had transferred control to the vehicle's internal autopilot.

Technology had long since bypassed the need for human guidance during the en route portions of the mission. Besides, the speeds at which the Corvair traveled made human control impractical. Even via redundant satellite links, the delay in transmission times made finite control inputs unworkable and unlike the Afghan theater of operations when drones were controlled locally from Kandahar Airfield, there was no infrastructure to support the Corvair on the opposite side of the planet. The aircraft needed to be able to accomplish its mission autonomously or it wouldn't be able to fly at all. Even so, this was the first time in the mission profile in which control would be completely ceded to the aircraft. The minute adjustments needed for midair refueling were better accomplished by the onboard computer.

At least that was the theory.

"Snake, this is Main, Corvair has the controls."

"Snake copies all," Bob said.

Though the Blackbird's thick windows didn't make for great sightseeing, Bob was only two hundred feet from the Corvair and had no problem picking out its distinctive shape. The UCAV resembled nothing so much as an ethereal spirit, an ink blot rendered across a canvas of blue. Though he could see no difference in the vehicle's flight profile as the onboard computer assumed control, the aircraft felt different to Bob. With live munitions and no human in the loop, the UCAV seemed like an attack dog whose leash had just been unclipped.

"There it is again," Charlie said.

"What?" Bob said.

"An anomaly in the maintenance data dump," Charlie said.

Building on a practice that was first instituted with the F-35 Joint Strike Fighter program, the Corvair leveraged machine learning algorithms to predict when it would need maintenance. This bit of magic was accomplished through a twofold process. One, the UCAV used its digital infrastructure and plethora of onboard sensors to collect data on nearly every aspect of its propulsion system.

Two, this telemetry was then archived into larger packets, encrypted, and transmitted back to Palmdale via scheduled data bursts. Once the information reached the maintenance professionals, it was run through predictive analysis algorithms that utilized different statistical tools to monitor the aircraft's overall health. In the event that a critical component was deemed to be performing outside of spec, the logistical hub would automatically order a replacement part and schedule the UCAV for maintenance.

By the same token, if the aircraft's onboard computer detected a component failure, it would include this information in the data burst so that a replacement part and maintenance crew would be standing by when the airplane landed at the completion of its mission. To Bob, who hailed from an era when pilots were expected to diagnose problems from the way the aircraft handled, the leap forward in technology was no less impressive than the Corvair's magnificent airspeed.

But in another lesson learned from the JSF, ten million lines of code took a while to completely debug. Charlie had been chasing anomalies of one sort or another since flight testing had begun and the issue with the maintenance reading was a prime example. That said, with only so many hours in the day and engineers to work them, the maintenance bugs had been designated as a lower priority than anything deemed to affect the UCAV's mission performance. While Bob understood the rationale behind this decision, he wasn't sure he agreed. If he'd learned anything in his years as a test pilot, it was that seemingly minute adjustments to complex systems often yielded unintended results. This was the mechanical and electrical version of the famous butterfly effect.

But this was now a philosophical argument, not a practical one. The President of the United States had decided that the Corvair was going to war. Bob's job now was to help facilitate this decision, not second-guess it.

"Any reason to think the glitch could affect the mission profile?" Bob said.

"No," Charlie said. "But I'm still wondering what—"

"Then call it in and get back to monitoring the refueling process," Bob said. "Our clock is ticking."

Bob could tell that his backseater wasn't happy, but for once, the engineer didn't push back. As their pre-mission briefing had made clear, President Ryan's decision had fundamentally changed the nature of the program. This was no longer a science project. Corvair was about to fly her maiden combat voyage and it was warriors like Bob rather than engineers like Charlie who were now calling the shots. Maybe his backseater had finally recognized the shift.

Or maybe he'd found another shiny object.

Charlie might be brilliant, but when it came to his airplane, the engineer was like a dog with a squirrel.

"Roger," Charlie said in an impressive display of radio protocol.

Perhaps the engineer was finally getting the hang of this military stuff. Or maybe the seriousness of the situation had broken through his carefully constructed startup genius façade.

Either way, Bob would take it.

The world's largest state sponsor of terror was on the verge of gaining a weapon that would allow its fanatical leaders to make good on their promises to incinerate their Jewish neighbors and bring about Armageddon. If there was ever a time for seriousness, it was now.

"Snake, this is Grip. Refueling commencing, over."

Bob eased his stick to the left, careful not to crowd the aerial ballet happening off his left wing, but wanting a better vantage point all the same. In the same way he still believed that he could feel what his jet was thinking through the flight controls, Bob believed the best test of the Corvair's autonomous flight capabilities was happening before his eyes.

Refueling in turbulent air was not for the faint of heart. In a real-world mission that now seemed like a lifetime ago, Bob had once lit a single afterburner in order to hold his position behind the tanker as the JP-7 fuel sloshed around in his Blackbird's tanks, adjusting the aircraft's weight and balance on the fly. If the Corvair's onboard computer could master this, a straight and level strike against a fixed ground target would be a no-brainer.

Literally.

The black form held its position with a dexterity that wasn't so much impressive as unnerving. Bob's head knew that the computerized flight controls could react with a speed far beyond what his human mind could manage, but seeing this in action was different than visualizing it. Normally the dance between aircraft and the tanker's refueling boom was a bit of a courting ritual.

Not today.

With a smoothness that defied reality, the Corvair slid into position and held its spacing like the aircraft was a paperweight resting on a desk rather than a machine the size of a school bus navigating the waves on an invisible ocean. The boom slid into the refueling receptacle and the two aircraft were mated.

"Damn. That was fast."

The words came from the boom operator in a radio call that was undoubtedly meant for his crew members rather than the outside world. But for once, Bob appreciated the breach of radio protocol. If the ease with which the refueling happened was an indicator for the rest of the mission, the Iranians would never know what hit them.

"Snake, this is Main. Confirm fuel transfer in process, over?"

"Main, this is Snake," Bob said. "That's a roger. Good flying on the bird's part. That's the smoothest docking I've ever seen."

"Snake, this is Main. Roger all."

For the next several minutes, Bob flew in formation to the mated pair as Charlie confirmed the fuel transfer and played on his laptop. As was his habit, Bob used this brief respite to review his mission profile. Once the UCAV departed, Bob would make his own hypersonic transition, transiting the continental United States and blasting out into the Atlantic.

In this regard, Bob's presence served two purposes. One, he would provide a plausible explanation for the sonic booms the Corvair would leave in its wake. Two, he would be there to meet the aircraft after it completed its mission. Navigating Iran's heavily defended airspace wasn't an easy chore, even for a sixth-generation hypersonic aircraft. There was a very real chance the UCAV would sustain damage, either from ordnance fired against it or, more likely, from the strain its extended mission would place on the aircraft's still unproven airframe.

Either way, the policymakers wanted Bob's eyes on the bird when it tanked again for the long flight home. If he thought the aircraft was potentially unable to complete the trip, the flight path would either be altered or the UCAV landed at a friendly airport. The administration had made it clear they would rather have the prototype fly into the ground at top speed than risk it failing in midflight and thereby falling into adversarial hands.

Bob was part of the contingency plan to make sure that didn't happen.

This wasn't exactly playing tag with Soviet MiGs or even overflying the communist governments in South America. As final missions went, Bob's role probably wasn't going to make the history books. Then again, he was taking the Habu out one more time, and for an old fighter jock, there was no better way to end a career. Besides, while boring missions didn't make for good war stories, they were a hell of a lot better than the ones that almost made you shit your pants.

"Snake, this is Grip. She's all topped off."

"Grip, this is Snake. Roger all," Bob said.

Bob moved his helmet visor as close as he dared to the hot glass, trying to get a better look. He could see the refueling boom retracting as the big tanker buffeted, but the Corvair still looked eerily calm, as if it were anchored in place. With a nonchalance that was unnerving, the Corvair's refueling receptacle closed and the aircraft slipped right, clearing both the tanker and Bob's flight path.

"How we looking back there, Charlie?" Bob said.

"All systems nominal," Charlie said. "We're go for flight."

"Roger that," Bob said. "I'll call it in."

"Main, this is Snake," Bob said after switching to SATCOM. "I confirm refueling is complete and the bird's configured for hypersonic flight. She looks ready to turn and burn, over."

"Snake, this is Main. Copy all. Stand by for hypersonic flight, over."

Bob replied with two clicks of the transmit button. To his right, the Corvair began to drift slightly left.

Then it was no longer just a drift.

"Bob," Charlie said, "I've got—"

"Not now," Bob said as he idled the throttle and yanked back on the stick.

With its minimal g-force rating, the Blackbird was not designed for aerobatics, but the Corvair hadn't given Bob much of a choice. In the blink of an eye, the UCAV had turned what Bob had taken for a small course adjustment into a steep left bank, bringing the aircraft directly across the Blackbird's flight path.

Bob stood his plane on its tail, but it was still close. With a casual disregard that only came with not having another living, breathing human being on board, the UCAV arced across Bob's nose before its twin afterburners ignited and the black wraith accelerated away.

"Man, that was close," Charlie said. "But you got your wish. That baby is going like a bat out of hell."

The Corvair was indeed rocketing away.

Unlike the weightier Blackbird, the UCAV wasn't weighed down with the mass of two pilots and all the associated equipment needed to keep them alive. The SR-71 had a blindingly fast top speed, but its acceleration was more like the stately march to altitude of the monstrous Saturn V rockets that had blasted men to the moon half a century earlier. Significantly lighter with even more powerful power plants, the Corvair accelerated like a sports car. Judging by the rapidly diminishing shape, the hypersonic bird was already approaching Mach 1. The kamikaze maneuver aside, the UCAV seemed to be proceeding to the next phase of its flight profile with great determination.

There was just one problem.

The UCAV's flight plan agreed to in the pre-mission brief charted a course that was basically due east, but the Corvair was not heading in the direction of the rising sun.

It was flying south.

40

"RUN THAT BY ME AGAIN, PLEASE."

Even though the command wasn't directed at her, Mary Pat still winced.

Under normal circumstances, the President of the United States was a levelheaded man who rarely raised his voice.

These weren't normal circumstances.

"We've lost contact with the UCAV, sir."

The silence that followed the Air Force general's pronouncement wasn't so much deafening as deadly. After Shannon Kent's very able overview of Project Chaos and the Corvair UCAV, the President had been intrigued, but had wanted to know more. Shannon had rightly pointed Ryan to the program's executive, an Air Force acquisitions officer by the name of General Perkins.

Mary Pat had been less than impressed with the man.

Unlike Kent, General Perkins had proven to be long on confidence and short on technical details. He'd unabashedly advocated for his new toy, and with few other options, Ryan had gone along with Perkins's recommendation.

That had been then.

Now, the patronizing confidence Perkins had displayed just a few short hours ago was nowhere to be seen.

But neither was he apologetic.

If Mary Pat were to label his tone, she'd call it defensive.

This was not going to end well.

"Forgive me if I wasn't clear before, General," President Ryan said, his voice sounding like steel rasping across leather. "I understood exactly what you meant by the words *lost contact*. My earlier question was a polite attempt to ask you to provide more detail. Since I apparently didn't communicate effectively enough, let me be more precise with my language. How did you lose contact with the aircraft and where in the hell is it now?"

"Yes, sir," General Perkins said. "As I said, the UCAV was a prototype aircraft and as such—"

"You've misunderstood me once again, General," Ryan said. "Perhaps that's because we haven't spent much time together before now, so let me be clear. I don't give two shits about fault or blame. The world's largest state sponsor of terrorism is about to join the nuclear club, and to ensure that doesn't happen, the nation they've promised to wipe off the face of the earth is prepared to use a nuke of their own. I gave my word to Israel's prime minister that I would ensure that didn't happen. So tell me in simple words exactly what happened to the UCAV."

Mary Pat shifted in her seat, considering her options.

While President Ryan didn't need her help, she viewed her job as more consigliere than adviser. The Air Force general was a pompous fool who deserved the dressing down he was receiving, but he was also a liability. If Ryan fired him on the spot, which was where this conversation certainly seemed to be heading, she had no doubt he would walk over to the *New York Times* or *Washington Post* and provide his version of events under the wonderful catchall of *anonymous source*. Ryan's adversaries in Congress would use the story to hammer the President, and suddenly the fight would be about politics rather than Iran.

Mary Pat couldn't allow this to happen.

On one hand, she found the notion of thinking in terms of politics rather than intelligence revolting. Then again, as a CIA officer, she'd had to undertake many actions that she'd found repugnant. It was part of the job then, just like it was part of the job now. Until Jack Ryan left the White House, her job was to guard her boss's flank just like she'd done in East Berlin all those years ago.

"After completing refueling operations, the UCAV unexpectedly deviated from its flight path," Perkins said. "We are still impacting the assessment of this deviation."

Ryan stared at the general without speaking.

Having witnessed enough stares from Jack Ryan, and just maybe having been on the receiving end of one or two herself, Mary Pat understood what was happening. The general did not. Rather than taking responsibility for his actions, the Air Force officer had chosen a different path.

"As I made clear, Mr. President," Perkins said, his back stiffening, "the UCAV was only eighty percent through its evaluation. There were bound to be some bumps in the road."

That the general had said nothing of the sort when they'd discussed the issue in private was of no matter. The acquisition officer now had an audience, and he was clearly playing to it. Maybe he thought the transcript of his words would one day be read back at his reinstatement hearing, or perhaps he was auditioning for a role in a future administration. Either way, the general was clearly covering his backside, and if there was perhaps one thing John Patrick Ryan hated more than an enemy of the American people, it was a bureaucrat more concerned with his reputation than the lives of the men and women he'd sworn to protect.

Things were about to reach critical mass.

"Mr. President," Mary Pat said, "I have an idea."

Mary Pat leaned forward in her seat as she spoke, purposely interposing herself between the President and his soon-to-be-former general. While she had no intention of taking a round for the pompous ass, Mary Pat wasn't above putting herself in her boss's gunline if it meant he'd hold his fire. While she would have loved nothing more than to see the general leave the Situation Room minus his stars, this wasn't the time or place.

At least not yet.

"I'm all ears, MP," Ryan said.

"It's clear that General Perkins is relaying information as he receives it," Mary Pat said. "Maybe we should go directly to someone on the ground."

Mary Pat's words had the effect of extending the blue-suited moron an olive branch, even though she wasn't at all certain he deserved it. One of the things she'd loved about working at the CIA as opposed to its bureaucratic cousin, the State Department, was that the pipe hitters who called the Agency home were about delivering the unvarnished truth to decision-makers in power, not smoothing out ruffled feathers. But as DNI Mary Pat was devoting more and more of her time to soothing bruised egos. In that moment she heard her husband's no-nonsense voice echo through her mind.

It means it's time to retire, Mary Pat.

Maybe her phantom husband was right.

Olive branch or not, General Perkins wasn't taking the hint. Either he didn't want the peace offering, was too dumb to see it, or he truly saw this moment as his opportunity to make a statement. The general opened his mouth, preparing to offer his rejoinder, but the President clearly wasn't interested in what the airman had to say.

"I think—" General Perkins said.

"What did you have in mind?" Ryan said to Mary Pat, speaking as if the general wasn't there.

In the most important way, Mary Pat supposed the man wasn't.

Jack Ryan was hands-down the best boss she'd ever had, but he still maintained his Marine Corps upbringing. In a town that celebrated effort but not outcome, Ryan was decisive and biased toward action. He encouraged his subordinates to accept risk and understood that taking big swings sometimes meant you struck out. Failure Ryan could handle. It was a refusal to accept your part in these failures that the President would not tolerate.

General Perkins had been given three chances to take responsibility for his actions. He'd refused each time. With President John Patrick Ryan, as in baseball, three strikes meant you were out. The acquisitions officer was no longer a voice in the Situation Room.

He apparently just didn't know it yet.

Mary Pat did.

"Before authorizing this operation, you sought out the counsel of the Air Force SR-71 pilot," Mary Pat said. "What was his call sign?"

"Lorenzo," Ryan said.

"Lorenzo, yes," Mary Pat said. "And as I recall, he gave you an honest assessment of the UCAV. Let's get him on the horn and see what he has to say now."

"I think that's a fine idea," Ryan said. "Put him through."

41

BOB EDGED THE THROTTLES FORWARD AGAIN AS HE TRIED TO KEEP THE CORVAIR IN
sight. Out of habit, he used the tiny rear-facing periscope to confirm that the elderly Pratt & Whitney engines were functioning correctly and was rewarded with the sight of twin flame pillars stretching a good two hundred feet aft of his aircraft.

That was the only part of the operation going correctly.

His spy plane was engineered to be most efficient at its cruising altitude of eighty thousand–plus feet and a speed of Mach 3.2. Bob was at neither, which meant he was burning through gas at a frightening rate in an effort to keep the much more aerodynamically efficient Corvair in sight.

Fuel that he didn't have.

Bob's eyes drifted down to the analog TEB counter located next to the twin throttles.

The gauge looked about as important as an old-fashioned odometer except that the black and white numbers moved down instead of up. Currently, their faded digits read 3. The innocuous-seeming number represented the amount of triethylborane, or TEB, shots Bob had remaining. This chemical mixture was required to ignite the Blackbird's afterburners. When the counter reached 0, so did Bob's ability to take his Habu supersonic. So not only was Bob devouring gas at a prodigious rate at an altitude and airspeed at which his aircraft was only slightly more fuel efficient than a brick, he only had three more opportunities to light the afterburners. If he slowed down, he risked not being able to speed back up again.

Perfect.

Just perfect.

Bob was preparing to key the radio in an effort to break the bad news to ground control, when Charlie chimed in.

"Hey, Lorenzo, we've got a call on the SATCOM."

SATCOM.

Back in Bob's day, missions were conducted with absolute radio silence. This meant that during an eleven-hour mission across the Atlantic to check on trouble hiding behind the Iron Curtain, Bob heard no one but his backseater and the refueling boom operator. While the world was undoubtedly a dangerous place back then, sometimes Bob really did long for the good old days.

"Who's on the horn?" Bob said, as he nursed the jet closer to the fleeing Corvair. "I'm kind of busy."

"The President."

This day kept getting better and better.

42

"HELLO, MR. PRESIDENT. WHAT CAN I DO FOR YOU?"

From the tenor of the SR-71 pilot's voice, he could have been reading off the arrival conditions at the Austin airport for a plane full of commercial passengers. Mary Pat didn't know whether this was a function of training paired with a life of high-stress interactions or just that at the pilot's age, nothing really upset him anymore. Judging by her own age-influenced dismissive view of the White House's internecine squabbles, she thought either explanation was possible.

"It's Lorenzo, right?" Ryan said.

"Yes, sir," Lorenzo said. "Good memory."

"I've got a thing for race car drivers," Ryan said. "Maybe when we're on the other side of this, you can come up to the office and tell me some flying stories."

"Love to, Mr. President," Lorenzo said, "but if it's all the same to you, I'd like to keep the chitchat to a minimum. I'm kind of busy up here."

Mouths dropped open all around the conference table, but Mary Pat had to fight to smother a smile. Lorenzo's no-nonsense response was the antithesis of the insufferable self-righteous general currently pouting to the President's right. If Lorenzo wasn't careful, he was likely to talk himself right into a cabinet position.

"I can appreciate that, Lorenzo," Ryan said with a smile of his own. "So I'll keep this brief. What in the hell is going on with my plane?"

The silence answering the President's question stretched for several beats, prompting Mary Pat to wonder if the communications link had failed. Ryan appeared to share his concern. He leaned forward, inching closer to the combination speaker/microphone located on the table in front of him. He was opening his mouth when Lorenzo's voice split the air.

"Sorry about that, sir," Lorenzo said. "This jet is an amazing piece of machinery, but it's no interceptor. I'm trying to keep the UCAV in sight while talking my backseater onto target with our sensor package. He's a good engineer, but he's not ready for prime time just yet."

Mary Pat felt a flash of déjà vu.

These were the same words Lorenzo had used when Ryan had asked for his assessment of the UCAV's readiness for a combat mission.

Hopefully Lorenzo's opposite crew member fared better than the runaway Corvair.

"Okay," Lorenzo said, "we are streaming video of the UCAV now. Are you receiving?"

Ryan looked toward the back corner of the room and the ever-present uniformed communications specialists. The pair were rapidly pressing buttons, which Mary Pat chose to take as a positive sign. A moment later, her optimism was rewarded as the screen opposite the President changed from a grainy satellite image to a high-fidelity video.

"Yes, we've got it," Ryan said.

While Mary Pat agreed with the President that video was indeed displayed on the LCD screen, she wasn't sure exactly what they had. To her, the images looked like a field of blue with a tiny black speck superimposed in the center. Then the field of view changed and Mary Pat was treated to a zoomed-in picture of the Corvair scything through the sky without a care in the world.

"Before we get to talking, I need to give you a warning, Mr. President," Lorenzo said. "The UCAV can do almost twice what my bird can do with the throttles firewalled and eighty thousand feet of altitude between me and the ground. Right now, I'm not able to do either of those for fear of losing her altogether. What I mean to say is that I'll do my best to keep her in sight for as long as possible, but that time might be measured in seconds."

"Understood," Ryan said in a clipped tone, "so I'll try to speak accordingly. We have lost all telemetry from the aircraft and it is no longer responding to commands. What can you tell us from your perspective?"

"A bit more than that," Lorenzo said. "She's flying on a heading of one three five degrees at approximately fifty thousand feet and about twelve hundred miles per hour ground speed. I can also give you a little insight into what she's thinking, but not much."

"What do you mean?" Ryan said.

"Fighter pilots aren't great with computers," Lorenzo said, "so you'll have to bear with me."

"No problem, Lorenzo," Ryan said. "Neither are presidents."

"Yes, sir," Lorenzo said. "Here's the long and skinny of it. The majority of the Corvair's telemetry is backhauled to the ground station through satellite links, and the aircraft receives flight commands the same way. But the engineers designed a larger data pipe for more in-depth, real-time monitoring of all the Corvair's software subroutines. Because the data volume is so large, the transmission range is relatively small, sort of like the difference between the Bluetooth aspect of your phone versus the cellular."

For a self-professed technological dinosaur, Lorenzo was doing a fairly good job of communicating the situation in terms understandable to even the boomers in the room, in Mary Pat's opinion.

Judging by the slow nodding of his head, Ryan seemed to share his view.

"With you so far," Ryan said. "What can your backseater tell us?"

"That's where the good news ends, Mr. President," Lorenzo said. "From what he can see, it looks like the bird is following some kind of preprogrammed flight profile."

"Preprogrammed by who?" Ryan said.

"Unknown, sir," Lorenzo said. "I'm not going to try and relay all the technical jargon he threw my way, but as I understand it, the refueling sequence triggered something lurking in the bird's code. Some kind of Trojan horse."

"Can your backseater establish control of the aircraft?" the President said.

"No, sir," Lorenzo said. "We've already tried. All incoming communications protocols are locked down. Most of the outgoing ones are, too. My backseater is guessing that whoever designed the malicious code didn't know about this telemetry back door as it was only designed to provide data to us during the testing phase. Once the bird went operational, the capability would be removed from the system. Or maybe they didn't care. The transmitter's range is small enough that only a chase plane like us can access it."

"Tracking," the President said. "Is there anything else you can tell us?"

"Actually, yes," Lorenzo said. "While we've been jaw jacking, my backseater has been working. He still can't influence the aircraft's flight profile, but he has managed to determine where it's headed."

"Where?" Ryan said.

"Texas."

Lorenzo's pronouncement caused a murmur of conversation to ripple through the room. Mary Pat shot a glance at Sam, but her assistant shook his head. A moment later, the President gave voice to her unspoken question.

"What in the hell is in Texas?" Ryan said.

"I don't know, sir," Lorenzo said. "But in a little while, we're going to find out."

43

BRIAR WOOD, TEXAS

JACK PULLED INTO THE LONG DRIVEWAY IN FRONT OF AMANDA'S HOUSE AND PUT
the SUV in park. For the last dozen or so miles, he'd been warring with two conflicting urges. Urge one was to dump the Escalade and put as much distance between himself and what had become a rolling crime scene as possible. While the gunman he'd killed was now hidden in a pile of brush along a remote stretch of Highway 79, Jack knew the man wouldn't stay that way.

Contrary to crime movies, it was extremely difficult to dispose of a body.

So he didn't try.

Instead, Jack figured that dumping the killer in the woods would buy himself time to unsort this mess. He had enough experience unsorting messes to know that it was a difficult task to do from a jail cell. But just disposing of the body did not put Jack in the clear. Besides the fact that the SUV's windshield was spiderwebbed and full of bullet holes, the interior was full of a dead man's DNA.

Not to mention Jack's.

If a police officer pulled him over, Jack would go straight to jail, assuming of course the officer didn't just shoot him on sight.

But ditching the SUV meant ditching his only mode of transportation, and Jack wasn't about to do that.

At least not yet.

How he'd become caught up in all of this was still a bit fuzzy even to him, but those convoluted details no longer mattered. Or if they did, the *hows* and *whys* were now subordinate to a much more pressing matter—Amanda and Bella's safety. While the single mom had been more than holding her own the last time he'd seen her, Jack didn't know whether that was still the case. The hit on him at Ray's BBQ had been just that—a hit.

And a professional one at that.

Jack had been taken down by professionals, which meant that the little altercation between Amanda and her daughter's boyfriend was too convenient by half. Plain and simple, the fight had distracted Jack, and his distraction had allowed a killer to jab him in the neck with a fast-acting sedative. It was not lost on Jack that his paramilitary career had begun in a similar manner, except back then Jack had been the one holding the needle. Ten years later, events had come full circle.

But that was neither here nor there.

Deeper analysis of the particulars of the interaction and the conclusions that would follow could wait. *Had* to wait. Bottom line, Amanda and Bella had been used as a distraction. Jack believed that the single mom's participation had been unwitting, which meant her life might now be in jeopardy. But even if that wasn't true, Jack still wanted a word with Amanda. Almost dying twice within eight hours tended to make Jack cranky, and while Graham would never make that mistake again, the rest of his crew were still out there. Jack had loads of unfinished business but next to nothing in leads.

Any way he looked at it, all roads led to Amanda.

Except this road felt rather empty.

Jack killed the vehicle's ignition as he surveyed her house. As before, the dwelling gave off a tidy appearance despite its well-worn exterior. With nothing but empty fields in either direction, it wasn't hard to picture this dwelling as it existed one hundred years ago. Back then, it had been a foothold of freedom. A stake in the ground, hammered into the soil by tough, independent people determined to claw a better life for themselves from the unforgiving Texas dirt.

In that respect, Jack didn't think Amanda was all that different from her forebears.

Though he'd lost his weapon and phone, Jack had secured replacements from Graham in the form of an Android device and a Glock. The pistol Jack could work with, but the phone took some fumbling to access. After switching the biometric data from the dead gunman to himself, he'd powered the device down.

As much as he'd wanted to call Gavin so that the hacker could mirror the phone's hard drive and begin a forensic analysis of the data, Jack didn't. The gunmen were sophisticated and well trained, and he imagined these characteristics went beyond just their tactics. At the very least, he had to work under the assumption that the men would use the phone to track his position the moment he activated it.

At worst, he should assume they might know some more nefarious tricks of the sort Gavin could manage. With this in mind, Jack had decided to consider the device the equivalent of an emergency flare. He had one shot once he powered the device up, and he didn't intend to waste it.

Besides, the person he most desperately wanted to contact was Amanda, but he didn't have her phone number. With this in mind, Jack decided his only option was to drive back to her house to see how things stood. This course of action still made sense from a logical perspective, but it had seemed far less foreboding as he was fleeing the men who wanted to kill him. Now that he was outside the single mom's house, Jack was having second thoughts.

What if Amanda had been a part of the plan to interdict him?

Or worse yet, what if the gunmen had dealt with her and her daughter in the same manner in which they'd intended to silence Jack? Was he ready to stomach whatever lay behind the unassuming front door?

Jack instantly knew the answer to this question.

No, but that didn't matter.

For the same reason he'd stopped to help a stranded motorist hours ago and then found himself shouldering the cause of a single mother desperate to see that her daughter didn't follow in her footsteps, Jack knew that he had to go inside. The concept of honor was not an abstract notion to him. Though at points in his life he'd found himself wishing that his last name wasn't Ryan, Jack had made peace with who he was and his lineage long ago. He'd been raised by an honorable man to be an honorable man.

That wasn't going to change today.

Jack slid the dormant phone into his pocket, picked up the Glock, and exited the SUV. Four quick strides brought him to the front porch. Jack paused for a second, gathering his thoughts and sharpening his will.

Then he knocked.

44

JACK'S FIRST SET OF KNOCKS WENT UNANSWERED. IN THAT TIME, HE CONSIDERED that perhaps he'd gotten all of this wrong. Maybe the confrontation he'd witnessed between Bella, Amanda, and Jeremiah had nothing to do with him. This alternate theory unspooled with the type of energy that only came from wistful thinking. In this version of events, Jeremiah had ceded the round to the indomitable single mother, and Amanda had driven Bella to school before heading home. Jack had already been forgotten as life in Briar Wood returned to the status quo.

Then Amanda opened the door.

Jack sucked in a breath.

While he hadn't known her long, he had shared enough time with her to gain a sense of who she was. Though her premature wrinkles and weariness around her eyes gave the impression of someone who'd been through much at a very young age, Amanda wasn't done. There was an intensity to her. A fire that refused to allow her to accept that what passed for her life now would be all that she could ever achieve. When it came to Bella, this determination manifested as a mama bear fierceness. Amanda would not sit idly by as the small town that had trapped her laid out the same snares for her daughter.

Amanda was a fighter.

Or at least she had been.

The woman staring at Jack was defeated.

In the time since he'd last seen her, Amanda seemed to have aged decades. Her shoulders slumped, and the fine lines that crisscrossed her forehead had deepened into furrows. She looked at Jack with red-rimmed eyes, and what he saw there wasn't fearlessness or spunk.

It was despair.

"What happened?" Jack said.

"I can't talk to you," Amanda said. "I can't talk to anyone."

Her words came out dry. Lifeless. Like the papery leaves strewn across her little yard.

"Why not?" Jack said.

"Because they'll kill her."

"Kill who?" Jack said, dreading the answer.

"Bella," Amanda said. "They showed me a picture of Brian's body when they took her. Just to make sure I understood they were serious."

Brian.

Amanda's boyfriend.

Amanda's cop boyfriend.

The pieces snapped together in Jack's mind as the image of the South African loosening the tourniquet cycled on repeat. Brian hadn't been on the take. That's why he was supposed to find Jack's body. When that hadn't happened, the gunmen had flexed to plan B. Once again, an innocent man had died for the crime of being too close to Jack Ryan.

And now those same monsters had Bella.

"Tell me," Jack said. "Everything."

"No," Amanda said. "They'll kill her."

She spoke the words with a finality that brooked no argument, but she didn't slam the door in his face. Instead, she stared at Jack, her pleading eyes at odds with her words.

She knew.

She might be the assistant manager of a no-name gas station in a no-name town, but Amanda wasn't stupid. She'd grown up way too fast and seen way too many things to believe that the killers who had her daughter were going to honor whatever deal with the devil they'd offered. Amanda still had fight left in her heart, even if she knew the coming brawl was beyond what she could handle on her own. Much like her headstrong daughter, Amanda had never accepted help from anyone.

Until now.

"What I told you before wasn't entirely true," Jack said, choosing his words carefully. "I don't work for the Department of the Interior."

"Then who?" Amanda said.

"Who isn't important," Jack said. "What I do is. I hunt men. Bad men."

"What do you do once you find them?"

"Make sure they don't ever hurt anyone else," Jack said.

Amanda stared at him without speaking, but Jack could see the war waging behind her eyes. On one side was cynicism. The notion that her daughter was already as good as dead, but that maybe, just maybe, if Amanda followed the instructions she'd been given to the letter, the monsters who had taken Bella might release her.

Then there was the other angel sitting on her shoulder. The one who knew from her own hard knock life that things that seemed too good to be true were. That you believe in the assurances of evil men at your own peril. This ember was all that remained of the all-consuming fire that had once animated Amanda. The coal was almost extinguished, but it was still smoldering.

Barely.

"I believe you," Amanda said. "But this job is too big for one man. Even I know that."

"I agree," Jack said, "which is why I have friends. Rough men like me. I'll call them, and they will come. When they do, hell and brimstone comes with them. But first, you have to tell me what happened. Everything. If you trust me, I will get Bella back. I swear it."

Jack wanted to pull the last three words back as soon as they left his lips. He'd been in this business long enough to know that only fools promised an outcome. As Ding was fond of saying, the enemy always had a vote, and when they voted, people died. Amanda was hanging on by a thread, and Jack was asking her to place what little hope she had remaining in him. Practically speaking, the odds that he could recover Bella alive were not great, and he shouldn't allow her to believe otherwise.

He owed her honesty, not happy talk.

Except Jack was being honest. In a revelation that was as shocking to him as it would be to Amanda, he realized that he did believe he could bring Bella home. He didn't just believe it. He knew it with every fiber of his being. Not because Jack thought he alone could take down an unknown number of highly trained operatives.

But Jack wasn't alone.

He had friends with names like Ding Chavez, John Clark, Cary Marks, and Jad Mustafa. Sons of thunder who drove fear into the hearts of men. He was not a betting man, but he would put the lives of his family in the hands of his Campus brothers and sisters any day.

On his own, Jack was just a man.

But with his Campus brethren, he was something more.

Something unstoppable.

Amanda held his gaze for a second more as a tear trickled down her face. Jack was asking her to do something far more difficult than trusting him with her daughter. He was asking a skeptic to find faith.

"Okay," Amanda said with a nod. "I'll tell you."

45

THE HOTEL WAS NO MORE INSPIRING ON THE INSIDE THAN IT HAD BEEN ON THE outside.

Jack had developed stringent criteria for the location. He needed something outside the city limits of Briar Wood but too close for the kidnappers to ignore. He wanted a place far enough off the beaten path that the likelihood of innocents getting hurt was low, but close enough to the main thoroughfare that the establishment wouldn't feel like a trap.

Most important, Jack needed discretion: a proprietor who would take his cash and not ask questions.

The Starlight Inn satisfied all three requirements.

Located in the town of Rockbrook, just ten miles east of Briar Wood, the Starlight Inn had seen better days. Or if not, it certainly hadn't seen many that were worse. The motel consisted of a single row of rooms stretched out along a decrepit length of parking lot from east to west. The establishment was located on the northern side of Highway 79 barely fifty yards from the road. In fact, the door to Jack's room rattled from the overpressure produced by the not infrequent eighteen-wheelers thundering past.

But what the motel lacked in aesthetics, or clean sheets, it more than made up for in location and discretion. Jack had secured the easternmost room by paying cash for two days along with an additional cash security deposit. The manager, a thin white man with stringy hair and droopy eyes, had ceased all attempts at conversation after Jack handed over the bills. For an establishment that probably did most of its business by the hour, a customer who wanted three entire nights must have been a godsend. Or one who could be leveraged for additional security deposits depending on what sort of shenanigans happened on Jack's side of the motel.

But that was fine.

The office was located on the opposite side of the parking lot, and a wood lot bounded the rear and sides of the hotel. In one fell swoop Jack had secured a place that offered both privacy and the seedy vibe he desperately needed. That he would need to shower vigorously when this escapade was over was a given, but Jack still appreciated this little gem. Sure, the room reeked of smoke, a suspiciously brown-tinged water gurgled from the faucet, and the sheets looked stiff enough to stand up on their own, but this was also exactly the sort of place where a man on the run might shelter.

Now that he had constructed his trap, it was time to set the bait.

Jack eyed the windows as the gauzy curtains fluttered in what passed for air conditioning wheezed from the combination heating and cooling unit mounted to the wall. Jack had been more than a little surprised that the device had lumbered to life when he'd set a temperature on the wall thermostat, but he'd rapidly tempered his expectations. While something that might have been a fan seemed to be laboring beneath the unit's cracked exterior, the air it was producing was neither warm nor cold. It did, however, circulate some of the mildewy smell that was competing with the odor of cigarettes for prominence. Jack's allergies had kicked into high alert about two seconds after he'd settled into a dusty chair. He hadn't hit the point of constant sneezing yet, but his throat was itching and his eyes were watering.

No matter.

Though his liberated SUV was parked around the side of the motel as would be in character for someone on the run, the nearly translucent curtains didn't do much to obscure Jack's view of the parking lot. And since his room sat on the property's far eastern edge, Jack had a great view of the traffic coming from Briar Wood. This was the direction from which he expected his eventual guests to arrive.

Now he needed to deliver their invitation.

Digging the dead gunman's phone from his pocket, Jack placed the inert device on the dirty plastic coffee table. The mobile somehow looked at home centered between a pair of cigarette burns to the right and a permanent condensation ring to the left.

Powering up the device was the first step in his plan, but Jack still hesitated. It wasn't that he doubted the wisdom of what he was about to do next. He'd thought through the courses of action available to him ad nauseam during his drive from Amanda's house. Bottom line, the police in Briar Wood were compromised, and he had every reason to consider himself a wanted man. His DNA would be all over multiple homicide scenes, most damningly by the railroad tracks where Brian had been killed. In the eyes of anyone who carried a badge and a gun, Jack was a cop killer, and cop killers did not fare well in the justice system. Even if he turned himself in, he'd immediately be isolated and interrogated. Sure, his story ought to eventually check out, and his employment with The Campus would certainly help there, but this all would take time.

Time that Bella didn't have.

He hadn't said as much to Amanda, but he agreed with the single mom's assessment of the situation. Whatever the shooters were after hinged upon some sort of timeline. Once their job was complete, they would have no need to exert further leverage over her.

Which meant they would have no need of Bella.

An optimist would view this as proof that the gunmen would honor their promise to Amanda and release her daughter. Jack wasn't an optimist, especially when it came to kidnappers.

The gunmen were professionals.

Experienced operatives.

By the time the deadline they'd given to Amanda expired, Bella would have been in their midst for hours. This was more than enough time for an observant person to note things about their captives, like mannerisms, accents, and nicknames. Any or all of these subconscious tells could be used by a trained investigator to build a profile of the captors. Professionals would recognize the teenager for the loose end that she was and eliminate her. It wouldn't be personal.

But Bella would be just as dead.

Jack wasn't going to allow that to happen.

He turned on the phone and watched as the device came to life.

The clock had just started.

Though he didn't know for sure, Jack was betting that the remaining shooters had engaged in some variation of the same decision-making process he'd just gone through. On the one hand, they could consider Jack's presence as sunk cost. Sure, he'd seen them and driven away with one of their members, but was he worth going after? No matter the skill of the operatives, sometimes a mission just didn't go as planned. Part of the difference between a good operator and a great one was knowing when to fold your hand instead of chasing the cards in the hopes of regaining lost money. Continuing an operation that had clearly gone off the rails was often the difference between a bad day and a catastrophic one. But that was a hard line to see, especially when your blood was hot and you were down a teammate or two.

Jack typed in the code he'd chosen after leveraging its previous owner's biometrics to unlock the device and then watched as it joined both the cell network and the motel's questionable Wi-Fi. Somewhere, probably not too far away, the shooters were more than likely clustered around a table not much better than the dilapidated one in Jack's motel room. They might have even been war-gaming scenarios. Arguing hypotheticals surrounding what they would do if their comrade's missing phone came back online.

And now it had.

The theoretical had just become the actual. Jack had chummed the waters and given the direct action team a tempting target—an isolated motel in an adjacent town. Were he the team leader in question, Jack would have looked at the blue icon representing the missing phone and posed the inevitable question to his teammates: *Is the risk of conducting a final cleanup operation worth the reward?*

He didn't know how the men would answer the question. Jack thought he knew what he would do in their shoes, but the cold hard truth was that he wasn't in their shoes. He hoped they'd be aggressive and that their bloodlust would get the better of them, but Jack had learned long ago the folly of relying solely on hope.

Which was why there was a second element to his plan.

Jack brought up the dialing app and then scratched a series of digits on a piece of scrap paper. Not for the first time in the last several hours, he found himself wishing for his own phone. He'd committed the number he was supposed to dial to memory, but was a bit shaky on the second and third series of digits. These he'd annotated on the Notes app of his mobile, where the information was currently doing him no good. After writing and then rewriting the message he wished to convey to ensure it was in the correct format, Jack prepared to dial.

The message service he was about to call was a relatively new addition to The Campus's bag of IT tricks. As with what seemed to be a more and more common occurrence, Jack was the driver behind this new capability. During his last operation, The Campus had been directly targeted and almost decapitated.

For an organization accustomed to operating below the radar and with the impunity that came with anonymity, this had been a wakeup call to say the least. In the grueling after-action review that followed, everything about the way the organization had historically done business had been examined. All aspects of The Campus were on the table and everyone was invited to participate and provide input. While painful, this session generated a number of beneficial changes, including the new capability Jack was about to employ.

The Campus's duress signal.

The previous attack against The Campus had incapacitated nearly every operator in the field and led to John Clark's capture, an event that the off-the-books intelligence organization was ill-equipped to deal with. When Clark had asked Jack what he'd wished for most during those first few moments as he'd tried to single-handedly sort through a mass casualty event and the kidnapping of a fellow operative, Jack's answer had been simple—a way to call for help.

Jack had made the comment without thinking, but Clark had immediately seized on the idea. Special operations teams that worked in denied environments each had a single duress word that could be broadcast in the event that an American was in danger of being killed or captured. One simple word that galvanized the battlefield and vectored all available resources to the stricken operator.

Clark was determined to implement a Campus equivalent.

Enter Gavin.

Campus operations were seldom conducted with military-style loadouts. Instead, operatives usually dressed as civilians with low-profile communications gear rather than tactical radios. This meant that any duress signal had to be accessible through cell phone. Or, in Jack's case, the grimy desk phone perched precariously next to the bed. Jack wasn't a germophobe, but he would have loved to be able to wipe the handset down with a pack of alcohol wipes before placing his call, but he couldn't. Then again, if his plan worked, germs from a hotel phone would be the least of his worries.

He didn't bother to think about what would happen if it didn't.

Instead, Jack lifted the handset and began punching numbers.

The call rang once.

Twice.

Then the automated voice belonging to an answering service clicked on. Ignoring the options the feminine voice presented to him, Jack dialed in the sequence announcing that a Campus operative was in duress.

The voice asked Jack to press the number 1 to confirm his entry.

He did.

Then he entered the telephone number for the mobile innocuously sitting on the table. Once again, he was asked to confirm his entry, and once again Jack pressed the number 1. The opening guitar riff for Van Halen's "Top of the World" echoed through the earpiece. This was the song Jack had chosen and was his audible proof that his unique Campus identifier had now been flagged as a duress mission. Jack listened to the song until Sammy Hagar's unmistakable voice cut through the guitar.

Then he replaced the phone in its cradle.

It might be heresy, but Jack was a Van Hagar fan. Diamond Dave was a great showman, but nobody could match Hagar's powerhouse vocals. Maybe when this was all over, he'd have to see Hagar in concert with his new band. Rumor had it that before cancer took his life, Eddie Van Halen was considering a tour featuring all of the Van Halen members past and present.

Now that would never come to be.

Jack thought about the life choices he'd made. Opportunities he'd seized and those he'd let pass him by. Jack couldn't travel back in time to see Eddie Van Halen one last time, but maybe he could start living today in a way that produced fewer regrets tomorrow. His pending marriage to Lisanne was a new beginning.

A chance to begin to live intentionally.

After a final glance at the docile-looking cell phone, Jack stretched out on the threadbare comforter and stared at the ceiling. He'd just done the equivalent of spray-painting his name in the sky with a red arrow pointing at the Starlight Inn.

Now he just had to wait for someone to come knocking.

46

TWO CONTRADICTORY URGES WARRED WITHIN JACK'S CHEST.

On the one hand, he couldn't help but think that what he'd set in motion was the most reckless action he'd ever undertaken as a Campus member. He'd just done the equivalent of illuminating the Bat-Signal. At this moment, the entirety of his team was reorientating their efforts toward a nowhere Texas town because they thought Jack was captured and/or in danger of losing his life.

Jack was neither.

At least not yet.

Though if his plan didn't come to fruition the way he intended, Jack thought that there was a better than fair chance his life would still be over. It would just be Clark, rather than a set of mysterious gunmen, who ended it. But that was a problem for later. The timeline that the kidnappers had presented to Amanda had been unambiguous.

Four hours.

Four hours of silence would buy Amanda back her daughter's life.

Jack didn't trust this bargain for a moment, but knowing the gunmen's timeline was still useful. Whatever was going to happen would occur before the deadline they'd given Amanda, which meant that Jack had closer to three hours. Maybe less. He'd pulled some rabbits out of hats during his time as an operator, but three hours was cutting it close, even for Jack. So with no other options available, Jack decided to play his hole card.

Himself.

The gunmen were desperate to keep the blowback from the last several hours to a minimum. Desperate enough to keep Amanda alive instead of just killing her outright and ridding themselves of the troublesome mother. To that end, Jack had to believe that he also represented a troublesome loose end. Though he still had no idea what the men's ultimate play might be, he felt fairly safe in his assumption that the gunmen would view him as a liability. What they would do to contain that liability was still a bit of a gamble.

Okay, perhaps more than a bit of a gamble.

Jack turned over on the bed, trying to mitigate the single spring that seemed determined to excavate his left kidney. The coffee table that had once held the gunman's cell phone was now empty, while the motel's landline had been moved next to the bed.

Both of these changes to the room's decor were by design.

The cell was now under one of the stolen vehicle's seats—a place where the device could have reasonably fallen undetected. The desk phone, on the other hand, had been rendered inert after Jack unplugged the line from the wall. He'd considered just taking the handset off the hook, but thought that would look a little too staged even though he did expect the room to soon be the site of a struggle.

At least Jack hoped there would be a struggle.

While he was pretty confident that the gunmen wouldn't be able to ignore the tempting sight of their dead comrade's stationary phone, he was less certain about their reaction. Jack was banking on his hypothesis that the extraordinary efforts they'd gone to to plug leaks in their operation would mean they would want to understand what level of risk he represented to their ongoing criminal enterprise by understanding what he knew. Which meant they would need to interrogate him.

If this was the case, the best place to do this would be wherever they were holding Bella.

But there were problems with this plan.

Many, many problems, beginning with the most urgent: What if he was reading the situation wrong?

The most conservative play would not be to interrogate Jack.

It would be to silence him.

There was a very real possibility that the shooters would breach his motel room, put a pair of rounds in his chest and one in his head, and call it a day. If that happened, the Campus duress alarm he'd triggered and the assets undoubtedly already moving his way would be for nothing.

And Bella would die.

But if he didn't use himself as bait, the gunmen would complete that operation and silence the remaining loose ends.

And Bella would die.

Jack eyed the door to his room as if to reassure himself that it was still closed as he turned the last thought over in his mind. During his time as a paramilitary operative, he had always tried to minimize the suffering of innocents, but he was no caped crusader. Sometimes, good people still died. Early in Jack's stint with The Campus, Ding had provided him with a bit of perspective on this subject.

You can't save everyone.

The words were simple, but the sentiment behind them profound. Not only was it physically impossible to right every wrong in the fallen world Jack called home, but attempting to do so was the path to madness. He hadn't known Bella for long and the interaction he'd shared with her had not been what anyone would term pleasant.

Was she an innocent teenager who'd had a rough go of her life?

Yes.

Did that mean he was obligated to risk his life on her behalf?

No.

So why was he doing this?

Jack sighed, almost willing the door to crash open.

What did it say about him that he'd rather face torture or death than wrestle with the question that he knew was driving all this? When Jack thought about Bella, he didn't see a sixteen-year-old blond-haired, blue-eyed Texas girl. Instead, he saw a defiant brunette with coffee-colored skin and blazing chocolate eyes.

Emily.

Lisanne's niece Emily.

This was always going to be about Emily.

At just over thirty years old, Jack knew that he was in no way qualified to become an instant dad to a troubled teenager. But he also knew that, just like Bella, if he said no, there was no one waiting in the wings to say yes. Jack loved Lisanne and he knew his fiancée loved him.

Loved him enough to choose their relationship over taking in her niece.

Jack would not force Lisanne to make that choice. He would reorder his life and learn how to be a father to Emily for the same reason that he was willing to risk it for Bella. Ding was right—you can't save everyone. But sometimes you can save someone. Or in this case, maybe two someones.

Jack started to smile as he pictured Lisanne's reaction.

And then his motel door crashed open.

47

"EXCUSE ME, MA'AM? I NEED YOU."

Mary Pat Foley paused mid-sentence at the interruption. After this long in government service, there weren't many things that caught the DNI flat-footed. Being interrupted during her weekly roundtable was one of them.

"Sorry, Sam," Mary Pat said, looking over her shoulder at her assistant, "but I'm in the middle of something. Can it wait?"

In the middle of something was a bit of a misnomer.

As the director of national intelligence, Mary Pat occupied something of a rare position in the sprawling government bureaucracy. As with the case of Homeland Security, her position sprung out of the ashes of 9/11. But unlike DHS, she did not helm a multitiered agency with thousands of employees. She was the notional head of the intelligence community, but she did not control the funds Congress allocated to the separate entities that made up this multiheaded beast.

This was a problem.

In Washington, D.C., more than perhaps any other place on earth, money equated to power. With Mary Pat not in charge of their budgets, the directors for the eighteen organizations that called the intelligence community home looked at her role as one that was largely ceremonial. To make matters worse, the directors who also held cabinet-level positions expected direct access to the President, further relegating Mary Pat's influence.

Early on in her stint as DNI, Mary Pat had realized she was at a bit of a crossroads.

Down one path lay the trail that most DNIs had followed. In this variant of her job, Mary Pat would serve as President Ryan's confidant, but her authority as DNI would end the moment she left the White House. Option two meant trying to establish herself as the genuine head of the IC, even though this route was littered with potholes, the largest inevitably being that she would have to find a way to bring her counterparts to heel.

It didn't take a genius to recognize that option one was the path of least resistance.

Mary Pat was not a path of least resistance kind of girl.

Though she intended to vacate this city the moment Jack Ryan climbed aboard Marine One for the final time, Mary Pat believed that her boss had put her in this role for a reason. Ryan could have just made her his national security adviser—a role that would have given her the President's ear without the hassle of the corresponding charter to lead an agency.

He hadn't.

For reasons that perhaps only he had understood, Jack Ryan had made her the head of one of Washington's most dysfunctional entities. With each year that passed, the lessons learned from 9/11 and the sense of urgency lent to those lessons faded a bit more. Though he hadn't explicitly said so, Mary Pat could only assume that her friend had made her DNI because he actually expected her to direct the entities under her notional control.

And that's what she would do.

"No, ma'am," Sam said. "It can't."

Mary Pat chose to ignore the groan that emanated from the far side of her conference table.

Bill Jones led the Department of Energy's Office of Intelligence and Counterintelligence.

Or at least that's what his job title implied.

The problem was that Bill was not very good at his job.

Though Jack Ryan did his level best to eliminate political considerations from his decision-making criteria, he was enough of a realist to understand the contours of the battlefield. He was President, not emperor, which meant politics was not something he could ignore. Everyone in elected politics owed something to someone and the list of *someones* grew larger every day.

From lobbyists, to peers, to party leadership, to colleagues across the aisle, to the American voter, the countless compromises and favors traded on a daily basis were the oil that greased the government's machinery. Bill's appointment was meant to pay back one political marker or another. Since her boss detested this kind of maneuvering, Mary Pat could only guess Bill's addition was Arnie's work, and while granting the man stature had worked to cement his caucus closer to Ryan, the result was an incompetent in a role he was by no measure qualified to hold.

But as DNI, this was Mary Pat's problem.

Which might go a long way toward explaining why Ryan had placed her in this job to begin with.

"I'm sorry for the inconvenience," Mary Pat said as she stood. "I know your time is incredibly valuable and I realize the sacrifice each of you make by attending my roundtable. Sam would not interrupt us for frivolous reasons. If you'll indulge me for just a moment, I'll be right back."

"Take your time," Bill said.

The comment was murmured just quietly enough that it could

be mistaken for an under-the-breath utterance, but just loud enough to carry the length of the crowded table. Mary Pat felt her face flush, but she resisted the urge to spin around and deal with the asshat in a manner appropriate with his boorish behavior. Mary Pat typically held these roundtables at her office in Liberty Crossing far away from the intrigue always surrounding the White House to help demonstrate that she was about results, not optics. By hashing through intelligence and threats there, Mary Pat had hoped that she could get people to let their guards down and actually work rather than audition for their next job.

Today, she was attempting to thread the needle by staying close to the President during the unfolding events while not breaking the battle rhythm she'd established with her roundtables. In Washington, crises were never in short supply. If she set the standard by canceling the gathering every time something bad happened, her attendees would find an excuse to do the same.

Bill hated being required to attend the meetings and would use any opportunity to push back. Mary Pat knew she'd have to deal with the pompous blowhard sooner or later, but today wasn't the time or place. Instead, she exited the conference room and eased the door closed behind her as if she hadn't heard Bill's outburst.

But she had, and judging by his clenched fists, Sam had as well.

"Let it go, Sam," Mary Pat said, forestalling the outburst she knew was coming. "We've got bigger fish to fry."

Her twentysomething assistant was smart, a hard worker, and fiercely protective of his boss. Mary Pat had hired Sam for the first two qualities and found the third secretly endearing, but she treaded that line carefully. She understood how Sam felt for her, because Mary Pat held her boss in the same regard. She would lie down in traffic for Jack Ryan, but she was also old enough to have gained the wisdom that allowed her to channel this instinct into productive avenues.

Sam, on the other hand, had the fiery, headstrong attitude that came with youth. While he was probably not more than one hundred and thirty pounds soaking wet, when it came to her, Sam was a honey badger. Were this two hundred years ago, she could imagine her staffer challenging Bill to a duel or, at the very least, a good old-fashioned brawl. Imagining Bill flat on his back with a dazed look on his face after being on the receiving end of a right hook was good for Mary Pat's soul.

But she didn't tell this to Sam.

Mary Pat was trying to mentor her protégé, not turn him into a mafia henchman.

Besides, when it came to punching Bill in the mouth, she had dibs.

Sam's eyes darted from her face to the closed conference room door, looking for all the world like a puppy who desperately wanted to chase a ball after receiving the command to *stay*. He was young, but his boyish looks made him seem even younger. To combat this image, he dressed like a middle-aged professor in a tweed sport coat and khakis, and he wore his brown hair long.

Even now, the mother in Mary Pat wanted to brush back the curl that was dangling across Sam's forehead and then steer him toward the cute girl in Travel who blushed every time he walked by. What did it say about her that she viewed her protégé through the same lens she saw her children?

That was a thought probably best left for later.

"Sorry, you're right," Sam said, returning his focus to her. "Clark's on the line for you. The red phone."

The warm, maternal feelings Mary Pat had been trying to hide vanished in an instant.

"Did he say what he wanted?"

He shook his head. "Just that he needed you. Now. I transferred the line to the huddle room."

Sam opened the door to a closet-sized room to his left.

"Okay," Mary Pat said, "but I need you to babysit while I'm gone. Make sure nobody leaves."

"Sure thing, boss," Sam said, a wolfish grin sliding across his face.

"Be nice, Sam," Mary Pat said. "I mean it. I'll deal with Bill when the time is right. That time is not now. Got it?"

"I won't do anything you wouldn't do, boss," Sam said, his grin widening.

Mary Pat shook her head with mock severity even though she wanted to smile. If he could survive his twenties without alienating the wrong people, her little wolf cub was going to be a formidable political operative.

But like her ongoing feud with Bill, that was a topic for later.

Mary Pat entered the room, waited for the soundproof door to swing closed behind her, and then picked up the red handset. "John? It's me."

"MP, we've got trouble."

48

THOUGH SHE KNEW THAT JOHN CLARK DIDN'T CALL HER ON THE RED PHONE TO shoot the breeze, both the words he spoke, and the tone he used to speak them, were instantly sobering.

John Terrence Clark was an anomaly.

Like Mary Pat, Clark had a history with President Ryan. A history drenched in blood. The two had solidified their relationship during a paramilitary operation gone wrong in the jungles of Colombia. But that violent fight was not Clark's first exposure to combat.

Far from it.

Clark had cut his teeth as a Vietnam-era Navy SEAL and SOG member. From there, he'd matriculated to the CIA as a paramilitary officer, during which time he'd served his nation in a variety of ways, usually as the stick as opposed to the carrot. Back in the nineties, Clark had come in from the cold for a time, serving as the first commander of the Rainbow counterterrorism organization before disappearing again, this time as the director of The Campus. In one form or another, John Clark had been doing bad things to bad people for a long, long time.

If he said there was trouble, Mary Pat believed him.

"What have you got, John?" Mary Pat said.

"Junior just sent out an operator duress signal."

Mary Pat sucked in her breath.

While The Campus was certainly not the Peace Corps, the paramilitary organization had taken more than its fair share of lumps over the last several months. The men and women who staffed the off-the-books entity were the epitome of high achievers, and the problem sets they encountered were not insignificant. Sooner or later, an organization that punched above its weight class as often as The Campus did would find itself the target of a foreign adversary.

That reality had come crashing home in a turn of events that found Clark captured and the rest of the Campus operatives reeling from a targeted attack. Mary Pat had used the event to push for The Campus's formal inclusion in the greater IC, but not because she wanted to exert more control over the nimble entity. On the contrary, she believed that The Campus's autonomy was one of the things that made the organization so effective. But an entity that boasted only a handful of paramilitary officers could not be expected to use only their own in-house resources to take on nation-states.

President Ryan had agreed with her argument in principle, but integration was being done in a slow and deliberate manner, primarily due to Clark's boisterous objections. While Mary Pat understood the need to move slowly in order to preserve what made The Campus most effective, she also believed that forewarned was forearmed. From her perspective, Pandora's box had already been opened.

The Campus had been targeted once.

It would be targeted again.

Now it seemed that her fears might have been prescient and

perhaps understated. This call wasn't just about any Campus operator. The duress signal had been triggered by Jack Ryan, Jr.

The President's son.

"What do you need?" Mary Pat said.

This was not the response Mary Pat wanted to give, but it was the right one. Though the former CIA station chief in her wanted to take charge of the situation, this was not her role. Clark was not a novice to blown operations and he had more on-the-ground experience than probably anyone she knew. Mary Pat needed to see herself as a resource for the Campus director of operations, not his boss.

"Nothing right now," Clark said. "I already have one Campus asset in place, and I'm moving more into position as we speak. If that changes and I need more hitters, you're my first call. As far as intelligence resources, Gavin's tied into the greater IC databases. Depending on what he finds, we might need some help tasking domestic collection platforms, but we're good in that area right now, too."

"Okay," Mary Pat said, dragging out the word as she thought. If Clark didn't need resources in the form of people or taskings, why was he calling her?

Then she understood.

"You want me to serve as a buffer to the President."

"Exactly," Clark said. "My guess is that the boss already has his hands full with what's going on with Iran. I want you to know what we're doing, but I don't want him distracted with something we can handle. If that changes, I'll let you know."

Mary Pat was silent for a moment as she sorted through the implications of Clark's ask. In an ideal world, this would never be an issue, but they didn't live in an ideal world. Until or unless the President told his eldest son that he could no longer work as a shadow warrior, this conflict of interest would continue to be an issue. The President could not be President if he was focused on his personal needs rather than the nation's. Maybe this wouldn't be true in every case involving Junior, but Mary Pat believed it was the right call today.

"Agreed," Mary Pat said. "And John?"

"Yes?"

"Bring him back."

Clark didn't reply.

He didn't need to.

49

LAS VEGAS, NEVADA

"YOU FAILED," HANS SAID, POINTING A BONY FINGER AT CARY'S CHEST.

The German's vehemence was enough to make the waitress serving the adjoining table glance over her shoulder.

"Don't worry," Jad said with a friendly smile. "He means us."

The waitress chuckled.

Hans did not.

"You were well paid to accomplish a simple task, and you failed," Hans said. "I want my deposit returned. Now."

"Hans, Hans, Hans," Jad said, reaching for his coffee cup. "This is no way to win friends and influence people."

"What?" Hans said.

"I think what my partner is trying to say," Cary said, "is that you might want to see the results of the operation before pronouncing judgment."

"I saw the results firsthand," Hans said, pounding his fist on the table. "You failed!"

Cary took a deep breath as he considered his life choices.

The three men were seated at the Peppermill, one of the many eateries that offered a breakfast of startlingly good quality. In fact, were it not for the angry European seated across from him, Cary might have been enjoying himself. The smell of coffee and fresh-cooked bacon saturated the air while the floor-to-ceiling windows along the far wall offered a breathtaking view of the sun rising over the famous Las Vegas strip. Though it was barely dawn, teams of groundskeepers and sanitation workers were already hard at work, doing their part to maintain Vegas's façade.

Unlike many other tourist destination spots, Las Vegas did not offer one version of itself on travel brochures and another after visitors happened upon its streets. For better or worse, Vegas was a city that delivered what it promised. Which was more than Cary could say of his would-be German employer.

"Actually, we succeeded in rather spectacular fashion," Cary said. "Perhaps a little too well."

"What are you—" Hans said.

"Shh," Jad said, holding up an index finger. "Have some respect for our fellow diners. Vegas hangovers are legendary."

Doing his best to maintain a straight face, Cary placed his cell on the table and turned the device so Hans could see the screen. "You asked for the target's driver's license," Cary said. "Here it is.

"His name is Sebastian," Cary said, swiping left to show the back half of the license, "but you already know that because he works for you."

For once, an expression beyond irritation or outright anger was reflected on the German's face.

Surprise.

Genuine and unadulterated surprise.

"How did you—" Hans said.

"Because we're good," Jad said. "Very good."

"You never got ahold of his wallet," Hans said, his face tightening. "This is a trick."

"How do you know we never got his wallet?" Jad said.

"Because I watched," Hans said. "Everything."

"Maybe you did," Jad said, "but how do you know you didn't miss something?"

"I know," Hans said.

"You're right," Cary said. "You do know. Because Sebastian wasn't carrying a wallet, was he?"

Cary took his phone back as he spoke, careful to grip the device only by its outer edges. The last question had been a bit of a gamble, but if there was ever a time to go all in, Vegas was the place to do it. Besides, the certainty with which Hans made the statement was a pretty good indication. As was the embarrassed flush stretching from throat to ears.

"He's messing with us, isn't he, boss?" Jad said.

"'Fraid so," Cary said.

"Hmm, hmm, hmm," Jad said, shaking his head. "Guess he's never heard the phrase *fuck around and find out*."

"He has now," Cary said.

"I think they're cops."

The statement came from behind Cary and to his left.

In a first, Cary and Jad were both seated with their backs to the restaurant's entrance. Since Cary had ensured that he and his spotter arrived at the eatery before Hans, he could have taken the adjacent seat with the view of the hotel lobby.

He had not.

This wasn't because he'd wanted to watch the Vegas sunrise. No, Cary had deliberately chosen a position of disadvantage to provide Hans with the illusion of control.

It was time to strip that illusion away.

"Hey, shitbird," Jad said, smiling over his shoulder at the newcomer. "We saved you a seat."

Without being bidden, the newcomer took the offered chair.

It was Sebastian.

"We're not cops," Cary said, locking gazes with Hans.

"Then explain to me how you obtained a copy of my associate's driver's license."

"The same way we now have a copy of yours," Cary said. He unlocked his phone as he spoke, spun the device around, and showed Hans his European driver's license. "As we told you during the interview process, my associate and I are former members of a military unit with a very unique mission set. As a result, we have a peculiar set of skills. One of those is sensitive site exploitation."

Cary touched another button and the phone's screen turned a vivid blue, illuminating three prominent fingerprints.

"These are yours," Cary said, pointing to the prints. "They're partials, so the quality isn't super great. Sebastian's, on the other hand, were perfect since he was kind enough to take several pictures for me. Anyway, the resolution for both of you was more than good enough to run through the database."

"What database?" Hans said.

"One maintained by the Department of Homeland Security's Office of Biometric Identity Management," Jad said. "It's a mouthful, I know. It's also one of the most comprehensive biometrics repositories in the world, with portals into the US intelligence community and Interpol."

"And you have access to this?" Hans said.

"Not anymore," Cary said, "but I do have a friend who owes me a couple of favors. At least I did. After reaching out to him twice in the last hour, I'm now the one who owes favors. As you can imagine, I don't like owing favors. So you're going to pay me the money you owe us plus another ten thousand for needless jackassery."

"Needless jackassery is expensive," Jad said.

"Exactly," Cary said. "You will pay us and we will amicably part ways."

Left unsaid was what would happen if Cary didn't receive his money. But that was fine. Hans seemed like the kind of guy who could read between the lines.

Most mercenaries were.

Hans pulled out his phone, stabbed an icon, and began to type furiously. After a second or two he looked up. "The money's in your account."

"Fantastic," Cary said. "I'd say it was nice doing business with you, but we both know that's a lie. As far as I'm concerned, you two jackwagons are persona non grata in my circle of friends."

"Wait," Hans said. "What you just did was a test run. There's another job."

"No shit, and not interested," Cary said, getting to his feet.

"Just listen," Hans said, grabbing Cary's arm.

Jad moved liked quicksilver.

One moment he was seated at the table. The next, he was standing with a blade at Sebastian's throat. Cary had been looking at Jad the entire time and still wasn't sure how his spotter had moved that fast. It was as if he'd teleported from one location to the other.

Impressive.

But maybe not to Hans.

"Easy now," Hans said. "Easy."

"Hands on the table or I will gut this dipshit like a fish," Jad said. "Now."

Hans placed both palms flat on the table. Cary looked from the mercenaries to his fellow diners, trying to gauge their reaction to the fracas. Based on the nonresponse, either their give-a-shit factor was exceptionally low or Jad was exceptionally fast.

Maybe both.

"Thanks, brother," Cary said.

"Anytime, boss," Jad said.

"Check it out, stud," Cary said, dropping his voice to a whisper as he leaned over the table to Hans. "My partner and I are gonna walk on out of here. I would not advise trying to follow us."

"Twenty-five thousand dollars cash," Hans said. "Each. That's how much the job pays."

"Details," Cary said.

"Come to my hotel room," Hans said.

"Not a chance," Cary said. "I will text you an email address. You will transfer a ten-thousand-dollar retainer into our account and send the details. We will read them and give you an answer. Either way, we keep the retainer."

"That's bullshit," Sebastian said.

Or at least that's what Cary thought he said. The second word came out a bit garbled, probably because it was hard to talk with Jad's knife pressed into the base of his jaw.

"Okay," Hans said. "You have—"

The opening riff to Van Halen's "Top of the World" blasted from Cary's phone, drowning out the mercenary.

"Hold that thought," Cary said as he pulled his phone from his pocket, "I've got to take this."

"Are you serious?" Hans said.

"Try the coffee," Jad said. "It's delicious."

The line was delivered in the same no-nonsense manner Jad had used with the rest of the conversation, but Cary knew his partner well enough to hear the undertone of concern. A concern that had not been there a moment earlier when the Libyan American had first pressed a knife to Sebastian's throat. Like Cary, Jad knew what it meant when this particular song emanated from any of their devices.

A Campus operator was in trouble.

Jack was in trouble.

"Hello," Cary said, doing his best to keep his voice light.

Though Cary hadn't known Jack for long, the Campus operative had already earned his respect. Jack was calm under pressure and a steady hand in a gunfight. He was not the sort of person who would sound an alarm unnecessarily. If Jack had triggered the duress alert, the shit was about to go down.

"Cary, it's Gavin. Jack's in trouble."

Cary resisted pointing out that he knew this already. While the team had done a test run of the alert system once Gavin had finished coding the new app, this was the first operational use. Each Campus operative's mobile would activate with the ringtone of whoever had triggered the duress alert, but only Gavin would have the details behind the call.

This was done for two reasons.

One, while it was good for the alert to go out to everyone, someone needed to exercise command and control over the response. Though Gavin occasionally ventured into the field, his area of expertise meant that he brought the most to the fight when he was behind his keyboard with access to The Campus's mainframes. Therefore, it was logical to assume that in any given emergency, Gavin was most likely to be at The Campus's headquarters and thereby in close proximity to The Campus's leadership team.

Two, in the event of a duress instance, the first actions The Campus would take would center around ascertaining the location and condition of the triggering operative. While The Campus had access to the greater intelligence community's resources, the initial triage would undoubtedly fall to Gavin. Actions like geolocating the missing operative and attempting to access the camera and audio functions of their phone would all be in Gavin's wheelhouse.

This was why Gavin was the one working the phones.

"Tracking," Cary said. "What's the location on the ping?"

He'd stepped away from the table, but didn't want to go far since Jad still had a knife pressed to Sebastian's throat and Hans was looking more antsy by the moment. But Cary was also conscious of operational security and he wanted the mercenaries to overhear as little of what was said as possible.

As Cary watched, Sebastian attempted to wiggle free.

Jad was having none of it.

As the man tried to scoot back, the Green Beret crowded into the booth next to the mercenary, transferring the blade from Sebastian's throat to his ribs. Hans caught Cary's eye and opened his mouth, but Cary forestalled the German's comment with an upraised finger.

"One more minute," Cary said, locking eyes with Hans.

"What?" Gavin said.

"Sorry," Cary said. "In the middle of something here. What have you got?"

"Oh, right," Gavin said. "The duress alert wasn't dialed by Jack's phone. Instead, it came from a landline associated with a cheap motel. The last ping from Jack's cell was nearby, but about fifteen miles west of the motel. The duress signal also contained the number of a second phone that I think—"

"Gavin," Cary said. "The location. Now."

"Oh, right," Gavin said. "The landline is located in the town of Briar Wood, Texas. The closest airport is in College Station."

"Got it," Cary said. "We're headed to the Vegas airport now."

"Make sure you go to the general aviation side," Gavin said. "This is a duress response, so time is of the essence."

"What's that mean?" Cary said.

"It means you're flying private. I'll make the arrangements."

"How will I know which jet?" Cary said.

"It'll be the one sitting on the tarmac with the engines running," Gavin said. "Money is no object. I'm gonna hire whatever can get you to Texas the fastest."

Cary could get used to this.

"Roger that," Cary said. "Out here."

He hung up and then turned to Jad. "Come on, partner. We've got a plane to catch."

Jad gave Sebastian a none-too-gentle shove and then stood, collapsing the blade and squirreling the knife away in one smooth motion.

"Wait," Hans said. "What about the job?"

"Get somebody else," Cary said.

50

THE BUZZING OF HER PHONE STARTLED LISANNE AWAKE.

Groggy from lack of sleep, she fumbled for the vibrating device twice before corralling it with her less than nimble fingers. Squinting at the clock across the room, she swore. She'd intended on grabbing only a catnap while waiting for the car service to drop off her rental. Judging by the incriminating red digits staring back at her, Lisanne had missed that mark.

"Hello?" Lisanne said.

Or at least that's what she tried to say.

Her voice wasn't any more well rested than the rest of her.

AFTER FINISHING WITH OFFICER BRADSHAW, SHE HAD FOUND THE NEAREST MOTEL on Google Maps and then summoned an Uber. In yet another surprise in a town that was full of them, the Brazos River Lodge wasn't half bad.

Though the motel's façade gave off a decidedly *Schitt's Creek* vibe, the rooms were both large and recently renovated. Rather than a single dingy domicile with furniture that had been outdated in the '70s and a sagging mattress that changed customers by the hour, the rooms sported chic decorations and updated furnishings.

The wall that had previously separated adjoining units had been removed, rendering each space into a suite of sorts. The bathroom was modern and clean, the tile floor sparkling, and the coffee station sported three different blends along with a note instructing the tenant to look in the stocked refrigerator for a choice of flavored creamer, half and half, and oat milk. Were it not for her current circumstances, Lisanne might have put the Jacuzzi tub and assortment of candles to use.

Instead, she'd hung her jeans and shirt to dry on the curtain rod ringing the shower and settled onto the bed to wait for the text announcing her rental car's arrival. She'd purposely refused to climb beneath the sheets, reasoning that the chill air would keep her from sleeping too deeply.

So much for that theory.

"LISANNE? IS THAT YOU?"

Gavin's high-pitched voice was easily recognizable.

As was the worry behind his tone.

"Yeah, it's me," Lisanne said.

The words were undecipherable even to her so she cleared her throat and tried again. "It's me, Gavin."

"You sound horrible," Gavin said.

"Been a long night," Lisanne said, pushing herself into a seated position. She thumbed to the Find My app as she spoke, and clicked on Jack's identifier, hoping to see him online.

The same three words glared back at her.

No location found.

"Jack triggered the duress signal," Gavin said.

The words hit her tired brain like a jolt of electricity. The fuzzy-headedness and fatigue vanished as adrenaline pumped into her bloodstream.

"How?" Lisanne said. "His phone still shows offline."

"He used a landline instead of his cell," Gavin said. "It's only a couple of miles from your location. Can you check it out?"

She could.

A FRIGHTENINGLY SHORT AMOUNT OF TIME LATER, LISANNE WAS PULLING INTO THE parking lot of yet another low-budget motel. How towns this small could sustain so many cut-rate motels was beyond her. It's not like this was a tourism hotbed and there really couldn't be that many people here using pay-by-the-hour rooms, could there? She put this line of thought into her "stuff to think about when I'm bored" mental pile. She had more important things to worry about.

Like the room at the far end of the parking lot with an open door.

Lisanne pulled into the spot across from the room and put the transmission into park. When booking her car, she'd asked for a sedan, but the service had delivered a truck. She'd intially been annoyed, but now was glad for the change. The elevated front seat offered her a sight line through the room's grungy window.

Pulling out her phone, Lisanne dialed Gavin.

"Are you there?" Gavin said.

"Yes," Lisanne said, ignoring his lack of decorum. The stress must be getting to everyone. Gavin was not just a faceless IT analyst. He was Jack's friend. "At least I think I'm at the right spot. There's a room at the far end of the hotel. It's the one Jack would have chosen."

"That's good news," Gavin said, some of the worry leaving his voice.

"Maybe not," Lisanne said. "The door's wide open and from my vantage point the room looks empty."

"What does that mean?" Gavin said.

Lisanne thought she knew exactly what that meant, but she kept her thoughts to herself. Instead, she said, "Who are my nearest Campus assets and what's their ETA?"

"Jad and Cary," Gavin said. "They're coming from Vegas so I would anticipate another forty minutes or so before linkup."

"That's some fast traveling," Lisanne said, holding the phone between her chin and shoulder so that she could draw her pistol. "Are they coming into Austin or Houston?"

"Neither," Gavin said. "I got them a private jet."

Lisanne filed that little bit of information away for later as well. While she was glad the Green Berets were headed her way, what she had to do next, she would need to do alone. Well, not exactly alone.

"All right, Gavin," Lisanne said, setting the pistol down on the seat next to her. "I've only got one hand, so I'm going to route the call through my Apple watch. You'll be on speakerphone as I take a look in the hotel room. Okay?"

Nothing about this was okay. To his credit, Gavin didn't point this out. Instead, he cleared his throat and reminded her why the operators loved him.

"Kick ass, Lisanne. I've got your back."

Lisanne opened the truck's door, grabbed her pistol, and prepared to do just that.

51

IT SEEMED TO TAKE AN ETERNITY TO CROSS THE TEN OR SO FEET FROM THE PARKING lot to the motel room. Though the transition lasted only seconds, it was more than enough time to consider a multitude of frightening scenarios that ran the gamut from finding that she had identified the wrong room to discovering a scene that would shatter her into a million pieces. The intense mental acuity that came with a fight-or-flight response allowed her to see every detail in high definition. She concentrated on this external stimuli in an effort to drown out the uncertainty roiling her thoughts.

This might have been a mistake.

Lisanne noticed things in her state of hyperawareness that she probably would have otherwise missed. The coolness of the breeze tickling her neck, the muddy boot prints on the cracked concrete outside the door, and the gauzy curtains billowing through the window's shattered remains. What she'd mistaken earlier for an open window was in fact the remains of a break-and-rake.

The preferred method a tactical entry team would use to secure a blind spot.

"I'm going in, Gavin," Lisanne half whispered, half spoke.

She wanted to believe the catch in her throat was because she was trying to be quiet.

It wasn't.

Lisanne brought the pistol up to the high ready position. She could now see the door resting against the wall and she understood why it was open. A blackened section of steel beneath the handle told the story. Someone had affixed a breaching charge to the locking mechanism.

With a shuddered breath, Lisanne barreled through the fatal funnel formed by the doorway and into the room proper.

"Police," Lisanne yelled. "Get on the ground."

She hadn't been a member of law enforcement for some time, but under moments of duress the mind and body both fell back on the familiar. She swept the room with her pistol's stubby front sight post. A bed to her left with a small nightstand was offset by a rickety-looking desk holding an equally rickety-looking TV to her right. A mirror and a tiny sink straight ahead.

A door to the left of the sink.

The bathroom.

Lisanne crossed the room with the rolling stride she'd practiced countless times on the range, trying like hell to compensate for her pistol's wobbling front sight post. Shooting accurately while moving was one of the most difficult tactical skills to master. Doing it one-handed bordered on impossible.

Lisanne hoped she wouldn't have to try.

She reached the bathroom at almost the exact instant she realized that having one hand made clearing a room a bit tricky. If the door was closed, she was screwed.

It wasn't.

At least not all of the way.

The door was partially cracked. Lisanne shouldered the door

open, allowing the handle to smash into the doorstop as she cleared the tiny space consisting of a toilet and a combination bathtub and shower. The shower curtain was open, revealing an empty tub.

The room was a dry hole.

"It's clear," Lisanne said, sagging against the door. "The room's empty."

"Any sign of Jack?" Gavin said, his high-pitched voice echoing from her wrist.

"Stand by," Lisanne said. Backing out of the bathroom, she surveyed the hotel room for the first time, looking at the room itself rather than just scanning for people. Reaching along the wall, she found the switch and flicked on the overhead light.

That's when she saw the blood.

52

COLLEGE STATION, TEXAS

LISANNE WAS SURPRISED BY THE RUSH OF EMOTION THAT SEEING THE TWO MEN deplane engendered. The pair looked more than a little at odds with their surroundings.

Easterwood Airport's FBO in College Station, Texas, did a thriving business for the rich and mostly famous. From Aggie sports to events held at the Texas A&M Hotel and Conference Center, there was no shortage of well-heeled visitors who used the centrally located airport as a landing pad for their private jets. Lisanne didn't doubt that the workers who staffed the FBO's front desk had witnessed all manner of glamorous, edgy, and chic fashionistas descend from the cabins of private jets.

Jad and Cary didn't fit this bill.

In fact, the two Green Berets looked almost sheepish as they shuffled down the portable steps in their contractor casual wardrobes. Even so, Lisanne felt her eyes tearing up at the sight of the two men. The last hour had passed agonizingly slowly, and while the commandos didn't make the problem set she was facing appear any less daunting, she was no longer alone.

That counted for something.

Lisanne waved from behind the sliding glass doors once the

men reached the concrete. The polite but firm man behind the desk had let her know that only passengers were permitted on the flight line, and Lisanne had nodded her understanding. But now that her fellow Campus operatives were just yards away, it was all she could do not to run out and greet them. Instead, she forced herself to wait stoically in the lobby as the two approached. Yes, she'd last been in a hotel room covered in Jack's blood, but in this moment Lisanne was an operative, not a fiancée.

At least that had been the plan.

"Hi," Lisanne said, offering Cary an awkward handshake as the Green Beret strode into the lobby.

He was having none of it.

"Come here, girl," Cary said, wrapping her in an embrace.

She stiffened for a moment at the unexpected contact and then found herself relaxing in the strong arms enfolding her. A moment later she felt Jad's chest against her back as the second Green Beret joined in the group hug.

"We're going to get him back," Cary said, his breath warm against her hair.

"Damn straight," Jad said from behind her. "That boy still owes me dinner."

Though her eyes still burned with tears, Lisanne found herself laughing instead of sobbing. In that moment, she believed Cary with an intensity that rivaled her love for Jack.

They would get him back.

And heaven help anyone who stood in their way.

"I WANT TO HEAD BY THE HOTEL ROOM FIRST," CARY SAID, "IF THAT'S OKAY. I DON'T doubt that you pulled everything of value during your sweep, but I'd still like to see the place for myself."

"Why?" Lisanne said.

Cary shrugged. "I can't say exactly other than my gut says that it's worth seeing. Jad and I are snipers, which means we're trained observers. When I'm developing a pattern of life on a target, I have some things I'm looking for, but often the most important detail finds me rather than the other way around. There's no substitute for seeing something with your own eyes."

Lisanne rattled off the hotel's address from her position in the truck's passenger seat as she turned Cary's answer over in her mind.

Could she have missed something?

Sure.

She was a cop and therefore trained on how to secure a crime scene and recover evidence, but she also couldn't ignore the fact that this crime scene was different than any she'd ever processed. The man she intended to marry had been assaulted in that room, and she couldn't pretend that her relationship to Jack didn't come with unwarranted blind spots. There was a reason why cops weren't allowed to work cases involving their loved ones. Being a good investigator required the ability to maintain an objective distance, and there was nothing objective about how she felt right now.

"Let's talk about the elephant in the room," Cary said as he activated his turn signal. "You're worried that being personally involved with Jack will adversely affect your performance. Don't be."

Lisanne stared at the Green Beret in shocked silence.

Was she really that transparent?

Pushing away her surprise, she considered how to answer and then just as quickly gave up the debate. As a fellow veteran, Lisanne felt a special kinship with the two commandos. She'd never served in special operations, but her time in the military had still taught her the benefit of calling a spade a spade. Instead of hedging or deflecting, Lisanne barreled into the conversation full steam.

"Why not?" Lisanne said.

"Because we're here," Jad said.

"That's right," Cary said with a nod. "ODAs consist of just twelve men."

"On a good day," Jad said.

"That's right," Cary echoed, eyeing his spotter in the rearview mirror. "Operating hundreds or thousands of miles away from reinforcements with only a dozen shooters teaches you what it means to be part of a team. Teammates don't hide their blind spots from each other."

"They acknowledge them," Jad said.

"Will you knock that shit off?" Cary said.

"What?" Jad said. "I'm helping."

"Not from where I'm sitting," Cary said.

"Fine," Jad said. "I'll explain what you missed *after* you're done talking."

Cary shot his spotter a murderous glare, which Jad replied to with a toothy, but silent, grin. "As I was saying," Cary said, turning back to Lisanne, "Jad and I are your teammates. You need to trust us to cover your blind spots when it comes to Jack. Otherwise, you're likely to second-guess yourself when you should be acting. That's when things go sideways. Got it?"

Lisanne slowly nodded.

She did get it.

"Do you guys take this show on the road?" Lisanne said.

"Shit," Jad said, "I'd need my own bus to go on tour with him. And don't get me started on his snoring."

"I don't snore," Cary said. "What you hear is an echo of your own obstructed breathing. Anyway, Lisanne, the point is that you need to consider us your guardrails. If we think you're making a decision that's emotional instead of logical, we'll let you know. Go with your gut and trust us to be your safety net. Okay?"

"Oorah," Lisanne said.

"You had to go and remind us you were a Marine," Jad said, shaking his head.

"*Am* a Marine," Lisanne said. "Once a Marine—"

"Yeah, yeah," Cary said. "Kumbaya time is now officially over. Instead of more hand-holding and feelings talk, how about you bring us up to speed on what you've been doing while my fellow commando and I were eating peanuts and reading the in-flight magazines."

Lisanne nodded and took a minute to gather her thoughts.

THE SCENE SHE'D ENCOUNTERED IN JACK'S HOTEL ROOM STILL MADE HER NAUSEOUS. Furniture had been strewn everywhere and the acrid scent of discharged explosives filled the air, but it had been the bed's tousled sheets that had torn at her soul. A splotch of dark crimson covered the dirty white pillow case and the cream-colored comforter as if the abstract artist who had painted it had extended beyond her canvas in a fit of artistic zeal.

But the crusty substance was not paint and Lisanne knew the work hadn't been done by an artist. The assaulting team had breached the door and window with a kind of cold-hearted efficiency. This was not a crime scene as much as the remnants of a raid executed by men who knew their business. As an MP in Iraq, Lisanne had both executed raids and seen their aftermath. She would put whoever had stormed Jack's hotel room on the same level as the Marine Raider teams she'd worked alongside.

With a shuddering mental effort, Lisanne had compartmentalized what had happened on the bed. Someone had been hurt, and odds were that someone was Jack. Beyond that, drawing further conclusions was both counterproductive and a waste of mental energy. It was a fool's errand to attempt to diagnose the injury by the amount of blood present at a crime scene. Sometimes minor injuries like scalp wounds bled profusely, while deep, life-threatening traumas to the abdomen might only bleed internally. Besides, if they'd wanted Jack dead right away, she would have found a body on the bed, not blood. Jack was either hurt badly or he wasn't. Either way, Lisanne could do nothing about that now. At that moment, she needed to gather as much intelligence as possible about who conducted the raid and where they might have taken Jack.

Then she needed to vacate the premises.

Chances are that whatever had gone down here went down loud. The police were probably already on their way, and Lisanne had needed to make sure she was gone before they arrived. The last thing she needed was another heart-to-heart with Officer Bradshaw.

Locking her emotions away, Lisanne had surveyed the place with cop eyes. She'd mentally set up a search grid and worked it quickly and efficiently, looking for anything the men had left behind.

She'd found nothing.

Perhaps even more important, other than the residue from the breaching charge, she'd smelled nothing. Gunpowder had a very distinctive odor. A sharp, almost painful assault on the nasal passages. As a Marine, cop, and now Campus operative, Lisanne had spent hours and hours on the range and she knew what the aftermath of a gun battle smelled like.

This hadn't been it. Whoever had taken Jack had done so without firing a shot. Lisanne had felt herself shudder as she'd digested these thoughts. With no body lying on the bed and no gunfight aftermath, odds were that her fiancé was still alive.

That had been the good news.

The not so good news had been that whoever had kidnapped Jack was good.

Very good.

Lisanne had found nothing that would have been left by the attackers, and more ominously, not a single trace of Jack. No pocket litter, articles of clothing, or clandestinely scribbled notes. He was gone and the hotel room had been completely sanitized.

Or at least that had been her impression during her admittedly hurried search.

Maybe Cary's suggestion to go back for a more thorough looksee wasn't such a bad idea.

"I WENT THROUGH HIS ROOM AND DIDN'T FIND ANYTHING," LISANNE SAID. "EXCEPT for blood. A lot of blood."

Her voice choked on the last word, and Cary reached over to squeeze her shoulder without taking his eyes from the road. One of the things she'd had to get used to when working with special operators was their fondness for hugs. They referred to each other as *brother* and did not use the word lightly. Each interaction started with a round of backslapping as if they hadn't seen each other in months rather than hours or days. Leaving involved the same ritual in reverse. Lisanne had observed this from afar while working adjacent to Marine Raiders or the occasional SEAL team while deployed, but she'd never been part of the pack.

Until now.

As a female, Lisanne had been a bit wary of being on the receiving end of a vigorous masculine hug, but to her surprise, she found that she enjoyed being part of the family. Cary squeezing her shoulder felt like exactly what it was—a brother reassuring his younger sister that everything was going to be all right.

Clearing her throat, Lisanne pushed past the emotion and continued her summary.

"Gavin told me you were coming, so I picked up some kit."

"You went shopping?" Cary said. "For us? I'm touched."

"And also a bit worried," Jad said. "My team sergeant's smedium shirts are not easy to find."

"They say *large* in block letters on the tag," Cary said. "I can't help that the manufacturers don't have man sizes."

"Then maybe you need to stop shopping at Baby Gap," Jad said.

"Please ignore my spotter," Cary said. "He's just worried about his dwindling supply of hair gel. What do you have?"

"I hit a military surplus store," Lisanne said. "I scored a couple of assaulter packs and a med kit. I'm assuming you're carrying your sidearms?"

"We don't leave home without them," Cary said.

"This isn't bad for the open market," Jad said, rummaging through her purchases.

"Welcome to Texas," Lisanne said.

"That's my girl," Cary said with a smile. "Now, how about a sitrep on what the hell is going on here?"

Lisanne nodded.

She'd expected this, but since Gavin had been the one relaying the duress signal information, she wasn't sure what the Green Berets had already digested during their short hop from Las Vegas to College Station.

"What do you know?" Lisanne said.

"That there's big trouble in little Texas," Jad said.

"For once my spotter is not exaggerating," Cary said. "We know that Jack was going toe to toe with highly trained shooters, but not much more than that. Apparently, he'd tasked Gavin to do some digging on a couple of leads, but Jack hadn't pieced together what was going on."

"Gavin didn't update you during the flight?" Lisanne said.

"He didn't get the chance," Jad said. "Wi-Fi on the bird wasn't functioning. Besides, we were sleeping."

Lisanne raised an eyebrow that Cary must have somehow caught from the corner of his eye.

"What?" Cary said. "Even Green Berets need their beauty sleep. Besides, we just rolled off an op in Las Vegas and were running on fumes. You read in on Vegas?"

Lisanne shook her head. "Not really. Jack and I were supposed to be on vacation."

"Famous last words," Jad said.

"No matter," Cary said as he navigated another bend in the road. "I think it was a dry hole, anyway. A merc company was looking to hire some ex–special operations bubbas. Not exactly a national threat."

She filed this away for further consideration.

She knew Clark well enough to know that The Campus's director of operations must have thought the lead had some merit else he would never have assigned precious members of his perpetually undermanned roster of operators to the task. But she also understood that whatever Jad and Cary had been working now took a backseat to recovering Jack.

The duress signal had been triggered, which meant that every Campus asset and operative should now be focused on Texas. Unfortunately, Clark, Ding, and their operational team were currently in Europe working a separate job. According to Gavin's last update, the men were in the process of disentangling themselves from the operation in order to head for Texas, but with flight time alone stretching more than nine hours, Lisanne wasn't expecting them anytime soon.

Cary and Jad were it.

"Okay," Lisanne said, "here's the CliffsNotes version. Before triggering the duress signal, Jack recorded an audio file that he attached to the alert. In the span of just a few hours, he'd witnessed two murders and taken part in a pair of gunfights."

"Sounds like another day at the office for our fearless leader," Jad said.

"Can you not?" Cary said.

"What?" Jad said. "I'm just saying what you're thinking. We've been in more tight scrapes in the ten months we've known Jack than the twelve years you and I were part of Triple Nickel. That boy is to trouble what honey is to bees."

"I don't disagree," Lisanne said, interjecting before the two siblings could get going again, "but this time, things are different. What's happening here goes way beyond a couple of shooters with bad intentions."

"How so?" Cary said.

"Jack's summary doesn't make a lot of sense," Lisanne said, putting into words what she'd been mentally chewing on for the last several hours. "It started with the murder of a man who was looking for his missing son. This in turn led to a woman named Amanda who had information that potentially contradicted the police narrative with regard to the missing teenager. But things escalated quickly."

"Escalated how?" Cary said.

"Jack was left for dead, and Amanda's daughter was kidnapped," Lisanne said. "Jack didn't die, but one of the small-town cops did. Amanda's boyfriend."

"Then what happened to our boy?" Jad said.

"He was taken to a spot outside of the town that the gunmen apparently intended to sanitize. Jack escaped, but not before the gunmen killed the people inside the building."

"Look," Cary said, "I'm not trying to downplay the severity of what Jack found, but from what you've described, things haven't risen to a level that justifies Campus involvement. Especially on American soil. I mean, aren't there rules about that kind of thing?"

Lisanne paused before answering.

That was actually a very good question.

There very well may be some sort of prohibition about operating in America. After all, The Campus had been conceived as a nimble organization meant to deliver the type of justice to America's enemies that larger, more bureaucracy-bound entities like the Central Intelligence Agency could not.

Still, that was a question for later.

At the moment, Lisanne had just one concern—rescuing Jack.

But that didn't make a portion of Cary's question any less valid.

"You're right," she said, "in the sense that Campus operations are not usually concerned with run-of-the-mill criminal activity. But I don't think this is that. According to his sitrep, the shooters Jack went up against were not gangbangers or even cartel members. They were mercenaries. Foreign mercenaries."

Once again Jad and Cary made eye contact via the rearview mirror. This time, Lisanne didn't think it was because the Green Beret team sergeant was irritated with his spotter.

"You thinking what I'm thinking, boss?" Jad said.

"Does seem like an awfully convenient coincidence," Cary said.

"What?" Lisanne said.

"The people we were scoping out in Vegas were foreign mercs," Jad said. "The guy doing the negotiating had a German accent, but his running buddy was South African. They were looking to hire Americans. Their first offer was somewhat legit, but it was a smoke screen for the real job."

"Which was what?" Lisanne said.

Jad shook his head. "We were in the process of figuring that out when we received the duress signal. Based on where things were heading, I don't think they wanted us to feed the poor in Haiti."

"Agreed," Cary said, nodding his head. "I pegged them as doing shady shit, but I was picturing somewhere overseas. Maybe we got that wrong. But even if this is the same bunch of hombres, Jack's kidnapping is a domestic issue. Why not rely on a domestic solution like federal or local law enforcement?"

"Because we're up against more than just mercenaries," Lisanne said. "The cop Jack saw die was shot by mercenaries, but the officer was murdered by fellow cops. One of them loosened the injured officer's tourniquet so that he'd bleed out. Jack watched it go down."

"Al'ama," Jad said, his Mediterranean complexion darkening. "That's some evil shit right there."

"It gets worse," Lisanne said. "When Jack first stopped answering his phone, I got worried. I reached out to a local Texas Ranger buddy of mine. I told him what was going on, and he got really excited. He arranged for us to link up just outside of town and told me not to talk with the Briar Wood police."

"What did he have to say?" Cary said.

"Don't know," Lisanne said. "He was T-boned in a hit-and-run."

"That's no bueno," Jad said. "What's the prognosis?"

"He's dead," Lisanne said.

"Of course," Jad said. "This is a Jack op after all."

"Easy now," Cary said to the rearview mirror. "We can't blame that boy for everyone who drops dead in his vicinity."

"True or false," Jad said, "when we work with Jack the body count goes up exponentially."

Cary huffed, but didn't bother to reply.

Instead, the Green Beret glanced at Lisanne. "I understand now why you're handling this the way you are. If your friend was ambushed by the same shooters who have Jack, whatever's happening here goes beyond just the local yokels. Texas Rangers are a state asset."

"I'm also cautious about the feds," Lisanne said. "FBI agents are human just like everyone else. Corruption spreads like cancer, infecting everything it touches. Anyone in close proximity to the Briar Wood cops should be viewed with a healthy bit of suspicion. I'm sure national assets like the Hostage Rescue Team are clean—"

"But they're in Virginia," Jad said, "not here."

"Exactly," Lisanne said. "Besides, Jack could have called for federal help, but he didn't. He called us."

"I can buy your reasoning," Cary said, "but I still don't understand Jack's play. He must have triggered the duress signal before he was captured, meaning he knew the bad guys were coming. But he still sat in his hotel room and let them take him. Why?"

"That part I know," Lisanne said, shaking her head. "He was using himself as bait."

"Seriously?" Cary said. "Why would he do something that boneheaded?"

"Come on, boss," Jad said. "We once rescued that boy from death by crucifixion. How did he thank us? By running back into the compound manned by the same bad guys who'd just tried to crucify him. When it comes to Jack, nothing surprises me."

Lisanne bristled at Jad's words, but she knew the Green Beret wasn't the target of her anger.

Not really.

She loved Jack with her entire being, but that didn't mean she didn't see his faults. Jack acted impulsively, and in the past, his propensity to listen to his gut sometimes got him in trouble.

Okay, so maybe *sometimes* was a bit too generous of an assessment. Jack was a magnet for trouble. But it was the kind of trouble men like him were born to create. Her fiancé was one of the most noble and selfless men Lisanne knew. Jack wouldn't have offered himself to the gunmen on a whim. There was a method behind his apparent madness, and she needed to believe in him as she tried to understand his thinking.

But that didn't make the Green Berets' concerns any less valid.

"Maybe there's something at the hotel I missed," Lisanne said. "Something that will help us better understand Jack's strategy."

Lisanne made this statement more as a consolation prize than because she believed what she was saying. Had she been in shock from the sight of what was most likely her fiancé's blood on the bed?

Probably.

Did this mean she'd missed something of significance during her assessment of the room?

She didn't think so.

Lisanne knew what happened to the fragile human body during a crash sequence. Even if the victim wasn't impaled by the steering wheel, crushed by buckling metal, or sliced open by chunks of glass, the g-forces produced when a vehicle traveling sixty miles per hour decelerates to zero in a fraction of a second wreaks havoc on flesh and bone. During these violent crash sequences, the heart can literally tear away from the surrounding arteries. She could handle seeing a puddle of blood on a bed without losing her wits.

Or so she hoped.

Either way, it didn't really matter.

Lisanne needed the Green Berets to buy into the notion that Jack hadn't just closed his eyes and leaped from a cliff, trusting that his Campus comrades would save him. She needed to build cohesion in her ad hoc team, and agreeing to another teammate's suggestion was an excellent first start. Besides, the motel parking lot was just ahead on the right. In a moment or two, the commandos would have their look at the room.

"Hey, boss," Jad said, "we got cop cars in the parking lot."

Or perhaps not.

53

LISANNE INSTINCTIVELY TURNED TO HER LEFT AS THEY DROVE PAST THE PARKING lot, giving whoever might be watching a look at her black hair and nothing else. With the advent of cheap, reliable cameras, surveillance was everywhere. While Lisanne hadn't noticed any overt sensors when she'd conducted her earlier survey of Jack's hotel room, it was better to assume there were some that she'd missed.

But that didn't mean she wasn't curious.

"What do you see?" Lisanne said.

"A couple of patrol cars," Jad said, "and at least one ambulance. Either another customer is experiencing a medical emergency, or Jack's kidnapping wasn't as clean as we'd thought."

Lisanne reviewed her earlier visit, thinking through whether she'd noticed anything else amiss. She hadn't. The parking lot had been empty. No, that wasn't quite right. There had been one vehicle. A battered, rusted hulk of a pickup truck occupying a spot on the side of the lot farthest from the rooms.

A spot where the motel's staff might park.

"An employee," Lisanne said, kicking herself for not thinking of this sooner. "Maybe the person manning the front desk."

"Probably right," Cary said as he motored past. "Either way, it looks like a recon of Jack's room is out. What else have we got?"

That was a very good question.

"Gavin's working a couple of different angles," Lisanne said, "but we don't have anything solid that points to Jack. At least not yet. He tried to localize Jack's phone, but no dice."

"All right," Cary said as the flashing red and blue lights faded. "Let's give Jack the benefit of the doubt. He's not insane, nor does he have a death wish. If he used himself as bait, then he either left us a way to locate him that we're still not seeing or thinks he'll be able to signal us once he gets to where the mercenaries are."

"Okay," Lisanne said, turning the Green Beret's words over. "Then where does that leave us?"

"I think we need to divide forces," Cary said. "You keep working with Gavin to find Jack's bread crumbs. You're the brains of the operation."

"What's that make you guys?" Lisanne said.

"The brawn," Jad said.

"Exactly," Cary said with a nod. "My spotter and I need to get ready for an extract. We have rifles to zero, kit to load out, and transportation to arrange. Chances are, the bad guys have Jack somewhere off the beaten path. If it were me, I'd want a remote location where I could see any hostiles coming from miles away and act accordingly. Once we get Jack's location pinned down, we're not gonna be able to drive up to the front porch."

"I have a suggestion," Jad said.

"I'm all ears," Cary said.

"Maybe pull over," Jad said.

"Why?" Cary said.

"So the helicopter that's been following us for the last three miles doesn't land on our roof."

Lisanne angled her head so that she could see out the window. Jad wasn't joking. A helicopter's skids dangled fifty feet above the pickup's roof. The acoustic insulation in this model must have been top-notch because she hadn't heard so much as a whisper.

"Huh," Cary said, activating his hazard lights as he pulled onto the shoulder. "What do you suppose he wants?"

"We're about to find out," Jad said.

54

TO THEIR CREDIT, THE GREEN BERETS WERE NOT OVERLY AWED BY THE FACT THAT A helicopter had almost landed on the truck's roof. Neither were they content to stay seated and wait for the chopper's occupants to announce themselves. Though neither commando said anything, Lisanne felt the atmosphere change as soon as Cary slid the transmission into park.

Both men released their seat belts and drew their pistols.

"What's the plan?" Lisanne said as she unfastened her seat belt.

The helicopter settled just in front of the pickup in a blast of rotor wash and engine noise. It was a smaller variant most often used by student pilots and sightseers and it vaguely resembled a tadpole. The transmission rose from the center of the aircraft via an elongated dorsal fin–type mast, and its tail boom looked thin and spindly. The helicopter lacked the roar associated with the jet engine–equipped higher-end models like the ubiquitous Jet Bell Ranger, but the rotor wash was still significant enough to hurl debris and dust against the truck while the wind gusts rocked the vehicle on its shocks.

"Jad and I are going to say hello," Cary said as the helicopter's passenger door opened. "Maybe you should stay in the car."

"Nope," Lisanne said.

Reaching into the glovebox, she withdrew her pistol, set it on the seat next to her, and then cracked open her door. Living with just one hand had required Lisanne to learn many tasks anew, but never was her disability more pronounced than the seconds before a gunfight.

"Thought you might say that," Cary said. "Stay ten feet behind us and to the right. Position yourself off the bird's nose. You've got the pilot."

That was more like it.

Lisanne nodded and pushed open her door. By the time she extracted herself from the vehicle, reached back inside for her weapon, and then oriented herself back toward the threat, the Green Berets had already halved the distance to the helicopter. With a curse, Lisanne put her long legs to use as she squinted against the debris kicked up by the man-made dust devil. If the helicopter's occupants were overly alarmed by the sight of three armed and evidently well-trained shooters converging on them, they didn't show it.

The helicopter's copilot door opened, and a man climbed out.

Lisanne wasn't sure what she expected the aviator to look like, but she knew this wasn't it. He was dressed in cowboy boots, blue jeans, and a white T-shirt with the black Gonzales flag prominently displayed. The cannon and single star were stretched over broad pectoral muscles with the COME AND TAKE IT slogan centered on his sternum. Oakley sunglasses protected his eyes from the whirling grit.

The man hunched as he shuffled beneath the swirling rotor blades and then straightened once he was clear. He waited for the approaching commandos with his arms folded across his chest.

Between his thick red beard, broad frame, and six-foot-plus height, the man looked more Viking than aviator. The wind gusts alternated between plastering the T-shirt against his lean torso and billowing the fabric like a sail. During one of the iterations, Lisanne saw the outline of a pistol printed against his waist.

Ignoring Cary's instructions, Lisanne altered course to converge on the Viking. While what the Green Beret had said made tactical sense, Lisanne thought it more prudent to focus on the man who had a weapon instead of the pilot who might or might not. Even if the aviators were up to no good, Lisanne didn't think the pilot would shoot through his own windshield.

Besides, she wanted to hear what the Viking had to say.

Since Lisanne ran, she arrived in time for the opening verbal salvo. At least she would have if there had been a verbal salvo. But instead of speaking, the men eyed one another like feral dogs from opposing packs. As evidenced by their many hours working as a tactical pair, Jad had offset to Cary's left, putting him close enough to hear the coming exchange, but angled so that the Viking couldn't cover both Green Berets with one gun. The commandos had their pistols out, but the muzzles were pointed at the pavement.

So far.

The Viking on the other hand might have been standing guard. While his eyes were impossible to see behind his sunglasses, his face was expressionless. Other than his slowly moving jaw, the big man could have been carved from stone. Leaning to the side, the Viking spit a brown stream onto the pavement, expertly missing his boots. While Lisanne had been a cop and Marine long enough to understand that there were rituals to observe when it came to rival alpha males meeting, she couldn't get the bloodstained sheets out of her head. Bad men had Jack and the clock was ticking.

There wasn't time for this bullshit.

"You got our attention," Lisanne said, speaking through the testosterone-laced air. "What do you want?"

Cary never so much as moved, but Jad turned his head slightly in her direction. Like his boss, the Libyan American's face was hard to read, but Lisanne thought a trace of amusement flickered in his dark eyes.

"You must be Lisanne," the Viking said.

"Great guess," Lisanne said, raising her stump to eye level. "Who are you?"

"The guy your boyfriend hired to watch his back. My name is Isaac Black, and we don't have much time. You guys getting in or what?"

"I've got a thing about helicopters," Jad said. "I try not to ride in them. Especially when the pilot just tried to run me off the road."

"Spoken like a true Long Tabber," Isaac said, his lips twisting into a smile. "For the record, that was just my pilot's way of saying hello."

"Maybe he should try waving," Jad said.

"Nah," Isaac said. "This is about as friendly as Kyle Hogan gets. He spent his formative years as a Black Hawk pilot air assaulting infantrymen onto mountaintops in Afghanistan. You should see how he behaves if he doesn't like you."

"What about you?" Cary said. "Where'd you spend your formative years?"

Isaac smiled before replying.

"Unlike you Triple Nickel boys, I didn't spend my career lollygagging at Fort Campbell," Isaac said. "Where I come from is Pineland."

"Fayettnam," Cary said with a smile. "You Third Group guys are okay. For prima donnas."

"Shit," Isaac said, "you Triple Nickel boys get all the glory, we do all the work. You guys are the SEALs of Special Forces."

"If you were in Third Group, you must have served with Big Fred Apicella," Jad said.

"Never heard of him," Isaac said. "But if you mean Angry Frank Apicella, he and I came out of the Q Course together. That crazy bastard is still in, if you can believe it. Now, if we're done playing who's who in the zoo, maybe you can step inside my office. Aviation gas ain't cheap, and you're on the clock."

Lisanne thought this was true in more ways than one.

55

"CANDY, THIS IS REAPER. RADIO CHECK, OVER."

"Reaper, this is Candy," Lisanne said. "Read you Lima Charlie, over."

"Roger that, Candy. Have you the same. Reaper is standing by, over."

While Lisanne was all for conducting a final communications check before executing an operation, she thought her exchange with Cary had little to do with testing the low-profile combination speaker and mike resting deep in her ear canal. For one thing, she and her fellow Campus operatives had used the comms gear on multiple operations and the Bluetooth link that paired it with her phone was both secure and reliable. She thought it much more likely that the Green Beret was enjoying the process of christening her call sign.

A call sign that she detested.

Then again, call signs were seldom awarded with their recipient's feelings in mind.

Lisanne forced herself to stop clenching the steering wheel as she motored up to the turnoff leading to a gravel road that climbed a series of rolling hills before disappearing from view.

This was the moment of truth.

The team had agreed that the mercenaries holding Jack would have covered the applicable avenues of approach with a ring of sensors. In practical terms, this meant assuming that from here on in, Lisanne was being watched and she needed to behave as such.

Turning from the highway onto the gravel path, Lisanne pulled forward far enough to ensure her rear bumper would be clear of the road's sixty miles per hour traffic and then threw the transmission into park. With a deep breath to calm her thundering heart, she opened the door and stepped out of the truck.

ISAAC AND HIS PILOT, KYLE, HADN'T WASTED ANY TIME.

No sooner had Lisanne squeezed into the backseat in between the two Green Berets than the bird had shot skyward like a champagne cork bursting from the bottle. With one hand, Lisanne hadn't been able to fasten her seat belt as quickly as the commandos, but she was still in good hands.

Literally.

The helicopter's abrupt motion caused her to tumble forward, but not far. Jad and Cary had each grabbed one of her shoulders and helped her settle into place. While she appreciated the help, she hated feeling dependent on someone for something she could have easily managed before her injury. With this in mind, she'd intended to make use of the headset Cary passed her to vent her displeasure to the helicopter's pilot in at least two languages, but Isaac was already speaking. Once she heard what he had to say, Lisanne's anger dissipated, replaced by another emotion.

Fear.

Jack had really done it this time.

Isaac and Kyle were the co-owners of a company that serviced a niche customer. This part of Texas was full of two things—gun aficionados and feral hogs. After meeting at the local VFW post, the men had hatched a business plan that would make use of both. For a reasonable price, the veterans provided guided aerial hog-hunting trips. For those who fancied putting steel on target rather than eradicating one of Texas's most resilient pests, customers could make use of an aerial gunnery range that included everything from standard shots at stationary silhouettes to precision engagements taken at moving targets.

Business was brisk. Even so, the phone call he'd received this morning was in a class all its own. After providing his bona fides and verifying Isaac's in a manner similar to the one the Green Berets had employed, Jack had tempted Isaac with a once-in-a-lifetime proposition—provide aerial overwatch on Jack's hotel room and then follow whoever kidnapped him to their bed-down site.

In a move that had surprised him, Isaac found himself agreeing. The former Green Beret might be retired, but he was still a patriot. A fellow operative needed help, and Isaac was only too happy to provide it.

Also, the nice retainer and bonus Jack had promised Isaac hadn't hurt, either.

Isaac had provided this running narration while Kyle piloted the helicopter to within sight of a ranch located on the outskirts of town. Isaac had spent enough time prowling the skies around the area that he didn't think the presence of his helicopter would attract the mercenaries' attention, but he didn't want to take any chances.

Cary agreed.

Instead of overflying the ranch, the helicopter tracked a parallel course while Cary and Jad surveyed the property with the

Bushnell binoculars that the hog hunters kept aboard for customers. After the quick reconnaissance, Kyle had taken up a reciprocal course that would bring the Campus operatives back to their hastily abandoned vehicle.

Then the real negotiations had begun.

Over the course of the fifteen-minute flight, promises had been made and markers called in. That Jad and Cary had never served with Isaac didn't seem to matter. The names of fellow commandos had been invoked, along with debts both owed and incurred. In the end, an agreement was reached and the matter resolved. Texas Hog Hunters would see its largest single-day earnings ever. In exchange, the enterprising entrepreneurs would provide Jad and Cary with the tricked-out AR-15s their customers used, ammunition, and a stable firing platform.

Which left Lisanne.

CLOSING THE TRUCK'S DOOR, LISANNE MADE A GREAT SHOW OF EXAMINING BOTH sides of the road for some form of address marker. That no such marker existed had already been well established, but Lisanne still played up her confusion for the benefit of any unseen cameras. After much shoulder shrugging, head shaking, and at least two instances of frustratedly waving her stump in the air, Lisanne got back into the pickup and slammed the door.

Unlike her feigned confusion, the anger was not an act.

Lisanne really hated her call sign, even though she knew it was fitting.

"Candy, this is Reaper. Solid performance. We're in position. Head for the house."

"This is Candy," Lisanne said. "Roger all."

Shifting the transmission into gear, she dropped the hammer. The truck's tires spun, spewing gravel and dust as the vehicle fishtailed. While the Green Berets were playing sniper, Lisanne had a different role.

She was the eye candy.

While the role to which she'd been relegated didn't exactly make Lisanne happy, she knew it was an honest assessment of what she could contribute to the operation. Odes to gun fu movies aside, there wasn't much call for a one-handed shooter in a gunfight.

But being the eye candy didn't mean she was extraneous to the coming rescue. If anything, the entire execution depended on Lisanne's ability to sell the role she'd been given. Perhaps now that her days of clearing a room as an assaulter were over, Lisanne might want to devote her time to a skill set more complementary to her new assignment.

Like community theater.

"Candy, this is Reaper. Be advised we've got activity on the white side of California. I see two Military Aged Males exiting the front door. One is armed with a long gun, the second just holstered a pistol in the small of his back. Shooter with the long gun is taking up an overwatch position in a carport at the corner of the white and red sides. Second MAM is standing in the driveway, over. Your show, Candy."

Your show.

Two Green Berets flying overhead in a helicopter owned by a pair of vets just asked a one-armed Marine whether she wanted them to kill the bad guys who might be holding her fiancé captive. Lisanne's mom was always irritated with her for not discussing her work.

She was glad she'd stuck to that rule.

Her mom would never have believed this level of craziness.

"Roger that, Reaper," Lisanne said. "Continuing with the mission. Candy out."

She understood what Cary was really asking: *Do you still feel comfortable with this?* Lisanne didn't feel particularly comfortable with anything that was happening. Then again she had to imagine that Jack, if he was inside the house, probably wasn't feeling too comfortable right about now, either.

Pushing her apprehensions to a dark corner of her mind, Lisanne focused on what she did know how to do—play her role. All jokes about her future in acting aside, Lisanne had worked undercover a handful of times to support drug buys, prostitution busts, and the like. None of her previous gigs had been long-term deep-cover assignments, but they hadn't been walks in the park, either. She'd once played the girlfriend of a prominent jeweler in a setup that was aimed at enticing a ring of thieves to target her while she transported diamonds from one buy site to the other.

Turned out Lisanne had played her role a bit too well.

While it was department policy to use a SWAT team to provide overwatch during high-risk undercover meets, the jewel thieves took matters into their own hands. Seeing Lisanne as nothing more than the pretty but mindless girlfriend, they'd decided to steal rather than pay for the jewels she was selling. Instead of exchanging money where the SWAT team was waiting, the thieves had ambushed her while she was waiting at a stoplight.

That had been a mistake.

A very costly mistake.

In her first use of her service weapon, Lisanne had killed two of the would-be robbers and injured a third. The SWAT team commander heard the sound of gunfire and responded, his men rounding up the rest of the crew. Losing her arm had done nothing to affect her mind. This was just another UC assignment, plain and simple. She needed to focus on her part and trust that the Green Berets would respond faster than her old SWAT team.

Winding around the driveway's final bend, Lisanne flipped the radio to a rock station, rolled down the windows, and turned up the volume. She summited the final incline accompanied by Eddie Vedder's growling vocals thundering the chorus to "Even Flow." Though she'd been far too young for the grunge craze, Lisanne always figured herself for a flannel-wearing hippie at heart. There was something about the music's raw, visceral sound that resonated with her soul. With one hand on the wheel, the wind in her hair, and a pair of avenging angels circling overhead, Lisanne felt ready for whatever challenge might be coming her way.

Including the man standing in the driveway.

The man with a gun.

56

HAD HE KNOWN ABOUT IT, CARY WOULD NOT HAVE SHARED LISANNE'S OPTIMISTIC view of the pending engagement.

Where Lisanne was now firmly committed to her part of the rescue, Cary was still hip deep in the operational concerns. While he had great faith in his ability, as well as that of his spotter, to put steel on target under a variety of conditions, their circumstances were still not ideal. He was shooting from a moving platform with a new-to-him rifle and an untested crew. He had no idea of the number or disposition of the hostiles on the target, and no insight into the status or location of their hostages.

But those were problems that would be resolved later.

For Cary, the more immediate threat was the pistol-holding man standing in the center of the driveway and his partner with the long gun.

His partner Cary couldn't see.

"Still red on Two," Jad said, as if reading Cary's mind.

The Green Berets were wearing headsets with boom mikes that were plugged into the helo's intercom system as well as Bluetooth-enabled transmitters that were synced to their phones.

Both comms systems were in voice-activated mode so that Cary didn't have to take his hands off his rifle to trigger a transmit button.

But this flexibility came at a cost.

With no way to change channels between the chopper's intercom and his phone, Lisanne heard his instructions to the pilots just as the pilot heard his transmissions to Lisanne.

To put it bluntly, the situation was not ideal.

Just like everything else in this goat rope of an operation.

Cary tried to mitigate any potential confusion as best he could by using Lisanne's call sign each time he wanted her attention, but he knew that the extra radio traffic would be playing hell with her concentration.

And he needed her locked in for whatever was coming next.

"Roger red on Two," Cary said, echoing Jad's update. "Candy, this is Reaper. We still don't have eyes on the long gun. If you can, try to position yourself so that One stays between you and the house, over."

A guitar solo assaulted Cary's eardrums as Lisanne keyed the radio twice in acknowledgment.

"The girl is definitely getting into character," Jad said, "even if she does have terrible taste in music."

Cary was more of a country boy himself, but he didn't answer. This was neither the time nor the place to debate music. That Jad was doing so was only a reflection of his spotter's anxiety at not being able to identify his target. As with most operations over his long Special Forces career, Cary had been relatively pleased when events had unfolded exactly as they'd planned. Lisanne's ruckus at the front gate had garnered the mercenaries' attention. Two men had exited the front door and he and Jad were able to identify both of them.

Then Murphy's law asserted itself.

Rather than follow his partner down the driveway, the merc with the rifle walked over to the covered carport that sat adjacent to the house and disappeared beneath the roof.

The helicopter's four crew members hadn't seen him since.

"I've got nothing, either," Isaac said. "Want me to flush him out?"

The former 3rd Special Forces Group commando was seated beside Cary with a pair of binoculars pressed against his face and an AR-15 between his legs. Cary believed the rescue attempt was on dangerous ground in more ways than one. Putting aside the lack of planning, rehearsals, and team members, he was entirely unsure of the legal status of what they were about to do. Sure, The Campus was created to be a nimble organization that was unbound by the horde of lawyers who prowled the Seventh Floor at Langley and inhabited the SES suites at other paramilitary entities, but this was not a foreign country, and the men holding Jack could very well include Americans.

While Cary hadn't really troubled himself with the details around which national authorities might encompass Campus work, he knew the statutes that applied to the Posse Comitatus Act intimately. The FBI's Hostage Rescue Team existed in part because federal law prohibited the military from conducting operations on American soil. Whether or not he and Jad were covered by some obscure Campus carveout, Cary didn't know, but he was sure that Isaac was offered no such protection. Accordingly, he wanted to keep Isaac out of the tactical arena as much as possible.

Unfortunately, the enemy wasn't cooperating with this part of Cary's plan.

"Not yet," Cary said, answering Isaac's question. "I'm afraid that if we start splitting our forces, we'll dilute what little combat power we have. Keep searching for him. Kyle, bring us around in a nice, smooth loop. It's about to go down in the driveway."

As a sniper, Cary was well versed in engaging targets from a helicopter, but not like this. For aerial gunnery, he was usually in a Black Hawk's passenger area with the doors pulled back and his feet in the breeze. Or, if he could finagle a bird from the 160th, on an MH-6 Little Bird strapped to one of the troop-carrying benches that ran along the helicopter's exterior.

This was not that.

While the rear doors to the Robinson they were riding in had been removed, it had been configured with weekend warriors, not Green Berets, in mind. There wasn't room for Cary and Jad to sit shoulder to shoulder, so his spotter was in the helicopter's copilot seat in front of Cary, while Isaac was next to him. This gave both Green Berets the same view of the battlefield, but it meant that Isaac wasn't of much use during an engagement.

That was only part of the problem.

Sniper engagements from helicopters followed exacting protocols that maximized the tradeoff between wind disruption from the helicopter's forward motion and the downdraft effect on the bullet's trajectory, which was more pronounced when the bird was at a hover. Most military pilots threaded this needle by keeping the helicopter at a steady fifteen- or twenty-knot orbit around the target.

In this scenario, that tactic wouldn't work.

While Isaac had assured Cary that he flew customers around this part of Texas daily, Cary was worried that a slow-moving helicopter loitering overhead would still arouse the kidnappers' suspicions. This wouldn't do. If Cary's meager plan had even a snowball's chance in hell of working, he and Jad had to achieve tactical surprise. This meant mimicking the faster flight Isaac normally employed when he transitioned from one hog-hunting site to another.

Time for that to change.

"Game time," Cary said as Kyle finished a long, slow turn. "Keep us at twenty knots. I'm on One. Jad, you have the fight."

Cary knew that Jad said something in reply, but his spotter's words sounded like Charlie Brown's teacher. This wasn't because the helicopter's intercom had suddenly gone spotty. Jad could have screamed a reply just inches from Cary's ear, and he wouldn't have heard. Instead, the sum of Cary's existence was focused on the holographic crimson dot projected by his EOTech reflex sight.

A dot that was hovering just above Target One's right ear.

57

THINGS WERE NOT GOING WELL.

While this state of affairs was not a new one for Jack Ryan, Jr., his current circumstances were a bit of a doozy, even by his standards. Which was to say that any sane person would regard the situation in which he now found himself to be an unmitigated disaster. Admittedly Jack had a higher standard than the average Joe when it came to disaster, but in this case, he thought they would be right.

This was a clusterfuck, no two ways around it.

The argument that had been simmering in the corner of the room was heating up. That it was being conducted in Spanish made understanding precisely what was being said a bit of a challenge, but the foreign language didn't make comprehension impossible. Jack was somewhat of an expert when it came to body language, and right now, the body language emanating from the two thugs was crystal clear.

They wanted to kill someone.

Jack was also pretty sure what someone they had in mind.

While his looming homicide was a problem, it was not *the* problem occupying the vast majority of Jack's frontal cortex. Put another way, it wasn't so much that people wanted to kill him that worried Jack.

It was the kind of people who wanted to kill him.

MS-13.

As if he could sense Jack's thoughts, the gangbanger closest to him turned his way.

Though the man was probably barely over twenty, his body was a living testament to his harsh and vicious upbringing. In addition to the tears inked under both eyes, the gangbanger sported the letters *M* and *S*, the number 13, devil's horns, and a pair of laughing and crying cloud faces. And while inked achievements could be faked, the same couldn't be said about the puckered flesh around his shoulder or the wad of scar tissue running lengthwise across his abdomen. The first disfigurement was from a bullet, the second from an edged object.

Probably a machete, if Jack had to guess.

"Hey, shitbag," Jack said with a smile. "Why don't you come over here for a minute?"

Jack didn't know how well the men spoke English, so he did his best to get his point across by employing a universally understood gesture of peace and understanding.

The double middle finger.

The effect was ruined somewhat by the fact that Jack's wrists were manacled to a chain that connected to leg irons before terminating in an eyebolt that was discolored with what Jack was choosing to believe was rust. The chain was short enough that he was forced into a permanent crouch, so to give the gangbangers the finger, he had to rock back, making him look more like a turtle that had flipped over on its back than a tough guy taunting his captors. But judging by the uptick in the intensity and frequency of the Spanish being exchanged between the men, Jack's message had come across loud and clear.

"Hey, *puto*," Jack said. "Come here."

Like most operatives who worked overseas, Jack could make himself understood in a language or two, but he could swear in a plethora of dialects. Though he understood the general meaning of the profanity he'd just employed, he believed that its significance in Spanish was more profound than its literal translation.

Judging by the man's reaction, Jack's intuition was correct.

Turning from where he was standing in the doorway, the gangbanger leveled his gaze at Jack. Though he was far from a shrinking violet, Jack still had to make an effort not to shiver. It wasn't so much that the gangbanger's look contained malice or the threat of violence. Those Jack could handle. No, what made Jack's stomach quiver wasn't the emotion he was sensing from the killer.

It was the lack of it.

Those cold, dark eyes might have belonged to a robot for all the humanity Jack saw in them. To this man, he held no more relevance than a bug he'd mistakenly trod upon. Jack had witnessed the type of depravity one man could visit on another in gruesome detail. In Syria, he'd come upon the aftermath of a thermobaric munition that killed by vacuuming up the available oxygen and thereby asphyxiating the victims who weren't incinerated outright. In Spain, he'd narrowly survived a terrorist bombing that had leveled a pub, killing and maiming men, women, and children without remorse.

That was nothing compared to this.

"Hey," Jack said, forcing his smile wider, "you do have a brain in your thick skull. Let's try a different word. How about *pendejo*? Does that ring a bell?"

Jack was not taunting the men because he fancied himself a matador to their bull. A matador at least had a chance of surviving his encounter with the two-thousand-pound animal intent on goring him with horns or trampling him with hooves that could split bones and rupture internal organs. Weaponless and bound hand and foot, Jack had no illusions about how an encounter with the killers would end.

But still he baited the men.

This was because Jack was the equivalent of a rodeo clown. He needed the pair focused on him so that their collective attention would not drift back to the room's second captive.

Bella.

The teenager was similarly bound, but unlike Jack, Bella was doing her best to disappear. Where Jack's earlier interaction with Bella was marked with equal parts sass and sarcasm, this Bella might have been carved from stone. Ever since the gangbangers had strolled into the room, she'd gone silent. Unlike Jack, who had scooted toward the eyebolt in an effort to ease a little slack into his chain, the rusty links securing Bella were as taut as a violin string. Bella sat with her head down, allowing her blond hair to hide her face, but Jack could feel the cold terror radiating from the girl in waves. In the same manner in which a rabbit could sense the danger represented by a snake, Bella seemed to instinctively recognize that the men's arrival signified that her circumstances had just changed.

And not for the better.

WHILE JACK'S UNCONVENTIONAL ARRIVAL PROBABLY HADN'T INSPIRED BELLA'S confidence, seeing the teen once the mercs had yanked the black hood from his face made him believe that his plan was working.

In a manner of speaking.

To Jack's way of thinking, the most dangerous aspect of

allowing himself to be taken hostage occurred in the few seconds after the assault team had breached his hotel room. His entire gambit had been predicated on the notion that the mercenaries had gone to a considerable effort to eradicate any trace of their presence. From the hapless father who'd simply been searching for his missing son, to the Briar Wood police officer who'd been allowed to bleed to death rather than speak, the mercs were both ruthless and efficient.

But they were also careful.

Rather than killing Amanda and Bella, the men had gone to the trouble of kidnapping the teenager in order to exert leverage on the mother.

Temporary leverage.

This suggested two things to Jack: One, whatever the men were actually in Texas to accomplish was on the verge of being completed. Two, the reverberations of their earlier kinetic activity were now expanding beyond their ability to contain the fallout. Put another way, the shooters would rather deal with the inconvenience of a hostage than risk the attention two more dead bodies might bring to the little town.

Following this same logic, Jack believed that given the chance, the mercs would rather interrogate him than eliminate him outright. And this interrogation would best be conducted away from prying eyes, which probably meant the location where the men were holding Bella. Without a doubt, the reasoning was thin, but it was all he had, or more precisely, it was all Bella had.

So Jack bet his life on his intuition and used himself as bait.

In the first moment or two after his hotel room door had nearly blown off the hinges, Jack hadn't been quite as confident in his trap. The assaulters who'd flowed into his room hadn't commanded him to remain still or hit him with a Taser. Instead, the number one man had leveled his shotgun at Jack and pulled the trigger.

Repeatedly.

That the weapon was loaded with less than lethal beanbag rounds instead of buckshot or slugs hadn't been much consolation to Jack. At least not in those first few seconds. The beanbags traveled at a velocity of three hundred feet per second and were filled with lead shot. Getting hit with one was like getting clobbered with a rubber mallet.

And he hadn't been hit by just one.

The pain that had scorched through his abdomen would have dropped Jack to his knees were he not already stretched across his bed. He instinctively curled into a fetal position, which only served to give the shotgunner a fresh target. Jack lost count of how many bags impacted his torso. While one part of his brain seized on the fact that the unbearable agony was radiating from his midsection rather than his head, where a beanbag strike could very well have proven fatal, that intellect was far, far away. Mostly he'd made animal sounds as his hands and feet were hogtied and a hood cinched over his head.

Once while playing high school baseball, Jack had taken a ninety-five-mile-per-hour fastball to the kidney. He'd pissed blood for days. That had been painful.

This was agony.

And then the real suffering began.

Lost in Jack's clinical calculations was the fact that the mercs, while professionals, were also very much human. Jack had been directly responsible for the deaths of two of their comrades, and while their orders had apparently been to take him alive, there must have been a bit of latitude given to his physical condition.

Or they were just pissed about their dead friends and looking for a little payback.

Either way, the beating had commenced as soon as the bindings were in place and hadn't ended until Jack was dumped onto the rough concrete. On the positive side, other than a couple of shots to the face, the men had mostly left his head alone. This meant that while his nose was still killing him, his left eye was swollen shut, and his front tooth was a bit loose, Jack could still form coherent thoughts. On the negative end of the ledger, he had a feeling that this time around he'd be pissing blood for a bit longer.

Like maybe forever.

Also, Bella had been less than impressed with Jack's arrival.

"Why are you here?" Bella had said the moment the mercs left the room.

"To save you," Jack had said.

He hadn't been sure what he'd expected, but it hadn't been tears.

Unfortunately, he wasn't given a chance to explain. No sooner had he gotten the words out than his mercenary captors had reappeared. One by one, the men each took turns beating him. The blows, while vicious, were controlled. Instead of his midsection, the punches targeted his legs and arms. This was a softening up for the questioning to come, not a death sentence.

At least not yet.

At some point, Bella began to weep. During the brief intervals between mercenaries, when they were alone, she asked Jack again and again why he was here. He always answered the same way.

"For you."

She pressed for more information, but Jack refused to provide it. For all he knew, the room was wired for sound. Perhaps more important, his plan depended on time. More specifically, giving his teammates time to find him. As long as the mercenaries believed that he was at their mercy, Jack was cautiously optimistic that he could last the hours it would take for help to arrive. But if for any reason his captors believed he was playing them, they would see Jack as a liability rather than an asset.

And he knew how they dealt with liabilities.

So while he had confidence in his ability to deceive them, he had no such assurance in Bella. Other than assuring her that she was no longer alone, he kept any semblance of hope from the teen. As awful as it was to endure her tear-filled, pleading looks, Jack couldn't risk an inadvertent change in her demeanor alerting the mercenaries that Jack wasn't quite as helpless as he seemed.

From that perspective, Jack didn't think he'd have to do much acting. His body was one mass of bruises, his legs felt dead, and his arms tingled, but still he prepared himself for more. As he'd learned to do in SERE school, Jack had already made a plan for his looming interrogation. A strategy for doling out information one chunk at a time. But to make his break realistic, he would have to make his interrogator beat the story out of him.

This was the tightrope Jack had prepared himself to walk.

Give in too easy, and the interrogator would become suspicious.

Give in too late, and Jack risked incurring permanent damage.

Just like with Goldilocks, Jack was going to have to play this thing just right. So far, Jack thought he was doing a pretty good job threading that needle.

And then the MS-13 thugs had arrived.

58

WHILE JACK DIDN'T UNDERSTAND HOW THE GANGBANGERS PLAYED INTO THE situation, one look at the men convinced him that things had just taken a turn for the worse.

A drastic turn.

Being on the receiving end of the mercs' rage hadn't exactly been all roses and unicorns, but the scenario had unfolded in a predictable, if brutal, fashion. Jack was trading pain for time. Each fist that smashed into his arms or legs represented another chance for his teammates to come to the rescue. And each time a merc vented his rage without asking questions was another delay to the inevitable interrogation.

That was what Jack truly feared.

For once the mercs began questioning him in earnest, they would begin to do irreparable harm to his body. Not to mention that after they were convinced his utility had ended, his life would soon follow. Until the questioning started, Jack was relatively safe.

Or so he'd thought.

But once the tattooed killers arrived on the scene, he knew that the jig was up. These weren't the people you used for delicate tasks.

They were the cleanup crew.

Jack didn't know what had changed, and he didn't have time to figure it out. After entering the room and closing the door behind them, the men had glanced at Jack with the casual disregard a slaughterhouse worker might show a steer. The MS-13 killers didn't want information or payback. They didn't want anything.

From Jack.

Bella was a different story.

The moment the two men spied the pretty girl, their entire demeanor changed. Bella felt the shift and responded by trying to make herself small. Unnoticeable.

Jack tried the other tack.

By becoming larger, he hoped to give the men something to focus on.

Something other than the shaking teenager just inches away.

"Hey, shitbirds," Jack said. "I've got something for you."

Then he let loose with every curse and slur he knew. He insulted the men, their parentage, and their progeny. Jack exhausted his limited Spanish fairly quickly, so he hopped to other languages, looking for any sign of recognition in their lifeless eyes. But the black beady orbs showed nothing. With a final burst of desperation, Jack gathered up the mixture of phlegm and blood that coagulated at the back of his throat and spat it at the closest man.

His aim was true.

The mixture of blood and phlegm splattered against the gangbanger's chest with a satisfyingly wet *splunk*.

"You like that?" Jack said with a manic smile. "'Cause there's more where it came from."

Jack cleared his throat again, but he didn't get a chance to spit. Crossing the distance between them in two angry strides, the gangbanger backhanded Jack across the face.

Then he drew a knife.

59

THE MAN STANDING IN FRONT OF HER HADN'T YET DRAWN THE PISTOL LISANNE knew was secreted at his back.

Then again, he didn't have to.

Thanks to her eyes in the sky, Lisanne knew that the man's partner was somewhere in the carport about eighty yards to her left. At that distance, even a novice shooter could hit a target with a half-decent rifle and iron sights. With the tricked-out AK-47 the mercs were running, she had no doubt that the sniper could put two bullets through her cranium without breaking a sweat. Her first platoon leader back when she was an MP used to say that information was power. This might be true, but right about now Lisanne favored the ignorance is bliss philosophy. Either way, the sniper was Cary's concern, not hers. She needed to focus on what was in front of her.

The man with a gun.

Lisanne slammed on the brakes, bringing the pickup to a halt in a cloud of dust.

Then she laid on the horn.

The blast startled the man. His right hand drifted toward his back as his left gathered the base of his untucked shirt, preparing to clear his draw. Lisanne appreciated his training, but she didn't want things to get kinetic just yet. If lead started flying, the unseen sniper would have the advantage and she would be in the kill zone. So rather than give the duress signal that would clear Cary to drop the merc, Lisanne thought about what her character would do.

Then she acted.

"Hey," Lisanne yelled as she hopped out of the pickup. "Get out of the way."

"What?" the gunman said, confusion etched across his face.

"I said get out of the way," Lisanne said, over-enunciating each word. "I've got a delivery to make." She punctuated her statement by blowing an impressively large bubble from the wad of pink gum she was chomping.

If the merc looked confused before, he now appeared dumbfounded. Then again, Lisanne supposed that were she in his place, she might also be a bit perplexed. As part of getting into character, Lisanne had made a wardrobe change. Gone was her earlier sensible wardrobe. In its stead were a tight T-shirt and even tighter jean shorts. Aviator-style glasses shaded her eyes, but with her makeup freshly done and her hair hanging loose around her shoulders, Lisanne knew she could pass for a decade younger.

Hopefully that would be young enough to do the trick.

"What delivery?" the gunman said.

Suspicion still colored his words, but the gunman's hands were no longer lurking in the vicinity of his concealed pistol.

Progress.

"Uber Eats," Lisanne said in her best *I'm over this conversation already* voice. "Are you gonna accept delivery or what? I've got three more drops to make."

The merc took a step closer, sliding to his right so that he could look over Lisanne's shoulder into the still-open truck door. His eyes narrowed as he presumably saw the cluster of white bags nestled in the passenger seat.

"We didn't order anything," the mercenary said.

Lisanne reached for her pocket, pretending not to notice as the merc tensed in response. "Look," Lisanne said as she consulted her phone, "I'm just the delivery girl, okay? Somebody bought a bunch of wings. You've got to take 'em, or I don't get paid."

"We did not order anything," the merc said, his anger making his accent more pronounced.

Lisanne recited the house's address. "This is it, right? Here, check for yourself."

She handed the merc her phone, which the man reflexively accepted. He seemed to realize his mistake the moment his fingers touched the device.

"Buckeye," Lisanne said.

A nanosecond later the mercenary's head snapped to the side as a 5.56mm projectile entered his cranium at 3,250 feet per second. The gunman dropped like a puppet whose strings had been cut, but Lisanne didn't pay the dead body any mind, either.

She was already sliding across the front seat.

As soon as her butt touched the leather, she shifted the transmission into drive, gunned the engine, and wrenched the steering wheel to the right. Judging from the lack of radio traffic from the Green Berets, she had to assume that the merc with the long gun was still in play.

Her plan to draw the man out of his hidey-hole had failed.

Time for an audible.

60

THE GANGBANGER FLICKED THE BLADE OPEN ONE-HANDED.

The length of steel glittered in the dim lighting.

Jack watched tiny points of light dance along the killing edge and felt time slow down. He heard Bella scream as the knowledge of what was to come broke through her protective cocoon. He had time for a million thoughts as his mind raced at light speed through the quarter of a second that had elapsed. These flashes of insight began with notions of how to defend himself against the knife, but quickly transitioned to other topics. Jack was bound hand and foot and unable to so much as sit up on his own.

There was no defending against the blade.

His subconscious seemed to both realize and accept this inevitability, and within a nanosecond, his thoughts fled down other paths. He briefly dwelt upon the coming pain and what it would feel like when the steel plunged into his flesh. Jack had been knifed before and knew the wounds burned.

Would his mortal one feel differently?

The gangbanger drew back his leg, and Jack saw how the final moments of his life would unfold. A vicious kick to his ribs would cause him to curl into a fetal position. Then the killer would drop a knee onto Jack's side to hold him steady and draw the blade across his jugular in one swift slice.

Strangely enough, this realization brought with it a sense of peace. As if by knowing how he was going to die, Jack no longer had to consider it. Instead, his thoughts turned to his raven-haired beauty and her niece.

Lisanne and Emily.

Jack still didn't know how all of this would work any more than Lisanne did, but that didn't matter. He loved his fiancée, and she loved her niece. They would make it work, that's what people who loved each other did.

But first Jack had to survive this killing room.

The gangbanger grunted as he began his kick, Jack's heightened senses slowing the sound down into a long exhalation as his brain furiously returned to the tactical problem confronting him. Jack had just one advantage, though in truth, the opportunity was too fragile to bear the weight of that optimistic term. It wasn't so much an advantage as an inconvenience to the killer. One thing that he had to overcome before he could set about the task of murdering Jack.

Distance.

By choosing to employ a knife rather than a gun, the killer had to close the distance separating him from his intended victim. The gangbanger had to come to Jack. In the truest sense of the word, Jack controlled the terms of the engagement. He could ambush his would-be killer.

In theory.

The practicality of the situation was much different.

But if theory was all that Jack had, then theory would have to do.

A horn blast cut through the air, surprising everyone. Bella jerked, the killer paused mid-kick, and his friend turned toward the sound.

The unexpectedness caused everyone to pause.

Everyone but Jack.

Like a striking viper, Jack grabbed hold of the man's stationary leg and yanked.

The gangbanger toppled.

The fight was on.

61

"WHAT THE HELL IS SHE DOING?" JAD SAID.

"Improvising," Cary said.

In truth, he didn't have a clue what Lisanne was thinking, but that was often the way of combat. Like a quarterback sizing up the defense at the line of scrimmage, the element in contact had the latitude to change the play on the fly.

Everyone else was expected to adjust.

The pickup with Lisanne behind the wheel was bouncing across the lawn to the right, radio still blaring and horn honking. For a long moment, Cary couldn't figure out what the former Marine was trying to accomplish.

Then he got it.

"Be ready, Jad," Cary said. "She's using the house to cut off the sniper's field of fire. He's gonna have to break cover in order to get a shot on her."

Cary was right, after a fashion.

Though between the helicopter's engine and his headphones, Cary couldn't hear anything on the ground, he could see the bits of metal flying into the air as high-velocity rounds tore divots from the pickup's frame. The merc was trying to engage, but in just a few seconds Lisanne would be out of his line of fire.

Assuming she lived that long.

"Anything?" Cary said, panning his red dot across the carport.

"Negative," Jad said. "He's either still beneath cover—"

"Or we're looking in the wrong place," Cary said. "Fuck me running."

"Gentlemen, far be it from me to interrupt when you're having so much fun, but perhaps I could make a suggestion?"

While Cary wasn't in the habit of taking suggestions in the middle of a gunfight, this was also not his first rodeo. As a result, he recognized what was happening even if he didn't want to admit it.

He was losing control of the battle.

As the team sergeant of Triple Nickel, Cary was accustomed to controlling multiple elements of the fight. This often took the form of leading the assaulting element while his team leader managed indirect fires or the close air support assets. On occasion their roles might be reversed, and Cary would find himself managing the support-by-fire elements such as the sniper teams or mortar crews. Then, like now, the tactical scenario could unfold in unexpected and confusing ways. Cary's problems in the current fight didn't stem from task saturation as much as an inability to focus his elements. He and Jad were the only assaulters, which meant that they needed to make entry in the house and start the process of finding Jack.

But they couldn't do that.

As long as an unseen sniper continued to cause havoc, Cary needed to be focused on controlling Lisanne's movements so that he and Jad could engage the hidden gunman. The problem was that every second the Green Berets spent searching for the sniper was another second they lost the element of surprise and gave the bad guys in the house a chance to prepare for the assault.

Or worse yet, kill their hostage.

Between himself, Jad, and Lisanne, Cary knew that there simply weren't enough guns to go around. Which meant he had to add more gunfighters to the equation. Cary looked over his shoulder to see Isaac staring at him from the opposite seat, a bright smile on the former 3rd Grouper's face. The grizzled veteran had already worked out what needed to happen and was patiently waiting for Cary to arrive at the same conclusion.

As Cary's first team sergeant drilled into his head so many years ago, with enough hair gel and a pair of floaties, anyone could be a SEAL.

It took brains to wear the green beret.

"All right, Isaac," Cary said. "Welcome to the team. Here's how we're going to skin this cat."

62

LISANNE ROBERTSON WAS HAVING AN EXISTENTIAL MOMENT.

Just seconds ago, she'd been confident almost to the point of arrogance. Yes, her tearing across the front yard like a bat out of hell hadn't been part of the pre-mission brief, but she'd seen a solution to their tactical problem and acted.

This was what it meant to be an operator.

At least that had been her conclusion before the sniper started punching holes in the pickup's cabin. While Lisanne had been shot at before, she'd always been part of a larger tactical element in the middle of maneuvering to close with and destroy the enemy.

This was not that.

Instead, Lisanne was playing the decoy—and that sucked.

Her passenger-side window had shattered just seconds into the engagement and now the windshield was spiderwebbed, too. Puffs of upholstery fabric from the shredded seats drifted through the air, and her face and arms were scored with bits of glass. Lisanne had thought that she'd be out of the sniper's kill zone by now. This had not proven to be the case, meaning either the gunman had changed locations or someone else was now taking potshots.

Either scenario ended with the same result.

Lisanne catching a bullet.

The world's angriest hornet snapped by her ear and Lisanne reflexively ducked even farther behind the dashboard. She could barely see through the cracked glass before. With her eyes this low, she had no idea where she was driving.

Where were her teammates?

"Candy, this is Reaper. Great job so far, but I need one more thing from you, over."

Lisanne let go of the wheel long enough to spin down the radio's volume knob so that she could better hear the Green Beret. Unfortunately, the truck's front tires took the opportunity to dig into a rut the size of the Grand Canyon. The vehicle swayed from side to side, forcing Lisanne to sit up higher in her seat as she grabbed for the wheel. Seeing the ground sloping to the left, Lisanne steered into the turn, keeping the truck upright but turning the vehicle broadside to the sniper in the process. The singular hornets became a swarm as the shooter fired a burst into the stricken pickup. A line of fire opened across Lisanne's shoulder and she cried out, almost letting go of the steering wheel in response.

Her heart thundered and her breath came in shuddering gasps as she relived the moment when a similarly placed round had clipped an artery, costing Lisanne her arm and nearly killing her in the process. Gritting her teeth, Lisanne forced herself to examine the shoulder wound as she prepared for the worst. She saw a furrow leaking blood, and sobbed in relief.

It would hurt like hell, but it was just a graze.

She was okay.

For now.

"Reaper, this is Candy," Lisanne said, trying to keep the emotion from her voice. "I don't have much left to give, over."

"Roger that, Candy. That's why we're going to keep this easy peasy. Here's what I need you to do."

Lisanne listened to Cary's soothing voice as she tried to ignore the metal-on-metal *thuds* as dozens of rounds raked the pickup. At this point, she didn't know whether the truck was rocking on its shocks because of the rifle fire, rough terrain, or her poor driving. Her world had shrunk to just her racing heart and Cary's voice. While the Green Beret's plan did sound simple, Lisanne still didn't know whether she had enough in the tank to get it done.

But that didn't matter.

Lisanne would go down swinging.

She was a Marine.

63

PIETER CHANGED MAGAZINES ON HIS AK-47 WITH THE SMOOTH, PRACTICED MO-tions that suggested this action was second nature.

It was.

At fifty-nine years of age, Pieter had been selling his expertise since he'd been forced to leave the South African military twenty years ago. In the ensuing decades, he'd lent his rifle to causes far and wide across the sprawling continent that was home.

Some of those causes he'd agreed with.

Many he had not.

But those ideological quandaries had never bothered Pieter. When he'd worn the red beret of the South African Recces, no one had asked his opinion about where and why his services were to be employed. His government told him to go and fight, and as a good soldier, he had obeyed. He viewed his time as a mercenary no differently. Sure, there had been some instances in which he had fought for clients he found utterly repulsive, but not any more so than some of the politicians who had helped steer his nation into lawlessness and corruption. Then as now, Pieter approached life with a practicality that people who didn't know him might have labeled indifference.

But Pieter wasn't indifferent.

Far from it, in fact.

When he was young, Pieter had taken mercenary contracts because he'd had a family to feed and no other appreciable skills. Now that he was old, Pieter's obligations had only increased. His wife of forty years suffered from diabetes, and like many in South Africa, his children struggled to put together a meaningful life. His eldest had tried his hand at farming and had been brutally murdered by militants. Pieter's youngest had just finished university and now looked longingly across the ocean at the booming economies of Europe and the United States.

But starting a new life did not come cheaply. Nor did covering Pieter's wife's ever-growing healthcare expenses, not to mention the education and welfare of his fatherless grandchildren. So when most of his Western contemporaries were trading their vocations for retirement life, Pieter was still selling his sword in the hopes of one day cashing out. At its start, this particular contract had the potential to move that *one day* from the fuzzy future into the very real here and now. But that required actually surviving to spend his earnings, a proposition that Pieter was now beginning to think was entirely unrealistic.

"Contact front," Pieter said as he changed magazines and racked the charging handle. The metallic sound of the bolt stripping a round from the newly seated magazine as it slid home was comforting even if the scene playing out in front of him was not. "I am engaging an assault force of an unknown size, and Jan is down. I say again, Jan is down. Request immediate reinforcements, over."

The South African mercenary community was both small and tight knit because South Africa had been contributing an outsized number of fighting men to the continent's wars for years. Partly this came from the nation's martial history and partly from necessity. South Africa's fighting men were highly sought after. Regardless of the larger geopolitical considerations, for Pieter, life was simple. He and his family needed money to survive, and he had but one thing to offer in exchange for payment—his rifle.

Pieter's earpiece crackled as his comrades answered his call for help, but for the old campaigner, these voices were background noise. In his world, only two things mattered—the red carrot-shaped reticle projected into his eye by his reflex sight, and the pickup lurching across the lawn toward the house.

If he were being honest, Pieter would have to say that he'd hoped his earlier barrage might have driven the truck off. He'd already violated the mercenary's cardinal rule and caught a glimpse of his target as he'd been shooting. The brunette at the wheel looked both young and pretty. Perhaps at an age with his own daughter. Contrary to what pop culture projected, Pieter did not relish killing, and he certainly didn't like the idea of putting his next hollow point into the brunette's brainpan.

But she'd left him no choice.

The woman was steering straight toward the house and Pieter had a job to do. With a sigh, he moved the rifle's selector switch back to single, placed the red carrot just above the woman's left ear, and began to take the slack out of the trigger. Pieter might not be able to spare the brunette, but at least he could make her death quick.

He only hoped that one day he was granted the same consideration.

64

"COME LEFT, CANDY. *LEFT.*"

Lisanne jerked the wheel to the left as she applied more gas. True to his word, Cary's instructions had been pretty simple— ram the front of the house. Also as promised, the helicopter pilot was giving her a target talk-on, providing her with steering instructions so that she could keep her head down and hopefully out of the sniper's murderous line of fire.

There was just one problem.

It wasn't working.

"Half a turn to the right, Candy. Now!"

Lisanne adjusted as the pickup bounced over another rut, banging her head into the vehicle's frame. Cary's plan had been a sound one and might have been successful if Lisanne still had two hands with which to steer.

She didn't.

While she was trying to use her stump to help steady the wheel, it wasn't working. The combination of high speed and uneven terrain ripped the wheel from her hand again and again, sending her off course. While she was still doing a great job as a bullet magnet, she knew something needed to change if she were going to actually do her part for the assaulters.

She'd have to stop hiding.

"Kyle, this is Candy," Lisanne said. "You can stop with the directions. I've got it from here."

Lisanne didn't bother telling the aviator her plan. He seemed like a smart guy and would undoubtedly arrive at the correct conclusion.

Besides, she had shit to do.

Popping above the dashboard, Lisanne took stock of her surroundings. What she saw wasn't encouraging. Cary wanted her to put the truck's grille right through the front door, but that was no longer an option. Despite Kyle's best efforts, she'd drifted off course and there wasn't time for a do-over. A round snapped past her head, shattering the sunroof. Another quarter of an inch, and it would have been her brains all over the roof.

Time to adjust fire.

Yanking the wheel to the right, she centered the hood ornament on the large bay window situated just to the right of the front door. Nicotine-colored river stone framed the window and she had a fraction of a second to wonder whether her pickup had enough energy to punch through the rock.

Then the time for wondering was over.

Mashing the accelerator to the floor, Lisanne fought to keep the window in the center of her splintered windshield. Whether it came from a rifle bullet or the stone, Lisanne knew she was in for one hell of a jolt. For a fraction of a second her agile mind pondered the insanity of her current situation. What did it say about your life when your preferred course of action was to drive into a stone wall at forty miles per hour?

Then steel met stone.

65

PIETER'S FIRST SHOT BROKE LEFT.

He chose to believe this was because the truck had taken an unexpected bounce rather than because he'd wasted precious seconds firing a final warning shot past the pretty brunette's face.

Regardless of the cause, Pieter would not miss a second time.

In the way of all good riflemen, Pieter blocked out the rest of the world as the sum of his existence coalesced onto the tiny crimson carrot. The woman was no more than fifty yards away. Her profile loomed large enough in the aiming reticle that Pieter could have just placed the carrot center mass and let fly.

He did not.

As a young soldier, Pieter had learned the value of the adage *aim small, miss small*. Even though a child could have put the next round in the woman's head, Pieter still selected the point just above her ear where a single midnight curl cascaded down the side of her face.

Pieter exhaled.

Waited for the natural pause between breaths.

And pressed the trigger.

The rifle barked.

But the round missed.

This was not because Pieter had experienced a second attack of conscience. If anything, the mercenary was cursing himself for not ending the fight earlier. This was because the crimson carrot no longer rested against the woman's face. Where once he had seen a lock of raven hair, Pieter now saw a metal fuselage.

A metal fuselage belonging to a helicopter.

He looked over his sight, attempting to make sense of what he was seeing.

He never got the chance.

Pieter's subconscious registered the image of a man leaning out of the helicopter's open door.

A man with a rifle.

The rifle flashed.

Pieter saw nothing more.

66

JACK CURLED HIS LEGS TO HIS CHEST AND LAUNCHED BOTH FEET AT THE KILLER'S
face. The chain brought one of Jack's legs up short, but the second hit the mark. His right foot glanced off the gangbanger's chin, snapping his head to the side.

Absent the chain and his manacled hands, Jack could have ended the fight right then.

He wasn't absent the chain.

With agility born of desperation, the gangbanger kept hold of his knife. Even worse, the gangbanger's friend spun his AK-47 so that the butt was facing downward and darted across the room.

Right into Bella's money-making right leg.

A ninja the teenager was not, but the soccer star knew a thing or two about slide tackles. With a ferocity that Jack could respect, she snapped a kick into the second man's shin, knocking him from his feet. Then Jack's gangbanger reversed his hold on his knife and jabbed the glittering end toward Jack's midsection.

Snapping his hands up, Jack caught the tip with the chain binding his hands. Then he clamped both hands around the man's wrist, trying to control the knife.

Outside, the honking continued, now punctuated by gunshots.

"Fight, Bella," Jack said, grunting. "Those are my friends."

Jack had no way of knowing whether this was true, but his words seemed to galvanize the teenager. Bella screamed and the sounds of scuffling continued. Jack tried to smash an elbow into the gangbanger's head, but once again the chains brought him up short. Then he tried to run out the clock by controlling the knife until help arrived.

That wasn't going to fly, either.

While both of Jack's hands were locked around the gang-banger's wrist, the killer had a free fist. One he put to good use by launching a series of hooks into Jack's jaw and temple. Jack weathered the first two punches, but the third caught him just above his ear. Stars exploded, and he felt the gangbanger's wrist slipping from his grasp.

Jack was a dead man.

Screaming, the gangbanger wrenched his hand free.

Then he plunged the knife downward.

67

"REAPER, THIS IS ANCIENT," ISAAC SAID. "CROW IS DOWN. I SAY AGAIN, CROW IS down. You are cleared hot, over."

"This is Reaper," Cary said. "Copy cleared hot. Reaper is breaching."

Cary removed his left hand from his rifle and squeezed Jad on the shoulder. Though the second Green Beret had undoubtedly monitored the radio transmission between Cary and Isaac, Jad would not move until his team leader gave him the physical cue to do so.

On the surface, close-quarters battle was a simple concept—enter a structure, find the enemy, and kill him. But the simplicity of the objective belied the complexity of the execution. In some ways this conundrum was like the difference between humming a melody and composing a symphony. Both activities produced music, but one of the undertakings was infinitely more complex than the other.

Though the thundering of the Robinson's rotors was comforting, Cary felt the hairs on the back of his neck stand up all the same. Breaching an objective was always the most dangerous portion of the assault. No matter how much planning, rehearsal, and preparation a tactical team undertook before hitting an objective, the moment the lead assaulter crossed the structure's threshold, he was crossing into enemy terrain. Like charging headfirst into a wolf's den, the number one man would be going toe to toe with a wild animal on its home turf.

Today, Cary was the number one man.

Jad grabbed the door handle and slowly rotated it.

Unlocked.

Normally, this part of the assault was the most kinetic. Successfully executing CQB required a strict adherence to three very basic-sounding tenets—speed, surprise, and violence of action. During the breach, this was accomplished through a dynamic entry that was usually heralded by explosive charges, flashbangs and/or fragmentation grenades, and a tactical stack of six to eight assaulters ready for war.

Cary had none of that.

Instead, he and Jad were stacked on a door leading from the house's green side. While Lisanne was still doing an admirable job of causing a ruckus at the front or white side of the house and Isaac had been given permission to engage any targets of opportunity from the orbiting helicopter, the yeoman's share of the work would fall to him and Jad. For a target this size, Cary would have allocated a minimum of six Green Berets and would have tried to squeeze in eight.

He had two.

But nothing was ever simple when it came to Jack Ryan, Jr.

His lack of assaulters meant that Cary had to turn the traditional method of clearing a building on its head. Instead of the dynamic entry most often favored by tactical teams, Cary was banking on surprise in the hopes that the shenanigans being perpetrated by his partners in crime would keep the structure's occupants focused elsewhere.

Now he was about to put that theory to the test.

Jad eased the door open, and Cary slipped past him.

His first impression upon transitioning from outside to in was of space. Or, to be more precise, the lack thereof. The side entryway spilled into a mudroom that was barely wider than Cary's shoulders and about two body lengths deep. The narrow enclosure would force him and Jad to enter single file and its narrow confines formed a perfect killing zone. If there were bad guys on the other side, this was where Cary would get zapped.

Cary pushed into the space and continued to the next room, trusting that Jad was stacked behind him. The can attached to the end of his AR-15 offset the rifle's balance a bit. He compensated by moving his lead hand closer to the muzzle as he swept the crimson dot from his reflex sight across the dim room. While he knew that he was losing the element of surprise by the second, Cary would still prefer to wait until he and Jad were clear of the fatal funnel imposed by the mudroom before they started engaging targets.

His hopes were in vain.

He was at the mudroom's midpoint when a scruffy-looking Hispanic male appeared in his sight picture. The man's eyes widened as he began to orient the AK-47 in his hands toward Cary. Cary pressed the trigger twice and the rifle barked, sending two slugs into the gunman's face. Even with the can, the report was incredibly loud in the tight confines.

But not as loud as the AK-47 rocking and rolling on full auto in the next room.

Gritting his teeth, Cary ignored the instinct to retreat in the face of the fire. If he pulled back now, they were done. The shooter only had to stick his rifle around the corner and spray. If he did that, both Green Berets would be caught trying to exit.

It would be like shooting fish in a barrel. Instead, Cary charged forward, exiting the mudroom and buttonhooking toward the sound of gunfire.

What he saw turned his blood to ice.

Five men with AK-47s were standing in front of the bay window.

CQB doctrine was pretty clear when it came to clearing a room using two people. The lead assaulter, in this case Cary, picked his entry style and the second man, Jad, reacted accordingly. Cary had buttonhooked right, which meant Jad would mirror him to the left. This would allow Cary to engage targets in his assigned sector without worry that he would be shot from behind by unseen assailants.

Jad would protect his back.

But in this case, it was Cary's front that needed help.

As if summoned by his thoughts, the grille of Lisanne's pickup tore through the stone wall, sending one man hurtling across the room.

Four gunmen remained.

Four gunmen were still too many for one shooter to successfully engage. But this sentiment, while true, did nothing to modify Cary's actions. As soon as he saw the first shooter, muscle memory created from countless hours in Fort Campbell's shoot houses kicked in. The crimson dot settled on the first target's chest and Cary fired twice. Seemingly of its own accord, the red circle floated to the next target and Cary put two rounds into the gunman's center mass. He was in the process of transitioning to the third, and what would in all likelihood be his final, target when the rifle reports he'd been expecting sounded.

Except the shots came from over his left shoulder rather than in front of him.

Jad.

Jad was standing next to him.

The final two men flopped to the ground, but they were no longer Cary's concern. Instead, his sight was locked on to the closed door that led off the main room. The door behind which he hoped to find Jack. Cary kept his weapon pointed on the door like an English setter pointing at a grouse. Then he felt a squeeze on his shoulder, and Cary was moving toward the final objective. At some point, he'd have to talk with his spotter about Jad's unorthodox method of clearing a room.

But that was a discussion for later.

Cary had bad guys to kill.

68

HAD THE GANGBANGER GONE FOR AN UPWARD THRUST INTO JACK'S MIDSECTION, the fight would have been over. Flat on his back with his arms and legs bound, Jack would have had no defense against such an attack. The six-inch blade would have entered his abdomen, parting flesh and muscle before rupturing his liver. Death might not have been instant, but it would have been imminent all the same.

That was not the attack the gangbanger chose.

Instead, the tattooed man let his passion rather than tactical sense dictate the fight. He plunged the knife toward Jack's face with a modified hammer strike. Jack's unforeseen attack had hurt the gangbanger, angered him, and probably filled him with embarrassment.

He wanted the pleasure that came with driving the blade into Jack's eye socket.

He didn't get the chance.

Rather than trying to intercept the knife's downward trajectory as he had previously, this time Jack added his weight to the strike. As the knife flashed toward him, Jack latched on to the gangbanger's forearm and pulled as he twisted to his right. The unexpected momentum threw the knifeman off balance, and Jack rolled with the motion, trapping the man's arm, and by extension his knife, under Jack's side.

The gangbanger reacted by trying to free his knife arm.

Jack had something else in mind. The chain binding Jack's hands was too tight to wrap around the man's neck, but it allowed just enough play for something else.

A cross-collar choke.

Jack crossed his wrists, gathered the fabric around the gangbanger's collar in his fingers, and rolled his hands together, driving his knuckles into the soft part of the man's neck above the carotid arteries. The choke worked by restricting blood flow to the brain, not air to the lungs.

This distinction was important.

A person choking due to lack of air recognized their predicament immediately and acted accordingly. The recipient of a blood choke, on the other hand, often experienced a sense of euphoria before blackout, especially if they were concentrating on something else at the time.

Like their knife.

Jack felt the blade bite into his side as the gangbanger worked to free the knife. He forced himself to ignore the line of fire burning above his ribs as he ground his knuckles ever deeper into his assailant's flesh. If the gangbanger wiggled free, there would be no second chances.

Jack either ended the fight now or he was a dead man.

A slap echoed from the scuffle next to him followed by Bella's scream. Jack was guessing that employing soccer as a martial art had reached its zenith, but he didn't dare look. Instead, like a pit bull latching on to a feral hog, Jack ground his fists into his opponent's neck, picturing the man's windpipe collapsing beneath his knuckles. His arms shook with the effort as a second and then third line of fire scored his abdomen.

Then the gangbanger fell limp.

Jack pushed the man off his chest knowing full well that the knifeman wasn't dead.

At least not yet.

He'd passed out from lack of oxygenated blood, but unless Jack held the choke in place for the next several minutes to ensure the man's brain died, the gangbanger would regain consciousness.

But Jack didn't have several minutes.

Scrambling for the man's knife, Jack gripped the plastic hilt and then turned to see what aid he could offer Bella.

None.

The teenager lay sprawled against the wall, her limp limbs splayed out lifelessly.

Jack screamed, looking for a target on which to vent his rage.

He found one.

The cold steel of a rifle barrel prodded the back of his head.

Jack lunged, swiping with the knife, but he cut only air. Once again, the chains brought him up short and he found himself staring into a killer's cold, lifeless eyes. The second gangbanger made a hawking noise.

Then he spat in Jack's face.

Though he knew the gesture was pointless, Jack made a futile stab at the gangbanger anyway.

He was a Ryan, and Ryans didn't go out cowering in fear.

As expected, the chain snapped taut, stopping Jack's blade inches from the gunman's inviting calf. The gangbanger chuckled, a deep, grating sound, and Jack prepared for the flash of light that would reunite him with his grandfather.

It didn't come.

Instead, the gangbanger's head snapped to the side, and his brains splattered against the wall with a wet slap. The corpse dropped to the floor like a pile of laundry as a pair of men assaulted through the door.

Cary and Jad.

Cary's rifle coughed twice, and the first gangbanger jerked at Jack's feet.

Then only the smell of cordite and blood remained.

"Clear," Jad said.

"Clear," Cary echoed.

"Well shit, boss," Jad said, letting his sling catch his rifle as he squatted down beside Jack, "looks like you got yourself into trouble once again."

"The girl," Jack said, pointing at Bella. "Check on the girl."

But Cary was already on it.

Bella looked impossibly small next to the big Green Beret, but Cary touched her forehead with a gentleness that belied his massive frame.

"Hey, sweetheart," Cary said as he triaged her neck and head. "Can you hear me?"

"Who . . . are . . . you?" Bella said.

The question came out long and slow, but the words were understandable. The teen's eyelids fluttered open and her gaze centered on Cary.

"A friend," Cary said, peering into her eyes.

"He said you'd come," Bella said, still sounding drugged. "He promised."

"Well, of course we came," Cary said, helping the teenager to a seated position. "That's what brothers do."

Jack suddenly found it difficult to swallow around the lump in his throat. The sound of a ringing phone cut through the air. Jad reached into his pocket, removed the cell, and answered.

"Hello?" Jad said.

The Green Beret listened for a moment and then nodded. "Just a second," Jad said.

Then he turned to Jack.

"It's for you."

69

"HELLO?" JACK SAID.

His voice sounded unsteady to his own ears. This time, the quaver didn't have anything to do with the very much alive teenager receiving medical attention from Cary, the two dead bodies he was sharing the room with, or even the knife blade slick with his own blood staring at him from where it had fallen on the dirty floor.

No, the catch in his voice came from the sight of the raven-haired beauty rushing into the room.

Or more specifically, the look on the raven-haired beauty's face.

Though she wasn't crying, Lisanne's ashen expression left no doubt what she'd been thinking. With a start, Jack realized the truth.

His fiancée had thought he was dead.

Putting the phone against his chest, Jack opened his arms.

Or at least, he opened them as wide as the chains would permit.

"Come here, baby," Jack said. "I'm okay. I promise."

He was not okay, a thought reinforced by the explosion of pain that surged through his body as Lisanne wrapped herself around him. The fierceness of the gesture surprised him. She more than he was conscious of the fact that they worked together and always went overboard to ensure her work demeanor was professional rather than personal.

But not today.

"I thought you were—" Lisanne half sobbed, half hiccupped. "I thought you were . . ."

"Shh," Jack said, burying his face in her hair, "I'm fine. Everything's fine."

Everything was not fine.

Judging by the dull ache coming from his entire body, Jack was pretty certain he was black and blue from head to foot. He'd singlehandedly pursued a lead that had resulted in a trail of bodies and necessitated The Campus operating on US soil. Not to mention the effort it took to rescue him. The town of Briar Wood was in shambles, Amanda's life was still at risk, and God only knew what a company of foreign mercenaries was doing poking around Nowhere, Texas.

But all that was still okay.

Bella was alive and Lisanne was in his arms.

Jack could work with that.

"Uh, boss," Jad said, tapping Jack on the shoulder. "You might want to answer the phone."

At this moment Jack didn't give two shits about the phone. "Who is it?"

"Mary Pat," Jad said.

Some days he just couldn't win.

"Mary Pat?" Jack said, once again holding the cell to his ear.

"Jack—are you all right?"

That was a difficult question to answer.

"I'm functional," Jack said. Or at least he would be after he got the damn manacles unlocked. "What do you need?"

"This is going to sound crazy," Mary Pat said, "but I need you to check something out. I'll fill you in on the way, but we're in crisis mode and the nexus is just thirty miles from you."

Jack looked at the two dead MS-13 members as he spoke.

"We're on it," Jack said, his words sounding weary even to him. "Give me a grid."

Mary Pat wasn't wrong a lot, but she was this time.

What she was saying didn't sound crazy at all.

70

LEON LOOKED FROM THE SILENT PHONE IN HIS HAND TO THE MONSTROSITY ON THE ground in front of him, trying to determine what concerned him more.

It was a tough choice.

The silent phone spoke volumes about the state of the men he'd left with the MS-13 gangsters while the monstrous blue shape that was rapidly expanding to a teardrop shape also silently screamed for attention. The azure hue of the material was meant to mimic the blue Texas skies that were usually clear this time of year.

Not today.

Today, iron gray clouds gathered overhead in clumps, perfectly mimicking Leon's state of mind.

"What do you think, Captain?"

He turned to his second-in-command with a sigh, trying to determine what he thought. When the client had first proposed this operation, Leon had been skeptical but intrigued. Though America was a melting pot of ethnicities and people, operating on US soil was notoriously difficult, especially for foreign intelligence services whose members were often shadowed by FBI counterintelligence officers.

This went doubly so for the venue required for this undertaking—a small town in middle-of-nowhere Texas. The client had understood these challenges and had been willing to pay an exorbitant contract fee if Leon accepted the job.

Actually, *exorbitant* didn't do the scale of money justice.

If Leon earned the success bonus, he would be able to move all his remaining comrades onto his company's payroll. No more visits from wives on behalf of husbands who were too proud to ask for help, no more old men trying to do young men's work with a weakened body for unvetted contracts and employers who would sell them out in a heartbeat if the price was right.

Just this morning Leon had touched base with his financial adviser. With the latest influx of capital, the Veterans of Africa would be solvent and ready to begin payments. Like an endowment, the principal would not be touched as the interest alone would be enough to pay the healthcare and stipends of the forgotten ones.

Except now Leon was seriously considering pulling the plug on the entire venture.

"I always thought that Namibia was the worst we'd ever face," Leon said as the azure puddle of fabric slowly began to take shape. "Now I'm not so sure. I brought this on us, Hendricks. Not a corrupt client or an inept government bureaucrat. Me. I'm responsible for more dead men."

"You have done nothing of the sort," Hendricks said. "Each man who signed up for the contract knew the risks, same as always. Before you, I was days away from living on the street. Others were already there. You gave us hope. Remember that."

Leon nodded, but Hendricks's warm words didn't cause the silent phone to ring or relieve the waves of fire that burned from his missing hand. Noble intentions were fine things, but Leon had learned long ago that results, not lofty sentiments, were what mattered. He led soldiers for hire. His job was to satisfy the customer and care for his men.

But what about when those two goals were in conflict?

"Pieter and Jan are probably gone," Leon said, the words bitter on his tongue, "but we could still fold up shop."

"What about the contract?"

Leon shrugged.

"I think we could argue for a breach of terms based on the events of the last twenty-four hours. Without the completion and success fees, there won't be enough to keep the fund solvent. On the other hand, we'll still be alive. We can always pick up more work."

Hendricks stroked his beard in silence.

The mercenary always did this when he was thinking. On more than one occasion, Leon had asked his friend whether his face actually itched or if Hendricks just thought the gesture made him look wise.

Leon didn't ask today.

The old joke felt flat, and besides, he could use some wisdom.

"I think we're done," Hendricks said, his words coming slowly. "I still don't agree with your decision to withhold the name of the client."

Leon stirred, but Hendricks held up his palm. "Peace. I'm not arguing with your choice, though I don't agree with it. One doesn't have to be Sherlock Holmes to compile a list of likely suspects. The number of entities who both want the plane and could afford to pay us the exorbitant fee we demanded to help them steal it is not exactly lengthy."

Hendricks softened his words with a smile and then paused as if waiting for Leon to object.

He didn't.

His friend wanted to speak, and Leon was going to allow him to do so uninterrupted.

Hendricks nodded as if he could sense the unspoken thought. Turning back to the staging area, he continued.

"Either way, I don't think your plan to protect us is going to work," Hendricks said. "Whatever the client intends to do with their shiny new toy is going to produce fallout. Fallout that will splash back on us. Not to mention that the little cleanup we envisioned has now become radioactive. No, I think this is our last chance. We either close this deal and ride off with the money or the fund dies. Either way, retirement is looming."

Leon said nothing.

Though part of him knew that his friend was right, he wasn't ready to accept it.

Not yet.

"I'll make sure that thing gets airborne," Leon said, pointing at the pile of fabric. "You see to the perimeter."

"Are we expecting someone?" Hendricks said.

Leon held up his still-silent phone.

"We'd be fools not to."

71

JACK RYAN WAS TIRED.

No, that wasn't quite right.

He was exhausted.

The kind of bone tiredness that only came after you'd given every last piece of yourself to the mission. His torso was a mass of bruises and his arms and legs ached. His broken nose throbbed in time to his heartbeat. Cary had taped Jack's nose. He'd offered Jack some pills for the pain.

He'd refused them.

Not because he was any kind of tough guy. Right about now, Jack thought he stood a good chance of losing a fistfight to a stiff breeze. No, he hadn't accepted Cary's offer for one reason—the operation wasn't over.

"Where'd you serve, Jack?"

The question came from Isaac, who had once again taken up his rightful spot in the copilot's seat. The Robinson was not a big helicopter under normal circumstances, and with five barrel-chested freedom fighters in its diminutive cabin, Jack was beginning to feel claustrophobic. It probably didn't help that he was sandwiched between Cary and Jad, but the Green Berets hadn't given him much of a say in the seating arrangements.

Probably because they were afraid that if they let him have a door seat, he'd fall out.

Jack adjusted his boom mike, careful to avoid his cantaloupe-sized nose and his newly split lip. The MS-13 gangbanger hadn't looked like much, but he'd fought like a demon. Then again, Jack seemed to have a gift for pissing people off.

"I didn't," Jack said.

His words sounded slurred to his ear, but that might have been due to his newly shaped mouth. While his jaw wasn't broken, Jack did have a couple of new gaps that had once been occupied by teeth.

"Come on," Isaac said. "This is the circle of trust. We're all from the special operations community except our flyboy. But he's too busy wiggling sticks to pay attention."

"Heard that," Kyle said.

"More flying, less talking," Isaac said. "You're not pretty enough to be a SEAL, Jack. And Green Berets know better than to take on a team of mercenaries solo. That's some Ranger bullshit right there. You a Batt boy?"

"I've never been in the military," Jack said. "At all."

"Really?" Isaac said.

"Really."

"Then how did you—"

"My last name is Ryan," Jack said.

"Here we go," Jad said.

"Ryan, huh?" Isaac said. "Kind of like—"

"Yes," Jack said. "Exactly like that."

Jack didn't know if it was his bone-weary tone or the subject matter that did the trick. He didn't care. All he knew was that for once Isaac was blessedly silent. The five had been winging their way westward for the last twenty minutes, tracking to a GPS coordinate that signified God only knew what.

Mary Pat's instructions had been short on details and high on urgency. For reasons known only to its computer brain, an experimental aircraft that bore on its stubby wings the only chance of preventing Iran from obtaining a nuclear weapon short of all-out war had decided to take a detour to Texas.

A detour that was only fifty miles away from Briar Wood, as the crow flew.

While Jack couldn't imagine what a crew of South African and European mercenaries had to do with a billion-dollar X-plane, his was not to reason why. With Bella in Lisanne's capable hands and every law enforcement entity ranging from the FBI's Houston office SWAT team to the entirety of Texas state law enforcement now converging on Briar Wood, Jack felt pretty confident that the lawless and corrupt men who had been running things were about to receive an enema. But all the king's horses and all the king's men could not get to the random grid coordinate the UCAV was now approaching faster than Jack and his ad hoc team.

Once again, he was it.

"Widow's Peak's coming into sight now," Kyle said. "Ten o'clock. Two miles."

Jack leaned forward, trying to see past Cary's broad shoulder.

Though he'd examined images of the peak on his phone, the pictures didn't do the gigantic terrain feature justice. The egg-shaped dome was made of pink granite and stood almost three thousand feet above sea level. At its summit, the rock was table-top flat and the size of almost three football fields. Unlike Enchanted Rock, the Widow's Peak's more benign cousin located in Fredericksburg, Texas, the path to the top of the dome was not welcoming. The routes were treacherous and often closed due to shifting rocks or washed-out trails. A road of sorts led into the park surrounding the dome from the highway, but the park's website said that the gravel drive was currently closed for resurfacing.

The people on top of Widow's Peak seemed to disagree.

"What the hell's going on up there?" Cary said.

That was a very good question.

Cary had the set of binoculars, but even with his naked eye Jack could see the makings of something very peculiar among the stunted trees and bits of scrub brush that poked up from the granite. A cluster of off-road vehicles formed the points of a lazy triangle. A gaggle of men were arrayed in what looked suspiciously like a defensive perimeter, leaving the triangle's center open.

Or mostly open.

"Cary, what's that in the center of the perimeter?" Jack said, trying to make sense of what he was seeing.

"Not sure," Cary said, adjusting the binoculars' focus, "but if I had to guess, I'd say it's some kind of winch. It's spooling out cable."

"To something over the side of the mountain?" Jack said.

"No," Cary said. "The cable's going up in the air."

"To what?" Jack said.

"That."

The answer came from Kyle. The aviator was pointing at the top of his plexiglass cockpit. Jack followed the man's finger and swore.

That was a balloon.

And it was ascending into the gray Texas sky like a homesick angel.

72

"WE MIGHT HAVE TROUBLE."

Leon looked from the balloon to his lieutenant, wondering what else could possibly go wrong with this operation. While the kit for the balloon was the very best the client's money could buy, the procurement team had apparently scrimped on the giant trailer-mounted winch. The winding mechanism had been rusted and it had taken considerable effort to break the cable free and get the line to play out smoothly.

As expected, the balloon had zero trouble going up.

But without the winch, guiding it back down would be significantly more difficult.

Though at this point Leon was seriously considering cutting the cable loose and letting the balloon and the client's representative drift wherever the Texas winds might take him. Banishing this tempting thought, Leon rested the hammer he'd been swinging on the dirt and asked the question he knew Hendricks was expecting.

"What do you have?" Leon said.

"Company," Hendricks said, pointing upward.

The industrial-sized winch was powered by an equally industrial-sized forty-kilowatt generator. The skid-mounted generator was attached to a trailer, which in theory made it portable, but getting it up the road hadn't been easy. With its one-hundred-gallon diesel fuel tank full, the generator weighed more than four thousand pounds. Unlike the winch it was powering, the generator worked fine, but quiet it was not. As a result, Leon was more than a little bit surprised to see that Hendricks was pointing at a helicopter.

A blue civilian helicopter.

"What about it?" Leon said, shouting to be heard over the generator's roar.

"One of Pieter's last transmissions," Hendricks said, "mentioned a helicopter. Before he went dark."

The words *went dark* provoked an unexpected reaction.

Unlike some of the new hires, Pieter was a friend. A close friend. The two had served together in the Recces before becoming mercenaries. This final operation was supposed to secure the futures of men like Pieter, not end them.

Pushing aside his anger, Leon concentrated on the task at hand. Recriminations and second-guessing were best left for after the mission, not during.

"Can you deal with it?" Leon asked.

Hendricks gestured toward a Pelican case resting on an adjacent truck's tailgate. "You say the word, and we'll bring it down."

Leon nodded as he examined the aircraft more closely.

Though he did not fancy himself an expert on rotary wing aviation, Leon did know a thing or two about air assets employed by military or paramilitary forces. In the United States, most police forces, and all military units, used jet-powered helicopters— and the small, tadpole-looking helo was obviously not that. Besides a larger engine, Leon would have expected to see sensor pods dotting the tiny craft's belly if it was being utilized in a paramilitary capacity, but the fuselage was smooth. By all signs, the helicopter was what it appeared to be—the property of an aviation enthusiast out for a recreational flight.

And yet.

And yet, Pieter had reported a helicopter overhead before he'd gone silent.

After almost four decades spent living by his gun, Leon had long ago ceased believing in coincidences. But swatting the helicopter from the sky was not the same as tying up a few loose ends in Briar Wood. Helicopters had radios, and even if the pilot wasn't in contact with air traffic control, an aviation crash would attract attention, and attention was the last thing Leon needed. Until the client's representative finished his work, Leon needed his team to remain under the radar.

Literally.

"Put a man on it," Leon said. "If the helo comes any closer, take it down. I'll light a fire under the client's guy. Make sure everyone is ready to roll as soon as he gives us the green light."

Hendricks nodded and then turned to his team and issued instructions. Leon watched for a moment, impressed as always by his lieutenant's work. Then he unclipped the walkie-talkie from his shirt, pressed the transmit button, and prepared to do some motivating of his own.

73

"I'VE GOT IT."

Bob winced in response to the shout from his backseater. While the rest of his body was airworthy enough to pass his reinstatement flight physical without too much cheating, Bob's hearing was a train wreck. Earplugs and flight helmets were no match for the roar of Pratt & Whitney J58 engines and the four million combined horsepower they produced. Bob had flown long before the advent of noise-canceling technology, and his eardrums were the worse because of it.

Like any self-respecting aviator, Bob had memorized the eye chart long ago, but his ancient ears were no match for the soundproof room and the hearing test's subtle beeps. After failing miserably three times in a row, Bob had persuaded the technician he could overcome his hearing deficit through liberal application of the volume control knob on the aircraft's radio panel. The woman had signed him off, partly due to pity and partly for civic duty, and Bob had been flying with the audio cranked to nine ever since. The decibel level was still hard on his eardrums, but Bob had gotten used to it.

Unless Charlie screamed.

Then it felt like someone was shoving a red-hot ice pick down his ear canal.

"For the love of God, Charlie," Bob said, "we don't yell in this profession. Ever. If you're going down in flames, you die like an aviator. Quietly. Now what have you got?"

"Sorry," Charlie said. "I thought you might want to know that I figured out why the Corvair is loitering here."

Okay, so sometimes there might be cause to shout just a little.

"Well, don't just sit there," Bob said, "spit it out."

Bob's wife claimed that he'd begun to mellow in his old age. Bob thought that was because she'd never shared a cockpit with him. Their marriage was probably still intact for this very reason.

"The Corvair is receiving new flight instructions."

Bob eyed his center console, which showed video from Charlie's sensor pod. The engineer had backed out to a wide field of view so the Corvair more resembled a black shadow flitting across the sky than an aircraft.

Even so, from Bob's perspective, the bird wasn't doing much of anything.

Though the Corvair had gotten to Texas in a hurry, the UCAV hadn't traveled at anywhere close to its top speed. Accordingly, Bob had been able to keep pace.

Barely.

While the UCAV had enough thrust to plow through the denser air at lower altitudes, Bob had been forced to head up north of sixty thousand feet where the thin air offered much less resistance. Though Bob hadn't said so to Charlie, the engineer's prowess with the sensor had saved the day. Charlie had kept the Corvair's thermal plume locked up, allowing Bob to mirror the UCAV's flight path. If the Corvair had jumped all the way to Mach 5, or if a cloud or two had obscured the clear skies separating the aircraft, the UCAV would have vanished for sure.

But luck had been with the Habu crew.

Bob had arrived on-station only slightly behind the Corvair, and that's when things went from strange to unexplainable. After decelerating down to what had to be its loitering speed, the Corvair had taken up a long, lazy orbit. Bob had been more than a little convinced that the UCAV's digital brain had a screw loose, but Charlie had insisted the aircraft was here for a reason.

Apparently, he'd been right.

"That's good news, then, right?" Bob said. "The ground crew at Palmdale has regained control?"

"No," Charlie said. "The update isn't coming via SATCOM or any of the normal data channels. The upload is happening on the UCAV's maintenance data dump frequency. The same short-range radio link I use to collect flight telemetry."

"How short are we talking?" Bob said, a sinking feeling gathering in the pit of his stomach.

"Line of sight only," Charlie said. "A mile. Maybe two, tops. I don't know where the signal could be originating."

"I think I do," Bob said, peering at the sensor feed from the wide-angle field of view. "Whatever you do, don't lose sight of that bird. I've got a radio call to make."

74

"MISS KENT, YOU HAVE THE FLOOR," PRESIDENT RYAN SAID.

If Shannon Kent was at all nervous at the prospect of briefing the President of the United States, she didn't show it. Nor did she display any trepidation about the fact that she was presenting in her boss's stead. After his less than stellar performance, General Perkins had been effectively fired by President Ryan with instructions to relay any further information through his deputy, Shannon, instead. Now Shannon was in the hot seat, though to Mary Pat's eye, the young woman seemed more than up to the task.

"Thank you, Mr. President," Shannon said. "I'm going to try to shed light on three simple questions: Who has control of the Corvair? What are their intentions? And why is it headed for Texas?"

"I like simple," Ryan said.

"So do I, sir," Shannon said. "Unfortunately, simple questions don't always beget simple answers. I will tell you what we know and what we think, and I'll be careful to distinguish between the two."

Shannon paused as if giving Ryan a chance to push back.

The President went a different direction.

"Miss Kent," Ryan said, "are you former military?"

"Yes, sir," Shannon said with a slight blush. "Navy."

"Thought so," Ryan said. "I'm a Marine, so I think we'll get along just fine. Here's what you need to understand: I don't shoot the messenger, but I'm not much for BS. I want you to give me your thoughts without spin or filters. Understood?"

"Aye, aye, sir," Shannon said. "And it's Shannon, not Miss Kent."

"Okay, Shannon," Ryan said with a smile. "Lay it on me."

Shannon glanced at her notes, but Mary Pat was pretty sure she didn't need them. Shannon had arrived in the Situation Room before anyone except Mary Pat and had patiently waited while the President had solicited updates from the other attendees. Shannon reminded Mary Pat of someone.

Herself.

Now it was time to see how deep that resemblance went.

"This is what we know," Shannon said. "Control of the Corvair has been completely co-opted. The aircraft is not responding to any of the ground team's commands. Neither is it relaying telemetry or using its transponder. Due to its low observable design and stealthy profile, we probably would have lost the aircraft completely had the SR-71 not been able to track the Corvair."

And the hits just kept on coming.

"How is it being controlled at this moment?" Ryan said.

The President hadn't been entirely fair in his earlier declaration to Shannon. While he didn't believe in shooting the messenger, he rarely let the briefer proceed with their own agenda. Ryan's nimble mind worked at a quick pace, and he expected those around him to keep up.

Hopefully Shannon was up for the challenge.

"We don't know at this time, sir," Shannon said. "We believe a section of malicious code instructed the Corvair to alter course and fly to its current location."

"Why?" Ryan said.

"We don't know," Shannon said. "We also don't know who inserted the line of code or for what purpose."

"That's an armed plane," Ryan said. "Do you think this is some kind of prelude to a terrorist attack?"

"No," Shannon said.

"Why not?" Ryan said.

Shannon gestured at the LCD screen on the wall. The television currently showed a map of the United States with the Corvair's flight path from its origination in Palmdale to its current location in Texas denoted by a thin blue line.

"As you can see," Shannon said, "the UCAV bypassed a large number of potentially high-value targets by flying to Texas. The trip also cost the UCAV half its available fuel. We estimate that the Corvair has a range of about another thousand miles before its tanks run dry. That distance decreases with every minute it spends loitering in Texas."

Shannon keyed another button and a crimson ring appeared on the screen. The ring was centered on the UCAV's current location and depicted a thousand-mile radius. While the ring covered a massive amount of territory, the red circle's northeastern edge terminated around Roanoke, Virginia. In the first good news of the day, the Corvair wouldn't be visiting Washington, D.C., but a good portion of the flyover states were within range.

So did much of Mexico and northern Central America.

"Based on this analysis," Shannon said, "we assess that someone is trying to steal the UCAV rather than use it as a weapon of war."

"Who?" Ryan said.

Shannon shook her head. "Unknown, sir. But taking control of the aircraft requires a high level of sophistication."

"The kind of sophistication that only a nation-state could muster?" Ryan said.

Shannon nodded.

"I still don't get it," Arnie said, scratching his head. "If someone is trying to steal our plane, why fly it to Texas?"

"Range," Ryan said. "That bird only gets two thousand miles to a tank of gas and it can't aerially refuel without our tankers. If it headed west from California, the UCAV would run dry in the middle of the Pacific. But you know what country it could reach from Texas?"

"Cuba," Mary Pat said.

"Exactly," Ryan said.

"Those commie sons of bitches," Arnie said, a flush building at the base of his neck.

"Hold on now, Arnie," Ryan said. "Every good analyst knows that you can't let confirmation bias influence your reasoning. Cuba certainly makes a good landing spot, and the current regime is on friendly terms with any number of nations that would love to get their hands on this aircraft, but we can't jump to conclusions. First things first. We need to understand why that bird's in Texas."

"Mr. President? There's a radio call the switchboard wants to route here."

The comment came from one of the headset-wearing technicians charged with managing the Situation Room's impressive communications suite.

"Who is it?" Ryan said.

"Lorenzo," the technician said.

"Put him through."

75

"LET ME GET THIS STRAIGHT," PRESIDENT RYAN SAID. "YOU THINK THE CORVAIR IS receiving updated flight instructions from some knucklehead in a hot air balloon? Why?"

Though inwardly she winced, Mary Pat managed to keep her face expressionless.

Lesson one when running assets—never react to what they're saying. From Soviet secrets passed to her by the cardinal of the Kremlin to Stasi double agents she'd flipped in East Berlin, Mary Pat prided herself on maintaining a poker face while weathering even the most outrageous news. But what was currently unfolding in the Situation Room was putting these abilities to the test.

A flash of distortion echoed through the speakers before Lorenzo's disembodied voice returned.

"Sorry about that, Mr. President. We're having some comms issues up here. Whenever my backseater jumps into the conversation, he accidentally steps on you. I'm not an engineer, so I'm gonna keep this in terms that even old fighter pilots can understand. It wouldn't be very difficult for a bad actor with access to the Corvair's operating system to insert a subroutine instructing the aircraft to fly to a single GPS coordinate and loiter there. With tens of millions of lines of code in the UCAV's brain, the hacker could feel pretty confident that their intrusion would never be detected by the program's engineers. But actually taking control of the aircraft and exercising its complete functionality would be a much harder lift. My backseater thinks the hacker used the first Trojan horse to fly the bird to Texas and is now uploading the rest of their instructions as it orbits."

"That makes sense, sir," Shannon said. "So far the UCAV has done nothing more than fly to a waypoint. But if the hacker wants to land the aircraft, they'll need much greater access to the operating system."

"I assume the same logic holds true if the hacker wants to employ the Corvair's weapons system?" Ryan said.

"Yes, sir," Shannon said.

The President nodded.

Though he didn't say anything, the implication behind Ryan's silence was obvious to Mary Pat. Best-case scenario, someone was attempting to steal a billion-dollar stealthy hypersonic weapon.

Worst case, someone was intending to use it.

Ryan sat in silence for a beat. Then he nodded again as he'd finished his internal deliberations. Mary Pat would have loved to know what her boss was thinking, but she knew better than to ask. The analyst part of Ryan occasionally still preferred his own counsel.

He'd share his reasoning when he was ready.

"Lorenzo," Ryan said, "how do you think the hacker's access-ing the Corvair?"

Another burst of static heralded Lorenzo's return.

"The UCAV has a software back door that is accessible by short-range radio on a discrete frequency. My backseater uses the portal to monitor telemetry during tests when we function as a chase bird. Up until this moment, the technical team believed this back door only swung one direction. That apparently is not the case."

Voices murmured around the long table as attendees tried to make sense of the damning information. Senator Brown cleared her throat, but the President forestalled her and everyone else with a single upraised finger. For those who were not part of Ryan's inner circle, it was easy to dismiss him as just another career politician. But at his core, Ryan was something else.

A United States Marine.

"You're sure it's coming from the balloon?" Ryan said.

"I'm not sure of anything right now, sir," Lorenzo said. "But this balloon isn't the kind you take on a sunset cruise. It's military-grade, configured for high-altitude flight with some sort of sealed cabin beneath it instead of a wicker basket. The cabin has an antenna sprouting from the side that my backseater tells me is the correct type for the frequency band needed to access the UCAV's maintenance protocols. The cabin is also tethered to the ground with some sort of cable that plays out as it gains altitude. And this thing is climbing like a bat out of hell. My backseater believes the balloon is only able to reach the UCAV intermittently until it gets closer and can decrease the transmission range."

"Then why not just fly the UCAV lower?" Ryan said.

"The Corvair is a fuel whore, sir," Lorenzo said. "It's optimized to fly at Mach 5 at eighty-plus thousand feet. My guess is whoever is controlling it wants to save as much fuel as possible for whatever they have planned next. That means bringing the balloon within range of the Corvair, not the other way around."

"How do we stop the balloon?" Ryan said.

"Don't know, sir," Lorenzo said, "about the balloon, anyway. But I might have a shot at taking down the UCAV."

"How?" Ryan said.

"Ram it," Lorenzo said. "My Habu isn't made for fancy flying, but the holding pattern the Corvair is following is fairly predictable. It won't be pretty, but I think I could bring the UCAV down. Assuming it doesn't change course."

This time the room's silence wasn't instigated by the President. What Lorenzo was so offhandedly proposing seemed to have universally cowed the attendees. He was talking about purposely colliding with the UCAV at the cost of his own life.

Mary Pat's secure device vibrated.

Flipping it over, she saw two words.

ON STATION.

"Does anybody else have any ideas?" Ryan said, sweeping the room with his gaze. "Anyone?"

"Actually, I do," Mary Pat said.

Ryan's eyes softened as they found hers, but his expression was still hard.

"Let's hear it, MP."

"Yes, sir," Mary Pat said, formulating her thoughts as she spoke, "we were able to vector a nearby paramilitary team. They are on-site now."

The vagaries Mary Pat used when she spoke were for the benefit of the room's other occupants. The Campus's existence was still a need-to-know item, and the President was in the process of deciding who among his principals he would bring into the fold. But while her odd language might as well have been a neon sign for Ryan, Mary Pat could tell her boss had another question.

A more personal one.

He raised his eyebrows.

She nodded.

Ryan held her gaze for a beat without speaking.

Then he nodded in return.

"Lorenzo, stay on station," Ryan said. "For now, you're our backup plan. Mary Pat, you're clear to work the other angle. If the rest of you will excuse me, I have a call with the Israeli prime minister."

With the exception of Arnie van Damm and Scott Adler, the other attendees got to their feet.

Usually, Mary Pat was content to walk out of the room in the stately manner the setting deserved.

Today, she ran.

76

"GO AHEAD, MARY PAT," JACK SAID. "I CAN HEAR YOU."

This was an accurate statement, for the most part. While the Robinson had the noisy cabin typical of most helicopters, Jack's headphones had a dongle that could be plugged into a cell phone. But even with the headset's noise-canceling technology, the environment wasn't exactly conducive to telephone conversations. Not to mention that everyone else in the helicopter would hear the conversation via their headsets, too.

Hopefully Mary Pat was calling with good news.

"Jack, the key to this whole thing is that balloon," Mary Pat said. "Whoever's inside it is sending updates to the orbiting UCAV. We have another military aircraft shadowing the UCAV, but it's unarmed."

Jack angled his head to get a look out the cabin's open door. The balloon was headed for the layer of broken clouds several thousand feet above them. If a pair of mystery planes were orbiting somewhere in the slate-gray sky, it was news to him.

"Any idea what they want with the UCAV?" Jack said.

"No, but here's what I do know. We need that aircraft back, Jack. It is loaded for a combat mission. If it doesn't fly, the world is going to war, not to mention what would happen if it fell into Russian or Chinese hands. It would be the equivalent of a B-2 bomber pilot defecting with her plane to Moscow. We can't let the aircraft get away."

Jack closed his eyes and fought the urge to groan.

His fingers were midway to the bridge of his nose when he arrested the gesture, remembering the throbbing cantaloupe in the center of his face. Just once it would be nice not to have the fate of all mankind resting on his battered shoulders. For fuck's sake, this weekend was supposed to be about spending time with Lisanne and watching a college football game. Surely there was someone else who could take a turn saving the world for a change?

The man doesn't choose the moment.

The moment chooses the man.

The thought popped unbidden into Jack's mind.

He didn't know where he'd heard the saying before. Most of the wisdom in his life he attributed either to his parents or Ding Chavez. But these words didn't sound like something either of them would say. Hell, maybe Jack had obtained this wisdom from a fortune cookie the last time he and Lisanne had grabbed Chinese. But fortune cookie or not, the sentiment was correct.

There was a job to do, and he was the only one who could do it.

Time to saddle up.

"We'll take care of it, Mary Pat," Jack said.

"Jack, you need to understand that—"

"I've got it," Jack said, gently but firmly. "Tell Dad that I've got it."

The answering silence made Jack wonder if the call had dropped.

Then Mary Pat spoke.

"Okay, Jack. Good luck."

The call ended.

"Well, shit," Jad said. "Sounds like President Ryan needs us to save the day. Again."

"You think this will get us another invitation to dinner at the White House?" Cary said.

"Dinner?" Jad said. "Hell. Been there and done that. This time I want a ride on Air Force One."

In spite of everything, Jack felt his split lips twisting into a smile. This was a raging shitshow, no two ways about it. But if he had to stroll through the gates of hell, he could think of no better men to have by his side.

"He really *is* that Ryan?" Isaac said, his earlier levity gone.

"Goddamn, son," Jad said, "I know you Third Group guys are the JV team, but do try to keep up."

"All right, boys," Jack said, "seems like we need to take a look at that balloon."

"There's a problem with that," Kyle said. "The balloon's approaching the edge of my bird's service ceiling. If we want to get up there, I'm gonna need to offload three of you."

"Actually, there's another problem," Cary said. "One of the ground crew is uncrating a MANPAD."

"Hang on," Kyle said.

Jack slammed into his restraint harness as the helicopter seemed to drop out from beneath him. The dome flashed by on his left and then vanished altogether as Kyle arrested their descent with the Robinson's skids at treetop level.

"You sure it was a MANPAD?" Kyle said, bringing the helicopter into a tight left bank.

"I'm a sniper," Cary said, "I'm pretty good at target ID. That boy was unpacking an SA-7 Grail surface-to-air missile."

"Roger that," Kyle said. "If we stay low, I can use the terrain to mask us. But if that Grail gets line of sight to our engine, we're done."

Someone was going to have to take out the missileer.

Jack glanced at Cary.

The Green Beret was staring at him.

Waiting.

"I'm going after the balloon," Jack said. "I need you to do some sniper shit."

"Thought you'd never ask," Cary said. "If only I had a decent spotter."

"The sooner you stop flapping your jaws, the sooner we can get to putting steel on target," Jad said.

"I'm coming, too," Isaac said.

"Well, now, that depends," Cary said. "Do you have a Ranger tab?"

"Of course," Isaac said, sounding slightly offended. "Why?"

"Because we're about to make Ranger Rudder damn proud."

77

RANGER RUDDER, AS CARY HAD HURRIEDLY EXPLAINED, REFERRED TO MAJOR General James Earl Rudder. Rudder was a US Army lieutenant colonel during World War II, and he scaled the hundred-foot cliffs at Pointe du Hoc. That alone would have been quite the feat, but Rudder had accomplished the task while leading his Ranger battalion in an assault through withering German fire. The daring operation helped support the Normandy invasion and went down in the annals of Ranger lore. Unfortunately, Rudder's courage was not without cost. He was wounded twice during the fighting and half his Rangers were casualties as well.

Jack hoped that this hastily cobbled together reenactment ended on better terms.

"SCEPTER, THIS IS REAPER," CARY SAID. "WE ARE AT THE BASE OF THE CLIFF. Beginning our ascent time now, over."

While Jack had been talking with Mary Pat, Cary had been busy scouting for a position from which he could engage the mercenaries occupying Widow's Peak. The dome was uniformly flat, but the northeastern corner boasted a fifty-foot cliff that overlooked the rest of the terrain. Though the cliff was easily accessible from the dome via a series of switchback trails, the sheer granite walls prevented alternate approaches.

Or at least they prevented most people from considering an alternate approach.

As they had demonstrated time and time again, the commandos from Triple Nickel were not most people. Cary believed that he, Jad, and Isaac could summit the northern side and remain hidden from its defenders. From there, the Green Berets would set up a firing position atop the cliff and neutralize the missileer, allowing Jack and Kyle to climb to altitude and inspect the balloon.

At least that had been the plan.

Kyle had inserted the Green Berets at the northern base of Widow's Peak, using a series of rolling hills to hide his intentions from the mercenaries. After dropping off the commandos, Kyle had flown due west for a mile in the hopes of persuading the gunmen occupying the dome that he was not interested in them.

Now it was time for that to change.

"Roger that, Reaper," Jack said. "Call when set, over."

"So," Kyle said, "we never did talk about what you were going to do if I managed to get you up to the balloon."

Jack didn't particularly care for the *if* in Kyle's statement, but he understood why the aviator was voicing it. Kyle made no bones about their odds of success. The balloon had continued its climb and every additional foot of altitude made the aviator's job that much harder.

"No, we didn't," Jack said.

Kyle was quiet for a moment.

When Jack didn't elaborate, he tried again.

"Even if I can get us that high," Kyle said, "we're not going to have power to hover."

"Noted," Jack said.

"Mind telling me what you're thinking?"

"I'm thinking I'll figure out what I'm going to do once you get me there," Jack said.

"Interesting approach," Kyle said.

"Scepter, this is Reaper," Cary said.

Jack didn't think he'd ever been happier to hear the Green Beret's voice.

"This is Scepter. Go ahead," Jack said.

"Roger that, Scepter. We've got a situation."

Or perhaps not.

78

CARY CLUNG TO THE SLICK GRANITE FACE WITH BOTH HANDS, TRYING TO IGNORE both the fifty-foot drop below him and the gusts of winds buffeting his body. This was actually easier to do than he'd anticipated, mainly because Cary had a more pressing concern than treacherous winds or jagged rocks.

The man waiting to kill him.

"Scepter, Reaper," Cary said, his voice a whisper. "I think there's somebody on the ledge above us."

As had happened many times in their career, Jad had saved their collective bacon. While Cary prided himself on his hard-won skills as a commando, Jad had a preternatural ability to sense danger. Whether it was making a last-minute decision to lead the assault team through an alternate breach point and thereby avoid an ambush, or halting a patrol steps away from a minefield, Jad was in tune with his environment in a way Cary didn't understand.

But understand it or not, when his spotter had given the command to freeze just yards from the cliff's summit, Cary had plastered himself to the granite. Using hand and arm signals, Jad had conveyed his belief that a sentry was occupying the top. Cary couldn't hear anything over the gusting wind and could see nothing but the rock face, but he still took Jad's word as gospel.

"Reaper, this is Scepter," Jack said. "Roger that. What do you need?"

Cary looked to Jad.

The spotter was leading the ascent and was ten feet above Cary and to his right. While he didn't dare speak, Jad could still monitor Cary's conversation with Jack. Jad made his intentions known with another series of hand and arm signals and Cary nodded, thought for a moment, and then keyed the transmit button.

"Scepter, this is Reaper," Cary said. "We'll handle the sentry, but we need a distraction. Do you think we could get that orbiting friendly air to make a low pass?"

"Reaper, this is Scepter. Stand by."

79

"YOU NEED ME TO DO WHAT?" BOB SAID, EYEING THE RADIO AS IF THE DEVICE IT-self was responsible for the idiocy of the speaker's request.

The voice that had just posed the question was an unfamiliar one, and Bob thought that perhaps the radio operator had mistakenly transmitted on the wrong frequency. Bob had been passing updates via his SATCOM radio, and the plethora of call signs asking for clarification was getting cumbersome. Where before he'd been talking either to the White House or back to Palmdale, now it seemed that everyone in North America with a radio was calling into the party line.

Once again, Bob found himself missing the Cold War days. Back then, the amount of radio calls he'd needed to make from the time he left US airspace until he returned had been easy to tabulate.

Zero.

With SATCOM technology nonexistent and the need for secrecy paramount, Bob had flown entire combat missions without ever talking to a soul. Now he couldn't make a right turn without ten people asking him why.

Maybe there was something to this retirement gig.

"We'd like you to make a low pass over the mountaintop, over."

Same voice, same stupid request.

Bob was about to key his radio and give the operator a piece of his mind when another voice joined the fray.

One he recognized.

"Lorenzo, this is Jack. Can you hear me?"

"Yes, Mr. President," Bob said, sitting up just a little bit straighter.

He'd been out of the military almost longer than he'd been in it, but one question from Jack Ryan and Bob felt like a doolie back at the Air Force Academy.

"Great," Ryan said. "The last thing I want to do is to crawl into your cockpit, so let me lay this out—we have a team of operatives maneuvering up the cliff and they need a distraction."

"A distraction, sir?" Bob said.

"Something to get the other team's heads down."

"Got it, sir," Bob said. "That I can do."

"Roger that, Lorenzo," Ryan said. "Continue the mission."

Bob thought he could get used to working for this Ryan guy.

"Hey, Lorenzo, what are we doing?" Charlie said.

For once, Bob didn't mind his backseater's endless questions.

"Watch and learn, son," Bob said. "We used to call this Blackbird Diplomacy."

80

"REAPER, THIS IS SCEPTER. YOUR FRIENDLY AIR IS INBOUND."

"Roger that," Cary whispered. "He's making a low pass?"

"That's a negative, Reaper," Jack said. "I'm told he has a better idea. Oh, he also said you should hold on to something and plug your ears."

Cary was no stranger to jet jockeys performing show of force overflights. While facing Taliban dug into the side of a hill in Afghanistan, Cary had once radioed for help from an orbiting B-1 Lancer. That beautiful bird had come screaming down the valley with all four of its afterburners spitting flame. About a millisecond before it reached the Taliban-occupied hill, the pilot had stood the aircraft on its tail, sending the Lancer streaking skyward.

It had been awesome.

Cary checked to ensure Jad and Isaac had gotten the message. Like him, both Green Berets were plastered against the granite.

Not the most secure perch, but as good as they were likely to get.

"Scepter, this is Reaper," Cary said. "We're set."

Cary opened his mouth, pressed his right ear against his shoulder, and plugged his left with his finger. Regardless of what happened today, Cary was pretty certain that this part of their ascent would not be taught in the mountain phase of Ranger school.

"Roger that, Reaper," Jack said. "Snake is turning inbound. ETA fifteen seconds."

A trickling of pebbles pegged Cary in the face.

He looked up, thinking that the stones had come from Jad.

They had not.

"Ten seconds."

Jad was so still he might have been carved from stone.

Cary understood why.

"Five, four, three . . ."

A pair of toes peeked over the edge of the cliff.

The sentry was standing right above them.

"Two, one, execute, execute, ex—"

The third *execute* was interrupted by what Cary could only imagine was the hand of God. He'd thought he'd seen a show of force before.

He hadn't.

The sonic boom that followed the aircraft's pass made the overpressure from a breaching charge feel like a love tap. It wasn't so much an assault on his auditory senses as an unseen uppercut. Cary had been expecting the onslaught and was barely still upright.

The sentry hadn't stood a chance.

Like a mongoose, Jad scrambled up the last two feet of rock. Cary followed, though his movements were considerably less nimble. But nimble or not, he made it over the lip of the cliff in time to see the sentry sprawled on the rock and Jad grabbing the still stunned man by the feet. Letting his tactical sling catch his rifle, Cary snared the sentry by his arms and in concert with Jad tossed the mercenary off the backside of the cliff.

A moment later Isaac clambered up the rock face and joined them.

"Maybe a little warning next time?" Isaac hissed.

"About the plane?" Jad said.

"No, the flying body," Isaac said.

"You've been retired too long," Jad said.

"Save it for the after-action review," Cary said, settling into the prone position. "We've got work to do."

Did they ever.

81

"SCEPTER, THIS IS REAPER," CARY SAID. "WE ARE IN POSITION AND SET, OVER."

Jack glanced at Kyle.

While it was difficult to judge the pilot's disposition through his aviator sunglasses, Jack didn't believe Kyle's body language radiated confidence.

"You ready?" Jack said.

"Are those guys really gonna get to ride on Air Force One?" Kyle said.

"There's always room for one more," Jack said. "Get me up to that balloon and you can join the party."

"I don't want to ride in steerage," Kyle said.

"Only first class for you," Jack said.

"I was thinking the copilot's seat."

"Done," Jack said.

"All right," Kyle said. "Here goes nothing."

Not the encouraging words Jack was hoping for.

Then again, beggars couldn't be choosers.

"Reaper, this is Scepter," Jack said. "We're going for it."

82

"THE HELICOPTER'S BACK."

Had Hendricks not been pointing at the sky, Leon wasn't sure he would have understood what his friend was saying. In addition to nearly deafening him, the shock wave from a second ago had nearly knocked him off his feet. He'd grabbed hold of the winch to steady himself as the men surrounding him stumbled or fell to their knees.

His first thought had been that the blivets of diesel had somehow exploded, but a quick look at the rubber bladders showed that the storage units were still intact. In fact, other than ringing ears and a thundering heart, Leon didn't seem to be any worse for the wear. A quick look around the perimeter confirmed his assessment.

Men were picking themselves up and dusting off their clothes.

Everything was fine.

But Leon knew that it wasn't.

Earsplitting explosions didn't just happen. Something had changed, and the years Leon had spent as a mercenary suggested that when things unexpectedly changed in the middle of an operation, it was seldom for the good. He was in the process of calling the team leaders for an update when Hendricks got his attention.

While the little helicopter had been circumspect in its approach of the rocky dome before, the aircraft was no longer timid. At first Leon was convinced its crew was going to attempt to land on the Widow's Peak alongside them.

Then the helo rocketed upward.

"It's going for the balloon," Leon said, his voice sounding distorted in his still-ringing ears. "Take it down."

Hendricks nodded. Turning, the mercenary whistled and pointed at the helicopter.

The missileer hefted the SA-7 to his shoulder and oriented the tube skyward.

Then his head exploded.

83

"SCEPTER, THIS IS REAPER. WE ARE ENGAGING NOW. BE ADVISED, MISSILEER IS down. You are clear to the balloon."

"Roger that, Reaper," Jack said. "Understand we are clear to the balloon."

For the first time since Mary Pat had dropped this shit sandwich in his lap, Jack felt a twinge of hope. The balloon and its gondola were growing larger in his windshield by the moment, the UCAV was still somewhere overhead, and the Green Berets were taking care of business.

They might just pull this off after all.

"Scepter, this is Reaper. Suggest you expedite, over."

"Reaper, can you elaborate? Over," Jack said.

"Uh, roger. Reaper is engaging a force of approximately twenty to thirty well-trained and well-armed fighters. We will not be able to hold them off for long. Over."

Jack grimaced, angry at himself for not seeing that one coming.

He'd been so focused on getting to the balloon and so confident in Cary's abilities that he hadn't bothered to think the scenario through. Yes, the Green Berets could take out the danger to Jack, but in so doing, they would kick over a hornets' nest.

Now, the angry insects were looking for someone to sting.

"Reaper, this is Scepter," Jack said. "Real talk. How long do you have, over?"

"Scepter, Reaper. Things are gonna get pretty interesting in about two minutes, over."

"Roger, Reaper," Jack said. "Wait one."

"How long till we're even with that balloon?" Jack said, turning to Kyle.

"You haven't even told me what you're going to do once—"

"How. Long."

Kyle paused, looking from the balloon to his instruments. "At this rate of climb, probably another minute or so."

"Climb faster," Jack said.

"I can probably squeeze it down to forty-five seconds if I redline the transmission, but—"

"Do it," Jack said.

"Hey, man," Kyle said, "I understand the urgency. What I'm telling you is that if I redline the transmission, the stress will do structural damage to the metal. Once that happens, we either land or risk a catastrophic failure midflight."

"We only need to get the Green Berets off that rock," Jack said. "Land in the parking lot at the base of the dome for all I care."

"Okay," Kyle said, "but I'm going into my two-minute transient time now. After two minutes we either land or the transmission seizes and we become a lawn dart."

"Got it," Jack said. "Start your clock."

Jack meant the comment half in jest, but Kyle was having none of it.

The aviator yanked in collective until his gauges flashed red and then started a two-minute countdown on the timer situated on the instrument panel between him and Jack.

When it came to their helicopters, aviators were pretty damn literal.

"Reaper, this is Scepter," Jack said. "We're coming to get you in ninety seconds, over."

This time, instead of replying with his voice, Cary clicked the transmit button twice. Even so, Jack heard reports from multiple rifles each time the Green Beret broke squelch. Hefting his AR-15, Jack looked at the rapidly growing balloon. It was probably time for him to start thinking about what in the hell he was actually going to do once Kyle brought him alongside the contraption.

And then his phone rang.

84

"CHARLIE," BOB SAID, "HOW'S THE ONES AND ZEROES STUFF GOING?"

"Damn it," Charlie said. "Damn it, damn it, damn it."

"I'm guessing that means not well," Bob said.

"I was so close," Charlie said. "I figured out how the intruders are trying to reconfigure the Corvair's flight protocols. I was able to delete some of their subfiles, but the other guy saw me and walled off my access. Then I tried to get the Corvair to only recognize my IP address, but the intruder beat me to it. His radio signal is much stronger, so the Corvair keeps defaulting to his network."

"Like how your phone automatically jumps to whichever Wi-Fi network is closer?" Bob said.

"Well, yes," Charlie said. "Exactly like that."

The shock in the engineer's voice almost brought a smile to Bob's face.

Almost.

But the image of the Corvair on Bob's screen precluded any happiness.

"Charlie," Bob said, "is it me or is that thing changing course?"

The image widened as Charlie bumped out a field of view, but Bob no longer needed the sensor's assessment.

He could see the Corvair banking with his naked eye.

"Main, this is Snake," Bob said, "tell the President our time is up. The Corvair is breaking station. I'm interdicting, over."

Bob lit off the afterburners as he plotted his intercept point. Learning how to join a formation without crashing into your wingman was something every flight school student had to master.

Now Bob was putting those skills to use, but in reverse.

"We're going to die, aren't we?"

The fighter pilot portion of Bob's mind was plotting speed and intercept angles, but the human part thought he might have misjudged old Charlie. The engineer wasn't begging or pleading. He was simply asking an honest question.

Bob owed him an honest response.

"Yeah, partner," Bob said, "we sure are. I wish there was another way, but there isn't. Hell, if this bird was set up to let us eject one at a time, I'd tell you to punch out, but it's not. I'm gonna fly this baby right through the center of that Corvair. I guess there's a slim chance we might make it through the impact intact enough to eject, but I doubt it."

"Okay," Charlie said, "I understand."

Bob rested his left hand on the throttle as he made a final minute course adjustment with the pedals, ensuring that the Corvair's ethereal shape remained centered in his windshield.

"I'm gonna tell you the truth, Charlie," Bob said. "You're a damn good backseater."

"Good enough for a call sign?" Charlie said.

Bob was a little taken aback. Up until now, Charlie had showed zero interest in the military conventions that came with flying a former Air Force jet. Then again, as Mark Twain famously said, nothing so focuses the mind as the prospect of being hanged. If Charlie wanted to go out with a call sign, that seemed like a fair request to Bob. "You betcha," Bob said. "How's Cowboy sound?"

"I like it," Charlie said.

"All right then, Cowboy it is," Bob said. "Hold on tight, Cowboy, this will all be over in about a minute."

Bob firewalled the engines and breathed a prayer for his wife. She deserved better than this.

A millisecond later Bob's head slammed against the side of the canopy.

85

"GO FOR RYAN," JACK SAID.

"It's Mary Pat."

"Hey, Mary Pat," Jack said as he chambered a round in his rifle. "I'm kind of in the middle of something."

"The UCAV is pulling off station," Mary Pat said.

"Fuck!" Jack said.

And then his face reddened.

Mary Pat might be a Cold War warrior and the current director of national intelligence, but Jack had known her his entire life. To him, she was something between an aunt and a surrogate mother.

You didn't drop the F-bomb in front of your surrogate mother.

At least you didn't if your real mother's name was Cathy Ryan.

"We'll be on the balloon in fifteen seconds, Mary Pat," Jack said.

For the first time, the rectangular gondola was fully visible. It looked more like a space capsule than something that belonged beneath a balloon. Though small, it had tinted windows and an assortment of tanks and pipes on top of the cabin, suggesting that it was probably pressurized.

"Don't bother," Mary Pat said. "That's why I'm calling. With the UCAV breaking station, we can't wait any longer."

"What do you mean?" Jack said.

"We're as high as we can go," Kyle said. "Twenty seconds until the transmission overheats."

"The friendly aircraft is going to ram it," Mary Pat said.

"No," Jack said, suddenly frantic. "Give me a chance. I can—"

"Fuck!" Mary Pat said.

"Mary Pat?" Jack said.

"Our aircraft had a mechanical failure," Mary Pat said. "You're it, Jack. You're it."

Fuck.

86

"WHAT HAPPENED?"

"WHAT HAPPENED?"

Bob thought he might have smiled if he wasn't so busy trying to keep his airplane in the air. Old Charlie sounded positively disappointed they hadn't smashed headlong into the UCAV.

Cowboy was already living up to his call sign.

"It's an un-start on the number one engine," Bob said.

"A what?"

"The engine flamed out," Bob said, "so the computer automatically brought the number two to idle."

"Why?" Charlie said.

"To keep us from dying," Bob said. "With the number two at full burner and the number one engine at idle, the yaw rate would have put us into an unrecoverable spin."

"So what do we do?"

"For Pete's sake, Cowboy. Let me fly this bus for a minute."

Bob ran through the engine restart procedure, his fingers still moving off muscle memory even though it had been almost thirty years since he'd last dealt with an un-start.

In the old analog days, the pilot had to pull back the thrust-producing engine on his own to avoid the deadly yaw. Back then, the aircraft wasn't even equipped with an indicator to let the pilot know which engine had failed. After several accidents, a pair of red lightbulbs had been added to the cockpit's instrumentation. If the light on the left glowed, the number one engine was out while the light on the right equaled the number two.

Bob had never needed the lights.

When an un-start happened, the aircraft yawed violently, and Bob inevitably bashed his head against the side of the cockpit.

Right side meant number one out. Left side, number two.

Simple.

Bob finished the engine start sequence and was rewarded with the gauges climbing to their prescribed levels.

Then he lit off both afterburners.

The analog counter now read 0.

Bob had just used his final shot of TEB.

For better or worse, he was committed.

Normally Bob liked to verify that the afterburners had ignited by looking for the exhaust with his rear-facing periscope.

This time he didn't bother.

The kick in the pants from sixty-five thousand pounds of thrust was verification enough.

"Cowboy, tell me you've got the UCAV in sight," Bob said.

"Sure do, Lorenzo. Come right heading one one zero."

"That's my boy," Bob said, banking the Habu to the aircraft's maneuvering limit.

"It's pulling away," Charlie said. "What are we going to do, Lorenzo?"

"Catch it."

87

"FIFTEEN SECONDS," KYLE SAID.

"Know anything about balloons?" Jack said.

"That one's a stratospheric balloon," Kyle said. "It has a service ceiling of over one hundred thousand feet, and it's filled with nonflammable helium. Your AR-15 isn't going to punch a big enough hole in the plastic skin to have any effect. Ten seconds."

Jack looked at Kyle.

"What?" Kyle said. "There's a startup company about forty minutes east of here that offers passenger flights to the stratosphere. Kind of like SpaceX but cheaper."

"Do their balloons look like that one?" Jack said.

"Well . . . yeah, I guess."

Several responses leaped to Jack's mind, but none of them were helpful to the current situation. While it certainly would have been nice for Kyle to volunteer this information sooner, nothing the aviator said had really changed things. A capsule containing a hacker intent on stealing a UCAV was dangling beneath a tear-shaped balloon.

Out of habit, Jack panned his holographic sight across the capsule.

The boxy structure wasn't exactly the height of sleek engineering, but based on Mary Pat's call, it was getting the job done. While Jack was a firm believer in the notion that a liberal enough application of brute force could solve just about any problem, this might be the exception that proved the rule.

Even if the helicopter had the ability to hover, which it didn't, and even if Kyle could somehow maneuver close enough for Jack to board the capsule without the aircraft's rotor blades impacting the tether connecting the capsule to the balloon, which it couldn't, the capsule's smooth sides offered no purchase.

Jack saw a handle protruding from what he guessed was the entrance hatch, but there was no ledge on which to stand even if he magically transported himself onto the capsule. Not to mention that the way today was shaping up, the capsule was probably locked from the inside, moving this course of action from the realm of fantastical firmly into impossible.

Jack wasn't getting aboard the capsule.

Which meant he needed to interrupt the hacker's work.

"Five seconds," Kyle said.

Jack centered the EOTech's red dot on the capsule's window as he took the slack out of the trigger. The capsule was pressurized, which meant that the windows would most likely be constructed of thick, double-paned glass. The light 5.56mm round his AR-15 fired would probably fragment before penetrating the window.

Even if Jack somehow managed to puncture the glass, then what?

Odds of him hitting the hacker inside were minimal.

Odds of killing him and stopping the broadcast were zero.

Stopping the broadcast.

"Time's up," Kyle said. "Transmission's cooked. We're done."

As the helicopter's nose tilted downward, Jack saw it.

The parabolic antenna mounted to the capsule's side.

"Wait," Jack said, grabbing the cyclic with his left hand and yanking the stick aft.

"What the hell?" Kyle said.

Jack didn't answer.

Releasing the cyclic, Jack tracked the holographic dot over the antenna as he steadied the muzzle with his left hand. He began pressing the trigger the moment the crimson circle alighted on the disc-shaped antenna. The shot broke and Jack continued to fire, squeezing off round after round.

Sparks leaped from the aerial as Jack hammered through his magazine.

Then, the AR's bolt locked to the rear, and Kyle nosed the Robinson into a dive.

Jack was out of both time and bullets.

88

"I'VE GOT IT," CHARLIE SAID.

"You've got to be more specific, partner," Bob said. "Kind of busy up here."

The SR-71 was still a cutting-edge airplane even almost sixty years after its inception.

It was good at a great many things.

Midflight linkups weren't one of them.

Though the Corvair had yet to transition to hypersonic flight, it was through Mach 1 and accelerating. Even if the UCAV had been on a straight and level trajectory, the speeds involved would have made Bob's job difficult.

The Corvair was not flying straight and level.

The robotic aircraft was climbing while turning and increasing its velocity. Short of doing a barrel roll, there weren't too many more variables the nimble UCAV could introduce that would make Bob work harder. Not to mention that while ramming the Corvair was both noble and the right thing to do, the idea of committing suicide did not get any easier the longer Bob had time to dwell on the idea.

"The Corvair," Charlie said. "The intruding signal's amplitude has dropped off significantly. It's still there, but ours is now more powerful."

"English, Cowboy," Bob said.

"Our Wi-Fi network is now stronger than the neighbor's," Cowboy said. "If you get me closer, I think I can take over the Corvair and then reinstall its original flight protocol system to overwrite the intrusion."

As if its ears were burning, the Corvair leveled its wings, coming to a steady altitude and course. Bob adjusted his bank angle accordingly, centering the aircraft in his windshield before rolling level.

He was now at a decision point.

"Okay, partner," Bob said, "we only get one shot. I can either bring that thing down or get you closer to do some computer magic. Not both. If you're wrong and the Corvair transitions to hypersonic flight, it's gone for good."

"I can do it," Charlie said. "I swear to you I can do it."

Bob looked at the Corvair's shadowy form, considering.

As the mission commander and pilot in command, the decision was ultimately his. And while Bob didn't have a death wish, he did understand what was riding on his actions.

He would not be the first pilot to sacrifice his life for the mission.

Nor the last.

But Bob was not just a singleton pilot. He was part of a crew, and his backseater was asking for his trust. Would Bob even be having this mental debate if it was Skunk or one of the other Air Force officers he'd crewed with making the ask?

No.

Either Charlie was a part of his crew, or he wasn't.

"All right, Cowboy," Bob said, adjusting course to slide into formation behind the UCAV, "it's your show."

89

"MR. PRESIDENT, THIS IS LORENZO, HOW DO YOU READ ME?"

"I've got you loud and clear, Lorenzo," Ryan said. "Go ahead."

Mary Pat had sat with Ryan during some pretty tense moments.

This just might take the cake.

"Yes, sir, we're tucked in behind the Corvair," Lorenzo said. "Whatever magic your ground team was trying might have just tipped the scales back in our favor. Again, I won't try to convey the technical details, but the bottom line is that my backseater thinks he can regain control of the bird."

Murmurs echoed down the table and smiles appeared.

Mary Pat didn't smile.

The case officer in her said that Lorenzo hadn't finished his update.

"Good news, Lorenzo," Ryan said, leaning forward, "but something tells me there's another shoe that needs to drop."

"Right again, sir," Lorenzo said. "If my backseater's wrong, and the Corvair transitions to hypersonic, it's gone."

Smiles were replaced by puzzled looks.

Lorenzo's unasked question seemed to go over most of the attendees' heads.

Not the President's.

"You're asking if I think you should crash into the Corvair and bring it down while you still have the chance," Ryan said.

"Yes, sir," Lorenzo said. "That's exactly what I'm asking."

There were no murmurs or smiles this time.

A tomblike silence enveloped the room. Even Senator Brown seemed to have lost her trademark smirk. Everyone knew that the presidency prematurely aged its holder, but few people ever witnessed the critical moments that stole years from the President's life.

Moments like this one.

"What do you think, Lorenzo?" Ryan said.

A burst of static sounded from the speaker.

Then Lorenzo returned.

"I think my backseater is a smart kid, sir," Lorenzo said, "but a lot of people are going to die if he's wrong."

For a long moment Ryan stared at the table in silence.

Then he raised his head.

"Yes, they are, Lorenzo," Ryan said. "So tell your backseater he better damn well get my plane back."

90

JACK THOUGHT THE HELICOPTER HAD BEEN FALLING OUT FROM BENEATH HIM before.

He'd been wrong.

The helicopter dropped with such suddenness that Jack's empty AR bounced off the cabin's ceiling. Had he not been strapped into his seat, Jack had no doubt that he would have joined the rifle. As it was, his limbs flapped in the air as his torso tried to escape the restraint harness.

Fortunately, the seat belt held.

Jack wasn't quite as certain about the helicopter.

"Five seconds out," Kyle said.

The aviator might have been discussing the score of the Cubs game for all the emotion in his voice. Though Jack hadn't been particularly impressed with the pilot's attitude before, he might have to reappraise his opinion.

"Reaper, this is Scepter," Jack said. "We are five seconds out, over."

"Roger that, Scepter. This is a hot LZ. I say again, hot LZ, over."

Kyle banked the helicopter to the left, giving Jack his first look at the battlefield.

Hot LZ might have been a bit of an understatement. While the three Green Berets were still lying prone on the cliff and firing at targets of opportunity, they were no longer shooting fish in a barrel. The mercenaries had segregated into three groups. A team of four men was arrayed behind vehicles, boulders, and equipment on the southwest corner of the dome. Their muzzles flashed with the even, disciplined cadence of professionals as they covered the Green Berets with a continuous stream of lead.

Two assault elements located to the south and southeast of the Green Berets were moving beneath suppressive fire provided by their teammates. The assaulters leapfrogged forward in successive bounds, one team providing covering fire as the second moved.

Were the mercenaries not intent on killing his friends, Jack might have just watched the mesmerizing performance. These were not thugs with automatic weapons. They were practitioners of death executing a synchronized react-to-contact battle drill that rivaled anything Jack had seen from his fellow Campus operatives. The Green Berets were caught in a crossfire and would soon be overrun. The assaulters would have to fight their way up the switchbacks leading to the overhang, but based on the battlefield choreography currently unfolding, Jack had no illusions about how this skirmish would end.

His friends would die.

"Two seconds," Kyle said. "Coming in hot."

Coming in hot did not do justice to what the aviator accomplished. The rate of closure to the cliff was so quick and the approach angle so steep that Jack had initially thought Kyle was doing a go-around.

He was not.

At the last second, Kyle spun the helicopter's nose and dropped the skids onto the northernmost point on the cliff, directly behind the still prone Green Berets. Jack slammed against his harness as the rough landing rocked the helicopter from side to side. Fumbling for the quick release mechanism, Jack unlatched his seat belt and half stepped, half rolled onto the cliff.

As was par for the course in situations such as this, Jack's body had propelled him into motion before his mind had processed the repercussions of his actions. Jack had been beaten within an inch of his life and could barely walk. His empty rifle was still in the helicopter, and the air was thick with incoming fire.

What exactly had Jack thought he could contribute to the situation?

The truth was, he didn't know.

But that wasn't the point.

His team was in the shit, and Jack wasn't about to sit it out in the helicopter.

"Go, go, go!" Jack screamed.

The Green Berets were arrayed from west to east beginning with Cary and ending with Isaac. The men were facing south and began to move at Jack's command. Cary raised to one knee, continuing to engage targets while Jad and Isaac sprinted for the helicopter.

They didn't make it.

Isaac's knee erupted in a fountain of blood and gore.

The big man tumbled to the rock.

Jack covered the distance in slow motion, his aching legs barely making headway despite the efforts of his adrenaline-fueled muscles. Isaac was easily two hundred and sixty pounds. Even with Jad's help, Jack knew there was no way he could get the big man into the helicopter.

So he didn't try.

Instead, Jack scooped up Isaac's fallen rifle, took a knee, and began to engage targets.

"Cary, get him to the bird," Jack said in between trigger pulls. "I'll provide covering fire."

The Triple Nickel team sergeant didn't bother to answer.

He just moved.

One moment Cary was crouched at the edge of the cliff's lip.

The next, he was somehow beside Jack.

"Come on, Third Group," Cary said, "I'm used to carrying deadweight, but you gotta help me just a little."

Jack could hear Isaac curse, Jad grunt, and Cary shout, but the Green Berets were no longer his concern. For a moment, the sheer scale of what he saw caused him to hesitate. Like a shark facing a school of fish, Jack didn't know where to start.

But these fish bit back.

Jack's shirtsleeve snapped as a high-velocity round passed within millimeters of his skin.

Time to get to work.

Panning the reflex sight across the dome, Jack centered the crimson reticle on the nearest assaulter and pulled the trigger. Ding always said that when in doubt, start with the fifty-yard target. While the mercenary wasn't quite fifty yards away yet, Jack knew the man soon would be if he didn't do something.

The mercenary flopped to the ground.

Jack selected his next target and fired again.

And the target after that.

And the target after that.

Jack settled into a rhythm. The world faded away until he saw nothing but the floating reticle, felt nothing but the trigger under the pad of his index finger, and heard nothing but the rifle's report. He was consumed with his intensity of purpose, feeling neither courage nor fear. He just panned from one fighter to the next. He might have been in this Zen state for seconds, hours, or years.

He had no concept of time, only the now.

Until something smashed him in the back.

Turning, Jack found himself eyeball to eyeball with Cary.

"Get your ass in the helicopter!"

Jack clambered to his feet, his flow state shattered. All at once the external stimuli he'd been blocking slammed into him like a physical force. He could feel every ache, hear the helicopter's roar, and smell the pungent odor of cordite. Jack stumbled over a rock, powerless to arrest his fall.

"No, sir," Cary said, grabbing Jack by the scruff of his neck, "you're not staying here."

The Green Beret threw Jack into the helicopter. Jack sprawled across the seats, smashing into Jad while trying to avoid Isaac's bloody leg. Then Cary was on top of him and a passenger compartment meant to hold two grown men now contained four.

"Fucking go," Cary screamed.

The world tilted as Kyle obliged.

If Jack had thought the helicopter ride resembled a runaway elevator before, this time he was on a rocket. But instead of blasting off for the moon, the spaceship was heading straight to hell. Though between Isaac's screams, Jad's curses, and Cary's grunts, Jack thought they might have already arrived. The air was thick with the smell of blood, sweat, and fear. The helicopter's transmission shrieked, and wind snarled through the open cabin, tearing at Jack with invisible talons.

Kyle's voice was the only calm in the storm.

"Brace for landing," Kyle said.

Judging by the aviator's cool tone, Jack thought he might be exaggerating the seriousness of the situation.

He wasn't.

The helicopter didn't so much land as impact the earth at a velocity that was slightly less than lethal.

Slightly.

The crash brought Jack into contact with parts of Cary he hoped to never meet again. The collision between flying machine and terra firma shot Jack into the helicopter's cabin like a pinball launched by the plunger.

He felt his body collide with too many hard objects to count.

Then he felt nothing at all.

91

JACK REGAINED HIS SENSES TO THE SOUND OF ISAAC SCREAMING AND SOMETHING a bit more pedantic.

A ringing phone.

With a groan, Jack pushed himself upright and spilled from the bloody cockpit onto the ground. True to his word, Kyle had gotten them off the rocky ledge. Also true to his word, the aviator had flown them no farther than the Widow's Peak parking lot.

But what a parking lot it was.

Jack tried to sit up, but the spinning world convinced him this wasn't such a good idea. Even so, his brief foray into the vertical had revealed much. Somehow, Jad and Cary were still functioning and the pair were busy applying a tourniquet to Isaac's leg. Kyle was standing at the nose of his once proud helicopter, perhaps pondering the skids that were now wrapped around the crew compartment rather than resting flat on the ground.

The landing really had been a doozy. But it was the sight beyond Kyle that warmed Jack's heart. A sea of flashing blue and red lights were hitting the turnoff from the highway and pouring down the access point to the park. In about another fifteen seconds, he knew he would be on the receiving end of an interrogation for the third time since this little adventure had begun.

Hopefully this time his interrogators would use words rather than fists.

The phone continued to ring, each shrill blast threatening to rupture Jack's aching head. Digging the offending device from his pocket, Jack pressed the green button and put the mobile to his ear.

"Hello?"

"Jack?"

"Hey, Mary Pat," Jack said.

His mouth tasted of gravel and his throat felt like he'd swallowed shards of glass.

Given the state of the helicopter, this was a distinct possibility.

"Oh, thank God," Mary Pat said. "You're alive."

"Yep," Jack said.

The single-syllable word seemed to sap his remaining strength. Jack closed his eyes, intending to rest them for a moment. It must have been for a bit longer.

"Jack? Jack?"

"Still here," Jack said.

He decided to keep his eyes closed as he talked.

The world looked better that way.

Besides, the abominable sirens sounded right on top of them, which meant if he opened his eyelids, he'd be assaulted by pulsing red and blue lights. His stomach didn't seem up to that right now.

"You did it, Jack," Mary Pat said. "We've got control of the UCAV again. You really did it."

"Grrreaaaat," Jack said.

His answer seemed slurred even to his ringing ears.

"Jack? You don't sound good."

"Tired," Jack said. "Really, really tired. Head hurts."

"You're probably concussed," Mary Pat said. "Police and EMS should be there soon. Do you need anything?"

"Yessss," Jack said, his eyes drooping. "Probably need you to bail me out of jail. Again."

Then he put the phone on speaker, set it on his chest, and let the darkness claim him.

92

"SO THAT'S IT, THEN?"

Leon looked from the army of red and blue lights screaming down the road toward them to Hendricks. Like his second-in-command, Leon was standing atop the section of cliff the mystery gunmen had just vacated.

The mystery gunmen who'd ruined everything.

"I think so, *bru*," Leon said. "Don't imagine we're fighting our way out this time."

The granite beneath his feet was littered with shell casings.

Hundreds of them.

Though he would gladly shoot the gunmen in their heads if given the chance, Leon couldn't help but feel a bit of grudging respect for the men. They'd scaled a rock face Leon wouldn't have thought passable, opened fire on a numerically superior force, and then escaped in a manner worthy of an action movie. Though judging by the sticky puddle of red near Leon's foot, the men hadn't made it away scot-free.

No matter.

Hendricks was right.

This was the end.

"What about that?" Hendricks said, pointing at the balloon.

Leon eyed the azure monstrosity, considering.

Much of this operation had not played out the way Leon had envisioned. While using a brothel protected by MS-13 and several corrupt Briar Wood police officers to target the engineer Daniel with a honey trap had been a smashing success, working in the small town had still been challenging, as the last twenty-four hours could attest. Leon's MS-13 counterparts had been amenable to sacrificing the coyotes who ran their brothel as part of the cleanup effort. But with several of his mercenaries dead or missing, Leon was now worried that the operational loose ends hadn't been tied off quite so neatly.

Perhaps the balloon offered an off-ramp.

"Cut it free," Leon said.

"You sure?" Hendricks said.

Leon nodded. "Maybe the client's man floats away, and the Americans don't learn the client's identity."

"How does that help us?" Hendricks said.

"This hasn't gone the way we'd imagined," Leon said, "but we're still at the bargaining table. The Americans are going to want to know who tried to steal their precious plane. That information has value."

"To the Americans?"

Leon nodded his head. "Yes, but to the client even more so. They'll pay to keep their anonymity."

"Pay who?" Hendricks said.

"You," Leon said. "You saved me once. Now I'm returning the favor. You're going to scamper down the backside of this mountain the same way the gunmen scampered up. Then you'll arrange payment terms with the client using the knowledge in my head as collateral. My silence for their money. Take care of our mates back home and the spouses and families of the boys here.

We came up short, but that doesn't mean we have to walk away empty-handed."

"What about you?" Hendricks said.

Leon sighed.

"I'm the commander," Leon said. "The commander goes down with the ship. Texas is famous for the Battle of the Alamo. Have you heard of it?"

Hendricks shook his head.

"Texas freedom fighters made a last stand in a tiny church against a numerically superior Mexican force," Leon said. "A stupid tactical decision, but it turned those men into legends. Maybe this hilltop will do the same for us."

"I won't abandon you," Hendricks said.

"You will," Leon said, his tone turning cold. "If you don't escape, none of this was worth it. I'm your commander, and I'm ordering you to leave the battlefield."

"What of the rest of the lads?" Hendricks said.

Leon's face softened.

"We're all prisoners of war now. I'll negotiate the terms of our surrender as best I can. We'll make some noise up here to buy you time. The Alamo defenders held out for thirteen days. We can last at least twenty-four hours. That should be long enough for you to follow our original exfil route to Cuba and then secure terms with the client. American law enforcement loves to talk, and I'll give them plenty to jabber about before we lay down our arms."

Hendricks slowly nodded. "I see the sense in it. But you'll need to tell me the client's identity."

"That I do," Leon said.

Leon spoke a name.

Hendricks's face lost its color.

"*Yebo*," Leon said with a smile. "Now you know why I kept

that bit of information to myself. They have deep pockets and I intend to leverage them. Here's the phone I use to contact the client. The information is stored in preset one."

Leon dug the mobile from his pocket and handed it to his lieutenant.

"Good luck, Captain," Hendricks said.

"My luck ran out long ago," Leon said, holding up his prothesis. "Now go. Hurry."

Hendricks rendered Leon a salute worthy of the parade ground.

Then he started down the mountain.

93

FOUR HOURS LATER
SAGHAND, IRAN

DAVID MILLER WAS TIRED.

Some of his exhaustion was physical.

While a good part of the selection process administered to special operations candidates was designed to test a person's physical and mental toughness, the grueling exercise regimens also served to get the soldier into operator shape. At the time, David had likened the endless loops through the obstacle course, constant calisthenics, timed runs, and long overland marches with a full pack and equipment to the equivalent of running a marathon. Sure, the race was hard, but once you finished and were awarded your medal, you were forever a marathoner.

This analogy had proven to be painfully incorrect.

In a philosophy stolen from their American counterparts, Israeli special operators lived by the maxim that selection begins anew each and every day. After receiving his Shaldag unit pin, David was convinced the hard work was done.

It was not.

His welcome to the unit had been a twenty-four-hour-long

grinder of physical fitness events, shooting, and long-distance navigation with full kit. Though not every day in Shaldag matched the intensity of his "welcome," David came home most nights spent.

Now he understood why.

Moving through the Iranian mountains loaded down with equipment was physically taxing. Doing so with the knowledge that he was surrounded by people who wanted to kill him was mentally challenging. Twelve hours ago, David would have welcomed the opportunity to escape the hot sun.

Now, he knew that nightfall brought its own challenges.

The temperature had dropped to fourteen degrees Celsius and the rock he was lying upon had long since shed the day's heat. The constant breeze chilled David's body and his exhausted muscles begged for a chance to stretch. But in spite of his constant discomfort, David was battling an even more determined enemy.

Fatigue.

"Are you awake, David?"

David was very much awake, but he still jerked.

As one of his many talents, Elad had the ability to move like a ghost. This was a very useful skill for a man who made his living creeping unseen and unheard through his enemy's homeland. But as grateful as he was for his team leader's stealth, Elad's sudden appearances still scared the bejesus out of David.

"Yes," David said, "I'm awake."

At 0130 Iranian local time, David could be forgiven for not being awake, if he had a normal vocation.

He did not.

Instead of lying in a bed fast asleep, David was taking his turn manning the thermal imaging camera that was trained on the entrance to the clandestine enrichment facility inside the Saghand mine complex.

The rest of the team were in their usual places.

Nimrod was on the far side of the hide site, dug in next to Yossi, who was behind the scope of his DAN rifle. Benny was again pulling rear security. Tonight, the nearly constant quiet bickering between the team members was conspicuously absent. Only minutes ago, Benny had received an update via the SAT-COM radio.

One way or another, their mission was about to change.

"Good," Elad said, "because you're about to learn why you joined the Shaldag."

In that instant, David was very grateful that his eyes were pressed to the camera's viewfinder so that Elad couldn't see his face. The last forty-eight hours had been some of the most terrifying of David's life. While he understood the need for units like Shaldag, he no longer was certain he had what it took to be one of its members. How Elad could know what he was thinking was beyond David, but at this point, he wouldn't have been surprised to learn that his team leader could also read minds.

"Ten seconds," Benny hissed.

David felt his heart rate spike as the dark forms to either side of him made minute adjustments to their weapons and kit. Short of coming into contact with an enemy unit, this was the most dangerous moment for a reconnaissance team. Somewhere, an aviator was using the coordinates they had provided to drop ordnance on a target the pilot had never seen.

This was the epitome of operational trust.

"Five," Benny said.

"Get ready," Elad said, placing his hand on David's shoulder. "You never forget your first."

For a moment David wondered if his tired brain had translated the Hebrew words correctly. Then Benny was counting down.

". . . three, two, one."

A flash of light split the night sky followed a moment later by a clap of thunder. The ground beneath David trembled as a shock wave buffeted him, almost knocking the camera from his hands. A groaning like tectonic plates shifting deep within the earth emanated from the mine as sirens began to wail. David's screen was a mass of white and he frantically shifted from spectrum to spectrum, trying to find a clear picture through the mass of dust.

A heartbeat later, the clouds parted, and David could see.

"Oh, my God," David said, unconsciously reverting to English. "Oh, my God."

"What do you see?" Elad said.

"The facility . . . it's gone."

"Yes, it is," Elad said, clapping him on the shoulder. "Do you want to call it in?"

For the first time, David looked from the camera to his team leader.

Elad was smiling.

"Yes," David said. "Yes, I would."

"Yossi," Elad said.

"Coming," Yossi huffed as he crawled across the ground.

David turned to see that Nimrod was already in Yossi's vacated position pulling rear security.

The team had planned this moment.

All of them.

David took Yossi's offered headset with trembling fingers. Then he slipped the earmuffs over his head, adjusted the boom mike, and nodded.

Yossi keyed the transmit button.

David waited for the tone that signified a secure connection.

Then he spoke.

"Alpha 1 is Barak. I say again Alpha 1 is Barak, over."

A voice answered back from two thousand kilometers away.

"Well done, Alpha 1. Continue the mission."

David intended to do just that.

EPILOGUE

TWO DAYS LATER
NATIONAL HARBOR, MARYLAND

"HOW'S THE NOSE?"

"Hurts," Jack said, resisting the urge to touch the length of tape.

Though his nose no longer felt like a cantaloupe had been grafted to his face, it was still tender. The doctor claimed that tape would help press the swelling out. Jack had his doubts, but this was the least of his worries. Between his black eyes, busted lips, and still-missing front teeth, he looked like he'd been on the losing end of an epic beatdown.

And those were just the visible injuries.

His torso was a mass of black and blues from the less-than-lethal beanbags as well as his captors' fists and feet. Two of his ribs were cracked, and even getting up from a chair sent lightning arcing through his nerve endings.

But injuries or no injuries, there was no way Jack was missing this meeting.

"Well, I think you look cute."

Though he was wearing his favorite suit and tie, Jack did not look cute.

The same could not be said of his dining companion.

494

Lisanne was dressed for the unseasonably warm weather in a white sundress and sandals. Her black hair cascaded across her brown shoulders even though one of them bore a row of stitches from a bullet that had passed by a little too close for comfort.

The hostess had done a double-take before seating the pair. Jack had smiled at her stricken expression and assured the woman that he and his companion were both fine. She'd nodded politely and suggested that perhaps the couple would like a table outside.

Jack had readily agreed.

"Nervous?" Lisanne said.

"No," Jack said.

"Liar."

Jack was nervous.

Extremely so.

The events that occurred in Briar Wood, Texas, were still fresh in his mind. Twenty-four hours of blood and tears that intersected with the potential theft of a hypersonic UCAV and a nuclear-armed Iran. Though the immediate threat of Iranian nuclear weapons had been mitigated, agencies across the United States government were still picking up the rest of the operational pieces in the quest to discover what exactly had happened and how. In his usual bull-in-a-china-shop method of operating, Jack and his ad hoc team had neutralized the fifty-meter target.

The aftereffects were not his concern.

After all, his beat was not America.

In theory.

In any case, Isaac was going to be okay, Amanda was reunited with her daughter. Bradshaw and his cronies had been arrested, and a murdered father and son would receive justice. Kyle would get a new helicopter and the aviator, along with Jad and Cary, was going for a ride on Air Force One. Whether Kyle would be enjoying his flight from the copilot's seat was still to be seen, but this, like what happened in Iran, was out of Jack's control.

Not to mention his field of concern.

"Do you think she'll come?" Lisanne said.

His fiancée's earlier joking tone was gone, and he could see the worry in her eyes.

Jack wasn't the only one who was nervous.

"Sure," Jack said, threading his fingers through Lisanne's. "We have a table at the best sushi restaurant in town. It's a beautiful day, we're sitting on the waterfront, and she gets to miss school. Of course she'll come."

While everything he'd just said was true, Jack was not certain the girl in question would come. Were it not for the circumstances of their meeting, Jack might have ordered a beer and taken the rest of the afternoon off. The National Harbor really was an amazing place. Full of hip eateries, great shops, and the Capital Wheel, the setting was magical. Their table offered an unobstructed view of the Potomac River flowing by just feet away with the slowly turning Ferris wheel as a backdrop.

But whether any of this mattered to a teenage girl, Jack didn't know.

"Is this your party?"

Jack turned at the sound of the hostess's voice to see Emily standing behind him. In what seemed to be her uniform of sorts, Emily was wearing an oversized black Marvel Universe T-shirt, a short skirt, and matching black Doc Martens boots. Her hair was done and her makeup applied. A tiny stud sparkled from one nostril.

She could have been a college coed.

She was a fourteen-year-old girl.

A girl whose mother was losing her battle with addiction.

"Hi, Emily," Jack said, getting to his feet. "Want to join us?"

Emily eyed him for a beat.

She reminded Jack of a wild horse he'd once tried to feed. The mustang had desperately wanted the apple in his hand, but its untamed nature recognized the threat of domesticity Jack represented. On that occasion, a Red Delicious had bridged what seemed like an uncrossable divide.

Maybe today a plate of sushi could do the same.

"Okay," Emily said, pulling out a chair.

Jack settled back into his seat and glanced at Lisanne. He'd met Emily a time or two, but he didn't really know her. This was Lisanne's show.

"How are you doing, sweetie?" Lisanne said.

Emily regarded her aunt in silence, her shoulders tensed, and her fists clenched.

"Why am I here?" Emily said.

Lisanne stuttered for a minute, seemingly taken aback by her niece's hostility.

Not Jack.

While not any kind of expert on teenage girls, Jack had spent some quality time with Bella. The lesson he'd learned from the small-town Texas soccer player applied here as well. Teens like Bella and Emily wanted the truth, not flowery small talk.

Jack decided to give it to her.

"We want you to come live with us, Emily," Jack said.

Emily turned toward Jack like a tank's turret tracking a new target.

"I already have a mom," Emily said, her flashing eyes daring Jack to say otherwise.

"I know you do, honey," Lisanne said, her eyes tearing up, "and she loves you oh so very much. But she's sick, and we don't know how long it's going to take for her to get better. No one does."

"I want to stay with my mom," Emily said.

"You can't," Jack said, pitching his voice low and soft. "She's about to go into court-ordered rehab. After that, she'll be in a halfway house for a while. You're going to have to go somewhere. Your grandma has dementia and your grandfather is busy caring for her. They both love you, but they can't take you in. We can."

"And we want you," Lisanne said, touching Emily's forearm. "Very much. We aren't trying to be your new parents. We're just offering you a safe place to land until your mom is healthy."

Again, Emily regarded them in silence.

This time Jack didn't try to break it.

Instead, he reached across the table and squeezed Lisanne's hand.

She squeezed back.

After a long moment, Emily spoke.

"You guys aren't even married," Emily said.

"You're right," Jack said, "but we're going to fix that. Once you're settled in with Lisanne and we see how things shake out with your mom, we'll schedule the ceremony. Until then, it will be just the two of you."

Emily stared back at Jack.

"You're going to plan your wedding around me?" Emily said.

"Of course we are," Lisanne said. "You're going to be one of my bridesmaids."

"But, but I just made you cry," Emily said, her voice breaking.

"Oh, honey," Lisanne said. "I love your mama so much. If a few tears are the price I have to pay to take care of her little girl, I'm happy to shed them."

Emily hiccupped through her own tears. She didn't throw her

arms around Lisanne's neck or lean in for a hug, but neither did she pull away.

Maybe that was enough.

"Okay," Emily said. "Okay. What happens now?"

"Now we go meet my parents," Jack said with a smile. "Ever been to the White House?"

THE UNMISSABLE
JACK RYAN, JR. SERIES

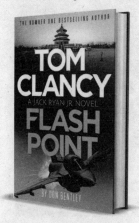

Jack Ryan, Jr. is in a world of trouble. A mid-air collision between aircraft from rival nations in the South China Sea threatens to serve as a flash point for the entire region. As Jack frantically tries to put the pieces of the conspiracy together, the Campus is hit with a crippling attack. When the dust settles, Jack is one of the few operators still standing and the Campus's de facto leader.

But the fight is just beginning.

As tensions escalate, Jack's mysterious adversary executes a brilliant campaign to paralyze the American government even as China inches closer to invading Taiwan.

With the odds stacked against him and no help in sight, Jack and his shattered team must stop the world's two remaining superpowers from stumbling into war even as the noose around the Campus grows ever tighter.

Every operation has a cost. This time the bill might just be too much to pay.

OUT NOW

DISCOVER THE
JACK RYAN SERIES

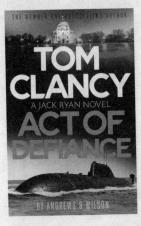

When a Russian superweapon is let loose under the waves,
it's up to President **Jack Ryan** to find a countermove in the latest
entry in this #1 *New York Times* bestselling series.

US intelligence says there's something going on in Russia. While their
land forces have been decimated by corruption and incompetence,
the Navy seems to be pouring money into some secret project.

Analysts are stumped, until the knot is untangled by one particularly
bright young woman at the Office of Naval Intelligence – Katie Ryan,
the youngest daughter of President Jack Ryan. Like her father, she sees
patterns where other don't, and she's determined that the Russians
are about to launch a super missile submarine, the Belgorod.

Now the race is on to determine where the sub is and
whether it poses a threat to the continental US.

ORDER NOW

President **Jack Ryan** travels to Colombia to support the president who is facing a challenge from autocratic forces. What seems like an ordinary opportunity to preach the values of democracy quickly turns into a nightmare when a full-blown military coup erupts.

President Ryan and his Secret Service team are cut off and out of communication. In Washington, the Vice President is coordinating a military response, but there's still one more obstacle.

The Russians recognize an opportunity when one presents itself. They've hired a private military contractor to do the unthinkable – use the cover of the coup to assassinate President Jack Ryan.

OUT NOW